SWITCHBACK

A SPY THRILLER BY

J.K. KELLY

Copyright © 2023 by JK Kelly Consulting, LLC

JK Kelly Consulting, LLC,
P.O. Box 4069, Media, PA 19063 USA
Library of Congress Control Number: TBA
Philadelphia, PA USA

ISBN: 978-1-7363592-8-0 paperback
ISBN: 978-1-7363592-9-7 eBook

TO JUDY, DON, DAVE, AND DAN

CHAPTER ONE

THE SCENT FROM the night's inferno reminded him of his Uncle Pete's fireplace and the many campfires Bryce Winters had enjoyed in his younger days in rural Vermont. Charred wood always left an unmistakable aroma. As dawn broke over Park City, Utah, Bryce navigated through coals and what was left of torched, massive beams that had formed the cathedral ceiling over his trophy room. This was no redolent, sentimental reverie. This was a nightmare.

"CIA bastards," he muttered with disgust.

The sheriff called out to him from what was left of the front entry: the carved grizzly bear on the door that had greeted guests and welcomed him home so many times was now nothing more than a fond memory.

"Damn it, Bryce, come on," he shouted. "It's not safe."

The look Bryce gave the lawman when he turned to respond was enough of an answer. For someone who lived on the edge racing in Formula One for a living, taking his life in his hands at over two hundred miles per hour, the danger from the smoldering remnants of the now ruined, rustic mountainside home – his retreat - wasn't a concern.

Finding who did this and making them pay would come next. For now, he wanted—and needed—some space.

"Strange - they didn't torch the garage," the sheriff said as he stared at the untouched building across the courtyard from the debris field. "All that gas in those cars would have been easy."

Bryce didn't respond. He just focused his stare on the structure for a moment and nodded.

"I'll be out of here soon," Bryce said as he kicked at some debris. "I've got to head down to Daytona for testing." He paused as he saw yet another prized possession in the rubble. "I guess this will get me there a bit early."

Seconds later, a crystal flake drifted gently onto Bryce's nose, and what was left of his mountainside home, his oasis, was now in stark contrast: everything burned black was now frosted with snow. The skiers in the area would be thrilled, but for him, this could just as well be karma putting a sheet over the corpse. He had been living a dangerous life on and off the track—it might be closing in on him yet again.

Bryce kicked at more debris with his hiking boots and kept searching. When he finally found what he was looking for, his reaction suggested to the sheriff that he should get back in his patrol car and drive away. Bryce knelt, brushing away soot and ash with his hand before picking up what had been, until today, his most prized possession—his Formula One World Championship trophy.

He lifted the once magnificent symbol of ultimate racing success by one of its handles. He pulled it close, inspecting the mark a bullet had left on it less than two months ago. Suddenly, the handle snapped off, and the partially melted cup fell back into the rubble with a thud. Bryce looked around and focused on the only thing other than his gun safe and fireplaces that had somehow survived the blaze: one windowpane overlooking the valley.

He threw the severed handle at it, smashing it to bits.

"Got that out of my system," he said to himself. "Now, let's go find the assholes who did this and return the favor."

He turned to look one last time at what was left of his home. He recalled the night his kitchen was shot up by a renegade CIA agent in a botched kidnapping. He thought of the Thanksgiving weekend he'd spent there with his Uncle Pete before he passed....

Then, something caught his eye: movement in the trees, up on the hill across the road from his gated property. It wasn't a moose this time.

The police had cleared the street of television trucks, reporters, and the curious assembled to see the spectacle. Still, the few remaining photographers were perched on the slope above, recording his every move. Someone else was also watching, dressed in black from head to toe and hidden in the trees another fifty feet up the hillside.

The photographers had no idea who they were really hounding. Bryce wasn't just a champion race car driver— he was a CIA-trained hitman. Taking a life was all in a day's work—under the fitting codename "Deadly Driver."

He took a few long, slow breaths of crisp mountain air to calm his rage and clear his head, but the charred wood smell and the moist snow brought him back.

He wouldn't consider asking the CIA, or the FBI for that matter, for help in tracking the arsonist. He couldn't trust anyone at either agency—not with his life. He'd done work for England's MI6 but didn't trust anyone there now either – he couldn't. He stood quietly in the rubble and then looked to the four-car garage across the stone courtyard from his once majestic home. He walked to it, waving at the few paparazzi who had come off the hillside and were shouting questions as their cameras lit up the area like a Hollywood movie premiere.

"Who did this, Bryce," one yelled. "Any chance Tony Bishop's sent you a holiday card?" called out another. Bishop, his racing nemesis, had been at odds with Bryce their entire racing career. "Piss someone off, Bryce – maybe someone's husband?" shouted another. They were trying to get under his skin. Bryce stopped in mid-stride halfway to the garage and smiled.

"Merry Christmas, Happy Holidays, and go f- yourself," Bryce said with a broad smile. Once at the side door and out of view of the bothersome bastards, Bryce bit his lip and walked back out into the view of the crowd.

"That last one was for Tony Bishop, wherever in the world he is tonight, and to whoever did this," Bryce said in a milder tone. "And for your information, I'm driving through that gate in three minutes. If you're in the way, I might skid on the ice and accidentally run a few of you buggers over, so be advised." Bryce laughed as the photographers studied the dry stonework under their feet. He tapped the entry code into the touchpad on the wall and reached for the door handle to the sound of the locking bolts releasing. He stopped just short of it. He looked back to the rubble and remembered what the sheriff had said. *Yeah, it is strange that the bastard didn't burn this too.*

I wonder if anyone checked inside. He cleared his throat and turned the knob.

Soon, he was inside the temperature-controlled garage, set to a mild sixty degrees. He pushed the door closed behind him and threw the bolt. He took a deep breath and rested his head against the door. He slowly turned toward the vehicles, tears in his eyes. He took a few deep breaths and stared at the vehicle closest to him. It was his late Uncle Pete's ten-year-old four-wheel drive Toyota Tacoma pickup with an empty rifle rack at the rear window. He walked to the front of the pickup and glanced at the white-on-green Vermont license. "Glad I didn't waste the effort getting Utah plates. It might be time for me to call someplace else home," he said softly. Bryce placed both hands on the front fender.

"I miss you, Pete. Wish you were here, now." He shook his head and let out a laugh. "You old bastard."

He walked past the pickup to the heavily performance-modified black Subaru WRX sedan he'd acquired from his friends at Vermont SportsCar in New England and driven cross country.

"Not tonight," he said fondly. He continued to the next ride, the brand new vibrant red Mercedes AMG coupe the manufacturer had shipped him from Germany. As he raced one, they felt he should also play in one.

"Nein," he whispered in one of the four languages he'd had to learn in recent years.

Then he walked to the fourth vehicle and nodded with approval. He climbed behind the wheel of his two-year-old black Chevy Tahoe Z71. With heavily tinted windows, it had always blended in well in Park City with the Land

Rovers and Mercedes SUVs driven by the town's countless celebrities – especially during the holiday weekends when the film festival or the ski slopes had drawn them there. He pushed the start button and smiled as the modified V8 engine came to life, and the custom exhaust gave off its distinctive purr. He checked the center console for the black semi-automatic pistol and three spare magazines at the ready.

He looked to the overhead console, tapped the garage door and gate openers, and then tapped the horn twice. He sped from the garage and through the now open gate as if he'd just come in for a pit stop and was gone. As the photographers ran for their cars, a sheriff's deputy quickly blocked the small road with his Dodge police cruiser.

Nearing midnight, with much of his life in ruins, Bryce sat quietly in the Tahoe and then caught his eye in the rearview mirror. He focused and reached for his phone. "Okay, enough of this pity party."

Miles from there, at a roadside hotel near a small truck stop just off a state road east of Park City, a woman struggled hard to free herself from the plastic zip ties that were cutting into her wrists that were cuffed behind her. The closet her abductors had stuffed her in this night, for what she thought must be her ninth or tenth night, had a particularly offensive aroma rising from the cheap, worn carpet she had been laid on. She could hear the television in the room on the other side of the creaky sliding doors and was frustrated it drowned out the conversation the men, she thought two but maybe three, were having. She prayed, no matter what, that if they remembered to feed her tonight, it might be something other than a burger and fries. They left her bloated, nauseous, and wanting her freedom even more. Suddenly, she heard footfalls coming toward her. Would it be food or another drunken beating? As the door slid open, she wished she were dead. What she saw in his eyes scared her. She didn't recognize the man, the stranger, now standing over her. His face was familiar. She'd seen those beady eyes somewhere before but couldn't remember where or when. Maybe it was the Xanax or whatever they had been giving her in her water to keep her mellow – and quiet. The man studied her for a moment. She followed those eyes as they moved from her face all the way to her toes. It sent chills down her spine. But then, as quickly as the man had appeared, the closet door slid closed. She listened but couldn't understand what her captors and this new face were saying.

∽

Chadwick pushed back in the worn, creaky wooden chair and rested his head against the wall. He took another few sips of beer and watched Russo and McCarthy walk to the door.

"You sure you don't want any of that," he heard Russo ask. "I know you like exquisite objects." He watched as McCarthy seemed to have second thoughts as the man turned and looked back toward the closet.

"She is a beautiful creature, even with the bruising," he heard McCarthy say and then sat forward in his chair, the legs slamming to the floor. He watched as Russo and McCarthy startled and then stared at him curiously.

"You okay, buddy?" Russo asked. Chadwick nodded.

And I'm not going to let either of you son of a bitches rough her up again, especially you, partner or not.

"Yeah, just tired of sitting around," he said. Russo reached for the door to let McCarthy out and then heard the man who was paying them joke about something he didn't find funny.

"Maybe Chad should take her for a ride. Relieve a little stress. It might do him some good," McCarthy joked and then left the motel room with Russo following him out. Not long after, Russo came back in with a smile on his face.

"Good news. We're moving. He's got a remote place out in the woods. She can make all the noise she wants, and nobody will hear it." Chadwick smiled and pushed his chair back against the wall.

"I don't like that piece of shit one bit," Chadwick uttered as he stared at his partner.

"Well, Winters cost us our jobs and pensions, and that 'piece of shit' pays ten times better than the CIA. We're here for revenge, but we're also here, at least I am, for the money. Remember that."

CHAPTER TWO

Bryce had parked in front of the five-star Grand American Hotel in downtown Salt Lake City, the intermittent wipers streaking the light snow that had begun to fall. He was alone, and it was Christmas. He searched his phone for their number and then made a call. "This is Bryce Winters. I need a room, and I'd like to get to it as quickly and quietly as possible. Can you help me?"

"Yes, yes, Mr. Winters. Everyone saw what happened to your home and on Christmas. Very sorry for your loss, sir," the woman began. "We can accommodate you in one of our presidential suites. Where are you now?"

"Right out front, but is there a way I can slide in without," he asked, but she cut him off.

"Oh yes, Mr. Winters. There is a parking garage ramp to the right of our front entrance. If you drive straight down, take the second left and stop at the black door with the letters PR painted on it. I will be there waiting for you and have an attendant park your vehicle if you have one."

"Perfect," Bryce answered. "What's your name?"

"Joan Glaser, Mr. Winters. I'll be waiting for you."

Minutes later, Glaser, a petite brunette with Bambi eyes and a warm smile, had led Bryce into a VIP elevator that went directly to the hotel's top floor. She swiped his credit card on her phone and handed him his card and room key as they arrived in front of Suite 1001.

"Is there anything else I can do for you, Mr. Winters?" she asked.

"Bryce, please call me Bryce. There might be. I have no clothes, no toiletries, nothing. Everything was lost in the fire except what I'm wearing." Glaser sized him up and smiled, blushing slightly.

"When are you leaving?" she asked. "The suite is yours as long as you need it."

"As of right now, mid-morning is the plan, but that can change," he told her. "But that, like this, is all top secret, right?"

Glaser nodded as she smiled. "I'll have toiletries delivered within ten minutes and a set of clothes, just like what you are wearing, plus a winter coat, by nine a.m. I take it North Face, Columbia, and Merrell size ten work for you?" Bryce smiled. "You're good, young lady, thank you." As Bryce entered his suite and began to close the door behind him, he heard a knock and felt the door push in. He tensed.

"Last question," Glaser said apologetically, "boxers or briefs?" Bryce smiled.

"Thongs. I only wear thongs," he told her, watching as her eyes grew wide and her skin regained that touch of blush.

"Kidding," he said with a laugh. "Briefs, please, but beggars can't be choosers." Glaser smiled and pulled the door closed as she backed away into the hallway. Bryce threw the bolt and chain on the door. *Like that's going to stop whoever wants me dead.*

As promised, the toiletries arrived along with an elegant room service cart full of hot and cold entrees and accompaniments he hadn't ordered. *Talk about five-star service.* Before leaving, the young male server handed Bryce a card that read, Merry Christmas With Our Compliments.

"Anything else we can get you, Mr. Winters?" the server asked. Bryce passed the man a crisp one-hundred-dollar bill.

"No, this is more than enough. Thank you so much." Bryce bolted the door again, ignored the chain, and inspected the food. He wasn't hungry. He walked to the bar and surveyed the imported beers, eighteen-year-old scotch, and ten other bottles of expensive liquor that came with the place.

He wasn't thirsty, and he needed to keep a clear head. Over the next few hours, he didn't eat. He didn't drink. He just sat there in the dark, heartbroken. He thought of all the good times he'd had in the home he had just lost. Time hiking there with Pete. A mother moose and her calf at the gate. The Christmas feast he hosted for the young Olympians who remained in Park City over the holidays. The night the beautiful blonde CIA handler he nicknamed Nitro had tried to lure him to bed. The massive trophy room that had been his pride and joy. The night he shot and killed an intruder and, most recently, the last night with Kyoto.

He got up slowly and quietly, put on a pot of coffee, then sat at the elegant dining room table and began studying his phone. Anyone and everyone was leaving voicemails or texting. There were some well-wishers and a ton of global media, but there were two people he wanted to hear from, but neither had called.

Kyoto must be gone for good, he thought. *Smart girl. Someone just burned my house down, and we could have been there.* He stared at his phone and shook his head as he deleted her contact info. The time had come; he was sure they were done—*nothing from Jack either*, he thought, which hurt him deeply.

He came across another contact in his phone: Sandra Jennings. She'd been his handler of late until she was kidnapped and killed in Singapore on the eve of the race there.

"Who was it she asked me about?" he questioned aloud. "What the hell was that guy's name?" As he grew tired, somewhere around two in the morning, he posted holiday greetings to his five million followers on Instagram and other social media.

"Guess my Christmas barbeque wasn't a good idea after all," he posted with a photo of him shrugging his shoulders while standing in front of the smoldering ruins.

"I'm fine. No worries. Merry Christmas to All!"

Jack Madigan had been at Bryce's side for years. The former Army Ranger grew up around stock car racing in North Carolina. He was eventually hired first as a pit crew member and then rose to technical consultant on the NASCAR and IndyCar teams Max Werner had put together for his prodigy. When Werner grew tired of watching his cars go in circles, he decided to go big, go international, and go for the global exposure that Formula One would afford his Werner Industries. He had tired of all the trips to America to watch his driver and teams go round and round.

"After all, going in circles can't be that hard," Werner once told Madigan and Bryce. "Strippers do it all the time." Both men had protested their bosses' characterization. Still, Madigan had followed Bryce overseas, continuing to serve as a technical consultant for the team, an occasional bodyguard for his driver and friend, and eventually working with Bryce for another team – the CIA. Sitting in the darkness, Bryce remembered Jennings and the moment she delivered an emotional bomb.

"He's trading with America's enemies, Bryce," she had told him. "Werner makes tech and arms, and he's playing shell games and trading with Russia, Iran, North Korea, and a few more. You have a choice. You can visit him and dose him with something that will look like a heart attack, or we can have a contractor do it with a sniper rifle. Your way, his wife and daughter have something to look at when they say their goodbyes. The contractor won't be as thoughtful. Either way, Werner's dead, and the arm's flow stops." When she saw him in the crowded church, Bryce thought of little Mila's expression at the funeral. Her sorrow turned to joy. It crushed him then, and it did again there in the dark.

He hadn't been able to bring himself to call his pilot, not on Christmas, to arrange a more exotic escape, and he also opted not to reach out to the former SEALS and Rangers he knew in the area. He often hired them as armed bodyguards depending on crowds and other circumstances. He had been ready at least twice to call for their security, but when it dawned on him that he wasn't sure who he could trust, he killed the idea. But now, as he stared at the clock through tired eyes, it was the day *after* Christmas.

As the morning sun lit up his east-facing windows, Bryce sat on the sofa and surveyed the room. He brewed coffee, ordered a pot from room service, and stared at the unit, trying to will it to work faster. Once the room began to fill with the scent he appreciated more than racing fuel or victory lane champagne, he stood at the floor-to-ceiling window in the master bedroom and smiled at the new day. *Enough with the damn pity party. It's time to get back to work.*

His F1 race team owner, Ameer Kazaan, who was on holiday at Mount Tremblant north of Montreal, had invited Bryce to come north and stay with him and the family at his ski chalet at Mont Tremblant. When Bryce called Kazaan early that morning, he had something else on his mind.

"Ameer, thanks for the invite, but I'm going to head to Florida and warm up there until the big track opens for the Roar. Getting back in a race car will do me good." Bryce began. "I appreciate the invitation, but this is your family time. Enjoy it because we'll be testing the new car in Barcelona before you know it."

The skies over Salt Lake City were clear, and the temperature was hovering around a tolerable forty degrees. *A great day for flying,* he thought. He showered, put on a luxurious gold-colored robe, and then watched the huge flatscreen, switching back and forth between CNN and the BBC. With the new day, another news cycle had begun, and any word of the arson at his American home had been relegated to an occasional streaming ribbon at the bottom of the screen. *Good.* Right at nine a.m., there was a knock at the door. Checking the privacy eye first, he smiled when he saw it was the concierge from the night before, Glaser.

"Did you get those thongs I ordered?" he asked jokingly. Glaser smiled and handed over two large shopping bags of clothing, new shoes, a jacket, gloves, a scarf, and a backpack; everything he had requested and then some.

"I can't thank you enough for your help - Joan, wasn't it?" he said. She nodded and smiled again. "I'll be out of here within the hour. I can just reverse what I did last night and wind up back down in the garage, right?" She nodded.

"You sure can, Mr. Winters. It was my pleasure helping you. I hope everything turns out okay." Bryce smiled, removed a sealed hotel envelope from a robe pocket, and handed it to her.

"Thank you," Bryce said as Glaser tried to refuse it. Then, a raspy voice was heard in the hallway.

"Take it, girl, he wouldn't be offering if you didn't deserve it," the voice continued. Bryce tensed as he stared at Glaser and began to step back into the room. His gun, the one Kyoto had taken exception to under his pillow, was a few feet away under a magazine on an end table.

"It's okay, Bryce, it's Johnson and Johnson." Bryce relaxed and let out a breath. The voice was now very familiar. He knew it well. As Bryce stepped out into the hallway, to the left stood Danny Johnson, and to the right stood Danny's brother Alan. They were brothers, identical twins, both dressed in jeans and black golf shirts. Danny, a retired Army Ranger Bryce had befriended when he first moved to Park City, and Alan, a retired Utah State Trooper. The only way anyone could tell the difference was when they walked; Danny limped from an IED wound he'd suffered years before while serving in Afghanistan.

"Well, what do you know," Bryce said as he smiled at the two.

"They've been out here all night," Glaser told Bryce. They showed up at the front desk around ten o'clock and showed their credentials and photos of them guarding you at the race in Texas last year. They said you were in harm's way, and they were here to guard your door. Was that okay?" Bryce smiled at Glaser and nodded. "Yep, looks like they're with me." Bryce thanked Glaser again, clasping her hands with his, sure that the thank you envelope was in her grasp. The three men watched as she walked to the elevator and waved goodbye as the doors closed. Then, it was time for Bryce to invite the heavily armed brothers inside. As they served themselves coffee and picked at the breakfast tray Glaser had sent up, Bryce went into the master bedroom and began to dress. A minute later, he laughed as he walked to the doorway, holding up a red and white Christmas thong she'd bought him.

"She likes you," Alan said as he chomped a mouthful of well-done bacon.

❦

Danny stood in the bedroom doorway, coffee in hand, and watched as Bryce folded and packed his bag.

"So, is there a reason you didn't call us yesterday?" Danny asked. "We could have been there at the house in ten minutes." Bryce stopped folding a pair of new Wranglers and looked at Danny.

"Yep. It was Christmas, and I didn't want to ruin anyone's day. I didn't want to take you guys away from your mother," Bryce explained. Danny moved aside as Alan walked into the room.

"Wish you had. That woman can't cook worth a damn," Alan said with a fond grin.

"Yeah, she's great at everything else, but burnt to bits is her style in the kitchen."

"See, I didn't want you to miss a moment." Bryce stopped and looked at the men. "Someday, she won't be here to give you guys something to laugh about, and you'll miss her cooking." Bryce paused. "There's not a day that goes by without me thinking about my dad and Pete." Bryce watched as Alan picked up the thong and then dropped it as if it were contaminated.

"So, how long can you guys hang?" Bryce asked through a laugh.

"As long as needed," Danny answered.

"How about thirty days in Daytona?" Bryce watched as the brothers locked eyes.

"That's why there are two duffel bags in the pickup down in the garage. We're ready; we even have our passports this time. We're in. Whatever you need." Within minutes, the three men were buckled into Bryce's Tahoe and headed for the airport, the driving champion in control at the wheel.

"Really," Danny asked. "You have to do ninety in this traffic?"

"Buck, buck, buck," Alan chuckled from the backseat as he mimicked a chicken's clucking. Bryce looked at Danny and saw he was scanning everything on the highway, his black assault rifle resting on his lap, his trigger finger resting on the guard. Bryce looked in the rearview mirror and saw Alan turn toward the rear of the vehicle, watching for anyone or anything out of the ordinary. He saw the weapon was the same as Danny's, ready to engage if needed.

"You guys drink too much coffee this morning?" Bryce asked. "If someone was going to shoot me in traffic, they would have done it by now, don't you think?"

"Hey Bryce, you might want to slow it down," Alan called out. As Bryce looked at Alan in the rearview mirror, he saw it. It was the bright blue light bar atop a white Utah Highway Patrol vehicle, and at ninety miles per hour, it was now right on his bumper, drafting as if they were racing at Daytona.

"I haven't told you guys the whole story," Bryce offered as he looked at Danny. Bryce watched as the now wide-eyed man riding shotgun cocked his head.

"Maybe I should have. Since that bastard who got fired from the CIA tried to kill me, I'm not sure I can trust anyone with a badge." Alan turned toward Danny in the front seat.

"Danny, how do you want to play this?" Danny looked at Bryce and then back at his brother.

"Well, I'll bet prison food's still better than mom's."

Alan nodded and then repositioned his rifle.

CHAPTER THREE

STANDING ON THE shoulder of Interstate 80 just west of downtown Salt Lake, the impatient trooper gave Alan Johnson an earful. "I don't give a shit who he is or what *you* used to be. At first, I thought he was just speeding, but when I ran the plate and Bryce Winters came up, I lit the lights. There's a BOLO on him." Johnson showed his surprise.

"At ninety miles per hour and headed toward the airport, some might think he's running," the trooper continued. "So get him out of the vehicle, now, because if *I* have to, it will only make things worse, a lot worse, for all of you." As Johnson turned to walk back to the Tahoe, two additional highway patrol cruisers pulled up behind the first on the scene. The trooper followed Johnson to the passenger's side door and gestured for Bryce to lower the window.

"I've been told to bring you in, and that's what I'm going to do," the trooper continued. Then, he directed Alan to walk to the guardrail at the back of the vehicle and take a seat. Danny Johnson then spoke to the trooper in a softer, less confrontational tone than his brother had employed. The trooper did a double-take when he realized they were twins.

"Look, he's not running. Speeding, yes, but he's not running away from anything. We're trying to get away from here in case whoever torched his house wants to take another shot at him. You remember what happened last year with that CIA asshole?" The trooper reached for the microphone on his shoulder-mounted gear and spoke into it, the roar of the traffic muffling any chance Danny had of eavesdropping. The trooper let go of the mic.

"He's wanted for questioning," the trooper began. "They found a body under the rubble at the scene. If he refuses to follow me back to Park City, he and you two knuckleheads will be charged with attempted flight and aiding and abetting." The trooper stepped closer, the rim of his hat nearly tapping Danny's forehead. "You copy?"

At Park City Hospital, Bryce introduced the sheriff to his team before they followed him down a long, sterile corridor one floor below ground level. An occasional fluorescent bulb in the ceiling flickered in its final hours of life. The sheriff knocked as he opened the office door.

The coroner, a balding and thin man in his mid-fifties dressed in pale green hospital scrubs, greeted Bryce and got right to it.

"We found the body face down under one of the large beams from your great room—strangely enough, it was dressed in a race driver's fire suit." He looked at Bryce. "One of yours, I presume?"

Bryce shrugged. "I'm not certain." The coroner looked at the sheriff, who nodded.

"The body was so compressed against the stone floor by the weight of the beam that part of the suit, the center front torso with the vertical zipper, remained intact.

"The body was also wearing a full-face helmet, again one of yours, from what we could determine. It didn't fare as well as the front of the suit. Follow me," the coroner said as he pushed open a door and held it for Bryce. As he entered the room, Bryce stopped abruptly. There on a stainless-steel morgue table lay a badly burned driver's suit—one of his. Bryce turned and stared at the coroner and then walked to the table. An unsettling aroma now tainted the disinfectant smell of the room, one Bryce had never encountered before. He stood over the suit and looked at every inch from top to bottom. He reached out and touched what was left of the embroidery that read Bryce Winters in simple block letters.

"Yep, it's mine. It's the suit I wore when I won the World Championship." He paused. "So where's the body?" The coroner pointed across the room to three 3'x3' square stainless doors in the wall set three feet off the floor.

"It's in the first one, but you don't want to see what's left. It's unsettling," the coroner told Bryce as the sheriff and the Johnson brothers joined them in the morgue.

"You're right – I don't," Bryce whispered. All were quiet for a moment, and then Bryce spoke up.

"And my helmet? Where is it?" he asked.

"Already on the way to the FBI lab in Washington along with some physical evidence taken from the body. They'll try everything in the book to identify everything we sent them," the coroner said.

"Sounds like some twisted bastard wanted to be you,

clothes and all," Danny suggested. "Played dress up and then torched the place." The coroner shot him an impatient look, annoyed at the interruption, and cleared his throat. Bryce started to ask a question, but the coroner held up his hand. "The person, a male, was not the arsonist, and he *was* murdered. We found a bullet in his brain: it entered through the right eye socket. We found no smoke in the victim's lung tissue. His lungs stopped working long before the fire."

Danny removed his gaze from what was left of Bryce's suit and looked at his brother.

"How did you determine the victim's identity," Alan asked.

"His ID—someone shoved it into his mouth," the coroner said, shaking his head.

Bryce looked at the others standing about the room.

"Okay, what do you guys know that I don't? Who's the dead guy?" he asked.

The Park City Sheriff stepped to Bryce, placing a firm hand on his shoulder.

"It's Jon, Bryce. Jon Watanabe."

Bryce was stunned. He'd crashed into concrete walls while racing at two hundred miles per hour, the life nearly knocked out of him, but this was different. This was an emotional blow that dazed his thoughts with shock and confusion. He turned away from the others in the room and stared into space.

"Who the hell's Jon Watanabe?" Danny asked.

"He was the CIA analyst who was kidnapped and brought to Bryce's home the night all hell broke loose up there," the sheriff offered. "He was Kyoto's brother."

"No way – I remember that name now. What the hell's going on here?" Alan asked.

"Jon was a good kid. His got sucked him into a world he should never have been in," Bryce explained. "Who knew being a race fan could get someone killed."

"Has his sister been notified?" Bryce asked as he turned toward the coroner. "They were very close."

"Not to my knowledge," he answered.

"Wait – just because it was Jon's ID doesn't mean it was him. Someone might be playing some sick game," Bryce said in a hopeful tone. The coroner walked to him and shook his head no.

"Bryce, the sheriff called the FBI field office in Salt Lake, and they got the deceased's dental records from the CIA in Virginia. We confirmed it was Mr. Watanabe. Now, whether the CIA has notified the deceased's next of kin, I can't say. My office has no way of contacting her. Do you?" Bryce stared at the coroner. He felt as if his head was going to explode. It was through Jon's overzealous nature that the CIA first got their hands on the F1 champion, and now the young man was burned to a crisp in one of Bryce's fire suits, not in a race but under what remained of his home. Bryce looked about the room. He wanted to throw something. He needed to break something to vent his fury.

"Bryce," Alan said softly. "Save it, buddy. We'll help you find who cooked this kid and put them in a sewer with the rats."

"What was that Pete used to say – just breathe," Danny added. Bryce turned and looked past the coroner to his friends. He nodded and then turned back to the doctor.

"So why am I here? Do you need me to identify the

body? You already did that," Bryce said, his tone turning angry. "You want an autograph or a photo? Maybe we could pose with the body, and you can sell it to the Globe?" The coroner tensed and stepped back as he looked to the sheriff, gesturing it was time to explain.

"Sorry, Bryce, this was my idea," the sheriff offered. "I just needed to observe you here and when you got the news. It's procedural. If the FBI were here, they'd have done the same thing."

"That's fucked up," Danny said as he stepped close to Bryce. "Let's get out of here. We're done, aren't we, sheriff?" The sheriff nodded. "Just doing my job." Bryce shook his head and walked back into the coroner's office. As he opened the door to the hallway, apparent freedom, and better air, Bryce stopped and stared at the photos to the right of the door. They were of the coroner posing with a young girl waist-deep fly fishing.

"Your daughter?" Bryce asked. The coroner cleared his throat.

"Yes, that's Bella, my pride and joy." Bryce thought of the mounted photos that followed him wherever he raced. Bryce wasn't superstitious like some drivers. The pictures of him in victory lanes with his first love, his father, his uncle, and his car owner – all now dead and buried – warmed the spot in his heart that had grown colder with each loss. He thought of little Mila.

"She's beautiful," he whispered, walking from the room. It was time to come face to face with Kyoto and shove another cold blade into his heart.

With the flight plan's destination changed from Daytona, Florida to Washington's Dulles, Bryce stood on the tarmac alongside his pearl white Bombardier 6500 jetand placed a call to the Park City Sheriff.

"I'm outta here," Bryce said abruptly. "You have my cell if anything comes up. Sorry for this morning. I know you're just doing your job, but from now on, I'm bringing an attorney."

"Don't blame you one bit, Bryce," the sheriff said. "The FBI and ATF are in charge now. They arrived just after you left. Their forensic teams are at the house and have your number."

"I'm surprised they haven't called me yet. We're headed to Washington to check on Kyoto and then to Daytona. The Johnsons are flying out with me. Once I get a chance to step back and take a few breaths, I'll be able to figure out what I'm going to do next."

Bryce's full-time pilot and co-pilot, Bill Miller and Lou Thompson, two seasoned former Air Force pilots who had done damage to America's enemies from the skies over Iraq and Afghanistan, were at the controls and ready to roll. As he entered the cockpit, Bryce apologized profusely for interrupting their holiday break with his last-minute plans, but they waved him off. They both protested as they jokingly insisted he leave their office pronto, gesturing with their fingers that it would cost him.

"One way or another, you'll pay us back," Thompson called out. "Who knows, maybe you'll take us to the South Pole like you've been promising for what - three years now?"

Bryce shook his head as he smiled, turning to greet the last-minute addition to the flight crew. Susan Livingston wore a red polo, tan khakis, and white sneakers and gushed at the chance to meet Bryce, her southern accent in full bloom.

"It's an honor to be flying with you today," she began, but Bryce shook his head and raised his hand.

"Where'd you get that outfit," he demanded. Livingston was taken aback and turned to the cockpit, where both men tried to withhold their laughter.

"He plays with everyone on their first day," Miller said. Livingston turned to Bryce and studied him for a moment.

"You do know I prepare your food, right?"

"Oh, you're going to fit in just fine," he answered. "Do me a favor and bring the Johnson brothers aboard. I need to get to the back and make some calls."

Bryce took his seat at the rear cabin of his Bombardier and laughed to himself as he watched the attendant scold the Johnsons before letting them into the main cabin.

"And keep your boots off the furniture," she warned and then prepared the cabin for the eastbound excursion. Once at cruising altitude, after the aroma had drawn him to the galley, she served Bryce lunch, cheeseburger, and fries with a side of mayo and a Coke Zero.

"Anything else I can do for you, Mr. Winters?" she asked. He smiled.

"No, this is perfect. Just do me two favors – call me Bryce, and if I fall asleep, please wake me with coffee an hour before Dulles." She nodded and turned from him.

"Oh, one more thing," he called out. He laughed

inside as he watched her turn and force a smile. He got up from his seat and walked to her as a slight wave of turbulence nudged the jet at 42,000 feet.

"I want to thank you for taking the job last minute. I know it's holiday time for most people, and I appreciate it." She smiled.

"My pleasure. It's not every day you get to work with a Formula One world champion – especially one who's an American," she told him with what he read as a sincere smile and then left the cabin. Now back with his burger, Bryce stared out the window as he picked at his meal.

Who the hell's playing with me? Is it another renegade at the CIA? Is it Russo? What the hell ever happened to that prick? Maybe some shithead who found out it was me who planted a bug? Did someone find out it was me who killed that Russian mobster? I can't talk to anyone about this other than Jack. Nobody else is left.

Bryce spent most of the eastbound flight's four hours staring out the window, lost in thought. He had no idea what he would say to Kyoto or how she would react to seeing him at her door. As the sun faded behind them as they neared the nation's capital, Bryce steeled himself for what was to come. The ride from Dulles to Kyoto's residence at the Watergate in Washington went by in a flash. Bryce had been taught a lot by his late father, a Burlington police officer, and his late uncle, a battle-hardened Marine, and had used their lessons in dealing with anticipation well in life. Waiting for the perfect moment when the twelve-point buck stood still just long enough for the kill shot. Waiting for "lights out" at the front of a field of twenty million dollar race cars preparing to launch from stationary positions on the starting grid. Waiting for the moment, he'd plant a bug, feign enthusiasm for a terrorist when MI6 had used Bryce's celebrity to lure to a celebrity function and a set of cuffs, maintaining calm as he sat across from Max Werner as he watched the man drink his last drink. Bryce smiled at his bodyguards as he insisted they wait in the chauffeured black Cadillac Escalade.

"I need to do this alone, and with this hat and shades, nobody'll notice me. I'll be fine," he assured them. Nonetheless, Alan followed Bryce from the car and took a position in the lobby of Kyoto's building. Danny remained at the ready, sitting up front with the unsuspecting chauffeur.

The elevator traveled as smoothly as Bryce had remembered it. Aside from the ever-changing floor number display above the control panel, there wasn't any sensation of movement. When the doors opened, Bryce stepped out into the hallway; he looked down at the yellow-gold carpeting and remembered how Kyoto and Jon had talked fondly of watching the Wizard of Oz film as children in Japan and how they had once joked, "Follow the yellow brick road" after a day of sightseeing in DC the year before. Bryce followed that path until he reached #434 – Kyoto's.

He rang the bell once and then a second time. He leaned close to the door and listened. It was silent until the door behind him suddenly flung open, and soon after, his heart dropped again.

"She's gone," Bryce told Alan as he and Danny returned to the Escalade. Her nosy neighbor told me she moved back to Tokyo before Christmas.

"Shit, boss, that sucks. Now what?" Alan asked. Bryce stopped and stared at Alan until he did the same and turned toward him.

"Daytona," he said. "I'll try to get a message to her somehow, but I'm not flying to Japan to get a door slammed in my face. I owed her this, but now I'm done. It's time to say sayonara to that chapter in my life, put this behind us, and focus on who's screwing with me -and then deal with them – how do they say it in the movies – with extreme prejudice?"

"Fuckin' A," Danny said, "That's what we do best."

Quickly passing through Atlantic Aviation's private jet facility at Dulles, Bryce and his team were quickly back in the air. He'd stepped aboard as if he'd had blinders on, not even regarding the flight crew he usually spent time with. For thirty minutes, he sat quietly in the rear cabin of his Bombardier, alone with his thoughts. Only days before, Winters had been in a much friendlier environment. Lying on one of Ibiza's beautiful beaches after concluding four days of F1 racing practice at the Catalunya Circuit in Spain, he had much to appreciate: the anonymity, the ideal weather, warm Mediterranean waters, and a beautiful Spanish blonde he'd met days earlier. Testing had gone better than expected, and he looked forward to the coming season. His hand, badly injured during the murder attempt in Park City months before, bore scars but was functioning perfectly as he brought a cold beer to his lips...then...something entered his peripheral vision: she was headed for the turquoise water.

It was as if a storm cloud had suddenly covered the

sun. A tanned beauty with flowing silk black hair and wearing a yellow bikini and thong reminded him of Kyoto, the first woman he'd been able to open his heart to in years, only to have her run as far from him as she could. *Who could blame her?* She had fallen in love with a famous race car driver and moved from her home in Japan to the States to be closer to her brother—and to him—only to realize what a dangerous life her new man led and that she was suddenly caught up in it. Perhaps the kidnapper's shoving a gun in her face and brutally breaking her arm in Singapore had been enough to call it quits? *No*—Bryce couldn't; he wouldn't blame her. He recalled that last night together in the place he had called home.

"If you don't want to do this anymore, then why did you bother flying to Abu Dhabi to be with me and then back here for Thanksgiving?" he had asked her, fighting hard to control his frustration and tone. "That was just two weeks ago. What the hell's changed?" he asked. Kyoto had walked to him from just inside the front door after handing off her bags to an Uber driver. She reached up and gently placed her soft hands on his cheeks.

"Because right after we made love last night, I felt something under your pillow," she told him. "It was a gun. That wouldn't be there for fun; it was there for a reason, and I can't be a part of this anymore. I want to live a happy, *peaceful* life, not a risky one." Rather than make promises he probably wouldn't keep, he had let her go without another word. Once the door had closed behind her and the Uber drove out through the gates, Bryce marched back into the kitchen. He drank down a Heineken and then another, throwing the empty green bottles hard into the fireplace. He looked at the well-stocked bar in the corner of the great room and focused on the collection of bottles. Twelve-year-old Macallan, a more senior Hibiki whiskey he'd been gifted after a race win in Japan, and the old faithful he'd become very familiar with in the woods back home – Jägermeister. He shook his head, reminded of how poorly he'd feel in the morning if he took any of those out for a ride, and then turned his attention to the special dessert he had made Kyoto. He ignored the sweet scent as he dug through the giant chocolate cupcake with vanilla buttercream frosting, her favorite, until he found the four-carat emerald cut solitaire diamond ring he had intended for her to discover as he took a knee to propose. As he held it under the sink's tap to rinse it clean, he let go of it and watched it disappear into the darkness—a *proper* ending, as his friends back in England might say. Her ring, his house, and their love were all gone.

His mind had been preoccupied; he hadn't noticed the personnel change that had taken place. When a familiar voice with an Australian accent asked if he wanted a coffee, he jumped up in surprise and wrapped his arms around the woman he'd flown around the world with year after year – Jenny Kim.

"What the hell are you doing here?" he exclaimed as he stepped back from her and embraced her again.

"The skipper called me once you left Utah for DC," she began. "After spending a few days with my parents in New York, I remembered why I can only take them in short doses, so I took Amtrak down, and here I am."

"I am so happy to see you," he told her. "It's been a strange few days." Jenny nodded.

"I met the Johnsons," she said. "They seem like their mamma raised them right." Bryce laughed. "She did, but be sure to ask them about her cooking." Jenny smiled.

"Speaking of which, let me go check the galley. I'll bet all of you are hungry."

Bryce followed her there and then stepped into the cockpit.

"Change of plans," he told the flight crew. "We're still headed to Daytona, but we have to make another stop first. Time to go check on Jack Madigan in Charlotte."

"You sure he's there?" the co-pilot asked. "You know Jack."

"I tried to reach him on Christmas Eve, but it went to voicemail. When the news of the fire hit CNN, I thought I'd hear from him, but nada and that's not like him. I'm going to have to go bang on his door. We'll probably find him half-dressed in a Santa suit, surrounded by two hot models and a lot of empty tequila bottles. He could be anywhere if he's not there, but I want to try."

Ninety minutes later, as Bryce pulled up to Madigan's house on Lake Norman in a white Suburban he'd rented, he stopped at the end of the driveway and stared in disbelief. Then he smelled it, even with the windows up. It was the same smell as the charred ruins in Park City.

"Holy shit," Bryce muttered as the Johnsons opened their doors and got out. What remained of Madigan's beautiful lake house was taking its last breaths, still giving off faint whiffs of gray smoke. Bryce got out of the vehicle and surveyed the surroundings. Everything else seemed in order. Christmas lights, inflated Santas, and reindeer dressed the houses on either side of Madigan's. Bryce stood silently and just stared.

Jack – where the hell are you? Then he walked closer to the house, stepping under the yellow police tape and ignoring the printed warnings that read CRIME SCENE – DO NOT ENTER. With the house in ruins, Bryce could look straight across to the dock and the boat Madigan loved to party on. The dock was gone; only the tops of charred bulkheads were visible above the waterline. All he could see of the boat was a single antenna – leaning to one side as the boat listed as it sunk. A second later, the whoop of a police car's siren startled Bryce.

"Wait a minute – that's Bryce Winters!" the patrolman called out to the Johnsons as he drove his patrol car onto the lawn.

"I'm used to seeing all the NASCAR drivers and crews up here, but this is a first for me," he said with a broad grin. Danny walked toward the patrol car and said, "He won a Daytona 500." As Alan arrived, he finished his brother's sentence. "And he won Indy too."

"What the hell happened here?" Bryce asked as he stepped between the brothers. Do you know where the owner is?" The officer climbed out of the vehicle and shook Bryce's hand, but his expression changed.

"Are you a relative of Mr. Madigan? Because if so, I have some bad news."

CHAPTER FOUR

Within seconds of hearing what had happened, Bryce was at the wheel, driving south on Interstate 77 toward Charlotte. A short time later, after following the police car as if they were drafting nose to tail at Daytona, Bryce and the Johnsons arrived at the Carolinas Medical Center. The Level 1 trauma center was where a badly burned Jack Madigan had been airlifted on Christmas Eve after his house exploded with him in it. The patrolman who led Bryce to the hospital had called ahead, and two Charlotte uniformed police officers were waiting for his arrival near the emergency ward entrance. The two vehicles screeched to a halt as if making a pit stop in front of the doors.

Alan got behind the wheel of the rental to move it as Danny shadowed Bryce inside.

So far, Bryce had been able to move discreetly about the country, but Charlotte was race central for NASCAR stock car racing, and it seemed like everywhere he turned, someone recognized him. He may be an international champion who lives half a year and a day in Monte Carlo, but he had raced stock cars before a crash ended his chase for that title.

As the facility's media director, a short, round man excited to meet Bryce greeted him at the entrance. They exchanged a curt greeting, and then Bryce wanted to see Jack.

"Where is he? What's his condition? Nobody would tell me anything over the phone," he insisted. People noticed and stared as the director led Bryce and Johnson through the trauma center. Some called out while others tried to take a photo. Once inside a small consultation room at the far end of a bustling hallway, the director briefed Bryce on Madigan's condition.

"Your friend is in the ICU's burn unit on the third floor. He's suffered third-degree burns over seventy percent of his body and second-degree burns over the rest. He's in a medically induced coma and on a ventilator. The prognosis, I'm afraid, is not good. Not good at all," the man said. "I'm very sorry, Bryce." Bryce looked around the room and plopped into a worn brown leather chair. The room was cold, and the leather gave him a chill. Bryce had dealt with loss his entire life. Left motherless while still in the crib, his father, a disabled and heartbroken cop, had left raising Bryce to his uncle, Uncle Pete, who was also gone. A drunk driver had killed his first love, Christy, while Bryce waited for her after work for their date. He didn't let many people in as a result of all that, except for his friend Jack Madigan and his Kyoto.

Bryce looked up somberly, locking eyes with Danny and then looking at the director.

"Can I see him?" His voice and tone delivered the request as if he knew the answer. The director shook his head no.

"You aren't family, so no, I'm sorry. That's against protocol and to protect the patient's privacy," he answered.

"Fuck protocol," Danny growled as he turned and opened the door. "Come on, Bryce; he's up on three. We'll find him." As Bryce stood up, he saw two women dressed in blue business suits standing in the doorway in Danny's way.

✄

"Move," Danny ordered. As two black badge wallets carrying identity cards and FBI gold shields were raised to his face, Danny uttered the f-word as he studied the men coming up behind them. Two fit-looking uniformed North Carolina State Troopers with chiseled jaws and high and tight haircuts stood tall behind the FBI.

"We're Special Agents Donahue and Williams from the Charlotte field office. We need to speak with Mr. Winters," Donahue stated as he peered around Danny for their person of interest. "And you are?" Donahue asked. Danny studied them. Donahue, a tall, fit-looking woman in her late fifties with short, graying hair and piercing blue eyes. White blouse, no make-up. The other, Williams, was short, stocky, and in her thirties; her suit looked like it had been slept in, a light blue blouse. Danny noted their other hardware as the agents returned their wallets to their jacket pockets. Donahue wore a left shoulder holster bearing a black semi-automatic pistol, while Williams hung one from her right hip, leaving a surprisingly noticeable bump in her coat. *Desk jockey* Danny assessed. Donahue stepped close to Danny.

"We're here on official government business, and we need the room," she stated. "Mr. Winters, are you armed?" Donahue asked as she stepped past Danny and into the room. "We know *he* is." One of the troopers stepped close.

"Let me see your carry permit," the trooper directed

with an attitude and a southern accent. Danny slowly opened his brown camo-colored jacket with his right hand to reveal his sidearm and then reached into his jeans pocket with his left hand and withdrew a money clip. Slowly lowering his right hand, he picked through his credit cards and IDs and held up his New Jersey concealed carry permit. The trooper took it and studied it, holding it up for his partner to see.

"Jersey. These are hard to get," he remarked. Danny smiled. *Depends on who you know.*

"But we're in North Carolina, in case you missed that part."

"My bad," Danny said with a smile as he removed a stack of cards from his left jacket pocket that he held together with a fat rubber band. He smiled as he fanned them to reveal the one the trooper was looking for.

"Okay, he's good. What about you, Bryce?" the trooper asked as he stepped further into the room and toward him. Bryce shook his head no and then got up from his chair. Bryce stuck out his hand and shook the troopers'.

"Danny, go ahead and wait outside with the troopers, or even better, see if you can find the cafeteria and buy them a round of coffee. This won't take long." Danny nodded and followed the trooper and the hospital director from the room.

As Bryce sat back in the warmer chair, he watched the agents prepare for the interview.

"Sorry about your loss," Williams began.

"Madigan's not dead yet," Bryce snapped.

"I'm sorry, I meant the victim in Park City and the loss of your home," Williams offered.

"Thank you."

"The sheriff stated it was arson, and our forensic team agrees. Nobody tried to hide anything. Whoever killed the deceased and torched the place must have poured gasoline all over the house. So far, they've found what's left of at least three charred jerry cans in the debris."

"Any idea who did this?" Donahue asked.

"Nope."

"You sure?" she followed.

"Yep."

"Where were you at the time the fire started?" Williams asked.

"At a friend's on the other side of town," Bryce answered.

"And you will give us their contact info so we can verify that?"

"Sure. I have nothing to hide. She's my masseuse. I've been training hard and needed to get some kinks worked out. She had no plans, and neither did I, so she ordered pizza. We watched a movie, and then the alarm company called me."

"What set off the alarm?" Donohue asked.

"Fire sensors. We already learned the hard way that smart people could work around entry and motion alarms," Bryce said as he held up his right hand, displaying the scars from the bullet that ended his chase for a championship the year before. Donahue nodded.

"What did you watch?" Williams asked. Bryce thought for a moment.

"Scrooged and then Love Actually, but no happy

ending for me, though," Bryce paused. "That's when the alarm company called."

"Is this masseuse an employee, a contractor, a lover?" Donahue asked.

"Just a friend I pay by the hour," Bryce answered as he looked at his watch and observed the agents looking at each other. Williams nodded, got up, and left the room. Donahue stood up from her place at the table and moved to the chair beside Bryce.

"Listen, we're on your side. We want to catch whoever did this as much as you do."

"Doubt it," he smirked. Donahue sat back in her chair and looked at the door.

"Okay, Bryce, we know you've had some dealings with the CIA. Our records show you did some team building with the State Department at a race track near D.C. We know you had a meeting there, a private one, but we saw the logs. You met with Sandra Jennings there that day. She wound up dead in Singapore harbor weeks later. We know all about the kidnapping and shooting at your property. Can you tell me how you and the CIA knew each other?"

"Nope," Bryce said, which made Donohue grind her jaw tight.

"I read the reports. Some of it was redacted, but can I be frank?" she asked. Bryce smiled.

"Don't shit a shitter. What were you, some sort of secret agent? Were you a spy for the CIA? You can tell me. This is all confidential." Bryce was about to say something, but suddenly, the door opened, and Special Agent Williams entered carrying three large coffees. She placed the tray on the table and handed Bryce a Starbucks Grande.

"With sweetener and hazelnut creamer as you like it," Williams said with a smile.

"You *are* good. Nice intel," he said as he took a sip.

"No, just lucky," he added. "Johnson was in the cafeteria with the troopers. He told me."

Williams retook her seat and slid a cup to Donohue.

"So, what'd I miss?" Williams asked.

"Nada," her partner replied. Bryce took another sip and nodded his approval.

"Two things," Bryce began. "First, I'm here for my friend who's burned to a crisp on the third floor. I know a lot about burn cases. I guess he's got a one-in-a-hundred chance of survival, and if he lives, he'll be miserable for the rest of his life. A shitty prognosis either way. So I'm pissed about what's happened to my friend, pissed about my house, and pissed you haven't caught anyone yet." Donahue leaned forward.

"So tell us," she said.

"Tell us what, what'd I miss?" Williams asked.

"Can't. It's above your pay grade," he told them.

"So there *is* a tie to the CIA!" Donahue said as if she'd scored a point.

"No, I'm just screwing with you," Bryce said, changing his expression to a very serious one.

"Okay, so let's mix it up since you're in a playful mood," Donahue said as her expression hardened. She leaned in.

"Why did you kill Jon Watanabe?" she asked.

"What?" Bryce shouted back with surprise.

"You blamed him for getting you caught up in the whole batshit crazy Deadly Driver covert ops at Langley, didn't you?" she pushed.

Bryce threw his coffee across the room, watching it smash like abstract art against a blank whiteboard. He returned his glare to Donahue, trying to hold firm, but his conflicted emotions and a lack of sleep washed over him. Then, he realized he'd exposed a vulnerability, and Donohue's eyes showed it.

"Bryce," Donahue questioned, "You're a CIA-trained assassin, aren't you?" Bryce stared at the agent, and the deep breath he took and then let out showed his frustration. But it also calmed him.

"Enough of this bullshit. I need to make a call," Bryce said as he pulled his iPhone from his jeans pocket.

"Good idea. You might want to call a lawyer," Donahue suggested.

"No, I have a better idea," he whispered.

Bryce scrolled through an endless list of contacts on his phone but stopped at one marked WH. He tapped the number, and a moment later, he smiled at Donahue.

"Hi, this is Bryce Winters calling for the president."

Williams looked across to Donahue and whispered, "Yeah, sure." Donahue grinned.

"Guess we're playing chess now."

"Starting to feel a bit more like career suicide to me," Williams offered as Bryce got up and turned his back to the women. After ending the call, he walked to the whiteboard and tried to clean up the mess he had made. Suddenly, as a knock was heard at the door, Donahue and Williams's phones vibrated. Then, just as the agents answered their phones, one of the troopers stepped in.

"We've been told to escort you to the airport, Mr. Winters. Please come with us."

CHAPTER FIVE

BACK ABOARD HIS jet and now climbing high and away from Douglas International in Charlotte, Bryce watched the ground grow further away as the Bombardier rose through a choppy, cloudy sky headed south for Florida. Bryce hadn't said much after his meetings at the hospital; he knew Madigan was gone, even if they hadn't pulled the sheet over him yet.

"Think the White House will keep the FBI off your ass now, Bryce," Danny asked from across the cabin. Lost in thought, Bryce ignored the question momentarily and then turned toward his friend and bodyguard. As the bright light from the fading sun in the western sky nearly blinded Bryce, Danny quickly reached to close the shade.

"I've dealt with too many feds in the last few years," Bryce began as he refocused on Danny. "The older one, Donahue, is going to be a pain in the ass. People like that, once they think they're on to something, never let go." The attendant interrupted the two as she delivered their drinks and servings of warmed assorted nuts.

"What's that, scotch? You don't drink scotch," Alan

Johnson said as he returned from the restroom in the forward cabin.

"Just one – this one's for Jack," Bryce declared as he raised a tulip glass that would typically hold his beer. The brothers raised their glasses, OJ for Danny and Coke Zero for Alan, and toasted Jack Madigan. One sip later, Bryce shook his head at the taste and smell and put the glass down. "My father drank that crap, only cheaper stuff, once he went on disability. I could never stand the smell of it or what it represented, especially now." Bryce sat quietly and turned his attention to the window, fighting back his emotion. He remembered the last time he'd seen Max Werner, the billionaire industrialist who had funded his rise to racing fame. He had poured a scotch for Max that fateful afternoon in Berchtesgaden, and the man had died shortly after. "They're all gone," he whispered and then focused through the window on a commercial jetliner headed north in the distance. After a moment, he turned back to the brothers.

"I'm going to find whoever killed Jon and Jack and make them pay, an eye for an eye. I'm not sure you guys want to follow me into the darkness, and I won't blame you a bit if you don't." Neither brother responded.

As Bryce opted to focus on the growing darkness in the distance, Danny and Alan moved to the front of the plane and sat across a table from one another. Jenny served them coffee for Danny and a Mountain Dew for Alan. They thanked her but waved off the dinner menus; they needed to talk.

"Dude, the troopers who boxed me in outside the hospital said Bryce killed at least two federal investigators in cold blood," Alan whispered, watching the curtain on the galley and the shadows cast by the attendant's long, athletic legs.

"So why isn't he in jail?" Danny pushed back.

"They said the FBI told them he was a hit man for the government. The president was using him to do covert hits overseas, and when two agents caught him in the act, he killed them both. They said Uncle Pete and Madigan were also part of it."

"Bryce? We are talking about the guy in the back who drives race cars for a living?" Danny asked, shaking his head as he surveyed the cabin. "They're full of shit."

"Remember that thing in Mexico with the two people he and Madigan were off-roading with? They weren't tourists like the news said. They were the agents and didn't just screw up and drive off the cliff. A Russian sniper took them out. Bryce paid for the hit." Danny sat back in his chair and stared at his brother.

"So the feds have him cornered in a room blocked by two state troopers, and he makes one phone call – to DC – and walks right out of there? This isn't a damn movie Danny, this is the real shit, and now we're in the middle of it." Danny sat back and pushed the call button. A moment later, Jenny was standing over them.

"Ready for dinner, I'll bet," she suggested.

"Yes – think you can rustle up some burgers and fries?" Danny asked.

"Both medium well. American cheese. Pepper Jack if you have it. Barbeque for him, mayo for me, please – on the side," Danny added. She nodded and retreated to her station as Alan sat forward again.

"This gig pays really well, bro, and hell, I have nothing to go back to in Utah. Let's ride this out, go to some races, meet some models, and cash in," Danny urged. "Plus, I don't believe a damn thing the feds are saying about Bryce." Alan shook his head.

"That's because you don't want to," Alan said as he slid to the edge of his seat.

"Where are you going?" Danny asked, sticking his arm out to stop his twin.

"I'm going to ask him point blank," Alan stated. "I'm not sure I can work for someone who kills any American who wears a uniform or carries a badge. I wore one." Suddenly, the seat behind Alan spun around. It was Bryce. He stood up quickly, and he wasn't smiling. Even more concerning, he was holding a gun.

CHAPTER SIX

SOMEWHERE HIGH OVER the Outer banks of North Carolina, Bryce press-checked the black Sig Sauer semi-automatic 45 and saw the round in the chamber.

"Bryce?" Danny asked. Bryce looked at Danny, took the gun by the barrel with his left hand, and held it out for Alan.

"Go on, take it." Alan looked at Danny and then reached for the weapon. Retaking his seat, Alan dropped the magazine from the gun and racked the slide, ejected the bullet, and caught it in the air. He placed the gun and magazine on the table but kept the bullet, a hollow point, and began to roll it between his right thumb and forefinger.

"Wow," Bryce began, "Look at those expressions." He stepped into the aisle, stood at the table, and stared at the brothers before him.

"So, what's going on here? What's up?"

Danny looked at Alan and nodded for him to answer the question.

"Bryce," Alan began. "Why don't you sit back down,

and we talk through a few things." Obliging, Bryce smiled, stepped back, and sat opposite theirs in a beige leather captain's chair. As Jenny arrived and freshened their drinks, Bryce told her he was famished.

"I'll take a burger medium well, please, Jenny, with onion rings or fries – whatever you've got."

"Mayo?" she asked. Bryce nodded.

"See Alan," Danny began, "I told you he's one of us. No Grey Poupon for the man from Monaco." Bryce forced a laugh. He knew there was an issue, and this last remark confirmed it. Here he was, cruising at 40,000 feet with two trained killers, and now, one of them was holding *his* gun.

⋘

"Bryce, I never was big on bullshit, so I'll cut right to it," Alan said as he pushed his plate toward the window side of the table and swiveled his chair ninety degrees so they'd be face to face. Donning a look of concern, Bryce studied Danny and then focused back on Alan.

"Back at the hospital, the two troopers who waited outside with me had quite a lot to say about you and your situation. I guess we should say *our* situation at this point."

"Keep going," Bryce urged as he sat forward and leaned forward toward Alan.

"Well, first they said you weren't shit, that anyone can win at Daytona."

Bryce laughed and let out a sigh of relief.

"Is that what's bothering you?"

"Nope. The one redneck said you should show up at Darlington or Martinsville. Win there, and you'd have his respect." Bryce laughed again. "Well, you know what they say about opinions and assholes; everyone has them." Alan didn't smile and turned to Danny, who had given Bryce's remark a laugh.

"So we talked for a bit out there, trooper to trooper, and they told me what they had heard about you from the FBI – that you had some U.S. government agents killed in Mexico, that the shoot-out at your home wasn't with a rogue CIA case worker; it was where you killed the guy who had something on you. And that you lured a CIA boss to Singapore and had her fed to the crabs in the harbor."

"Sounds like a James Bond movie, doesn't it," Bryce joked as he sat back in his chair. Alan watched as Bryce seemed to consider all that had been said.

"Nobody on the headset to help you with strategy on this one, Bryce. I don't give a shit about what those troopers said about your driving, but I do have a real issue if you took out someone in law enforcement. So I need to know – did you?" Alan watched as Bryce picked up the phone and called for service. A moment later, as Jenny arrived, Bryce smiled at her.

"Did you put the knock-out drugs in both of their drinks or just Alan's," Bryce asked and then watched as Alan's eyes widened, his body tense, as he stared at the woman.

"Oh damn, Bryce," Jenny began. "I dosed someone, but now that I think about it, I might have mistakenly dosed the two in the cockpit." Alan turned to Danny. *Now what?*

⁓

Bryce watched as Jenny laughed and walked back to the galley, but when he returned focus to the brothers, they looked dazed and confused.

"Alan, relax. I'm joking. I know it's a bit different from what you're used to from me, but I'm a bit out of sorts. We only dose bad guys and throw them out of the plane at low altitudes, preferably over shark-infested water. You're the good guys, remember?" Bryce watched as Danny kicked his brother's foot from under the table. Bryce sat forward again and looked up and down the aisle before proceeding.

"Listen, there's a lot of things going on and way too many moving parts to this. You guys signed NDAs when we put together your thirty-day contracts, and what I can tell you will fall under that. Alan and Danny exchanged glances. So, I *can* only tell you that I work for the State Department occasionally but always very unofficially. They use my celebrity status and the access that comes with it to pass a note or exchange a thought with people they may not have relationships with. Make sense?"

Alan nodded. "But you didn't answer the question. Have you ever killed any American in law enforcement or the military?" Bryce looked at Danny and read his expression; he wanted to hear the answer, too.

"Let me ask you this. This is way before our time, but if you found out that a CIA agent was the sniper who killed JFK – the President of the United States, would you have been okay with someone taking out *that* agent?"

"Holy shit," Alan blurted. "I get it now. You *are* a contractor for the CIA!"

CHAPTER SEVEN

It had been two days since Bryce's jet had landed in Miami. Bryce sat alone in his black gym shorts and red t-shirt on a private balcony on the fiftieth floor of the Aston Martin Residences overlooking Biscayne Bay. He watched the lights of three cruise ships as they sailed into the darkening horizon. As Jenny delivered a steaming mug of coffee, she plopped down on a cushioned seat two chairs over and shook her head.

"I can see how people once thought the world was flat. It does look like they will sail off the earth's edge. At forty-five thousand feet, we see the curvature of the earth all the time, but from here, yea, back in the old days," she trailed off.

"Speaking of flying, are you ready to get back to work?" Bryce asked.

"Really? Do we have to? Can't we stay here another week? I love Miami, and I *love* Ameer's condo!"

As Bryce sipped at his coffee and savored the aroma, he shook his head no and laughed.

"Sorry, luv, time to get back to work. It's time to get

back in front of all the questions and the cameras. I have to sign in at the track in the morning, so wheels up at eight."

"Are you okay with only having Danny and Alan on you for this event? Don't you need more bodies just in case?" she asked.

"I've been trying to remember the name of a guy Sandra Jennings had mentioned. He's former FBI, and she said he's helped some people in Formula One." Bryce sipped at the coffee once more.

"It's a shame those assholes in Singapore killed her. She left a young son behind."

"Sounds like the guy's a fixer," Jenny said as she strained to find the last cruise ship on the horizon.

"He's tough to track down, but I can't ask around. I need to keep all of this close."

"You do know we private flight attendants are privy to a lot," Jenny began. "I can if anyone in the circle knows who this is." Bryce smiled but shook his head no. "No, best let me do it my way." Jenny nodded, but Bryce locked eyes with her.

"Seriously, Jen, you need to stay out of this. I have no idea where this is headed, and you don't need to get caught up in this any more than you already are by working with me."

"You're the boss," she said as she reached for her drink.

Bryce got up from his chair and stretched. He'd enjoyed these quiet, restful days in South Florida but yearned for the cockpit. He loved racing; it was his life, and he was up for the challenge of competing in his first twenty-four-hour endurance race – IMSA's Rolex 24. He'd be driving a Mercedes AMG that, on the outside, might resemble what he'd left behind in his garage in Park City, but this one, in racing trim, would be even more fun to maneuver.

"You and Danny going out again tonight?" Bryce asked. She nodded with a grin as she undid the tie that held her blonde locks and retied it.

"You're not falling in love again, are you, young lady?" he asked. She blushed.

"Nope. He's just good in bed, and I find all the guns, ink, and war stories kind of hot."

Bryce shook his head and laughed as he walked through the flowing sheer that blew through the sliding door as he opened it.

"And what about Alan? How are you two getting along?" Bryce asked.

"Fine," she answered. "He's a good guy, but it's clear he's got some baggage."

"Who doesn't?" he said, laughing.

"Well, you guys enjoy your last night on the town, and I'll spend a few more hours on the simulator."

"Not the blow-up one, I hope," Jenny teased. Bryce shook his head and continued into the living room. "Then I'll take Alan to the tactical range and see what kind of trouble we can get into."

CHAPTER EIGHT

DAYTONA IN JANUARY wasn't known for high temperatures, and today was no different, but it's undoubtedly the hottest spot on the planet for auto racing at the start of each new year. Bryce stood in line with many other well-known racers, team owners, engineers, and mechanics and was in a great mood. He was back at a race track, back among friends, and physically and emotionally psyched to do what he did best – race to a win. As the sun played hide & seek behind the clouds that blew high overhead, he adjusted his sponsor's red, white, and blue racing jacket's zipper accordingly. Just as the sun went into hiding again, another form of darkness - his racing nemesis, Tony Bishop of Canada, came strolling up the line.

"Well, look what we have here, ladies and gentlemen," Bishop said to anyone interested. "It's Bryce -don't shoot-Winters!" Bishop stepped close to Bryce but was pushed off by another figure dressed in America's colors.

"Back off," Danny whispered, "or I'll break off your arm and shove it up your ass!"

Bishop stepped back and glared at the man as Bryce grinned.

"Yep, he's with me. Isn't he good?" Bryce asked. "Now tell me, why does your breath always smell like skunk, Tony?" Bishop began to edge closer to Bryce, but Danny stepped between them. "What the hell have you been eating?"

"You need a thug to protect you now, Bryce?"

"No, I've knocked you on your ass more than once, but if I do it here, you'll run off like a baby, and I'll have to spend the morning with the commissioner rather than in the race car. Do me, do us all a favor. Go buy some mouthwash and then fuck-off." The people around them in line had all tuned in to the confrontation, and a few recorded it on their phones. Then, a woman stepped between Bishop and Danny, and when Bryce saw her face, he felt the blood drain from his heart. It was Claudia Werner – not just a dear friend but the widow of a man Bryce had terminated for the CIA.

"Claudia," Bryce exclaimed. He stared at her for a time and then wrapped his arms around her. He felt her hands against the small of his back, pulling him closer. He closed his eyes and took in the same alluring scent she had worn the night Max Werner had introduced them at a gala at the Royal Automobile Club in London. Bryce hadn't spoken to Claudia since Max's funeral service in a six hundred-year-old Bavarian church six months before this. He'd seen her if for only a split second, standing behind Kyoto at a crowded press conference in Abu Dhabi after the last F1 race of the season. The look she'd given him that night, standing within inches of the woman he loved, had concerned him. He knew he could have called her but had decided to let whatever storm that was be.

"How's Mila?" he whispered as he stepped back and gazed at Claudia – *how's the daughter that will now grow up without a father thanks to me and my government?*

"Come on now, break it up," an awkward and appearing somewhat jealous Bishop joked as he put his hand on Claudia's shoulder. She turned to him, and from Bishop's expression, Bryce assumed she had burned a hole in the man's head with her eyes. She turned back to Bryce.

"Mila is the little angel she's been since the day she was born," she stated. "And she misses you." *Another dagger to the heart, this thrust felt rusty and deeper.*

"I miss her too. I saw you for a flash in Abu Dhabi, but then you disappeared. I wanted to talk to you, but the press conference was crazy."

"Come on, Bryce. You have a plane and a phone, and I bet they both still work. You can see her anytime you wish. But Abu Dhabi was two months ago. Have you been in a coma or something?" she asked jokingly.

"Listen, my number has not changed, and we are still in Zermatt or Munich, so any time you want to come to see us, just call."

"I will – I promise," he told her. Claudia began to turn away but suddenly turned back.

"Why put it off? Perhaps we could meet for dinner while we're here in Florida—just you and me. We can leave Tony to his simulator," she said with a grin. Bryce smiled as he watched Bishop take his turn, now burning a hole in her with his eyes.

"I'd like that, Claudia; I'd like that a lot," Bryce began.

"I promise to call and soon." She stepped close to him again and took him by the hands. She smiled at him while she squeezed them. He felt a twinge of pain in his still-healing right hand but didn't let on. "We have something to discuss, and I think you know what it is." As she pulled away, her expression had changed. *She knows.*

Inside the pearl white Prevost motorcoach Bryce used at events in North America as he began to dress for his first laps out on the speedway's massive road course, his phone sounded the familiar tone of his Formula One team owner Ameer Kazaan. After they chatted for a few minutes, Kazaan provided the intel Bryce had been searching for.

"Matt Christopher – he's the man who helped keep my son out of jail in Singapore two years ago," Kazaan said. "He's former FBI, got his own money – a lot of money– and runs a global security firm. He's a good guy, down to earth. You'll like him."

"Shit, Ameer, I don't want to work with anyone involved with the American government. Remember, the prick who shot me was from the CIA." The call went quiet.

"Ameer?" Bryce asked.

"Yes, Bryce, I am here. But I think you will be okay with Matt Christopher. He was framed by the FBI when he got too close to locking up some of your senators, so he left the job and moved overseas. But it's too late now. I already told him about you and your problem."

"Well, what the hell, what's the worst that could happen, right? But tell me about Abbas.

I didn't know he'd gotten into any trouble."

"Exactly! That's why Matt is so good. Nobody found

out about the unfortunate incident with my son. A young woman who turned out to be a rather enterprising prostitute had tried to blackmail him for money – my money. Matt took care of everything like it never happened. I think he can help you, Bryce. We must find out who did this to you and poor Jack." The call went quiet for a moment. The distant sound of race cars on the track made both men pause to consider Jack Madigan's plight.

"Yeah, it's not good, Ameer. They wouldn't let me see him, but I know it's not good." The call went quiet again.

"Ameer?"

"Bryce, you don't know?" Ameer asked.

"Know what?"

"It's Jack. He died during the night."

Bryce felt like he'd crashed hard again, almost knocking the life right out of him. Tears formed in his eyes as he added Jack Madigan's name to the list of people he had loved that he had now lost. He walked to the front of the Prevost to look at the faces in the photos that followed him wherever he raced. But - the three photos were gone. *They were there earlier, right, or were they?* He thought of Jack as he shook his head in disbelief. At first, he grew sadder, if that was possible, but then another emotion flowed through him in a flash as if he'd made a split-second pit stop. He was filled with rage.

"Ameer, I need a few minutes to get my shit together," Bryce said. "Please text me that guy's contact info, and I'll chase him down. I need to go now, Ameer. Thank you." With the news still swirling in his head, Bryce stared at the spot where his prized photos had always been. It had been three months since he'd last been in the Prevost, during the F1 in Texas. The first was a photo with his high school sweetheart, Christy. The second was a photo with his father, Paul, and his uncle, Pete. The third, and the one that reminded him that he took deadly risks on and off the track, was with Max Werner standing with Bryce in victory lane at Daytona just a few years earlier. A knock at the entry door shook Bryce back to the present. As the door opened, it was Danny.

"Hey Bryce, one of your crew guys said it's time to roll." Bryce nodded but continued to stare at the bare wall.

"Two minutes, and I'll be there, Danny. I just found out Jack didn't make it. I need a minute for myself." Danny's head dropped as the news hit him like a brick.

"No worries, boss," Danny said as he took a moment to gather himself. As Danny took a step down, he closed the Prevost door gently. Bryce then raised his phone and called Ameer.

"Bryce?" Ameer answered.

"Ameer, I need another favor. Can you have someone check my suites – the one on wheels and the ones they box up? I need to be sure the photos that go to the races with me are still there. Someone's taken them from my American rig."

"I'll take care of that right away, Bryce. Do you think it's an accident, or is someone toying with you?" Bryce placed the phone on speaker and sat it on the bureau in the master suite. He tensed as he changed from jeans and a polo shirt to fire-resistant underwear and a white driving suit with red and blue markings.

"I don't know Ameer, but I can tell you this – if the photos are gone from there too, then you have an internal security problem that you'll have to sort out. This is getting wild."

"I texted you Matt Christopher's info. Did you get it?" Ameer asked.

"It's here, but I've been distracted. I'll call him right after this first practice session. I have to go Ameer. Thank you for your help, and I'm sorry to have drawn you into this." Bryce stared at himself in the mirror. *Uncle Pete and Jon Watanabe drew me in, and now they're both dead.*

The first daylight test session went very well as Bryce familiarized himself with the car, the team, and the track. The layout at Daytona for the endurance races would be new to him and incorporated the high-banked, high-speed corners of the superspeedway but also ran on the infield's many left and right tight turns and the famous "bus stop" meant to slow cars on the backstretch. Getting acquainted with the white #55 Mercedes AMG he'd be racing in the GTD Pro class came quickly at 175 mph. It had to. With significantly different horsepower and handling than his F1 car, he had a blast getting used to the car. Frank Dini, the team's lead engineer, a short and stocky New York Italian in his 70s who had wrenched on cars that had won the twenty-four-hour races at Daytona and LeMans a handful of times had given Bryce a smile and a high five after he brought the car back to the garage without a scratch.

"Now keep it that way, and we'll win this thing," Dini had said with a confident wink.

Many hours later, after Bryce had somehow continued to shelve Jack Madigan's death until the end of the day when he'd be alone and let the tears flow, he buckled in for the first nighttime practice session. The temperature had dropped, and Bryce wanted to fire the engine, get back on track, focus on racing, and push everything down deeper inside. On the flight to Daytona, Bryce realized Madigan wouldn't survive and had already begun to mourn the loss. It had been the abruptness of the news that had delivered the gut punch. Now, it was time to park that emotion, at least for now, and go fast again because that's what racers do. This time, in the darkness and the rain. In Formula One, he had always done well in the wet, often attributing it to his experience growing up driving fast on and off the roads of Vermont and New Hampshire. As he sat quietly on pit road, buckled in, awaiting the direction to start the engine, Bryce thought about the field of international driving stars who surrounded him on the grid. He thought of his plight, a trained killer for the country he loved. He laughed to himself. I wonder how many of these people have ever done what I've done. Not just race but served their country in another type of uniform as a spy.

He thought of the film Ford versus Ferrari he had watched the night before, where two major brands, American and Italian, fought it out in endurance races just like this one. The fact that the actor Matt Damon had also been the star of the Jason Bourne spy films, something Bryce could also relate to, made him laugh. Maybe they'll make a movie about me someday.

An hour later, while racing around the thirty-one-degree banking of turn four, just as a light rain began to taper off and he moved low to overtake a slower car, his right front tire exploded, which made the car turn right and crash hard and fast into the white retaining wall at the top of the track. Within seconds, the hard crash and collision with two other race cars left three smoldering piles of recycling strewn across the track apron. He stood with the two other drivers, a lanky Italian road racing star and an up-and-coming rookie from Brazil, and surveyed the damage as a small fire erupted in one of the cars but was quickly extinguished by the safety crew as they arrived. After a short ride and visit to the infield medical center, a requirement for any driver involved in a crash, all three were released to reunite with their teams and assess the damage. As Bryce's destroyed Mercedes was brought back to the garage area on a flatbed, a crewmember had driven Bryce to his pearl white Prevost motor coach in a golf cart within seconds of leaving the infield hospital. The cause of the crash had yet to be discovered, but just after Bryce finished dressing back into street clothes, Danny knocked at the door and entered.

"Your crew chief wants to show you something in the garage," Danny called out. "He said it was very serious and not to say anything to anyone." The rain and late hour had sent most back to their hotels or into the warmth and dryness of the RVs and motor coaches that filled the infield and "Driver's Only" parking lot, so Bryce's quiet ride to the garage area went unnoticed, or so they hoped. Once inside the garage, the doors all closed for the night, Bryce began walking to Dini, who shook his head as he pulled the car cover off the nose of the Mercedes. Dini gestured for Bryce to come to the front of the car as he called out to Danny.

"Could you step outside and make sure nobody comes

in and that nobody takes any photos through the windows?" Bryce shook Dini's hand as he surveyed the garage.

"Other than a big repair bill, what did you want to show me?" Bryce asked.

Dini took a knee and pointed.

"Is that what I think it is?" Bryce asked, leaning in much closer to inspect the car.

"When I was in the Marines, I worked weapons and ballistics. Those marks, young man, were made by a sniper. Somebody took a shot at you tonight."

CHAPTER NINE

STANDING IN THE garage area at Daytona, a cold rain now pelting the windows and doors, Bryce was stunned.

"Who else has seen this?" Bryce asked as he ran his fingers along the marks left by the lead.

"The guys were looking at everything, but the minute I saw it, I told everyone it had been a long, cold day and sent them back to the hotel," Dini told him. "I don't think they realized what they were looking at. And then I called your security." Bryce took a knee while Dini leaned in, studying what had been found.

"A bullet did that for sure, Bryce. It went through the hood, marked this part, and then hit the tire before it wound up who knows where." Dini stared at his driver. "What the hell's going on here, Bryce? Did some deranged fan follow you here from Park City and take a shot? This is crazy." Bryce shook his head and watched Danny through a garage window. Bryce stood up and surveyed the garage again.

"Where's the tire?" he asked Dini.

"The tire guys came for it the minute the car was

dropped here. The damn thing had a hole in it; it reminded me of a top fuel drag racing tire when engine shrapnel tears into one. My bet is they'll figure it out before morning if they haven't already." The two men stood quietly, staring at the damage. Suddenly, the door opened, and Danny fast walked to them.

"We need to get you out of here," Danny suggested as he stepped toward Bryce and reached for his arm. Bryce pulled away abruptly. He was angry.

"Not yet, Danny; if someone wanted to shoot me while I was driving, they could have. This was a pro, a sniper. I think we all realize that." Bryce walked from the men and stepped to the garage door window. Dini followed him there.

"Bryce, what the hell's going on?" Dini asked.

"Someone's fucking with me," he began. "First the fire, then Jack, then my pictures, and now this." Dini scratched his head.

"Photos, what photos? Bryce, we need to call someone. IMSA, the FBI, the State Police, somebody," Dini insisted.

"Not yet, Frank. This was directed at me. Nobody's blown up the place or –"

"Wait a minute, Bryce," Dini interrupted. "Two other drivers were at risk out there because of this. This isn't just about you." Dini placed his left arm on Bryce's shoulder and stepped close. He began to speak but stopped, looked to his left and right, and then patted Bryce's shoulder as he leaned in close.

"Listen, I've wanted to work with you for ten years and finally got my chance, but I don't want any part of this if someone's going to get killed. Racing is dangerous enough." Bryce turned to look at Dini.

"Frank, you need to keep this between us. Give me twelve hours to develop a plan, or I'll withdraw from the event." Bryce checked his watch. "Give me until ten in the morning. Can you do that?" Dini stared at Bryce and nodded in agreement before returning to the destroyed race car. Danny let out a slight whistle.

"Bryce, we need to get you the hell out of here. I called the pilots and put them on standby," Danny said sternly. Bryce looked back at Dini and watched the racing veteran slowly cover the car, like a doctor covering the deceased.

"Frank?" Bryce called out. Dini stopped for a moment, as had the rain. He turned and then glared at Bryce.

"You've got eleven hours and fifty-five minutes, so get moving," Dini declared, his glare softening. Bryce nodded and left the garage, but before they could drive off, Dini called out to them as he approached the cart. He surveyed the area and leaned in.

"You two realize where the shot must have come from, don't you?" Dini asked.

"Where?" Danny asked.

"There," Dini said as he pointed past the men seated in the cart. Bryce got out of the cart to see where Dini was focused as Danny kept scanning the area around them. The vertical scoring tower for the speedway was sticking straight up toward the sky.

Bryce nodded in agreement, and then Danny hit the gas, headed for the Prevost. Moments later, the area lit up with red and blue lights from atop one Florida State

Trooper cruiser that came out of nowhere and pulled in front of the golf cart. Then, a second came up from behind and blocked them in. Danny turned to Bryce.

"What's your guess, friend or foe?" Bryce shrugged his shoulders, climbed out of the cart, and waved to the troopers approaching him.

"They don't look very friendly," Danny said, placing his hands high on the steering wheel.

"I guess we'll find out," Bryce said under his breath.

CHAPTER TEN

JUST PAST SIX, as the sun rose over the Atlantic and brought warmth to Daytona, Bryce sat up from the king bed in the rear of his suite on wheels. He hadn't slept, tossing, turning, and scrolling through his phone for hours as he waited for the new day to begin. Stopping in the bathroom on the way to the coffee maker, he stared at his tired face and bloodshot eyes and then spent thirty seconds figuring out how to operate the new coffee maker; he'd worn the last one out. Bryce placed four white ceramic F1 mugs on the kitchen table, then slowly, cautiously poked his head out the door. He waved to the uniformed state trooper who was standing watch.

"Come in and get some coffee," Bryce said in a low tone. Seconds later, the trooper who had said goodnight to Bryce just six hours earlier sat at the table and placed his tan campaign hat on a nearby chair. Bryce studied him for a moment, taking note of the man's flat top haircut and the massive arms, chest, and shoulders of a bodybuilder.

"How long have you been a trooper?" Bryce asked as he filled the man's mug and sat across from him.

"Seven years, Mr. Winters," the trooper answered. Bryce smiled and said, "It's Bryce."

For the next ten minutes, the two engaged in small talk. They talked about racing, cars, weapons, and their upbringing. Trooper Brian Kane was raised by two detective parents in Tampa and had served in the Marines for ten years before signing up for another type of duty.

"We have a lot in common then," Bryce began. "A police officer and a Marine sniper raised me and kicked my ass if they ever heard me being rude or disrespectful to anyone. Well, just about anyone. They didn't mind it when I decked some shithead for bullying somebody. I guess you could say I was raised old school."

"Doesn't sound like you came from money. How'd you get into racing?" Kane asked. Bryce opened a cabinet and pulled out a box of donuts. He stared at the fruit bowl on the table and then smelled the donuts. Smiling, he offered the trooper a donut and then devoured one with chocolate frosting.

"No, I didn't grow up with money. I snow-plowed every winter to make money to race. I grew up in Vermont, and back then, thank God, there was a lot of snow." Suddenly, a knock at the door interrupted them. Bryce got up to answer it, but Trooper Kane stepped before him.

"Let me, just in case," Kane told him, then moved to the door. It was the track's security director, Johnny Parsons, a tall and thin South Georgian in his sixties who had worked at the track for the twenty-five years since he finished seventh in his last NASCAR race there.

"Good morning, gentlemen; glad to see I'm not waking anyone," Parsons said.

"Want some coffee?" Bryce asked, holding the pot and a mug up for Parsons to see.

"No thanks, Bryce. One more cup of caffeine, and they'll have to take me to the hospital." Parsons took a moment to survey the motor coach's interior and then refocused on the day's center of attention.

"They'd like me, or the troopers, to bring you across the road to NASCAR-IMSA headquarters for a nine o'clock meeting," Parsons said. "There are a dozen chairs around the big conference room table, but I think it'll be standing room only from what I hear." Bryce laughed.

"You better wand everybody before letting them in. It looks like someone wants me dead," Bryce said as he refilled his mug and looked at the clock on the wall; it read 6:59 a.m.

"Just in time for CNN, Fox, and the BBC," Bryce continued. "Wanna bet I'm the breaking news on all three?" he said, his tone changing from enthusiastic to depressed as he said the words. As Bryce searched for the TV remote control, Trooper Kane thanked Bryce for the coffee.

"I'll wait outside with the other troopers, and we'll run you over in one of our unmarked SUVs if that's okay?" he asked. "Drive me over, please; that won't hurt as much." The men laughed as Bryce pushed the power button with one hand, and he gave the trooper a thumbs-up with the other. "Thank you, and thanks for the company. I enjoyed it, Trooper." As Kane disappeared out the door, Parsons stood in the middle of Bryce's living room and began watching the news on the TV. Bryce had been right, and all three networks on the split screen led with BREAKING

NEWS - SNIPER TAKES SHOT AT F1 CHAMPION. He turned to Parsons.

"Hey, I've got to get ready unless you need anything else?" Bryce asked. Bryce laughed to himself as he saw Parson's eyes go to the mugs on the table. Without saying a word, Bryce grabbed a sharpie from a drawer and signed To Johnny – Bryce Winters on a mug, blew on the ink to dry it, and handed it to Parsons. Shaking the man's hand, he said, "Thanks for doing what you do here. I love this place." Beaming, Parsons thanked Bryce and left the motor coach. Bryce finished his coffee and turned toward the rear of the coach to see Danny Johnson jump from a bunk bed and into the bathroom. Seconds later, Bryce could hear Danny singing over the sound of the shower.

"Oh, I don't think so," Bryce said as he opened a control panel in the kitchen and flipped a switch. Within a second, Danny's voice went from song to shouting. "There's no hot water!" Bryce watched the clock as he grabbed the remote and changed the channel from the news to the NFL Network. The football playoffs were in full swing, American football – not what everyone else called soccer. After thirty seconds, Bryce threw the switch back and heard Danny shout, "That wasn't funny!" Bryce walked back to his bedroom and began laying out his clothes for the day: blue polo, worn jeans, hiking shoes, and his favorite watch, the TAG Heuer his Uncle Pete had given him after Bryce won the Daytona 500. The Rolex he never wore, presented to him when he won the Formula One World Driving Championship, had been lost in the Park City fire.

~

The White House, Washington D.C.

The president's chief of staff, Roland McCarthy, a genius and master manipulator in political circles and formerly of Wall Street, was late, and that didn't sit well with his boss.

"That son of a bitch still thinks he's in charge," President Zach Johnson said as he sat behind the Resolute desk. McCarthy had indeed helped Johnson get elected, but he'd overstepped his bounds a few too many times recently, and the president had just about enough. He looked across the massive desk at the man he had appointed to run the CIA, former Senator Billy Reynolds of North Carolina. Just as he began to deliver another rant, McCarthy entered the oval to begin a hastily arranged meeting. Minutes later, Johnson had heard enough.

"Damn it, Rollie! Bryce isn't just an American hero; he's a friend." McCarthy shook his head in disagreement and sharpened his beady eyes, which tensed Johnson even more.

"He campaigned for you, Mr. President, and gave you a thrill ride in a race car. That's all. He's radioactive now, and you need to stay as far away from him as possible. You've got an election coming up," McCarthy said. Johnson was in a fighting mood, but Reynolds jumped in before it could get any worse.

"Stay away from him, Mr. President, and let nature take its course," Reynolds interjected. "He killed two of our case workers in Mexico and," Johnson waved his hand for silence.

"There's no proof of that, but he's killed for his country and with my approval. Don't forget how he got roped into this in the first place, gentlemen." Johnson said. McCarthy got up, poured the president a cup of coffee, placed it in front of him, and stood there.

"Bryce's uncle was involved in murders overseas – mostly drug dealers in bars and thugs he caught roughing up women in hotels. Winters and Madigan were caught on camera taking out the trash. Someone at the CIA picked it up on facial recognition and CCTV searches, and my predecessor went for it. She leveraged our American hero and his accomplice. They had talent, and Bryce's celebrity allowed some bad actors to get close, and the CIA took advantage of it. MI6 did too." Reynolds offered. Johnson pushed away the coffee and walked from the desk. He stared out the thick ballistic windows at the South Lawn and then turned.

"I want Secret Service protection on him, effective immediately," Johnson ordered.

"Mr. President, some of the enemies Winters has helped us with might see that as a connection to you. If this were to go the wrong way, protection or even contact with Winters, you're done," McCarthy insisted. Johnson shook his head in frustration and returned to his seat.

"Don't you mean we are, Mr. Chief of Staff?" Johnson questioned.

✖

At the speedway in Daytona at nine-thirty, Trooper Kane and Danny Johnson led Bryce to a waiting SUV. Danny ran to the other side as Kane entered the front passenger seat. Minutes later, two unmarked police cruisers took their places before and after the SUV and led it through the tunnel that ran under the track's Turn One and sped across Highway 92. Parsons greeted Bryce and Danny at the entrance to NASCAR and IMSA's corporate offices and led them immediately past two groups of heavily armed men and women and into an elevator. Soon, Bryce and Danny found themselves alone in a large, windowless conference room two floors up. Bryce worked his phone and sipped at what had to be his tenth coffee since he rolled out of bed. He looked at Danny, who was watching something Bryce thought had to be Thursday night football highlights on his phone.

"Danny, you don't have to stay here with me," Bryce called out. "Go get some sleep. Send Alan back if you think it's necessary, but I feel pretty safe with the FBI and State Police rapid response teams in the lobby. Danny stood up and walked to Bryce, leaning against the edge of the massive table surrounded by a dozen black leather chairs.

"I will, as long as you promise not to go anywhere without us." Bryce nodded in agreement and fist-bumped Danny as he stepped from the room. There, and finally alone, Bryce couldn't imagine what the day would hold for him. Fifteen minutes passed, but as Bryce got up to find a bathroom, he was met at the door by an entourage of officials. First in came Fred Simpson, the speedway president, followed by Joe Miller, the president of the sanctioning body, then two aides, two uniformed state troopers, and finally, the governor of Florida. Bryce shook every hand until he got to the governor.

"This must be a big deal if this pulled you off the campaign tour, governor," Bryce joked. As everyone but the troopers sat at the table, Bryce studied the room and wasn't encouraged.

"Bryce, you've had a tough run of it lately," Miller began. "On behalf of everyone here, I want to extend our condolences on the death of Jack Madigan. Bryce cleared his throat and prepared to respond, but Simpson cut him off and continued.

"But what's happened here has taken things to another level. When I heard the news, I thought I was watching Mission Impossible, not the racing news." Bryce nodded in agreement, stood up, walked to the credenza at the far end of the room, and poured another coffee.

"My first experience with a sniper was in Mexico when that Russian hit man tried to take me and Jack out," Bryce said. "I'm thankful whoever took the shot last night wasn't him, or I'd be dead." A knock at the door interrupted, and as one of the troopers opened the door, two familiar, frowning faces entered. Badge wallets extended for all to see, FBI Special Agents Donohue and Williams introduced themselves and took seats across from the governor.

"Governor, we've been instructed by the Attorney General to take over the investigation," Donohue said. The governor shook his head in disagreement.

"You can investigate anything you want, but you're in my state now, and we're going to do this my way," he retorted. Donohue began to object, but Bryce cut her off.

"And how is that exactly, governor?" Bryce asked as he retook his seat.

"Well, this incident has presented a clear and present danger to everyone at the speedway," he said. "From the people cleaning the grandstands, the fans, the media, the officials, the racers and crewmembers – you'd be putting everyone at risk if you think you're going to race this weekend. And because of that, you need to get on a plane and head to some tropical island somewhere until the FBI here sorts this out. You need to be anywhere but here." Bryce stared into space.

"I agree," Miller said as he glanced around the table. "This isn't a stadium where you can sweep the place and everyone before they come in. They're already here, in thousands of cars, trucks, and motorhomes." Everyone in the room looked at Bryce.

"And I agree," Bryce said. "I don't ever want to put anyone else at risk, but I would like to make a statement to the media in person, and then I'll get back on my plane and disappear for a while." The FBI agents both shook their heads no.

"What?" Bryce asked.

"We think it's best if we take you into protective custody," Williams began, but Bryce cut her off. "Fuck that! It was three assholes from the CIA – from the same city the FBI and the DOJ are from – who tried to kill me, and I'm pretty sure Russo is still on the loose and behind this too. You take me anywhere; you might as well just cut my throat." Donohue got up and approached Bryce.

"And you think running back to Monaco will make you safer? You're right, those two are still out there, and we know they can travel however they wish. They are trained in covert behavior." The governor got up and approached Bryce, staring at Donohue. Bryce stood up.

"Listen, unless you're going to charge me with being

a moving target, I'm out of here," Bryce said firmly. He looked to Simpson and Miller.

"Wait a minute, wait," Bryce shouted at Donohue. "Did you just say, 'those are the two'?" Donohue nodded.

"Who's the second one? Who's working with Russo?" Bryce asked as he stepped close, almost too close to the agent.

"Originally, it was thought that Chadwick was killed in Singapore, but we've found evidence to the contrary," Donohue said in a hushed tone. She turned and surveyed the room.

"Unfortunately, that and anything else involving this case is classified and need-to-know, so I have to continue this briefing in another area or ask the rest of you to give us the room."

Bryce dropped back into his chair. This news had completely blindsided him. The year before, in Singapore, when Russo and Chadwick had followed Bryce and Kyoto there for the F1 race, Chadwick had kidnapped Kyoto and tried to force Bryce to pull out of the race and erase any hope of winning the championship. Unable to ask the CIA for help, Bryce had called in a favor with Susan Lee, an intelligence official – a spy – for the Chinese government he had met in Paris.

"But Lee said she'd killed Chadwick," Bryce whispered. "If he's alive, she lied." Bryce sat quietly, slowly shaking his head in disbelief. He looked at Donohue and then took a deep breath.

"Okay, can we at least do an impromptu press briefing at ten in the track's media center?" Bryce asked. "I'll just walk in, make a statement, and then maybe the state police can give me a ride to the airport?" Simpson and Miller nodded in agreement.

"We're going to have to impound the race car," Williams said. Simpson nodded, saying, "State troopers have it covered and guarded in the garage area." Simpson checked his watch. "We better get you on the move then." Williams gave Simpson a thumbs up and then turned to Bryce.

"Are you sure this is what you want to do?" she asked.

"Yes. Formula One testing starts in Bahrain soon, so I'll get out of here and lay low until then." The governor spun around.

"What? You're headed to another racetrack? You're going to put yourself out in the open again?" he asked. "If he takes another shot at you, he might not miss."

"Governor, for your information," Donohue began, "that he could very well be she. Russia and China are just a few of the countries that produce some highly trained special operators. They're as good a shot as any man out there. We're assuming it's Russo and Chadwick, but we can't forget there could be something else going on here." The governor ignored Donohue's comment and refocused on Bryce.

"You're really going to face the danger?" he asked.

"Of course I am. It's kind of what I do for a living. So you better capture the assholes who have a hard-on for me because I am not missing another race, no matter what." As Bryce headed for the door, the governor called out to him.

"Bryce, can you wait a moment? I'd like to get a picture with you." Bryce stopped and turned.

"That would be a hard no governor. I don't do politics," he said, leaving the room.

Stepping into the back seat of a black and tan Florida Highway Patrol SUV, his identity obscured by heavily tinted windows, Bryce texted Danny and Alan as the three-car motorcade headed for the media center at the speedway.

PLAN ON BEING AT THE JET AT 10:30
SHARP. ALREADY TOLD THE PILOT TO FILE
A FLIGHT PLAN FOR MONACO. BRING
YOUR GEAR AND YOUR PASSPORTS. BW

Bryce waited and smiled as he saw Danny's thumbs-up response. He texted back.

TELL ALAN WE'LL LEAVE
WITHOUT HIM IF HE'S LATE!

Bryce nodded as he received another thumbs-up and then focused on what was to come. During the long night, he had called the two other drivers who had been scheduled to take shifts for the practice sessions and then race in the Rolex 24. Bryce had also spoken again with Dini and the car owner, assuring them he'd pay for the damages and the expense of flying another driver in to take his place for the race. Then, in the pre-dawn hours, he had taken his phone and scrolled through his contacts, ready to tap Jack Madigan's number to talk about all that had happened that night. When he realized that he'd never speak with his friend again, it punched him again hard. Sleep-deprived and emotional, somewhere around three a.m., he scrolled to Jack's contact info and, after a pause, deleted it.

As the motorcade stopped in front of the Media Center at Daytona International Speedway, Bryce was whisked through a side door and moments later stepped to the podium as the media shouted questions and photographers flashed away. With Simpson and Miller to his right and left, Bryce gestured for everyone to quiet. When they didn't, true to form, he stepped off the podium as he had done a few times over the years. The room quieted, finally. Returning to the microphones, he made it short and sweet.

"I'm going to leave all the details regarding the incident and the investigation to the authorities," Bryce began as he pointed to Agents Donohue and Williams, who he had spotted standing near the main entrance to the room. "They're FBI, and I won't speak for them, but the consensus is that the deaths of Jack Madigan and Jon Watanabe," Bryce said but stumbled. He collected himself and continued. "Their deaths and the fires that destroyed the properties in Park City and Lake Norman were carried out or orchestrated by the two former CIA case workers who are still on the loose." Someone in the crowd shouted a question.

"But what about last night, Bryce? Who shot at you out on track?"

Bryce shrugged his shoulders and continued.

"The investigators are impounding the car, but Frank Dini already has another car set up for practice, and Jason Melrose is flying in from England and will take my seat for the rest of the testing and the Rolex next week." Perhaps sensing that the presser was about to conclude, the crowd began shouting questions. Bryce shook his head and waved his hands for them to quiet.

"The best thing you can all do is plaster your news and social media with the photos of Russo and Chadwick – if the FBI will make them available to you. Help us find them, and we can all rest easy." A British journalist shouted another question, and the room went silent, anticipating the answer.

"But what if it wasn't those two blokes, Bryce?" The reporter asked. "What if it's someone else that's after you? What then?" Bryce thought for a moment, laughed to himself, and then answered.

"Well, then, it sucks to be me." As quickly as he had taken the podium, Bryce disappeared from view and followed two uniformed state troopers toward the exit. Moving quickly, the troopers led Bryce outside toward a collection of idling patrol cars and SUVs. Suddenly, Bryce stopped to pose for a picture with a young fan in a powerchair and, as he did, recognized two Brits he'd encountered a few times in his travels.

"Glad to see you are doing okay, Bryce, all things considered," the older of the two said.

"Well, at least it's not raining," Bryce answered as he looked up at the beautiful blue sky. "Hey, you two do Radio LeMans and the IMSA global race broadcasts, don't you?" Both men nodded and stepped close.

"Well, then, I have some breaking news I just decided on, and it's exclusive, just for you," Bryce began. "With the open weekend between the F1 in Spain and Canada, I'm going to run the 24 hours of LeMans."

"That's exciting news, Bryce. You've never raced it before!" the older man proclaimed.

"No, I've never even seen the place. So if someone doesn't shoot me before June, I'll see you there!"

The troopers gestured for Bryce that it was time to go and guided him toward the SUV, but someone shouted Bryce's name. Recognizing the accent and the woman's voice, Bryce stopped and turned to see Formula One team owner Claudia Werner working her way through the crowd to him. Bryce smiled as he waved to her and quickly signed autographs for young race fans calling out to him from a rope line. As Claudia arrived, he kissed her cheek.

"You're leaving?" Claudia asked.

"Yep, we don't know what this asshole has in mind for me, but I won't put anyone else and risk, and they won't let me race anyway, so I'm gone," he told her. Bryce hugged and held her until Trooper Kane tapped him on the shoulder.

"Bryce, you're vulnerable here. We should get going." Bryce held Claudia tighter for a moment longer and then turned and disappeared into the back seat of the SUV. Seconds later, as the motorcade began to drive off, Bryce saw another familiar face in the crowd. It was Tony Bishop, and he was scratching his cheek with his middle finger as Claudia walked toward him. Well aware of what was happening at the speedway that morning, people packed the roadway to see this American racing champion, a hero to many, leave Daytona for what could be the last time. There was a shooter on the loose who wanted him dead, but that didn't seem to faze anyone, not even Bryce. Minutes later, as the motorcade drove alongside Bryce's jet at the adjacent airport, the troopers received a radio call that blew Bryce's heart and mind.

"Be advised, one of Bryce Winter's bodyguards has been found dead in his hotel room."

CHAPTER ELEVEN

SITTING IN THE state police SUV in the shadow of his Bombardier, Bryce was ready to explode with emotion. He'd been sitting there for twenty minutes since the news about Alan Johnson had come over the radio. While a bomb detection dog from the State Police scoured the inside of the pearl white plane, Bryce finally gave in to Trooper Kane's suggestion.

"Bryce, Danny will be here in a few minutes. Say what you guys need to say, but then you need to get on that plane and disappear," Kane said. "If you go to the funeral, that could become a circus, and the last thing you or his family needs is to have that lunatic or a copycat decide to take you out while grieving at Alan's grave. Give them the privacy every family deserves." Bryce agreed.

"You're right," Bryce whispered, and then he took another punch to his emotions as he saw Danny arrive and climb out of the back of a Daytona Police cruiser. Bryce quickly exited the SUV, and the two met at the foot of the jet's stairs. They held each other and cried, like brothers, at the loss. After a minute, Kane approached and put his hand on Danny's shoulder. "I'm very sorry for your loss, Danny."

∽

Danny looked up and choked back his emotions. He'd found his twin brother Alan lying face down in the motel bed.

"He had the damn do not disturb sign on the door and didn't answer, so I jumped from my balcony to his and shoved the slider open," he began. "But I could tell right away something was wrong. He never slept on his stomach, never. I shook him, but he was cold, and I knew instantly that the game had changed. I rolled him over. They shot him in the head. They fucking shot him right between the eyes and flipped him." Danny took a moment to check his emotions and then continued. I drew my weapon and spun around. I checked the bathroom and the closet. I even checked under the bed, but there was nothing. No sign of anything. Not even a spent shell casing." Danny stepped away from Bryce and surveyed their surroundings as he cleared his throat. He turned to the trooper.

"Thank you," he said and then stepped close to Bryce.

"And now I have to take Alan home to our mom," he said, " and bury him next to our dad out on that hill. Now they can watch the sunrise together like when he took us camping as kids." Danny fought back the emotion again.

"What can I do?" Bryce asked. Danny answered in a second as he stepped close to Bryce, placing both hands on Bryce's shoulders.

"Kill this mother fucker for me and do it soon because

if you don't, right after the funeral, I'm going to turn this world upside down looking for this bastard. And I'm going to bring all of our friends." Danny watched as Bryce struggled to maintain his composure.

"This is my fault, Danny-" Bryce began, but Danny shook his head no.

"The hell it is. If I were going to blame anyone, it'd be the damn CIA, but that's for another time and place. Alan and I volunteered for this mission, you know that, and you paid us well to do it." Danny paused. "What scares me the most is that someone got one over on my brother. Nobody, including me, has ever been able to do that. Whoever got in there and did this is good, really good. So you need to get on that bird and get the fuck out of here," he said and then paused. "I have a few things to take care of here." Danny wrapped his arms around Bryce, held him for a moment, then broke off, turned, and walked back to the police car without looking back.

As Danny's ride sped away, a black SUV roared toward Bryce's plane, followed by a black sedan. So quickly that Kane and the other troopers took a defensive stance and placed their hands on their weapons, ready for anything. Kane tried to push Bryce back toward their SUV, but Bryce didn't flinch. He wanted a fight. Suddenly, the vehicles slowed, apparently reacting to the police's posture. The SUV's rear door opened, and Claudia Werner stepped out of the vehicle, waving to Bryce.

"It's her again," Bryce called out to Kane. "I'd know those legs anywhere."

Claudia stopped, waiting for the police to relax their stances. Once they did, and Bryce waved for her to keep coming, her SUV drove alongside her until they reached Bryce's jet.

"I just heard about your bodyguard; it's all over the news," she said.

"Yeah, that was his brother that just left. What are you doing here?" he asked.

"I had my pilot call yours. You're headed to Monaco. Can I hitch a ride?" she asked.

Bryce surveyed the private jets parked nearby and pointed to the red jet with the name WERNER in white letters painted on the tail.

"What's wrong with that one?" Bryce questioned.

"Tony needs it. He's doing media in Vegas for the F1, and after the 24, he'll use it to head over to Bahrain. Let me fly with you to Monaco. I can get home to Mila pretty easily from there. I miss my little one." Bryce smiled as he pictured Max and Claudia's beautiful six-year-old, but then a twinge of guilt struck him, and he struggled to hide his emotion. Suddenly, a German shorthaired pointer police dog wearing a camo body harness scurried down the jet stairs and led its uniformed State Police handler to the K9 unit vehicle idling near the tail of Bryce's plane.

"How is she?" Bryce asked.

"She's great but misses Uncle Bryce," Claudia replied.

Trooper Kane and two others approached the couple and gestured for him to get on the plane.

"No bombs aboard Bryce, so she's clear and ready to go," Kane said.

Bryce looked to the cockpit windows and saw Bill Miller, his pilot, giving him the thumbs-up.

He looked at Kane and then back at Claudia.

"Got your passport?" he asked. She nodded. "How about luggage?"

Claudia pointed to the black SUV driver standing nearby, holding small designer luggage in both hands.

"Where's the big one? The one with all the shoes?" he said, attempting, needing, some humor.

"The one on the left," she said, "I'm traveling light this trip." Bryce waved for the driver to approach with her bags.

"Can we check those?" Kane asked. Bryce laughed. If the troopers only knew what Max Werner had been up to before his sudden death the previous summer.

"No need. I trust her with my life," Bryce told them. Kane nodded and stepped to Bryce, pointing to the four men who had stepped out of the second vehicle.

"What about them? They going too?" Kane asked. Bryce shook his head no.

"No room," Bryce joked. "They look dangerous."

Kane stepped directly in front of Bryce and extended his hand.

"It's been an honor working with you, Bryce," Kane said as the men shook hands. Bryce didn't let go and stepped closer.

"No, it's been great to be around troopers like you and the rest of your team," Bryce said, then paused. "Normally, I'd be doing selfies and all sorts of stuff, but I don't think it's appropriate, all things considered."

"Neither do I, Bryce," Kane said.

"But I'll promise you that if I don't get shot, the next time I'm back in the States, I'll get down here and take you all out to eat. What do you think?" he asked.

"That would be great. We all like free food, so don't get shot, okay?" Kane said.

With that, Bryce waved to the other troopers and gestured for Claudia to board the plane. As she did, Bryce caught himself looking at her legs. The pink Coco Chanel minidress and the Jimmy Choo designer heels made quite the presentation, but then he looked down. He felt ashamed. People were dying because of him, and he guilted himself again, even more.

∽

Claudia Werner introduced herself to the flight crew, asked Jen for a beer, preferably a German beer, if they had any, and then walked the length of the plane and went into the large bathroom, Bryce's private bathroom, at the rear of the main cabin. Once inside, she opened her handbag and searched for her lipstick. After all, a woman, especially a German heiress who used to grace the covers of fashion magazines worldwide, always needed to look her best. She smiled as she withdrew her black Werner Industries 9mm compact semi-automatic pistol.

"I wonder what they would have done had they found this?" she asked as she checked her makeup in the brightly lit mirror and then freshened her lips. A tone sounded, and then the pilot made an announcement. "We've been cleared for an immediate, expedited take-off, so if every-one can take a seat and buckle up, we'll have you over the Atlantic and climbing to 42,000 feet very quickly."

Claudia finished her pit stop and then joined Bryce in the main cabin, where he was holding a steaming yellow and red Werner coffee mug in one hand and a Bitburger German beer in the other. She smiled, took the beer, and then sat in a rear-facing brown leather captain's chair in front of Bryce. As the jet taxied and then went to full throttle and charged down the runway, Claudia studied Bryce. His attention seemed elsewhere as he gazed out the window and watched his homeland disappear beneath the clouds.

∽

"You know, they should have checked me," she called out to Bryce.

"Why? What don't I know?" he asked.

"Well, in addition to some expensive shoes, I have a few special edition pistols I had intended to present as gifts to customers in the Werner suite this weekend. Maybe Jen and your pilots would like them instead?" Bryce smiled.

"Silver, small caliber semi-automatic compacts. What do you think?" she asked.

"Any ammo?" he responded. Claudia shook her head no.

"Do you have any weapons on you?" he asked. "You don't usually move without one."

"Maybe you should frisk me? How long's it been since the last time you did?" she teased.

Bryce studied her. She crossed her legs, her trademark move, and he took the bait.

"The one and only time, Claudia," he said. "How long's it been since Zermatt?"

"Well, Mila's turning six, so," she said. Bryce nearly choked on his coffee.

"What the hell's that supposed to mean?" he asked.

Bryce felt the plane level off and heard a tone and the seat belt sign turn off on the front cabin wall. He unbuckled his belt and moved to the edge of his seat. He watched as Claudia did the same.

"Seriously, you've never wondered?" she asked.

"Wondered what?" he replied.

"If Mila is yours. You must remember that night," she said as she raised her shoe and tapped his foot. Bryce sat back in his captain's chair and stared out the window. He remembered that night as if it were yesterday. It was a night he could never forget.

Max Werner's diverse portfolio ranged from producing and distributing small arms to highly technical military weapons for use by boots on the ground to drones, jets, and even satellites. Some were generally known, many top-secret, and a select few known to only a handful of people. His clients were law enforcement and military agencies worldwide. The diversity in his portfolio came from the ownership of a championship-winning Formula One team, a team that had taken the prestigious Indianapolis 500 and the stock car equivalent – NASCAR's Daytona 500. He also operated five-star hotels and restaurants throughout Europe, Asia, and South America. One of which was an exclusive ski resort with spectacular views of the Matterhorn in the Swiss Alps. That was where Max Werner and his young wife, Claudia, had first met and would spend their Christmas holidays and ring in the new year together. A few years earlier, Bryce had been brought there to recuperate from a vicious crash that took him out of the race and the title contention at NASCAR's Talladega Speedway in Alabama. A few years before, it was also there that Bryce consoled Claudia on the breathtaking balcony under the stars and a spectacular mountain.

As the chill of that night in Zermatt began to overcome them, Claudia had moved closer to Bryce.

"I'm finished with this," Claudia told Bryce as she emptied another bottle of champagne into her flute. "I'm finished with him. We made a deal. No more women, and he broke his word again, and this time, it will be for the last time." She cried out and fell into Bryce's arms. He held her and stroked her long brown hair, also feeling the effects of more alcohol than they usually would have consumed. Bryce remembered the night, every minute of it, but had struggled with the guilt from early that morning when Claudia snuck out of Bryce's suite until the day Max died. Looking at her in the present, he had a confession to make.

"I stole your panties," Bryce told her through a boyish grin.

"What?" she said, thinking back to that night.

"You left the room without them, and when I found them, I didn't know what to do, so I kept them," he said.

"Should I be flattered, or are you a collector?" she teased, amused.

Bryce sat forward and reached across for her hand. He held it tightly and continued.

"No, that night was very special and meant something

to me, so I kept them for the memory. Years later, they went up in smoke in Park City," he said. Claudia leaned forward.

"I'm flattered. I know you always kept the things that mattered to you there, not in Monaco. You kept them at your true home," she said as she put her other hand on his. "But the arsonist took them along with everything else from you." Bryce laughed as he sat back.

"No. Kyoto found them and threw them in the fireplace," he said as he phoned Jen to refill their drinks. They laughed and told stories as they waited for dinner service until Claudia said something that punched Bryce in the gut.

"But now you have another souvenir from that special night," she said. "You have – we have – our little angel, our little Mila."

Bryce had always found Jen's timing perfect, but he struggled for words as she arrived holding two food trays. He was caught in an emotional battle that tore at his heart and head. He'd betrayed a friend and mentor, later killed him, and left a child fatherless. Bryce looked up at Jen, and she appeared to read him perfectly, turning away with the trays. But he stopped her.

"Where do you think you're going," he called out. "We're starving." Jen studied Bryce's expression as she placed their trays, a filet for Bryce, and a half lobster for his guest. He smiled and nodded his head, which she returned in kind. For the next hour, Bryce and Claudia told stories as Bryce defended his steak once and twice from Claudia's far-reaching fork. As the trays were cleared, replaced by coffee for them both, the German said something that brought him back to reality.

"So tell me the truth, Bryce, you never wondered if Mila was yours?" she asked. Bryce stared at Claudia, his mind registering the hundreds of times he'd played with Mila in one of their suites at an F1 event, swimming with dolphins on holiday in the Bahamas, and at her birthday parties when schedules permitted. Sure, he had wondered. Every time he saw his eyes in hers.

"Max wondered on more than one occasion," Claudia said, interrupting his daydream.

Bryce almost jumped out of his captain's chair.

"Max knew we had been together?" he asked. When Claudia nodded, Bryce deflated, crushed.

"That night in Zermatt, he had returned to our suite to beg for forgiveness, but he didn't find me there. He knew how vengeful I could be, so he assumed I had found another warm bed to get me through the night," she said.

"But how did he know you were with me? He never said anything to me. He didn't change a thing in our relationship after Zermatt. He must not have known you were with me," Bryce insisted.

"He knew on Mila's second birthday," she began. "Someone commented on what beautiful eyes she had. I saw Max's expression. He looked at this little girl enjoying her party and then at me. He saw your eyes in hers. He glared at me, and I read his lips. He asked, 'Was it Bryce'? I turned away, and he knew."

Bryce had been on an emotional rollercoaster for days now. First his home, then his friends, and now this. He watched Claudia get up from her seat, collect her handbag, and walk to the bathroom. He didn't say a word.

After closing the door, Claudia gazed at her reflection and then smiled. She searched again through her bag, setting aside the pistol and freshening her makeup. She pursed her lips as if giving a kiss, closed her bag, and then reached for the unlocked door.

"The hook has been placed," she said confidently, returning to the main cabin. She studied Bryce's expression as she approached him and watched his surprise when she sat opposite him on the other side of the cabin. He swiveled his chair to face her and leaned toward her.

"Everything okay?" he asked. "Are you all right?" She stared at him for a moment and then leaned toward him.

"Now, we have something more to discuss," she said sternly. She watched Bryce's expression change to one of concern.

"There's more?"

"Yes. You killed Max, so there is much to discuss."

CHAPTER TWELVE

THEY WERE SOMEWHERE high over the Atlantic, between Greenland and the western coast of Ireland, when Bryce engaged the DO NOT DISTURB on his cabin light and phone. Claudia's bombshell accusation had knocked Bryce for a loop.

"Say that again; I must be out of it," he demanded.

"Max and I were on the phone that day. You had just left him. He told me you had come to warn him that the CIA, MI6, and Mossad knew he was selling illegally to their enemies and were going to have him killed," she said. "So they sent you."

Bryce stood up, stared at Claudia, and then walked to the flight tracking screen on the bulkhead wall. He studied it for a moment. *She knows.*

He retook his seat, took a deep breath, and let it out as he attempted to study her, looking for something he could take advantage of. An opportunity to deflect, deny, or perhaps come up with a story she might believe. The problem was, she hadn't flinched. If anything, she seemed at ease, having let the cat out of the bag. Her gun was within reach in her purse; his – one of an assortment hidden aboard, wasn't as close.

"Okay, tell me what you think happened that day," he said, calm and composed.

"As I said, we were on the phone. You had just left. He said the CIA had engaged you to approach him as a friend and warn him to shut down the flow of weapons to the bad guys, as he called it, and go find an island to spend the rest of his life on, or that a sniper would explode his head like a melon and leave nothing for me or Mila to kiss goodbye." Bryce nodded. "Go on."

"But Max responded just as you or I would have predicted. He didn't run from anyone or anything. He said he would stay and fight. He said he told you and reminded me that the bad guys have snipers, too." Bryce saw his chance and took it. He moved to the edge of the seat, close to Claudia, and reached for her hands. At first, she didn't move, but then slowly took one hand with hers and then the other.

"I tried to talk some sense into him, Claudia, I did, but his temper flared, and he told me that I should leave and let him get busy making calls," Bryce told her. "He walked me out to my car, and that was the last time I saw him." Claudia squeezed Bryce's hands but then let go and sat back in her chair.

"You've left something out, though, haven't you, Bryce?" she said, raising her eyebrows, wanting more. Bryce nodded but then got up and walked to the galley through the darkened cabin, past a sleeping Jen in a reclined captain's chair. Bryce took two German beers from the refrigerator and headed back toward Claudia. He stopped, looked fondly at Jen, and reached down, pulling the lightweight brown blanket over her shoulders. As he headed back to Claudia, he heard a whisper from behind him. It was Jen.

"Are you hungry? Do you need anything?" she asked.

"No," he whispered. "Go back to sleep."

"Okay," she said, drifting off.

Once back in his seat, Bryce handed Claudia a beer and raised his bottle, as did Claudia.

"To Max," they both said and then took long draws. Suddenly, Bryce realized he was in a race. Claudia often claimed she could outdrink him, so the challenge was on. Two empty bottles were set on the tray seconds later, and Claudia smiled.

"Okay, I won – again," she bragged. "Now tell me the rest."

Bryce took a moment to consider his words carefully. He wasn't sure if she was baiting him or genuinely interested in what else he and her late husband may have shared.

"It had been some time since Max and I spoke," he said. "I set up the meeting to clear the air between us, which I think we did."

"He told me why the CIA chose you to deliver the warning," Claudia said. "He told me about your Uncle Pete and how they blackmailed you." Bryce didn't answer. He simply nodded. Claudia leaned into the center aisle, apparently hearing something coming from the front of the plane. Then she sat back and refocused on Bryce.

"Now, I need your help," she said as the aroma of warming cinnamon buns and fresh coffee reached them.

"What do you need?" he asked.

"After Max died, I took control of the company, and the first thing I did was tell the executive team to shut it down. There was to be no more illegal sales of anything to enemies of the EU, America, or the United Kingdom," she said. Before she could continue, Jen walked up behind her and delivered a tray of warmed sweet rolls, hard rolls, coffee, orange juice, and everything to go with them. Bryce smiled but could see Claudia's frustration. She had something to say. After thanking Jen for her service, Claudia continued as Bryce went after the coffee.

"One night, perhaps a week later, a woman showed up at our home in Munich. She got inside, beating the security sensors and the guards. I woke up with Mila beside me, with this woman holding a knife to my throat."

"Holy shit," Bryce said, nearly choking on his coffee.

"She had one simple demand," Claudia said. "Keep the arms flowing or, and she pressed the knife harder against my throat as she looked at Mila, or this little girl's blood will." Bryce was infuriated. He stood up and paced the aisle in thought. Suddenly, he turned to her.

"So are these the people that are fucking with me? I thought all along with was the CIA fuckers but -," he said but stopped as Claudia shrugged her shoulders.

"Do you know if Max told them about me?" he asked. Claudia shook her head no.

"Did you say anything to them about me, to anyone at Werner?" he asked. Claudia shook her head no again. Bryce dropped down in his seat.

"We should have watched a movie," he said, laughing. "This is getting more insane by the minute." Claudia had picked at a warm cinnamon bun, taking bits of nuts and raisins from the one nearest her on the tray.

"Bryce, I think you have made enough enemies on your own, judging by what I know about what your CIA had you do for them," she said, reaching for a juice.

"Now you have your enemies, and I have mine, but both of us are now in the sniper's sights, don't you think?" she posed.

"I agree, and if our enemies take us out, Mila's left without any of us," Bryce said, suddenly realizing he might have a role in Mila's life – and in preserving it. He spent the next few minutes deep in thought as he watched Claudia pull a blanket over her and recline her seat.

∽

Claudia woke abruptly as the jet's wheels touched down at Nice's Côte d'Azur airport in France. As the plane taxied toward the small private terminal, she brushed her hair and freshened her make-up while looking down the aisle to see where Bryce had gone. Curious, she walked toward the cockpit, where she discovered Bryce and Jen standing near the open cockpit door, joking with the pilot about which they wanted more, a bath or a bed.

"I'll take both," she said as she thanked Jen for the in-flight courtesy and service. "And if this American ever takes you for granted, you can always come fly for Werner F1," she joked with a wink. Once the jet came to a halt, Bryce released the jet stairs and gestured for his guest to deplane. He followed her to the tarmac, where an older man dressed in a black suit and tie took her bags and placed them in the trunk of a waiting dark blue Mercedes sedan. Bryce surveyed the area and saw a red Werner jet, cabin lights on, parked nearby.

"Seriously, Claudia, you can't walk to your plane?" Bryce teased. Claudia yawned in his face and then began to walk to the car. Bryce called out for her to wait and caught up to her.

"You're headed to Munich to see Mila, but we need to finish our conversation," he told her.

"Then come with me. She'd love to see you, and we can talk more on the plane." Bryce looked back at his jet, watched as his flight team deplaned, and began walking toward the terminal. He shook his head and turned back to her.

"No, I need to get back to Monaco and develop an action plan," he said. "Let's meet in Bahrain and talk much more about Mila." He watched as Claudia's tired eyes studied him. She stepped closer and leaned in for a kiss on the cheek. Claudia held Bryce for a moment and whispered in his ear.

"You do know, the fact that they have not caught the renegades and that you are still alive makes me think the CIA is allowing this to happen. Looking the other way," she said. "You need to be very careful, my dear." Bryce wrapped his right arm around her and escorted Claudia to the sedan.

"You know, you should just sell the company and buy an island somewhere," he told her. Claudia stopped suddenly and turned to face him.

"Easier said than done, my dear," she said. "The woman who broke into my home made it very clear. I still hear her words; 'Status quo or blood will flow.' She didn't just threaten Mila; she threatened my parents." A slight drizzle began to fall on Nice, and the driver approached them with a large black umbrella. Claudia waved him off.

"The woman," Bryce said, "what nationality was she? You only saw her eyes. Tell me more." Claudia looked into space as she appeared to remember that night.

"Russian, probably, or Eastern European," Claudia told him. "I know the accents, but her cold blue cobalt eyes made me sure of it." Bryce took it all in.

"But she wasn't Japanese, so it wasn't Kyoto," she laughed. Bryce didn't smile.

"So tell me, is she gone for good? I liked her, and she was intelligent and exquisite," Claudia said.

Bryce tried to rub the sleep from his eyes, but suddenly, he had a revelation.

"You know, I just realized I never told her I loved her," he confessed. Claudia leaned in again and kissed Bryce on the cheek.

"That happens more than you know. Max was generous with gifts but selfish with words, except for Mila." Bryce stepped back and stared at her.

"Claudia, I have to know. Is she mine?" he asked. She laughed.

"I prefer to keep you in the lurch. After all, you killed my husband." Bryce grew angry.

"You have to stop saying that," he insisted. "It's not funny. Not funny at all." As the rain grew heavier, she appeared ready to say something but then turned and ran toward the sedan. Bryce stood and watched as she stepped into the vehicle's rear seat and then drove off, perhaps one hundred feet, to the Werner jet. He walked toward the terminal, watching Claudia leave the car and enter her plane. Once inside, he called her on his phone.

"Miss me already," she said with a laugh. Bryce didn't answer.

"Hello?" she said.

"You should just blow up the factories," he told her. "Blame the CIA or whoever you want," he told her.

"If it were only that easy," she said. "I think my customers have moles everywhere, watching everything I do." Bryce nodded in agreement.

"So now I have one last question for you," she said. "The CIA came for Max. Will they now come for me too?"

"I have no way of knowing Claudia. I wish I did," he said. "But if you haven't already, you need to replace anyone guarding you and Mila that night. They're either incompetent or complicit, and either will get you killed." Bryce heard Claudia sigh.

"See you in Bahrain," he said, ending the call. Minutes later, as he watched her jet take off for the one-hour flight to Munich, two trained killers approached him from behind.

CHAPTER THIRTEEN

IN THEIR EARLY thirties, Toby and Elaine Trudeau were former operators for France's elite special forces. Married, they lived in Monaco, as did Bryce and many Formula One drivers and principals who took advantage of the spectacular atmosphere and the tax-free status residents received. Married, the two often provided discreet security for Bryce and other celebrities as they attempted to have some semblance of everyday life in Monte Carlo. Despite being trained killers, the joke often made to them was that they looked more like brother and sister. To entertain or perhaps put someone off, Elaine often said, "Incest is best if it's kept in the nest." Once they got the drop on Bryce, which they often did, the three took to Toby's black Land Rover SUV and headed east on the A8 toward his European home and what he hoped would be twelve hours of undisturbed sleep.

Bryce thanked the Trudeaus for the ride as he climbed from the back seat of the SUV, hastily moved through the building's lobby, and tapped his fingers on the elevator railing as he waited impatiently for the doors to close. Once they did, he let out a sigh of his own. This wasn't Park City, but for now, he was home. After typing the keypad that released the two bolt locks on his condo's front door, Bryce pushed the door open, dropped his bags in the foyer, and walked toward the living room's floor-to-ceiling windows, bathing his place with the bright morning sun. The décor he had chosen for this abode made his guests believe they were in Santorini, including the only time Kyoto had been there. The blue and white were vibrant but also calming. As he dropped onto his blue cloth sofa, he took a deep breath and then another. He could feel his body and mind ease. But then, suddenly, his day took an immediate turn.

"Nice place," CIA case worker Jason Ryan said in a hushed tone. Bryce jumped to the opposite end of the sofa and reached under a white pillow for the pistol he kept there for special occasions. But it was gone.

"Bryce, it's me," Ryan called out. "Ryan from CIA." Shocked at the intrusion and angered by the presence of what he now perceived as the enemy, Bryce glared at the balding, middle-aged man in the tan suit in mirror sunglasses.

"Where's my gun?" Bryce demanded.

"It's in the fridge," Ryan said as he placed his shades on the coffee table between them. "Now take it easy, champ; I'm not here to hurt you. I'm here to help."

"How'd you get in?" Bryce asked.

"Did you miss the part where I said CIA?" Ryan answered.

Bryce stood up, rubbed his face with his hands, and then looked past Ryan into the spacious stainless steel kitchen he rarely used.

"What, you didn't bring coffee?" Bryce said, irritated. Ryan turned and looked to the kitchen.

"No, but I brought something better." Bryce brushed past Ryan as he stormed into the kitchen and turned as he searched the cabinets until he found the ground coffee he needed so badly. He looked at Ryan, who had followed him into the room and sat at the two-tiered kitchen island.

"So what's up, other than my pissed-off meter at seeing you here," Bryce said, smiling as he watched Ryan's body language.

"Scared I'm going to go for the gun?" Bryce asked.

"Curious, yes. Scared, no," Ryan said.

Bryce reached into the cabinet as the aroma of brewing coffee began to spread across the room. Pulling out a mug, a Werner mug, and sweeteners, Bryce then opened the refrigerator door. He studied the inside of it—juice, beer, soda, water, energy drinks, and a bottle of coffee creamer. As Bryce moved the creamer, he saw the magazine from his weapon, fully stacked with the eight hollow-point bullets he always loaded.

"Told ya," Ryan said. Bryce laughed to himself. *He doesn't know about the one on my ankle.*

"Where's the rest of it?" Bryce asked in a joking tone. "Let me guess, the toilet?"

"You'll come across it after I leave," Ryan answered.

Bryce poured a cup, treated it with a heavy dose of hazelnut, and then marched past Ryan and retook his seat on the sofa in the living room.

"So what's the news?" Bryce asked as he blew at the steaming cup and took a sip.

"We've found Chadwick and Russo," Ryan said proudly.

"Are they dead?" Bryce asked as he crossed two fingers on his left hand.

"Yes," Ryan told him.

Bryce nodded as he studied the CIA man. Ryan must have sensed he was more welcome now and retook his seat across from Bryce.

"It looks like Russo grabbed Jon Watanabe and did the damage in Park City while Chadwick took out Madigan. One of our tactical teams cornered them at a Holiday Inn off I-95 north of Daytona and took them out. We've been able to keep it quiet. The local news and police have no idea we were even there, and Langley wants to keep it that way."

Bryce turned his attention to the sea view and took his mug with him as he slid the balcony door open and went outside. As the breeze blew the white sheers, Ryan stepped through them and joined Bryce. The two stood within a few feet of each other until Bryce turned and leaned back against the railing.

"So now we know," Bryce said as he looked at Ryan.

"Not really," Ryan responded. Bryce's apparent relief, the one he feigned for his guest, also turned.

"What?" Bryce asked.

"Because they were both dead a half hour before that sniper took the shot at the track."

CHAPTER FOURTEEN

ORDINARILY, A RETURN to his Monaco home would come late on a Sunday night after completing another Formula One weekend in Europe, and quite often, with some impressive hardware, Bryce had been presented on a podium, but today was different in every way. His racing, at least his debut in the Rolex 24, had been curtailed, and instead, Bryce was jetlagged and sat staring not at a trophy but at what he considered an enemy.

"So why am I just hearing from you now?" Bryce asked. Ryan laughed slightly.

"You're kidding?" Ryan said. Bryce shook his head no. "Because you called POTUS, that's why," Ryan said in a raised voice. "He and the CIA need to stay as far away from you as possible, at least for now." Bryce got up from the blue sofa and stopped abruptly. *Do I kick his ass, throw him off the balcony, or play along?* Bryce knew the answer. He walked to Ryan and stood over him.

"So my country's leaving me out here on my own?" Bryce asked.

"I'm here, aren't I?" Ryan asked as he got up awkwardly, stepped around Bryce, and entered the kitchen. Bryce followed him there and stopped, leaning against the doorway and watching as Ryan fumbled with the coffeemaker.

"I'd feel better if you were with the Secret Service and had brought a few friends," Bryce said. After watching for long enough, Bryce walked to Ryan and took over the chore.

"God, you need a shower, champ," Ryan said.

"I'd have had one and been in bed an hour if your ass hadn't been here," Bryce responded. "So, it might be best if you got out of here and get a coffee in the Starbucks on the corner. I have a lot to process." Ryan nodded, but instead of walking to the door, he walked down the hallway toward the master bedroom. Seconds later, he returned to the kitchen, holding Bryce's semi-automatic pistol. Bryce watched as Ryan reached into the refrigerator, withdrew the magazine, and loaded the gun. He then cocked the slide and press-checked the weapon to be sure it was ready to roll. Ryan walked to Bryce and handed it to him.

"You might need this," Ryan said. Bryce studied the CIA man for a moment. What was this? Genuine concern, or was this guy just covering his Washington ass?

"Look, you have your security here and at the F1 venues," Ryan said. "I'll be in Bahrain, and we'll bring a few of our best to keep their eyes open. You won't see them, but they'll be there." Bryce nodded his head as he placed the gun on the kitchen island.

"You might want to see a doctor; something's come over you. Is it a conscience?" Bryce said, half joking.

"No way, Bryce; I'm still an asshole. If someone's

going to shoot you, we believe it will be live, maybe on a podium, broadcast and live streamed to millions worldwide," Ryan said.

"Gives me a headache just thinking about it," Bryce said, rubbing his forehead. Ryan stepped close.

"As long as you're wearing that American flag on your uniform and refusing to lay low somewhere safe, we'll do what we can to keep you alive. That's just come straight from the top." Bryce nodded and reached for the door.

"Bryce," Ryan began but paused. Bryce grew concerned. *Oh shit, there's more. This can't be good.*

"What? Tell me. After everything I've been through, I can take it," Bryce assured him.

"It's Kyoto," Ryan said. "Right after we were notified about her brother, we sent a team to her place at the Watergate-" Bryce interrupted him.

"I did too, but her neighbor told me she had moved back to Japan," Bryce said as concern for his former love came sweeping back.

"That's what the State Department said too, but-" Ryan stopped.

"But what?" Bryce shouted as he stepped close to Ryan.

"Bryce, she never made it to Tokyo," Ryan said before clearing his throat. "She's missing."

CHAPTER FIFTEEN

In Washington, the president's chief of staff, Roland McCarthy, drank another hot coffee as he masterfully orchestrated a Windsor knot on an expensive royal blue silk tie. The three monitors mounted horizontally on his bedroom wall were on, with CNBC, CNN, and the BBC early morning news broadcasts catching his attention occasionally. He checked his wristwatch, an Omega given to him during a going-away party at one of the Wall Street firms on the day he set out for the White House. He was right on time at 5:58 a.m. As he tapped the keypad to reset the alarm, McCarthy stepped outside and took a deep breath of morning air. He scrolled through his phone, took the three steps down to the sidewalk, and suddenly realized he was alone. His black U.S. Government SUV with the heavily tinted windows and the security team that typically took positions on the sidewalk and in the street weren't there. He tensed as he quickly called the Secret Service desk at the White House.

"Mr. McCarthy, good morning," the agent said.

"Where the hell's my detail?" McCarthy nearly screamed into the phone.

"POTUS pulled it," the agent said. McCarthy spun around on the sidewalk in a rage. He was so angry that he didn't hear what the agent said next. "Repeat that for me, please."

"I said, the president told me I was to quote him verbatim, so here goes again. 'Tell McCarthy now he knows what abandonment feels like.'" McCarthy raised his hand, prepared to throw the phone to the ground, but stopped and took a deep breath.

"You need to get my team here now," McCarthy insisted. "I could be in danger."

"No can do, sir. POTUS suggested you take an Uber." McCarthy was beside himself but calmed when he heard the agent's next words.

"Take it easy, Mr. McCarthy; you're not in danger," the agent assured him. "Look around. Two of your team are sitting in a white Dodge sedan two doors down on your right, and another two are in the black Cadillac to your left."

"You just wait until I get there," McCarthy shouted.

"Mr. McCarthy?" the agent called out.

"What?" McCarthy answered as he stormed toward the Cadillac.

"Please don't do anything aggressive when you arrive, or we will have to react appropriately," the agent said, then disconnected the call.

෴

Meanwhile, thirty miles south of the nation's capital, Kyoto woke from another night in a closet, only this one was a small walk-in and had come with an air mattress, pillow, and blanket. Her hands were still bound behind her, and her mouth gagged; she wondered when her chance at freedom would come or if this nightmare would go on forever. But the mask was off, and that gave her hope. She'd seen their faces and knew they'd never let her go. Inside her, what she had fought against all along, that emotion that kept creeping up – the violent one she had struggled all of her adult life to keep buried deep inside, the one that forced her to walk away from the only man she had ever loved, was coming back.

[❧]

Bryce paced his living room as the sun disappeared for the day over Monaco. He'd taken as much aggression out on the fitness equipment in his private gym as possible and then, exhausted, had returned to the balcony he loved only to be gut-punched by the sound of race cars in town for the annual Monte Carlo rally below. He'd missed out on running the Rolex 24-hour race at Daytona, and now another event he'd often admired was taking place without him – in the streets where he lived. That was it; he'd had enough. He grabbed his phone and called his pilot.

"I wondered how long you'd be able to sit still," Miller joked as he answered.

"You up for some time in Abu Dhabi?" Bryce asked.

"Leaving tonight or?" Miller asked.

"How about wheels up at ten a.m.? Pack enough to stay through the race in Bahrain," Bryce said.

"I'll call the others. See you then, boss," Miller answered and ended the call.

Bryce tossed his phone on the blue sofa and stood at the balcony door. He thought of Kyoto and where she might be. Was she still alive, or had she been cooked like Jack and her brother and just not discovered – yet? He looked at the wall clock and realized it was time for dinner, not from the clock but from the growl that rose from his stomach. He looked through his phone and stopped once and then again at casual acquaintances he dined with occasionally. Suddenly, he felt vulnerable and alone, as if he were the only person on the planet. He made a call.

"Have you eaten?" he asked when Elaine Trudeau answered the phone.

"Hi Bryce, no, we were just watching the Rolex-" she said but caught herself. The two went back and forth, Elaine being polite as Bryce realized he was being a bother. Thirty minutes later, Elaine knocked at Bryce's door, holding a six-pack of beer and a large half-pepperoni pizza. Bryce was surprised to see she was alone when he opened the door.

"Where's Toby? "he asked. Elaine dismissed her husband as she brushed past him and walked to the kitchen.

"He's babysitting tonight," she called out as Bryce entered the room and gave her a questioning look.

"He's shadowing one of the big shots in town for the rally," she said as she searched for plates and stared at Bryce.

"So where are we going to do it?" she asked, her French accent making her words sound even more alluring.

CHAPTER SIXTEEN

THE SOFT KNOCK at Bryce's door startled him. He looked across the room at Elaine Trudeau, fast asleep on the far end of one sofa under a throw Bryce had placed on her halfway through her favorite movie, *Pretty Woman*. With the second knock, Bryce got up from his end of the sofa and pulled his pistol from under the pillow. He looked at his watch. It read. 12:20 am. Standing beside the door, he asked, "Who's there?" When there was no answer, he slid the hammer back with his right thumb, raised the gun toward the door, and began backing down the hallway. Suddenly, he came to a stop as he bumped into Elaine, who was coming up behind him in the hallway holding her gun. Elaine's phone vibrated as she guided Bryce back into the living room. When she looked at her phone, she laughed.

∽

"It's Toby. That son of a —" she said as she shook her head and walked to the door, sliding her pistol back into her ankle holster as she threw the deadbolt. She peeked through the eyehole and then opened the door, shaking her head at her husband as he shook his head at her.

"So, what film did you watch?" he asked as he walked past her into the living room, dropping his black backpack in a corner. She closed the door, threw the bolt, and engaged the alarm system. When she entered the living room, she found Toby picking at a piece of cold pizza while Bryce collected the empty beer bottles from his end of the coffee table and returned from the kitchen with two more. She watched as Toby studied Bryce as the two men clinked bottles.

"What's the matter, mon chérie?" she asked. Toby smiled and told Bryce he should take a seat. Bryce took the remote and turned off the movies they had been watching until she fell asleep, bingeing on *Mission Impossible*.

"What's happened?" Bryce asked as Elaine took a seat beside Toby, sitting close.

"Some people are lingering down on the street in front of the building," Toby said. "What I am most concerned about at this point, here in Monaco, are copycats and crazy people. When things like an attempt on a star's life happen, oddballs come out of the woodwork, and now, they are here."

"Individuals or a group scoping the place?" Elaine asked.

"Not sure, but they didn't seem coordinated, so just loners, I believe."

"Not lone wolves?" Bryce asked as he got up and walked to the balcony door. Before the couple could stop him, he went outside. Elaine followed him there quickly as Toby went to the hallway to recheck the front door.

"Bryce, come inside," Elaine insisted as Bryce looked over the wall and down at the street below. "Or at least come away from there." Bryce didn't move. "Please, Bryce," she asked again. She watched as he looked up at the bright full moon casting its spotlight down onto the Mediterranean but shivered in the late-night January cold. Bryce noticed and gestured for her to go inside. Once she did, he followed her in and then pulled the curtains.

꙳

"I've already made plans to get out of here in the morning," Bryce told them as the Trudeaus stood side by side against a kitchen counter while Bryce loaded the coffee maker.

"I'll fly to Abu Dhabi and stay there until it's time to move to Bahrain for the race," he said as if speaking to the cabinet. When he turned to face them, he was conflicted.

"One minute, I feel like a caged lion," he said. "The other, I feel like a tethered goat – and I can't stand that." Toby nodded as Elaine looked into the living room.

"So we'll drive you to Nice, leaving from the underground garage, and then shadow you in the UAE until the F1 team picks up your security when you get off the plane in Bahrain," Toby said. Bryce poured a coffee and then shook his head no.

"I can use the ride to Nice; that would be great," Bryce told them. "But I'll be on Ameer's yacht at the Yas Marina, and his team will take good care of me there. Plus, anyone who's gotten too close to me has wound up dead, and with the baby coming, there's no way I'm putting either of you in harm's way." Bryce smiled as Elaine gave Toby a surprised look and then turned back to him, cocking her head.

"What are you talking about?" she asked. Bryce laughed.

"I've known you for almost three years?" he said. "In all that time, tonight was the first night you ever refused a beer. Ever. So don't play with me; when's the due date?" For the next ten minutes, Bryce watched and listened as the happy couple acknowledged the news and went on and on about their plans, but then, suddenly, Elaine got in Bryce's face.

"Listen, mister. Don't think being pregnant means I can't do my job or that I'll be preoccupied thinking about risks and not taking them because nothing's changed; you got that?" she said. "I won't go to Abu Dhabi, but only because."

"Because you get seasick, and being pregnant might make it worse." The three laughed and then moved to the sofas, where Elaine dove back under the blanket, and Toby turned the TV back on.

"Go get some sleep, Bryce," Toby insisted. "We've got you covered tonight and in the morning." Bryce stood and stared at the couple until he realized he'd only slept a few hours in the last twenty-four. With a bottle of Evian in hand, he said goodnight and walked quietly toward his bedroom. Friends, the friends with guns he paid to be with him, were nearby, but now, lying on his bed in the darkness, he felt very alone.

The morning came quickly. Bryce had the coffee flowing and warm croissants, plain, fruit, and chocolate delivered by a familiar face who worked in the building's restaurant. Once Elaine and Toby took turns showering, they joined Bryce at the kitchen island.

"So let's eat and then head for Nice," Bryce said enthusiastically. He loved flying and enjoyed spending time on super yachts almost as much. They were the only two places he could get away from it all, or so he thought.

CHAPTER SEVENTEEN

Within an hour, despite the morning traffic, Toby pulled up to the front of the private jet terminal at Nice's Côte d'Azur airport. Then, standing outside the black Land Rover, Bryce shook Toby's hand and reached for Elaine's. She knocked his hand aside and wrapped her arms around Bryce, tightening her grip until he joked that he couldn't breathe.

"Are you sure that baby is mine?" Toby joked, and everyone broke into laughter. But as Bryce waved goodbye and walked inside the terminal, his thoughts went to little Mila.

On a slow winter morning for air traffic, Bryce's jet was rolling down the runway headed for Abu Dhabi quicker than he could remember. Having joked with the flight crew as usual, he moved to the rear of the main cabin and became lost in thought as the plane took off and tore through the clouds. He was quiet until someone nudged him.

❧

"So, how are we doing, boss?" Jen said as she sat on the rear-facing captain's chair before him. Bryce ignored her momentarily, still lost in the clouds, but Jen wasn't having it. She nudged him again, this time a bit harder. Bryce turned and stared at her momentarily as if she'd interrupted his sleep, but then the smile she loved so much brought one to her face.

"All that racing's taken away your hearing, or you just being anti-social this morning, luv?" she asked. She watched as Bryce studied her. They'd had talks like this before, and she was often entertained by his delays in answering, knowing he was searching for a memorable response. This morning, though, she was disappointed.

"I'm good, Jen," Bryce answered. "How about you?" Jen shook her head and sat forward in her seat.

"Bullshit," she said. He laughed, so she knew she still had a job. He slid forward to the edge of his seat and reached for her hands. She took his.

"I've never been able to get anything past you, Jen, so I won't try to now." She sat back in her seat, pulled a pad and paper from the ledge, crossed her legs, and stared at him.

"Okay, as your therapist, I normally get three hundred an hour, but today, the first hour's free. So tell me, what's going on in that head of yours?" Bryce sat back. She laughed to herself as he stared at his empty coffee mug.

"We're probably on autopilot by now, so I'm sure the captain will happily get you a refill; just phone him. But you're not changing the subject, mister," she said. "Start talking."

She laughed as Bryce looked through the small storage cabinets beside his seat.

"Seen my gun anywhere?" he asked. She shook her head no. "Now start talking."

A slight bit of turbulence shook the plane briefly, calmed, and shook it again. She and Bryce had experienced rough air hundreds of times together before, but she knew from his now sullen expression that was how he felt inside.

"Other than testing in Barcelona and Bahrain, normally this time of year would be filled with all sorts of trips and adventures with the people I love, but between losing Pete, the house, Kyoto, Jon, and Jack, life kind of sucks right now," he said. "Of course, racing in the 24 at Daytona had been a dream of mine for a long time, and that literally got shot to shit. I just want to get back in the car; I need to put all of this out of my mind and focus on just going fast." Jen tapped at his hiking shoes with her black flats.

"And I'm sure not knowing what's next or who's still out there doesn't help," she said.

"Sure as hell doesn't, but," he paused. Jen saw something in his eyes, in his expression.

"Are you scared of dying or something? Come on, don't be a baby. We all have to go sometime." Bryce looked at her and broke out into laughter.

"Yeah, but I'm not quite ready to go yet. Still have a few things to do, like eat a huge piece of my next fifty birthday cakes," he said. Jen placed the pad and pen back on the ledge and began to sit up.

"Where do you think you're going?" he protested.

"Our session just started." Jen shook her head and gave Bryce a reassuring look.

"You're holding something back; I can see it," she said. "If you don't want to tell me, I understand. All kidding aside, I'm here for you, Bryce. You know I always have been." Bryce shook his head and gestured for her to stay put.

"So Claudia dropped a couple of bombs on me on the flight over," he said. "She led me to believe that Mila is mine." Jen's jaw dropped. "Shut the fuck up!" Bryce laughed.

"Okay, you owe me ten euros for that one," he said. Jen smiled and hurriedly reached into her pants pocket and handed Bryce a crisp twenty-euro note. "I don't want change; I can assure you I'm going to spend the other ten any minute now." She watched Bryce as he folded the note, slid it into the pocket of his black polo shirt, and continued.

"Yep, that was one part. The next was that someone threatened her and Mila, and that's got my head spinning." Jen felt her jaw drop again.

"Who'd do that, Bryce?" she asked. "I can't believe someone would hurt that little girl. Claudia can be a handful now and then, but hurt that little angel, no way. What can you do to help them?" Bryce got up and grabbed his empty mug.

"And the worst part is, we can't go to the authorities. Claudia and Mila would have to move to Mars to be far enough away from these bastards," he said. Jen was stunned. She sat still in her seat and shook her head, wondering if she might be in harm's way. Bryce took a knee in the aisle and moved close to her.

"Listen, none of this has ever come close to you or the two up front," Bryce told her. "But if you're concerned, I can see it in your eyes, and I'll understand if you want to take some time off until we figure it all out." Jen felt his eyes grow as her temper began to flare up. She stood up, grabbed the mug with one hand and the twenty out of his shirt pocket with the other, and stormed to the front of the plane. As she arrived at the galley, she looked down the aisle and saw Bryce walking towards her. He arrived as she finished filling his mug. She turned to hand it to him, but he took it and placed it on the counter. Bryce wrapped his arms around her and held her tight, whispering in her ear, "I just couldn't take it if anything happened to you, Jen," he whispered. Suddenly, the cockpit door opened, and the co-pilot stepped into the aisle.

"You two should get a room," he said, then stepped into the bathroom and threw the latch. Jen and Bryce began to laugh. It felt good, and from the look in Bryce's eyes, she knew he needed this and much more to survive.

❧

Bryce felt rested and relaxed as the plane taxied to the private terminal at Abu Dhabi's international airport. The talk with Jen had helped, as did the four hours of sleep he'd managed despite the half gallon of coffee he'd ingested on the way. Walking through the private terminal, he immediately recognized a familiar face: a tanned, fit, and trim man in his fifties walking toward him with open arms. Bryce had always assumed ex-military and more but never asked.

"Omar, how the hell are you?" Bryce asked as he

extended his hand and then embraced the man. He laughed as he felt Omar's discreet yet probing hands check him for weapons. Stepping back, Omar smiled.

"Good and good to see you are not carrying," he said. "There is great interest in your plight here, Bryce. The authorities will be watching you, and the last thing you or our boss needs is for you to be caught with a gun. That's my job, yes?" Bryce laughed as he surveyed the area around them. People were looking; they recognized the F1 driver and seemed torn. Some wanted an autograph, some a photo with the celebrity, but most kept to themselves out of respect or fear. As Omar took Bryce's suitcase from a baggage handler, he quickly led Bryce through an expedited customs check and then out the front door. There, two black Cadillac SUVs idled nose to tail at the curb. Suddenly, a dozen camera flashes lit up the scene as photographers pounced on the man they had heard had been coming their way.

"Bryce, Bryce, look this way," one man yelled as another flashed away, asking, "Who's trying to kill you? Is it safe for the other drivers if you race with them in Bahrain?"

Omar opened the side door for the man he had been tasked with keeping safe as two men, dressed and looking much like Omar, all wearing black Armani, stepped between Bryce and the paparazzi. Seconds later, without uttering a word, the two SUVs sped off as Bryce thanked Omar, who was now riding shotgun up in front.

"If you ever get tired of working for Ameer, let me know, Omar," Bryce called out. "You're good." Omar smiled at the driver beside him and turned to face their passenger.

"I'm good? Thank you for saying so, but I have some bad news. The boat, Mr. Kazaan's yacht, had an engine issue this morning. They will work around the clock to make the repairs so you can cruise the gulf for two weeks, but tonight, we have booked you a room at the Yas Viceroy Abu Dhabi hotel – the same suite you always use when you are here.

"What kind of engine issue?" Bryce asked as he leaned forward. Omar shrugged his shoulders and turned to watch the road.

"Omar?" Bryce asked. Omar turned back toward him. "Did someone sabotage the boat?"

Omar smiled and shook his head no.

"No, it wasn't sabotage. It was stupidity. While fueling the vessel this morning, they put petrol in one of the tanks instead of diesel. There is some new staff, and someone was, what do they say in America – a knucklehead? Everything has to be flushed and refilled, and the engine needs to be double-checked. But you know Mr. Kazaan. When he finds out which person grabbed the wrong nozzle, they'll be in hot water, maybe literally, for some time." Bryce nodded and watched as Omar turned to face forward. Then Bryce focused on the driver, a man he had never seen before and called out to him.

"I'm Bryce, by the way," he said. "What's your name?" Bryce and the driver's eyes met in the rearview mirror. The driver looked at Omar, who nodded his approval.

"Please to meet you, Mr. Winters. My name is Malik. My father and I are big fans of yours." Bryce smiled courteously in the mirror and sat back in his seat. Bryce thought of the Watanabe men from Japan. *Father and son*

race fans? Are you trying to torture me with this shit, or what?
Bryce thought.

"That happens a lot in car racing," Bryce said. "Just like with American football, soccer, any sport, I guess. Dad's take their kids to the games or races, and the tradition gets passed on." Malik smiled in the mirror as he nodded in agreement. Bryce took a breath and stared through the window at the illuminated skyline of one of the most exciting cities in the world.

Fathers and sons, he thought to himself. *Like my Dad and me, like Pete and me – like Kyoto's brother and their father.*

As the two SUVs stopped in front of the hotel, two men from the second vehicle walked to Bryce's door and waited for Omar to walk around from his side and open their guest's door.

A few photographers, the type who always lingered around five-star hotels hoping to catch a celebrity's comings and goings, or better yet, a couple who would prefer not to be seen, snapped away with their cameras, but the look Bryce saw Omar give them kept their mouths shut. They knew better.

Within minutes, Bryce was walking through the front door of his suite. As he entered the living room, Omar asked the man standing at the window if everything was in order.

"Yes, Omar. I've been here since you left. Nobody attempted to come in. Everything seems to be fine." Omar nodded, and the man walked past Bryce and from the suite without uttering another word.

"One of ours, of course," Omar said as he placed Bryce's suitcase on the floor against a wall.

"Two of my men will be outside your door and follow you wherever you go," Omar said. "If you tell them not to follow you, they won't, but your safety will not be their concern from that moment. Do you understand?" Bryce nodded and shook Omar's hand.

"Thank you, Omar. You've always been a professional, and I appreciate this very much," Bryce said as he walked him to the door. A minute later, Bryce was alone with his thoughts. He sat in front of a bank of monitors but then quickly stood up and changed into his workout gear. It had been a few days since he worked up a sweat, and he realized that was exactly what he needed.

Two tall, young, and fit-looking bodyguards, ex-military Bryce assumed, followed Bryce from his suite to the hotel's fitness center. In the elevator, they introduced themselves as Barhom and Suliman, and to him, they came off as quiet, confident, and extremely capable. *Hopefully, none of that will be needed while we're here,* he thought as he smiled at them both. Barhom took a position outside the door in the hallway as Suliman went inside and surveyed the room. There was only one person in the brightly lit gym, a man in his early thirties with curly reddish hair and a fair complexion, running on a treadmill, watching a rugby game on a ceiling-mounted monitor in front of him. Barhom walked before him, studying him, and then returned to Bryce.

"Everything looks okay inside; enjoy your workout," the guard said. "We'll be right here." As the two men took up their positions, Bryce looked at the fitness equipment and opted to step onto a treadmill two over to the right of the redhead. As the machine gained speed and Bryce began to move, the man looked at Bryce and smiled.

"Don't remember me, do you?" the man said with a British accent. Bryce studied him but didn't sense he was a threat, so he continued to move as he studied the man's face.

"Sorry, I don't," Bryce called out as he adjusted the speed on the treadmill.

"I was with you at a birthday party in London the day you put a bullet in a terrorist's face." Bryce laughed and focused on the monitors; one was rugby, and the other tuned to the BBC World News.

"Is that the one where they had me jump out of a cake? I do that so often I'm not sure which one you're referring to," Bryce joked as he brought the treadmill to a stop and wondered if his heart would soon follow.

CHAPTER EIGHTEEN

AFTER A COOL shower in his suite, Bryce walked into the hotel's massive bar an hour later. He was relaxed and comfortable wearing his designer black t-shirt, well-worn jeans, sandals, and his favorite watch, his Tag, tight on his left wrist. He sat on the tall barstool beside the man with red hair.

"Not sure what you drink," the man said. "I'm a scotch man myself." Bryce smiled politely while trying hard to avoid the smell from the man's breath. As the bartender arrived, she greeted Bryce in an accent he initially struggled to recognize.

"I bet you're here for the races," she said. "What may I serve you?"

"I'll take a hoppy IPA if you have one," Bryce said as he surveyed the room. "Hopefully, that'll be the only bitter taste left in my mouth tonight." Soon, an ice-cold green beer bottle was placed in front of him.

"Obrigado," he said, thanking her. "Are you from Portugal or Brazil?"

"Sao Paolo, of course," she said. "The home of the greatest Formula One driver ever."

Bryce raised his bottle and nodded in agreement. After she left the men, the two sat quietly for a time, sipping at their drinks as they looked across the room at the view of the Yas Marina and the million-dollar yachts docked there. Having been told the Brit was an old acquaintance, the bodyguards sat at a table together, twenty feet from Bryce, sipping at glasses of sparkling water, one knocking the lemon into the glass, the other knocking his to the table.

"That was quite a party," Bryce said to the MI6 agent beside him. "You did a great job for us that day. Most on the team felt you were a natural," the man said. Bryce nodded, finished his beer, and waved to the bartender for another round.

"I didn't get your name, by the way," Bryce said as he turned on his barstool to face the man.

"Jonathan Sproul, MI6, at your service," Sproul said as he extended his hand. Bryce fist-bumped the man instead and then spun his chair back toward the bar.

"Now I remember you had a beard the last time," Bryce said. Sproul rubbed his chin. "New girlfriend. She told me the beard or the dog had to go." Then, Sproul leaned in.

"Any chance we can go somewhere private to talk," he said. "We're a bit exposed here."

"Well, we're not going to my room, and you best keep your knickers on, or I'll knock you on your ass," Bryce said just as their drinks arrived. Bryce laughed as he saw confusion take over Sproul's face.

"No, no, no," Sproul said, seeming embarrassed and off balance. "Don't get the wrong impression. What I want to talk about, the only thing on my mind, is your relationship with the CIA and nothing else," he said. "We can only assume you don't feel safe working with them anymore, all things considered, but perhaps you can lend us a hand?" Bryce noticed two stunning brown-skinned brunettes enter the room and take seats at the left end of the bar. The plunging necklines of their tight-fitting designer dresses and their cover girl beauty gave him pause. Finally, he turned back to Sproul.

"Don't tell me it's another birthday party," he said. "It's funny. I was just talking about mine a few hours ago." Seeming frustrated at Bryce's compromised attention, Sproul picked up his scotch and sat to Bryce's left. Bryce grew annoyed with the move and looked past Sproul as he smiled at the women.

"Bryce?" Sproul asked. "No tethered goat this time, not bait, like London. I promise."

"What? What do you want me to do? Tell me because I need a distraction from all the bullshit I'm swirling in right now, and they just walked in." Sproul checked his watch.

"Just give me five minutes, and I'll be gone," Sproul begged. Bryce waved for the bartender, requesting she provide drinks for the newcomers, and then looked at Sproul.

"Five minutes, starting now," Bryce told him, then focused his full attention on the Brit.

"There's a woman in London, a powerful woman with ties to many of our elected officials," Sproul began. "We believe she's the middle man, the middle person, between the politicians and some special interests from countries that, shall we say, aren't U.K.-friendly." Bryce looked at his watch and moved his hand, gesturing for Sproul to hurry.

"We already know she's infatuated with you; she loves Formula One and men who live on the edge," Sproul said, "But she also has a weakness for rescue dogs, puppies, and the like. She thinks you need a hug, for starters, and that's your in - for us." Bryce quickly finished his beer and stood up from the stool.

"Send me some info, her photo, and bio for starters. If I bump into her at the Paddock Club or a VIP event, I'll fake an interest in her, and we'll see where that goes," Bryce said as he patted Sproul on the shoulder.

"Sure you don't need a wingman?" he asked. Suddenly, the wind was knocked out of Bryce. Yes, he needed a wingman desperately. But not here, not for this. Jack had been at his side for years, through it all, but he was gone. Bryce smiled, shook his head no, and walked toward the women. Suddenly, he stopped, turned, watching Sproul leave the bar, and held his finger to them. *One minute*, he worded and then walked through the doors onto the patio, reached for his phone, and threw it into the water below.

"Birthdays and tethered goats?" Bryce said in a whisper. "These sons of bitches. Who the hell else is listening?" Bryce reentered the bar, headed for the two women he'd been exchanging looks with, but then something, a subtle move by one of his bodyguards, made him slow. He saw Barhom discreetly move his head to the left and right, and Bryce understood. He brushed past the women, said, "Enjoy the drinks," and then passed his two shadows as he left the bar. In the elevator, his guards there with him, Bryce was tense and concerned. Once the doors closed, he looked at Barhom.

"What was that? Was there a threat?" he asked. Barhom smiled.

"Yes, if you had engaged them, Omar might have cut off your balls," the man said with a laugh. Bryce cocked his head, puzzled. He was tired but had been up for a good time until he was waved off.

"The woman in the yellow minidress," Barhom began. "That was Omar's daughter. She must have overheard him mention that you were here. I know she's a big fan." Bryce stared at the man and then looked at Suliman. As the elevator reached his floor, they stepped out.

"Okay, what about the other one? She was magnificent, too." Suliman cleared his throat as he followed Bryce toward his suite. "My sister," he grumbled as they arrived at his door, and Bryce swiped the keycard. Once the room was checked, Barhom waved him in. Bryce thanked them both, apologized for any accidental offense he might have made, and closed the door. Fifteen minutes later, Bryce answered the chime, opening the door to another beautiful woman. A hotel masseuse smiled at him with exquisite eyes and full lips as he regarded her head to toe. "Come in, please. You're just what the doctor ordered." As she entered, Bryce stuck his head into the hallway.

"She's nobody's mother, right?" he asked with a laugh. Both men smiled as they shook their heads no. As he stepped back in, Bryce affixed the Do Not Disturb sign, wished his team a quiet night, and closed the door. Early the next morning, as the woman blew him a kiss and left the suite, Bryce grabbed the remote and began to watch a replay of NASCAR's Daytona 500. He'd won the race before and had watched it on TV for years with his father growing up, but he switched it off ten minutes in. He'd considered buying a last-minute ride in this year's race, but the speedway and the governor had made it clear. You are not welcome here until they catch whoever's trying to kill you. Someone had ruined his plans, and they were still on the loose.

Two weeks later, Bryce was greeted by the morning sun as he stepped out on the rear patio deck of Ameer Kazaan's magnificent pearl white super yacht – *The Lilly*. He'd spent the last fourteen days and nights sleeping, training in the ship's extensive fitness center, listening to soothing music, eating well, and reading in the sun. Bryce had always appreciated reading autobiographies and thrillers and enjoyed the latest bestsellers from Jack Carr and Mark Greaney. Books, like binging on shows and movies, were his escape; the time cut off from the rest of the world had done him good. The first F1 race of the season, Bahrain, was just days away now, and he felt focused and ready to chase another championship.

He had come to terms with the fact that Jack wouldn't be there at the start, for the first time in years, and that pain was now behind Bryce. It had to be. When racing takes a life, the rest come back to race again. So he was ready, or so he thought, until his concern for Kyoto crept back into his head. Bryce sat at the table, placed his coffee mug off to the side, and stared at the sea. He thought back to Singapore and how badly her body and emotions had been beaten down by that piece of shit Chadwick and wondered where and how she might be. But then, a sense of guilt washed over him, demolishing his enthusiasm and outlook for the day ahead. He knew he could never find her and wondered if the CIA and FBI were looking for her or if she was just collateral damage and already dead and buried in their books. Suddenly, a shadow blocked the sunlight as a steward placed his breakfast plate of fruit and eggs in front of him.

"Is there anything else I can get you right now," the perky Brit dressed in a starched white shirt and shorts asked. Bryce continued to stare.

"Bryce, Mr. Winters, are you all right?" she asked. Slowly, he turned his head from the water to engage.

"Yes, yes, I am. Thanks," he assured her. "This looks great. I'm going to miss all of this. You do a great job." He paused. "Just getting into race mode. Getting ready for war, you know."

Well, pardon my French, but, 'leur donner l'enfer." Bryce smiled.

"I *do* intend to give them hell," and then turned his attention to his food and thought of Kyoto, hoping above all else that it would be for the last time. Early that morning, as he sat on the side of his kind bed and stared at himself in the mirror, he decided it was time to let her go, just like Jack finally, this time for the last time. She'd left him in Park City and had made it clear she was gone for good. He pictured her beautiful but sad face the last time he saw her and remembered how he felt as he watched her Uber drive away. *One way or another, I guess you are really gone. You have to be for me to move on.*

He stood up, walked to the railing, and looked across the water to the horizon. *But who the hell's still after me — and why?* Suddenly, gunfire erupted from the deck above him. Bryce assumed a defensive posture and turned, expecting to see his bodyguards racing toward him, but they were nowhere in sight.

CHAPTER NINETEEN

Fifty-year-old tech billionaire Ameer Kazaan loved his wife, son, money, and Formula One team in that order. A short, slight man with thinning black hair may have lacked a presence when it came to physical stature. Still, he was a lion with a dynamic personality and a drive that made him work harder than anyone he knew in tech, perhaps to make up for any shortcomings. His bank account and bodyguards dealt with threats of any kind. He'd met his Lilly while they were both students at MIT and moved to Canada after graduation for marriage and to start a family. He took great pride in his vessel, a trophy he'd given himself as a reward when his company had grossed its first billion. Not to show off, not to impress, but to treat as an oasis that could take him or his guests anywhere in the world. He'd offered Bryce the solitude needed to deal with the recent, violent past and prepare for a dangerous season driving on the edge. When he had heard two crewmen had taken it upon themselves to skeet-shoot with shotguns on the stern of the ship, *his ship*, he was beside himself in his penthouse overlooking Montreal.

⤜

"Throw them overboard," he screamed into the speaker-phone on his antique wooden bureau, but then a softer voice came on the line. It was Lilly Kazaan, a soft-spoken, petite woman with a French accent, a lioness, and she was speaking to the ship's British captain.

"Yes, throw them overboard, but do it when you are close enough to port that they can swim in. Maybe they can outswim the sharks. After all, we are peace-loving Canadians, for goodness sake."

Captain Billy Wells, a sea-worn Brit in his sixties, had first seen action as a much younger man serving in Her Majesty's Navy forty years earlier when the battleship he was aboard was dispatched to sail nearly eight thousand miles of quite often rough seas south to Argentina to deal with an uprising in the Falkland Islands.

"We're still operating in international waters," Wells responded. "We could keel-haul them like they did in the good old days if I had my way." Lilly looked to her husband, who was pacing their massive bedroom while trying his best to avoid tripping over the two cats, who seemed to take his movement as a desire to play.

"Throw their personal property overboard and toss them onto the dock the minute they throw the lines," Ameer called out to Lilly.

"Heard you loud and clear, Mr. Kazaan," the captain said. "I'll take it from here."

⤜

As the ship slowed as the Yas Marina came into view, Bryce shook his head as he looked at the two young Middle Eastern-looking men dressed in white and blue crew attire seated on the bridge floor to the left of the captain's big wheel. He looked to Wells and then stepped close.

"You ever seen anything like this before?" he asked. "Two new crewmen decide to try their hand with shotguns and clay pigeons at sea?" Wells shook his head no and then turned and glared at the men. Bryce nodded and then called out to the two bodyguards, Barhom and Suliman, who had been shadowing him since he first arrived in their country.

"Either of you?" he asked. Both men shook their heads no. Barhom gestured for Bryce to follow him from the bridge. Once outside, he turned to Bryce.

"Something is very off with these two," he said. "What they did is unheard of. My senses tell me they were paid to do it, paid to throw someone off. The big question now is, were they trying to send a message of some sort, and if so, to whom? Was it for you or Mr. Kazaan?" When Suli and I heard the gunshots, we were there in a second, and neither looked surprised or even scared to see us. This is very strange." Bryce nodded in agreement.

"You should do what you think best, but if it were my decision, I'd have some local cops who are into the rough stuff have a little talk with these two, if you know what I mean. Ameer can fire them, but my guess is that wouldn't be the end of this." Barhom agreed and made a call. Bryce watched as the man trusted with guarding his life walked thirty feet down the ship's starboard side, turned, and began walking back. By the time he returned, he had given Bryce the thumbs up. "They'll meet us at the dock, but-"

"But what?" Bryce asked.

"The word is out that you are on this vessel, and a crowd of fans and local media are waiting for us there." Bryce turned and stared at the marina in the distance.

"So tie these two up below; I'll get off and greet the fans. Then let's head for the airport. I think it's time to get to Bahrain. I am so ready to get back to racing." Moments later, the captain joined Bryce and Barhom at the railing.

"I've just been made aware of something," he said. "The two with the shotguns. We all assumed they were shooting skeet, but I've just been informed there weren't any clays loaded." Bryce watched as Barhom stepped close to Wells.

"This changes everything, captain," he said as Bryce stepped between them.

"It sure does, and I want to discuss this with those two downstairs as soon as possible. Can you change course, skipper, and take a few laps so I can enjoy my time aboard this beauty just a little longer?" Wells nodded. Bryce thanked him. Then another noise took everyone's attention as a small helicopter suddenly flew low over the vessel and then came around and landed on the ship's small heliport.

"These two are really in for it now," Barhom said. Bryce turned to him.

"Why? Who's that?" he asked. Wells patted Bryce on the shoulder and began walking toward the helicopter.

"That's Omar, and tonight, these two will be swimming with the fishes as they say in the Godfather movie, yes?" Barhom asked.

"Works for me," Bryce said as he followed Wells to greet Omar, but as the man climbed from the helicopter, he appeared agitated. He shook hands with Wells and then approached Bryce and Barhom.

"Give me thirty minutes, and we'll know what these two were up to," Omar said as he placed his hand on Bryce's shoulder.

"And then, we can talk about my daughter."

Bryce studied Omar and waited, hoping his expression would change.

"Okay if I get on that chopper? I'm sure I'm late for something somewhere."

Omar finally smiled as he waved to a steward and directed her to pack Bryce's belongings and load them on the helicopter.

"Yes, you shouldn't be on this boat anymore. Not with what I have planned. Go ahead to Bahrain, and I'll see you there when I arrive with our boss, and I can tell you in person what I found with these two. No phones." Bryce thanked Omar, shook hands with Wells, and stepped close to Barhom.

"Thank you all for taking such good care of me," he said. Minutes later, Bryce was out over the water, on the phone, and headed for the airport. His flight crew was still at their airport hotel, anticipating a departure later in the afternoon, but they got moving once Bryce alerted them he wanted to leave early. As his full-time pilot, co-pilot, and attendant entered the terminal, they found him drinking coffee, posing for photos with the staff, and raring to go. Jen was the first to him.

"What's the bloody hurry? You rob a bank or something?" she asked. He winked and followed her out to his jet. He had an agenda; race week started now, and he began making calls once up in the air. The first was to his homebuilder in Park City.

"I love the house just how you built it the first time," he told the woman. "But I want you to stop what you're doing and find me some land. Maybe two to three hundred acres, if possible. Enough land for some toys and animals. Lots of toys, horses, dogs, and whatever wanders in, okay? If that works for you, I'll stop home to check out what you've found between the race in Jeddah and Melbourne." Bryce smiled from his captain's chair as Jen approached with a tray of snacks, water, and coffee. She sat across the aisle and waited for him to finish the call. Once he did, he turned to her.

"You're lurking. What's up?" he asked.

"Everything good? You feel good – sound mind and body and all that?" she questioned.

"Yes, ma'am. That week on the boat did me wonders. I feel fantastic and am looking forward to suiting up and chasing the championship. Enough of this off-season shit. Let's go!"

Jen got up, high-fived her boss, and then returned to the galley. Bryce smiled as he watched her go and scanned the legal pad in his lap for the next call he needed to make. In what felt to him like the blink of an eye, they were landing in Bahrain, quickly driven to the Al Areen Palace, a luxurious resort whose design reflected the region, where he immediately headed straight to the bar. There, he found a room full of familiar faces, fellow competitors, engineers, team members, reporters, columnists, and broadcasters who were all a part of this global traveling circus. The first hour was spent accepting condolences for Jack Madigan, toasting his friend, catching up on the news and gossip of the paddock, and just soaking in the unique camaraderie shared among people who operate in a world where people risk their lives for a living. Jokes were told, pranks were played, and drinks were shared. It was a perfect evening until he bumped into Tony Bishop. If looks could kill, Bryce would be a dead man. Seven thousand miles west of where he was standing, the woman he had finally cleared from his mind was still fighting for her life.

CHAPTER TWENTY

IN THE RUSTIC motel cabin a few miles off Interstate 95 in Virginia, Russo sat on the edge of his double bed and watched Chadwick guide Kyoto into the bathroom. The worn-out bed springs squeaked in protest as he leaned forward to watch them go in.

"Cuff that ankle good this time; if I have to chase her again, I'm going to shoot the both of you," Russo called out. A minute later, Chadwick closed the bathroom door behind him and walked to the small wooden table and chair near the cabin door.

"Volume," he called out to Russo, who picked up the remote from the tired bedspread that looked old enough to vote. He held the button until the ESPN commentator's voice could be heard. After waiting impatiently for a few minutes, the video teaser finally appeared on the screen.

"F1 returns this weekend with the first race Sunday morning, at eleven Eastern time, eight Pacific, from the Sakhir Circuit in the Kingdom of Bahrain. Will American Bryce Winters be ready to go after his house was burned to the ground, his friend killed, and a sniper shot at him during a test session at Daytona, or will they even let him race? Find out after this short commercial break." Chadwick jumped up from his chair, knocking it back against the wall.

"Fuck that; they better let that asshole race," he shouted. Russo stared at his partner and listened as he heard the shower water turn off.

"Five minutes," he called out to Kyoto, then looked back at Chadwick.

"If he doesn't race the first two events, he can't win the title, which means he won't run Miami," Chadwick said as he walked to the little faded white plastic Mr. Coffee maker and refilled his Styrofoam cup.

"Oh, they'll let him race in Florida. It's all about the sponsors, global audience, and ticket sales. The American has to race in the first American event of the season," Russo said as he got up from the bed and knocked on the bathroom door.

"Four minutes," he shouted, then walked to the TV and stared at it, waiting for the show to resume.

"It'll be like he's entering the Coliseum for a life-and-death battle. He'll be in Miami, and we'll be there waiting for him."

⋘

Late Thursday afternoon in a small meeting room just off the circuit's media center, Bryce forced a smile as he stood and shook hands with Dev Kahn, a popular motorsports correspondent from the premiere sports TV network in India. Before the cameras rolled, the two men caught up.

"Last night was a lot of fun," Bryce said. "How is your head this morning?"

"Please, don't ask. So tell me, my friend, how many is this for you today?" Kahn asked as he double-checked his hair on his phone.

"Let's see; I may have lost count. We started at nine this morning. I think you're the thirty-first."

"Mine too, and I saved you, the best, for last," Kahn replied.

"Well, I'm pumped full of caffeine and energy bars, so I'm ready to roll when you are, but remember, Dev, no talk of a sniper or Jack or house fires. Focus on the new season and how excited I am to be here to begin the chase for a second world championship." Kahn smiled and gave Bryce a thumbs-up; "Then, let's begin."

The ten minutes went by in a flash, and the interview and Bryce were done in no time. After they shook hands and their social media reps took photos of the two standing close, Bryce escaped the room and sought an exit. He wanted some fresh air, hot as it might be, and a calming look at the setting sun. It had been a good day, but tomorrow would be even better; back in the cockpit, taking to the track at speeds nearing 200 miles per hour. He shook a few more hands and smiled at the drivers from the Ferrari team. They, too, needed air.

As Bryce strolled toward the balcony door, barely listening to the Kazaan team's two media reps suggest three or four more people they'd like him to meet, a full-figured, middle-aged blonde woman approached him, gushing with excitement. He recognized her immediately from the intel he'd been sent; it was the MI6 target – Penelope Charles.

"Oh, this is a dream come true," she said, nearing tears. "May I hug you?" Bryce opened his harms and felt the woman envelop him. "You've made my year," she said as she squeezed him once and then again. Bryce could smell her scent, a fresh dose of hairspray overpowering whatever Chanel she may have spritzed.

"Now, who's this little one," she asked as she stepped back, looking past him. In an instant, though, Bryce saw her expression turn to fear. He spun around and was overcome with joy as he saw Mila running to him. But coming up fast behind her, his arms outstretched, was a brawny, rough-looking Asian man with a shaved head. Bryce saw a gun as the man's tan suit coat flew open, and he took off toward them.

CHAPTER TWENTY ONE

THE MEDIA CENTER at the track in Sakhir had never seen a commotion quite like this. The plainclothes security operatives known for blending in suddenly appeared out of nowhere. Bryce grabbed Mila and spun so his back was to the gunman as the Asian in the tan suit was knocked to the ground. Pinned to the carpet, face down, he struggled briefly but soon gave in as a security team member's knee had been planted firmly on the man's arms, legs, neck, and back. Then, another figure came running toward them. A few tensed until they recognized the man; it was Tony Bishop, a look of shock and disbelief on his face.

As weapons were returned to their holsters, Bryce held Mila close and watched as Bishop tried to diffuse the situation, assuring anyone who would listen that, sadly, embarrassingly, this lummox was with him but was now officially without a job or a reason to be on the premises. As if that weren't enough excitement, Claudia Werner walked from the elevator to see the calamity in front of her, involving her daughter, her lover and team driver, and their racing nemesis. Worse, one of the camera crews, just about to turn off their equipment, had caught it all. When Mila saw her mother rushing toward her, she called out, "Look, Mommy, I found Uncle Bryce." Werner reached out and pulled Mila from Bryce's arms and held her close, kissing her cheeks and fussing over her. Bryce wasn't sure what to do next. He considered going over and slugging Bishop for hiring an overzealous lunatic but knew that would result in a grid penalty by the series or the sanctioning body. But then he suddenly realized why he stayed still. He didn't want Mila to see his violent side. That revelation was an eye-opener that left him wanting, needing fresh air even more. As he headed for the door, he veered toward the film crew huddled around their camera.

"That was exciting," he said. "What'd you get?" One of the four turned their viewer toward Bryce and hit play. Bryce hoped Mila's face wouldn't have been captured, but there she was, and he had to do something about it.

"Hey, I need a favor," he said to the group, unsure who was in charge. A tall, thin man in his twenties with short hair and massive sideburns moved forward, placing himself between Bryce and the camera.

"How can we help," the man asked. Bryce studied the man for a moment and then stepped close.

"You captured the little girl's face, so I have to ask you to delete at least that part from your video file.

"Why? It's news," he protested.

"Because she's an innocent minor, and I'm asking that as a professional and personal favor. Do that for me here right now, and I'll give you an exclusive of some sort. Tell me what you'd like to do." The man turned and spoke with the others. As he turned back, Bryce read the man's face and knew this might need to get dirty.

"What if we say no? What are you going to do? Send the CIA after us?" the man said. Bryce laughed and then stared at the man. As the seconds ticked by, Bryce's eyes grew more threatening and bore into the man. Bryce hoped the man would get it - that this was a man not to be on the wrong side of, and soon, he relented. The man turned, took the video card from the camera, and handed it to Bryce.

"Go ahead, take the whole file. We're good," he said. Bryce slid the file into his pocket and smiled.

"You know the schedule tomorrow. Stop by and ask for Billy, and she'll put us together. Maybe you want to see inside my private mobile suite? Nobody else has ever taken a camera in there." The man stumbled at first. Perhaps shocked that Bryce, the man who had just put the fear of God into him, would make good on his offer.

"That would be exceptional, Bryce, thank you very much," he said and then waved his arms for this team to get moving.

"No, thank you," Bryce said and then turned to see what was left of the mess.

He surveyed the hallway and was happy to see the Kazaan team's media people were still there, quietly gesturing for him to come their way. Past them, he saw the two Ferrari drivers standing together, shaking their heads, and there, now smiling again, was Penelope Charles. Bryce forced a smile but then took on a real one as Jacques Lafrance, the French president of the international sanctioning body, and a young aide blew past her and headed straight for him. As they approached him, Bryce said with a laugh, "It wasn't me," and let out a sigh of relief as they continued past him and stopped in front of Tony Bishop and his team owner, Claudia Werner. When he turned to head for fresh air, he nearly bumped into Charles as she came close.

"Does this sort of thing happen every day in Formula One," she asked. Bryce checked his watch and looked up.

"Only on Tuesdays. It's Thursday still here, I think, so," Charles smiled.

"You look like you've had a long day. May I buy you a drink? There has to be a high-dollar happy hour somewhere." Bryce had wanted to engage Claudia and Mila but knew now, especially now, was not the time and place. He waved to his social media team as he called out, "Are we done?" They both returned a thumbs-up as he held out his elbow for Penelope.

"Grab hold and lead the way, my dear; the first round's on me."

⁓

Charles studied Bryce on the barstool beside her as he nursed his apple juice. She waved to the bartender for another Dirty French Martini with Grey Goose.

"I love everything that's French. Clothes, bread, kissing. Are you sure you don't want something a little more exciting," she asked. He smiled.

"I'd love a tall glass of beer, but when it's race weekend, there's no alcohol. That's my rule." Charles studied him.

"Only beer? Not the most expensive champagne they have?" she said, prodding his arm.

"I prefer to be showered in it, not drink the stuff," he said, "Plus, I grew up on six packs back in the States, and aside from great coffee and Coke Zero, it's my go-to when I need to chill." Charles' drink arrived. She handed the bartender her credit card and whispered in Bryce's ear.

"I've never slept with a Formula One World Champion before," she said. "Let's go up to my suite and let me pop your cork." She watched as Bryce nearly choked on his drink and then seemed to consider the offer. He finished his drink quickly, leaned over to her, and whispered, "Would love to, but not tonight. It's that time of the month." Suddenly, she sprayed out the gulp of martini she had just taken and laughed loudly for some time. She was happy to see a genuine smile from this racing driver; she knew she still had game, and he looked interested. But then he got up and took her hand in his.

"So, do you go to every race?" he asked. She nodded yes.

"Even the long hauls like Melbourne?" She smiled and nodded as she took a drink.

"Of course. I love Australia, and I have a big client in Sydney, so I get to see them, take in the race, and write it all off," she said. Bryce smiled and then took and kissed her left hand.

"Penelope, it's been a pleasure getting to know you. I have a lot of commitments the rest of the weekend, so I'm booked up socially, but I'm sure we can connect again soon, and if we hang out after the race, who knows, there might be a few corks involved." Bryce nodded to the bartender and placed a hundred euro note on the bar. Minutes later, he was in his suite after navigating through the lobby and the islands of people there. He bolted the door, set his alarm, threw his clothes in a pile in a corner, and got under the lavish gold comforter. He took deep breaths, expelling the day and relaxing his mind and body. Then Mila came to him; her beautiful face filled his thoughts and heart.

Bryce looked at the digital clock to the right on the wall; it read 2:29. He cocked his head slightly back and forth, his helmet snug within the padding surrounding it. He surveyed the sea of instrumentation and displays on his steering wheel. Then he looked forward over the front of his red and white Formula One entry at the crewman, a young Frenchman with whom he often practiced his French, standing in front of him, preparing to wave him out of the garage and into the action. Normally laser-focused on the matters at hand, his mind wandered. He thought of the beast his rival Tony Bishop had hired for protection. It didn't make sense. Tony might have been an asshole, but he had good taste, was professional when he wanted to be, and typically surrounded himself with fit, lean men and women, regardless of the job's requirements. There was something off about it. He'd need time to figure that out, but-

Suddenly, something tapped his helmet once and then again. Turning to the left, he saw a team engineer, this one a young Brit who always wore shorts no matter the weather, standing alongside the car, gesturing for Bryce to look toward the pit lane. There, the Frenchman was waving repeatedly to get his attention. His Mercedes racing engine purred as it idled.

"Bryce, radio-check," a British race team engineer called out on his headset.

"I got you loud and clear," Bryce answered. "My bad. I was just listening to the engine. She sounds like she wants to go."

"Well, then hit the gas and let her eat," the engineer said. A second later, the Kazaan racing entry was speeding down the pit lane with Tony Bishop right on his tail.

Hours later, the second practice session of the Friday complete, Bryce took the time to shake hands, fist-bump, high-five, or hug each of the thirty-two Kazaan team members on-site at the track. Being the fastest in both practice sessions was something to be proud of, and he wanted to let them know that he appreciated their part. Once he returned to his trackside suite for a quick, cooling shower and a fresh set of clothes – this time a red and white Kazaan Ralph Lauren polo with pressed jeans and black Reeboks. Sponsors were necessary; they paid the bills, and on race weekends, subtle as they might have been, Bryce was a handsome, walking, talking billboard. When he came upon Claudia Werner, they exchanged a cordial greeting in front of fans and photographers and then walked to the Werner VIP lounge. Then, seated in a see-through cubicle, Bryce had a few questions to ask.

"Anything new as far as threats go?" he asked as if it was no big deal. Claudia shook her head no. Bryce waited until a server delivered coffee, fruit dishes, and assorted, warmed nuts.

"Thank you," he said as the man left the cubicle. Bryce surveyed the Werner lounge, looking for familiar faces, dangerous ones if they were to be found, and anyone out of place. He knew they were being watched. A driver or celebrity can barely take a leak without probing eyes, an outstretched hand holding a Sharpie, or a camera trying to capture the moment it often seemed. With everything and everyone seeming at ease, he returned his focus to Claudia.

"My heart took quite a ride yesterday in the media center," he said. "It raced when I heard Mila calling my name, and then when I saw that thug chasing her, it felt like it froze for a second." Claudia tensed as she sat forward in her seat.

"That was the last straw," she told him. "Tony and I are done. I'm telling him after the race. First, he pitched a fit when I flew to Monaco with you, and then he shared something I had never known." Bryce leaned in.

"He told me that late one night when he and Max were drinking after the race at Silverstone, Max went quiet and then told him he thought Mila was yours," she said. Bryce was stunned.

"So he's been racing me thinking that. I just thought he was a natural-born asshole. But now I get it." Bryce laughed as he stared at Claudia.

"Does this mean you'll be looking for a new driver come Monday morning?" Claudia shook her head no. "As long as he races his Canadian ass off, he has the seat." Bryce nodded.

"But does this mean you'll be looking for a new friend with benefits?" he asked. Now, it was her turn to laugh.

"My life is complicated enough as it is, Bryce; you in my bed is the last thing I need right now – not that I haven't thought of it quite a few times since Zermatt."

Bryce shook his head in agreement. "Me too." Claudia looked at her watch and then got up.

"Now, I have a dinner party to attend at the Ritz. Are you there?" she asked. Bryce stood.

"No, I prefer the Al Areen. It's closer. If you do get bored, though, call me." Claudia smiled and began to leave the cubicle as people positioned themselves to try to grab a moment of her attention. But she turned back to Bryce.

"By the way, who was the woman at the media center yesterday? I don't know her." Bryce wondered for a moment. Then he remembered.

"Some race fan from England. Penelope Charles." Claudia stepped close, grinning.

"She's a bit old for you, my dear," Claudia said. Bryce nodded in agreement.

"Which is why I slept alone last night in that huge bed in Suite 99 at the Al Areen in case you need to find me." Claudia waved her finger at Bryce as she shook her head no and engaged the people waiting for her. Bryce spent the next twenty minutes slowly but happily posing for photos, signing, and talking with fans and well-wishers as he worked his way to his vehicle and the team driver waiting for him near the paddock entrance. With the car in sight, he heard his name called by a familiar voice with a French accent. When he turned, he wished he hadn't. It was Jacques Lafrance, and he didn't seem happy.

"Bryce, just a minute of your time, please. I know it is late," Lafrance said. As Bryce stopped, a crowd of people began to converge, so he took Lafrance by the arm and led him to his car.

"Step in for a minute," Bryce suggested. "Nobody can read our lips or bother us in here."

Once inside the white Land Rover, a second security vehicle with four quick-response specialists inside pulled close to the lead car's bumper. Bryce instructed his driver to cruise around for a bit.

"So what can I do for you, Jacques?" Bryce asked.

"Nothing, we don't need anything more than what we ask of our other drivers here this weekend," Lafrance said.

"But?" Bryce asked.

"But we want the drama to occur on the track and in the pits, not in the paddock or anywhere else. I have to be honest with you. I voted to ban you from racing this season until the sniper is caught. It is in the interest of public safety. I hope you understand."

Bryce cleared his throat. This was news to him. *They had a vote?*

"I think whatever happened back in Daytona will remain in America," he said.

"So we should be concerned about Miami, Texas, and Las Vegas? Is that what you are saying?" Lafrance pressed. Bryce's temper was starting to rise. In the few years Bryce had raced under his organization's rules and authority, he and this Frenchman had battled over technical regulations and other trivial matters. Although he had never come right out and said it, it was clear to Bryce that this man had no time for him or any American.

"You know, look at us right now. We're riding with two men up front, both probably armed," Lafrance said. Bryce grinned as he caught his driver's eye in the mirror. The man winked. "And we are being followed by another vehicle, just like this one, and probably with armed men inside. This is different from everyone else. The other Formula One pilots drive themselves to and from the races." Bryce looked out the side window, deciding the direction he would take from here. Throw the guy in a dumpster, wishful thinking, or be as diplomatic as possible under the circumstances. He wanted to find a dumpster but took the more peaceful path.

"Look, everyone has security at some of the venues, you know that. We all have crazy fans, and stalkers, and there's the risk of kidnapping," Bryce said. "It comes with the job. It's just that one of mine decided to try to shoot me during a major racing event. My security does not interfere with anything we do here at the track. The sold-out track, I might add." Lafrance nodded but shook his head in disagreement.

"You don't read about a rogue MI6 spy going after any of our British drivers, do you?" he asked. But before another word could be spoken, the driver slammed on the brakes as two men jumped in front of the vehicle.

CHAPTER TWENTY-TWO

NOBODY WAS ENTERTAINED by the overzealous fans who had seen Bryce climb into the Land Rover and drive away from the paddock at the Bahrain Circuit, especially Jacques Lafrance. His sudden shriek when the fans first appeared left the man visibly shaken and embarrassed. Within seconds of the two fans forcing the vehicle to stop or be run over, the security team in the follow-up vehicle had left it and had surrounded the two at gunpoint nearly as fast as an F1 pit stop.

"Just fans, Jacques," Bryce reassured him. "No need for panic. But they'd have run them over if there'd been a weapon in view." Lafrance grew angry, exited the vehicle, and stormed off toward the paddock entrance. As the vehicles began to move again, Bryce laughed at what had just occurred, but inside, he knew the incident could have been deadly.

The weather was typical for the Middle East in March: hot. As Bryce entered the exclusive Paddock Club for a VIP appearance, he enjoyed the chill of the air conditioning as he greeted fans, signed autographs, posed for photos, and did his favorite thing – making a quick speech. He stood at the front of the room and thanked everyone for their support, promising them he'd do his best in the qualifying session to take the pole. As he scanned the faces in the packed room, it occurred to him that Penelope Charles wasn't in view, so much for being a rabid, die-hard fan. Maybe the snub at the bar turned her away. So much for helping MI6, or so he thought. Bryce took the pole an hour later, beating his teammate Mateo Mesa of Spain by two-hundredths of a second. By eight that evening, after doing media, Bryce participated in a debrief with the team inside the second of three extravagant, state-of-the-art hospitality and conference room trailers that followed the team on tour. The red and white team colors and logo of Kazaan Global Racing were everywhere and on everything. While Mesa gave the group his take on his qualifying run and outlook for tomorrow's race, Bryce scanned the room, studying the engineers. Some new, some familiar, but then Jack crept into his mind. He sat up abruptly, catching Mesa and the rest off-guard, and pivoted.

"Hey, how about the job we did today out there," he said as he stood and raised his can of Coke Zero. He gestured for Mesa to stand, which he did, taking his orange Powerade with him.

"Since all of you are Brits, Mateo and I excluded, I say bloody good job today, mates. Bloody good!" The seven men and women still seated raised their beverages in response.

"And here's to taking first and second tomorrow and kicking Werner's ass!"

Everyone applauded and suddenly realized their debrief was over. Bryce gestured for Mateo to follow him, and the two left the room as they high-fived or fist-bumped everyone they passed.

Outside, Bryce turned to his new teammate.

"We haven't spent that much time together, Mateo," Bryce began. "With you coming onboard after the Catalunya tests and me screwing around at Daytona, let's start tomorrow by finishing one-two and never let up from there." Mateo nodded and shook Bryce's hand. "Yes!"

From there, Bryce walked to his private area, where he checked to ensure everything was in order, then passed the lingering fans and well-wishers who slowed him once more. Fans have their favorites, but everyone migrated to the pole winner, especially the one somebody had tried to kill. Then, his Land Rover ride to the hotel, where Bryce made it to his suite without issue. Once inside, he ordered room service and searched the entertainment system for a movie. He was starving. He needed meat, and he needed a distraction. Not a massage with a beautiful stranger or a cigar with friends outside at the pool bar. He needed to get lost for a time; he needed to escape.

Just as it had been the day before and the one before that, the sun had toasted the circuit, and as the 6 p.m. start time crept closer, Bryce was dressed for the race and raring to go. As one of the team's aides reminded him he had five minutes, Bryce approached the race car parked on the front row of the grid, waved to the crowd in the nearby grandstands, and smiled as they roared with cheers and many waved miniature American flags. Suddenly, someone tapped him on the shoulder. As Bryce turned, a sixty-year-old Brit, a former F1 driver now doing grid walk interviews and commentary on live TV, began to speak.

"Bryce, just a quick word. We're live," he said. Bryce smiled, put his left hand on the man's shoulder, and turned toward the camera.

"Beautiful night for a race, don't you think?"

"It certainly is. Bryce, I know you've been asked this a million times, but do you feel safe racing here this evening?" Bryce nodded he did.

"Yes, I do. What happened back in the States is behind us. The bastards who killed my friends and burned down our homes are dead. So it's the season's first race, we're starting from pole, and I'm looking forward – not backward." The interviewer smiled as he nodded.

"Good to know. I feel safer out here already. We'll let you get to it then, Bryce. Best of luck." Bryce patted the man's shoulder and then turned and began getting ready to race, but another man put his hand on him. It was Bishop.

"Haven't seen Claudia today," Bryce said.

"No, after what happened with Mila, she wants to keep her away from all of this," Bishop said. Bryce nodded, then stepped close as engineers and aides from the Werner and Kazaan teams closed in, asking their drivers to get in their cars. The minute hand of the big white, gold, and green Rolex clock positioned high over the grid had ticked again.

"That's a shame. I was hoping for a good luck kiss before the race; she has the softest lips," Bryce said for everyone to hear.

"That's sick; she's just a kid," Bishop protested.

"I was talking about Claudia," Bryce said with a smile. The engineers separated the two drivers, and Bryce turned. He knew time was becoming an issue. But Bishop shook off his handlers and pulled Bryce by the arm.

"Enjoy watching me from behind all day," Bishop shouted, and Bryce knew just what to say in return.

"Just the way she likes it."

Bishop exploded with rage and went for Bryce, but the Werner team restrained their driver as members of Bryce's group chuckled despite their anxiety that they were running out of time.

As the Rolex clock ticked to 7:45, Bryce walked past Bishop to take the top position on the podium and waved to the cheers of his team assembled below on pit lane, and his country's national anthem began to play. Bryce removed his ball cap, tussled his short brown hair, and stood at attention, an electronic version of the American flag displayed on the monitor behind him, the red and white Canadian maple leaf behind Bishop, and the orange and red flag of Spain behind the third place finisher, Bryce's teammate Mateo. Two hours of trackside celebrations took place, and then at eleven, Bryce stood at the top, this time at the head of three tables in a private room at the hotel, toasting the assembled team and thanking them for their hard work.

He looked around at each of them, making eye contact with every person there, from Twigg to Scotty, Byron, Suzie, Jess, Boris, and on and on.

"I know it's late," he began. "But we can all sleep

in tomorrow. Ameer was disappointed he couldn't be here, but he told me everyone's got the morning off, so get drunk, celebrate, and let's do this again next week in Jeddah!" Mateo followed Bryce through the doors to the patio overlooking the pool as the drinks and food continued to flow. Bryce looked up through the palm fronds and then stepped clear of them to view a magnificent night sky.

"I am surprised Ameer didn't attend this first race," Mateo said. "I wanted to show him my appreciation for this opportunity to be a part of this great team." Bryce looked away from the stars for a moment.

"Between you and me, he doesn't like coming to the Middle East. I think he or his family has some history here. If anyone asks, he'll tell people his wife wasn't up for the trip, but it's understood by now." Bryce and Mateo smiled at each other. "This was a good start. Let's keep doing it," Bryce said. Mateo smiled.

"Yes, but I think I'll do better next Sunday in Saudi Arabia."

The next stop on the global tour was the fast but dangerous track built recently in Jeddah. As Bryce stormed into his private suite in one of the transporters and threw a bottle of water against the wall, Jason Ryan suddenly stepped out of the small bathroom, a stethoscope hanging from his neck.

"What the hell? What are you doing here?" Bryce shouted. "How'd you get in here?"

Ryan shrugged his shoulders.

"I hope you're happy. You just cost two security guards their jobs!"

Ryan shook his head and stepped closer to Bryce as he removed the lanyard holding his credential. Bryce read it and looked up, astonished.

"You're posing as an FIA doctor? Are you kidding me?" Ryan took back the credential and then sat down, gesturing for Bryce to do the same.

"I told them I wanted to double-check you after that hit," he said. "And they bought it. I had a credential, so I don't blame them. Come on, take a seat."

"This is *my* place, remember?"

Ryan nodded.

"I know it is, but you'll need to be seated for what I'm here to tell you."

Bryce's mind raced. He was exhausted from the intensity of the heat and the race and stunned by the high-speed crash he'd been involved in that eliminated him from the race. He pictured Kyoto's exquisite, smiling face. The one he had fallen for the first time he'd seen it. *No. They've found her.*

CHAPTER TWENTY-THREE

IT WAS TOO much. Bryce had done everything he could to wipe the haunting memories of his past from his mind, but they kept creeping back, and this, he was sure, was going to hit him harder than the concrete wall had just done at 155 mph. Bryce took a few breaths and then looked directly at Ryan.

"Go ahead, I'm ready."

"It's okay, Bryce; you'll like what I have to say."

"You've been thinking about suicide a lot?"

"No, we found out who's behind the Daytona sniper."

Bryce let out a deep breath, and his mood changed in an instant. He reached into a mini fridge, withdrew a bottle of orange Powerade, and drank it in one very long draw. He tossed the empty over Ryan's head into a trash can in the corner.

"Well, well, well. You son of a bitches haven't forgotten about me."

"Bryce," Ryan began. "Do you remember Alistair Marshall in Sydney?"

It only took a moment to remember the disastrous

race in Australia last year and the encounter the CIA had planned for the man they code-named Deadly Driver.

A crash on the very first lap of the race had ended his day early and meant the 8,000-mile flight from the U.S. had been a waste unless he included the work the CIA had planned for him there. All the pieces had fallen perfectly into place when Bryce was introduced to Marshall in a VIP suite while the race was still being run. Marshall, a devout racing fan, had told Bryce he wanted to make up for the lousy day and make him his guest at one of his exclusive, high-end resorts on Bondi Beach. The private jet ride from Melbourne to Sydney was over before his host could open another bottle of champagne.

"Drown your sorrows or celebrate life; your choice, my new friend," Marshall had said. Much like Max Werner, a billionaire, Marshall was passionate about everything, especially Achara, the young twenty-something beauty he wore on his arm like an expensive watch. He had his hands in nearly everything else down under, from constructing skyscrapers and his exclusive beachfront resorts to owning cable news networks and print media around the globe. Tonight, though, he was focused on impressing his new friend and bedding the woman he'd met on holiday in Thailand just weeks before. On arrival in Sydney, Marshall's team was waiting and whisked Bryce off to his luxurious home for the next few days.

"I have business in Singapore that I have to take care of," Marshall had told Bryce. "I'll send a car for you in two days. You can come to my office, and then we can dine like kings."

Bryce had plenty of time to relax. The next race would

be back in Europe in three weeks, and he needed to get inside Marshall's office.

Sitting in his private quarters across from a CIA case worker he had little time for, Bryce remembered it all. The massive Lion's head was impressive, as was the rest of Marshall's office. The mounted heads of lesser animals, who weren't kings of anything, filled the room. Now, they just gathered dust as their acrylic eyes, at least to Bryce, seemed to reflect their better days. The rugby trophies Marshall had acquired as the championship team owner lined the old-world, classic mahogany shelves. Bryce didn't see the sense in killing animals like these just so the rich would have something to brag about. In other circles, he'd suggested the big dollar, big game hunters should seek their prey as they did in olden times to make things more of a challenge with a spear or bow.

As he inspected the man's trophies, he thought of the last time he and Pete had been in Africa, not long ago. Pete had indeed bagged the water buffalo he'd been after for years. When he put it on display at his cabin, they had toasted the animal and its head. The difference between the two hunters was simple: Pete ensured the meat from the kill went to the local village. Bryce was unsure what happened to the rest of the magnificent lion but assumed it was left in the dirt and became part of the circle of life.

Back home in Vermont, Bryce had killed for food before he could afford to buy meat in any quantity at a store. Trophy hunting – at least this type – did nothing for him, but he faked his enthusiasm, not wanting to offend his host and bring the night to an early end. To him, killing needed to make sense, and he still had work to do.

Marshall's view from his office of the Sydney Bridge, the familiar Opera House, and the city skyline was very impressive. When Bryce had first entered the space, he was startled by the sudden move of a man in a tailored dark blue suit who approached him with a wand, much like the ones used at airport screenings. This instrument appeared smaller and more sophisticated.

"No need, Julius," Marshall called out. "He's a friend." As he talked about Singapore, Achara poured a drink for both men: scotch rocks for Alistair and a Carlton Draught, a popular beer and Bryce's new favorite – at least down under. As she began fixing herself a cosmopolitan, Marshall called out again. "No need, my dear," he said, his tone softening with every word. "Our guest and I have business to discuss, so nighty-night for you, all dressed up in blue."

Marshall then led her to the door. She turned to tell Bryce that she had enjoyed meeting him, and seconds later, her silky black hair and tight figure disappeared from view as the door closed behind her.

Marshall turned to face his guest. Bryce sensed an immediate change in his demeanor. Sitting down beside Bryce on a massive sofa covered in hides, perhaps from the plains of Africa, Marshall leaned in. His breath was of scotch, but his eyes were that of a hunter eyeing his prey.

"So, what are you doing here, Bryce Winters?" he asked without taking his eyes from his guest.

"Meaning?" Bryce responded. "Dinner; I thought we were going to dinner. Look, I've had a great time here this week. Your hospitality has been exceptional, and Achara has been—"

Marshall had put his hand up for Bryce to stop. "Listen, mate; I can hunt. I can sniff out a big cat like that one on the wall. More importantly, at least for right here and now, I can sniff out bullshit. And you're shoveling it."

He leaned in closer, forcing Bryce to lean back and consider punching him in the throat. "You sought me out at the track; I saw it. I see that look constantly: people wanting to get close to me. That happens when you're bloody rich."

Bryce cocked his head. "Really? I thought I saw the same look in your eyes. I see that all the time from fans, stalkers, and women looking for someone to give them the good life or just a ride. Then there are the brokers, the land agents, you name it – and in every country. People who say they want to pay me to promote everything from deodorant to diapers, for God's sake. What was that look in *your* eye, Marshall? Why am I here?"

The stare-down continued. Marshall leaned an inch closer, sniffed, and then burst into laughter. "So, you didn't connect to ask me to sponsor you or the team?" he asked.

"And you don't want me to do commercials for your beach resort?" Bryce replied, continuing the laugh, more from relief than anything else. The two got up, fixed another round of drinks, and gazed at the skyline again, the sun now fully set.

"You still buying me dinner?" Marshall asked with a smile.

"Of course, Alistair, it's what I would like to do to show my appreciation. You have my permission to publish some of the photos of me at the resort – the ones you had Achara take." They laughed again.

"Okay, down that beer while I use the boy's room. It's a bitch getting older, nothing to look forward to, I can tell you." *That's okay; I'd like to find out for myself.*

Marshall disappeared down the hall into what Bryce assumed was a private restroom.

Now was his only chance, and he moved about the man's office with the speed of a finely tuned pit crew. He peeled the paper-thin, transparent devices from the back of a card the CIA had given him; one bug here, another bug there, until four were placed. He was back at the window, empty beer glass in hand, and smiled as Marshall reappeared. But something was wrong, different.

"Now, what have you been up to?" Marshall asked. Bryce stared at his host and smiled.

"Nothing, why?" he asked.

"You're up to no good," Marshall said, his voice louder, his expression meaner. Bryce remained cool under pressure, another reason his country's clandestine service had wanted him as a spy. Marshall walked to his desk and stood within a foot from where Bryce had placed the first bug. He picked up the desk phone.

"I need security in here right away!" he shouted.

Suddenly, the office door was thrown open, and Julius and two other men, all with handguns raised, stormed in and took positions between their boss and his guest. Bryce kept his cool and looked at the windows. *Well, they don't look like they open, but I guess we'll find out.*

"That man's trying to steal my lion!" Marshall shouted and then began laughing.

In Bahrain, Ryan shook his head as Bryce finished telling the story.

"So, did he find the bugs? Is that why he's after me?" Bryce asked. "Did you get anything out of them?" Ryan didn't answer. Bryce grew frustrated as he watched the man choose his words.

"What I can tell you is that he has an adult son. A former military sniper, his only child, is set to inherit the business. We know he flew into Miami a week before the incident at Daytona and flew out on a private jet the next morning." Bryce got up and began making coffee. He turned and held up a mug to Ryan.

"No thanks; I've got to be back in Washington in the morning and need to sleep."

Bryce stared at the coffeemaker for a moment before retaking his seat.

"What's the prick's name?"

"Andy," Ryan said.

"And is the guy's mother still around?" Ryan shook his head no. "Drowned off the great barrier reef ten years ago."

"So where is he now?" Ryan shrugged his shoulders and then held up his hand.

"We lost track of him, but if they're going to take another shot at you, it would make sense for them to do it in their backyard." Bryce got up and mixed his coffee. He brought the mug to his lips and inhaled the aroma. It was the only thing that made him smile so far today.

"Melbourne's in a few weeks," Bryce said as he leaned against the counter, "and Alistair likes Asian women."

"What?"

"He collects them like his trophies. He had his catch of the day show me around while I was there. Achara was from Thailand, and she was stunning. When you put all this together, I know where Kyoto is now. Alistair's got her. I'm sure of it." The mini suite was small but had room enough for Bryce to pace, and he did until he stopped and demanded action from the CIA.

"You need to find his kid and grab him. Make it look like a kidnap for ransom because that's what it will be. Keep him locked up somewhere until I've been there and gone, and then trade him for Kyoto." Ryan looked at his watch and got up; a sigh of frustration made Bryce pause.

"If it were only that easy, Bryce. The guys connected. By default, he's tied to the Prime Minister, the Defense Minister, and someone else."

"You're killing me. Who?" Bryce asked.

"Claudia Werner, and Werner Industries. Marshall's shell companies channel some of Werner's weapons to the bad guys."

"So give me an untraceable gun, so I won't have to get one myself, and I'll kill both of them, father and son. To put a nice bow on the present, I'll do it with a Werner gun." Bryce watched as Ryan stared into space as if considering the option. Ryan looked at his watch again.

"Last question," Bryce called out. "Could he be the bastard who killed Alan Johnson?"

Ryan shook his head no.

"Our techs got an image from some cameras of someone stalking outside the hotel in the middle of the night. But they were much shorter. And most probably a woman."

Without saying a word, he nodded at Bryce and left the room. For a moment, Bryce considered going after Ryan and perhaps putting him in one of the track's dumpsters, but then he thought of something better and made a call. It answered on the second ring.

"Well, this is a pleasant surprise," the woman said.

"Where are you? We need to meet."

"Hong Kong," she said.

"Can you meet me at the Peninsula in twelve hours?"

"Sure, but it will cost you," she said.

Bryce ended the call and then phoned his pilot.

"Hey, change of plans," Bryce said.

"Where to boss? All I need is time to file a new flight plan and top off the tanks."

"Hong Kong. I need to be there in the morning," he said. "Can we make it?"

"Sure thing, boss. Just get your butt out here, and we're gone."

Bryce nodded, quickly packed the room into a black Pirelli duffle bag, and left. It took him twenty minutes to navigate through the screaming fans and media, but soon he was back in the Land Rover, the second car in tow, headed for the airport.

This is the second time I'll be forced to work with a Chinese spy.

CHAPTER TWENTY-FOUR

THE PENINSULA HOTEL in Hong Kong was one of Bryce's favorites. As Susan Lee, a beautiful representative from China's MSS, the Ministry of State Security, approached him in The Bar, the intimate lounge with the lights turned low, she smiled as she placed her soft right hand on his cheek, her nails pained a vibrant red, and kissed him softly.

"We've got to stop meeting like this," he said as he studied her and remembered how attractive she was. He remembered her guns her finely tuned muscular arms, and she had them on display again this evening in a sleeveless dress.

"The last time I saw you, there was a CIA official floating face down in the Singapore Bay, and your girlfriend was getting the shit kicked out of her," she said. The British accent she'd adopted while growing up in London had always intrigued him. She pulled the seat closer to Bryce and got on, gesturing to the bartender. "How is she?"

"Missing," he said.

"You've lost her again?"

"It's complicated. Very complicated. Can we take our drinks and go upstairs to talk?"

Lee reached for the martini the bartender had just delivered. She sipped at it once and then again as she stood up.

"Sure," she said. "But we're not going anywhere near your bathroom this time."

Bryce laughed as he signed the bill and slid the thin black book back to the man. He reached for his beer glass and turned, surprised that Lee was nowhere near him. He surveyed the room and saw her tapping her gold high heel on the marble floor at the doorway. Minutes later, they were inside Bryce's Harbourview suite. Lee dropped her small red bag on an end table and sat on an elegant beige sofa as Bryce placed his empty beer glass on top of the bar and studied the stock, returning with a Heineken and a vodka on the rocks with a twist for the lady. He handed her the drink and sat at the opposite end of the sofa.

"Okay, let's get the business end of this out of the way," she said. "Is she really missing? What was her name? Kyoto, I think?" Bryce stared at his guest. He wondered if she had another Sig compact pistol in her tiny bag, replacing the one he took from her in Paris. They made a deal; he kept his promise and her gun. When he visited Beijing later in the year, he didn't plant bugs or kill anyone for the CIA. In return, Lee owed him a favor, and he called it in during the F1 race weekend when the CIA bastard Chadwick showed up in Singapore, killed his CIA handler, and kidnapped and tortured Kyoto. Lee and her team had found the victim, one arm badly broken, the other handcuffed to a rusty vertical pipe as she sat on a cold, wet floor. Lee had reversed the table and turned Chadwick into a victim, shooting him three times and assuring Bryce he was no longer a threat.

"So, who has her?" she asked, concerned. Bryce didn't answer as he looked across the room at the skyscrapers across the bay.

"You can't go to the CIA or anyone in America now, can you?" she said more like a statement than a question. "Even the White House has turned its back." He shook his head again.

"And that's why I asked you to meet me."

"What, you're ready to come to work for the MSS?" she joked.

"Not hardly, Susan, but I need your help, and I want to make a deal, same as before. You help me with this, and I'll owe you." Lee smiled.

"We have a deal. Now, tell me," she said.

Bryce laid it out for her. The connection Alistair Marshall in Sydney had to Max Werner and their illegal arms dealing. The CIA hadn't entirely left him out to dry; they fed him the intel that Marshall's son Andrew had been the Daytona shooter.

"So, do you want me to kill him for you? One or both of them?"

"I want you to grab his son a few days before the F1 in Melbourne. If I know you have him, then I can race without that hanging over my head," he said.

"How do you want him? Upright, restrained and muzzled, roughed up, or dead in a body bag?"

Bryce laughed.

"I feel like I'm ordering from a Chinese menu. A or B is fine, but I need him alive."

Lee got up from the sofa, swallowed her drink, and walked past Bryce toward the bedroom doorway.

"Coming?" she asked and then disappeared into the room. Bryce walked to the window as he finished his beer. He drew the curtains as he heard the bathroom door close. Then, he walked to Lee's bag and opened it. He saw her gun, another Sig, and closed her bag. As he entered the bedroom, he looked at the bathroom door and laughed as he remembered his overzealous security team kicking one down in Paris to find him with Lee making a deal.

So you lied about killing Chadwick, he thought. *I'll wait until you grab the shooter for me, and then your lying ass is mine.*

Lee had snuck out of the suite in the early hours; Bryce had heard her but decided to play dead. Once his desire for coffee crept into his head and blood, he was on the phone to room service, and Bryce had a morning ritual that he didn't like interrupted, no matter where he was. Coffee and lots of it, CNN or the BBC on the TV, fifteen minutes of stretching and core work, and then a shower. Hot at first and then cold. His yoga, workouts, and bike rides typically would be accompanied by his personal trainer and masseuse back in the States or at the races, but he'd decided to keep her away for her safety. After this stop in Singapore and then the race in Melbourne, he hoped to return home to Park City to check on the land he wanted to build his new home on and then get back to training, heavy training, during the three weeks between Australia and a return to Europe and the Azerbaijan GP. Now out of the shower, Bryce checked his watch; it was 10:30, 8:30 in Sydney. *It's still early – but who knows where in the world he is right now.* On the second ring, Alistair Marshall answered.

~⁙~

"Bryce Winters, how the hell are you, my boy?" Marshall said as he waved to his son Andy, who was standing near the galley, flirting with a flight attendant.

"Doing well, all things considered, Alistair. How about you, my friend? Will I see you in Melbourne?

As Andy Marshall approached his father, Alistair gestured for him to sit across from him.

It's Winters, Alistair worded and grinned as he saw his son's eyes light up.

"How's that massive office décor coming along? Bagged anything bigger than that lion since I was there?" Bryce asked. Marshall held the phone against his shoulder and ear as he gestured to his son with his hands as if reeling in a catch. Andy shook his head in disagreement and raised his arms as if shooting a hunting rifle.

"You'll have to come see, but this time, after you win the damn race," Alistair said. "And as always, a beachfront suite will await you."

"How's Achara? She's quite the catch," Bryce asked. Alistair tensed.

"Oh, she's long gone, my boy. Back to Phuket or wherever the hell she came from." Alistair listened, expecting something more, but Bryce said nothing. "We caught her up to no good, so we shipped her home."

"Well, I hope it wasn't in a box. If I know you, there's another more angelic beauty on your arm. Where the hell are you anyway? I hope I've not called you too early," Bryce said.

"My son Andy and I are high over the Bengal Sea,

headed home after some business in Mumbai. He's home from the Army and learning as much as possible about the business."

"Well, I'll find you at Albert Park," Bryce said. "See you there." Alistair put down his phone and looked across the aisle to Andy.

"You sure you can pull this off?" Alistair asked. "It should have been done at Daytona. I would prefer he loses his life in America. There are enough guns and shooters to keep law enforcement searching for years, but she wants him dead now, so it's time." Alistair watched his son raise his arms again, this time shouting "Bang" as he jerked back from the pretend recoil.

CHAPTER TWENTY-FIVE

BRYCE STOOD AT the window and looked down at the hustle and bustle in the busy harbor below. He'd always found Singapore entertaining and intriguing but, until now, had spent very little time there. Fly in, practice, qualify, race, fly out. He wanted to explore the city, hiding under a ball cap and behind his Oakley sunglasses, but a ring of the suite's doorbell reminded him there was work to do. He reached for the gold knob, looked into the small door viewer, and laughed as he saw an eyeball peering back at him. Then, her familiar voice called out as she rang the bell again.

"Room service," the woman's voice called out. Bryce opened the door and found a sharply dressed Susan Lee, shopping bags in hand, smiling at him. She stepped past him, dropped her bags in the foyer, closed the door, and wrapped her arms around him. They kissed.

Hours later, Bryce leaned across the rear seat of the black van and kissed Lee goodbye.

"You do know you will owe me about five favors now," Lee said as she placed her hand on his cheek.

"If your boys pull this off, then, yes, at least that," he said as he kissed her hand. He held it for a time and then studied it. She pulled it back and looked at him. He saw the confusion in her eyes.

"How many lives has this hand taken?" he asked.

"You look exhausted," she said, "You need to get some sleep. I'll see you when I see you." Bryce forced a smile and stepped out of the van that had stopped in front of Singapore's private jet terminal. It was past midnight as raindrops began to pelt the tarmac; he didn't look back. Normally, things would be quiet at that late hour, but this was Singapore, and like New York, the place never slept. It took Bryce fifteen minutes to make his way through the crowded space, making small talk with the Hollywood actress just arriving to start shooting a thriller there, posing for a photo, and doing the usual until he was finally standing in the cockpit door, happy to see his team and ready to roll.

"Let's get out of here," he told them. "I've seen enough of this place for now."

"Melbourne, here we come," the pilot called out as Jen followed Bryce into the main cabin; the tray of a burger and onion rings with a Coke Zero he'd requested on the ride there would soon be devoured.

A year earlier, the race in Australia hadn't been very good to Bryce. He'd crashed out on the first lap, and then his interaction with Alistair was at the CIA's direction. Bryce had fared better the two other times he had raced here and desperately wanted a win this time around. With so many people pissing on his party, as he had thought to himself more than once recently, he needed to get this trip and the Marshalls far behind him. He'd arrived there just past nine in the morning, recharged from a good night's sleep on a flawless flight in, and was at the Albert Park Circuit for press day energized and happy to answer any questions about racing. The Friday practice sessions and Saturday's three qualifying rounds had gone well, with Bryce securing the pole position in the Kazaan car. As he left the circuit late that afternoon, he'd hoped for a quiet evening, perhaps dinner and a movie in his suite at the Ritz Carlton, before falling asleep in a good book, but as luck would have it, someone crashed his party. Just as Bryce finished signing autographs at the front entrance to the hotel, his phone vibrated. Once inside the lobby, he checked it. Alistair Marshall had texted him.

JOIN US FOR DINNER. SUITE
1901. 19:00. JEANS ARE FINE.

Bryce scrolled through his other messages while riding the elevator to the seventeenth floor. Once inside his room, he dropped onto a massive orange and gold sofa and set his alarm for 6:30, just in case. He'd have dinner; why not? *It's not like anyone's ever been killed in a hotel before*, he joked. Plus, he didn't run from danger. He thrived on it on and now off the track. The quick nap helped him, although he checked his phone, praying Alistair had suddenly flown off somewhere, but the cold shower got his blood flowing. By 6:58, he was dressed and walking from the elevator on nineteen to the suite situated a few doors down on the left. He'd barely raised his hand to knock when the door flew open, and Alistair greeted his guest as if they'd been lifelong friends.

"So glad you could join us," Alistair said as he shook Bryce's hand and led him into the suite. "So much more personal, breaking bread in a quiet room. It's much better than with all the wanna-be players at the track venues. As Alistair stepped out of the way, he called out to his other guests.

"Well, our star attraction has arrived," he said as he waved for Penelope Charles to come forward and greet his guest. Bryce was surprised to see her there but took only a split second to process it. *MI6 connects me with her, and the CIA had me after this bastard. Yeah, maybe tonight's the night I fall off a balcony.* Suddenly, Bryce heard someone else enter the room.

"You must be Andy; I can see the family resemblance," he said as he grasped the man's hand.

"And you're the world-famous race car driver from America, hunting for another winner's trophy," Andy said as he prepared drinks at the bar.

"I've followed your career. You and your uncle used to hunt off the Kruger in Africa. I've never been there, but the old man says we'll get there someday once I earn him a few million." Bryce smiled as he looked at Alistair and thought of the trophies he'd taken there.

"No, Pete used to hunt big game while I hunted for poachers," Bryce said as he joined Andy at the bar. "Pete may have taken a few heads, but he always gave the meat to the people who needed it the most." Alistair joined them at the bar and dug through a drawer for a cigar lighter.

"Andy's quite a shot, well at least, that's what he tells

me. Mostly taken out terrorists and who knows what on some black ops for our special forces. Isn't that right, son?" Andy sipped at his drink and winked at Bryce.

"That's top secret."

Bryce walked to Penelope. While the men had all dressed down in polo shirts and casual jeans, she was decked as she had been in Bahrain, and as they embraced and kissed cheeks, he remembered her now trademark scent, a concoction of hairspray and Chanel.

"Where'd you disappear to in Bahrain?" Bryce asked, buttering his target. She stumbled for words until Andy delivered her martini, and she seemed to relax.

"I must admit, Bryce, I got a little flustered with all the excitement," she said.

"What? Nothing exciting ever happens at auto races; come on, P," Alistair said.

Bryce was curious and figured, why wait until dinner? He might not last that long. He took Penelope by the hand and guided her to the sofa, where she sat down, Bryce joining her just close enough to make her feel wanted.

"Oh, Alistair and I go back a long way," she said. "My father and Alistair did some international business before he died a year ago.

"Oh, I'm sorry to hear that. Was it sudden?" Bryce asked.

"I'd say," she said. "A hit-and-run driver drug him fifty feet before anyone realized what had happened. Daddy was dead there on the cold, cobbled street, all alone." Bryce took her hand and held it.

"He was a good mate, Johnny was. We made a lot of money together back in the day," Alistair said. Bryce surveyed the room. He saw Andy more preoccupied with his phone than the famous race car driver who had come to dinner. *Strange*, Bryce thought. As the evening continued, the four sat close at one end of a large dining room table, telling stories, jokes, and drinking – everyone but Bryce. He stuck to water and fruit juice; he had a race to win tomorrow and perhaps his own life to save tonight. As four uniformed servers cleared the dinner plates and dessert was being presented, Bryce declared he needed to call it a night. He thanked his host, kissed Penelope again, and fist-bumped Andy. As Bryce walked to the door, Penelope got up from her chair and followed him. Out of sight of the Marshalls, she stepped close and asked Bryce, "Is it true what they say about athletes?" He cocked his head.

"I've always heard they shouldn't have sex before a big event; it takes something out of them, if you know what I mean," she said, blushing. Bryce began to answer, but she cut him off.

"What suite are you in? Let me come up and tuck you in, no strings attached." Bryce took a step back and looked at her from head to toe.

"Come on now, what's a girl got to do to shag a world champion," she asked.

Bryce felt a wave of concern. This woman didn't seem like a spy. Here, tonight, she appeared vulnerable and alone. He felt for her; he had felt the same way a lot recently.

"Okay, here's the deal. You can come up and watch a movie if you'd like, but no funny business. We can save that for another time, perhaps on my boat in Monaco." Penelope smiled and called out to the Marshalls.

"Bryce is going to make sure I get home safely; thank you for dinner."

Once in his suite on seventeen, Bryce dropped onto the sofa and began scrolling through the movie options. When Penelope returned from using the bathroom, her clothes were gone. The only thing between her and Bryce was a luxurious white Ritz Carlton bathrobe. Suddenly, there was a knock at the door. Bryce managed to get up from the sofa before Penelope could pin him there. To his surprise, he checked the door viewer and saw Jonathan Sproul standing in the hall wearing a server's uniform. Bryce opened the door and stared at the man.

"Room service," Sproul said loudly enough for anyone to hear and rolled in a food cart.

"Hey, I didn't order-" Bryce protested as he closed the door but followed Sproul into the suite. Penelope had tightened her robe, sat on the far end of the sofa, and smiled politely at Sproul. Suddenly, he raised a small pistol and shot Penelope in the neck. Bryce froze for a moment. He considered going for the gun as Sproul shook his head no and pointed to the dart sticking from her neck.

"She's not dead. Just sleeping," Sproul whispered as he searched the suite for the woman's belongings and found them in the bathroom. When he returned to the living room, Bryce looked at the man's hands. He was holding pills, a small baggie, and a syringe. Sproul picked up the remote, raised the volume on the TV, and motioned for Bryce to follow him into the bathroom. He turned the sink faucet on and stood close to Bryce.

"She was going to drug you. They'd have found you dead of a heroin overdose in the morning. You'd have been a national disgrace to your country. And you'd be dead. Did I say that enough for it to sink in?"

"But why would she want to kill me?" Bryce asked.

"She didn't. She just wanted to shag. But now, she'll be found dead of an overdose in *her* room." Bryce raised his hands in protest.

"If I hadn't knocked, you'd have died long before dawn, mate."

As he approached his car on the grid Sunday morning, Bryce was shocked, this time a much happier but conflicted one. Surrounded by crewmembers in headsets, there was a sudden commotion as someone was shoving their way through the crowd to get to him. Then he saw the cause. It was Mila, and she jumped into his outstretched arms a moment later.

"Well, what do we have here? Are you a kangaroo or perhaps a wallaby? No, no, I know what you are – you're one of those Koalas they have down here!" Mila took Bryce's smiling face in both hands.

"I wanted to give you a big kiss for good luck," she said, kissing his cheek and wrapping her arms tightly around his neck. Bryce held her as he scanned the crowd, looking for who he hoped would arrive soon. Seconds later, followed closely by two fit-looking young women wearing shades, earpieces, and Werner team uniforms, Claudia Werner worked her way to them. She leaned close to greet Bryce with a kiss on the cheek.

"I thought you said you were keeping her hidden away, safe," he whispered. "What the hell is this?" A hand pats Bryce on the back. He turns, Mila still in his arms. It's a crewman.

"Bryce, we've got to get you in the car. We've got four minutes." Bryce nodded and then spun back to Claudia.

"Now everyone watching knows we're connected, making her an even bigger target – for whoever is after me." Bryce jostles Mila and then hands her to Claudia.

"Thank you for my good luck kiss, little lady. I'll see you after the race, okay?" The crewman tugs at Bryce's arm as he reaches across to Mila, patting her head. Behind his sunglasses, though, he holds back a tear. *What the hell is this?* Bryce shook his head and removed his sunglasses. Quickly putting on his balaclava, red, white, and gold full-face helmet, and Hans restraints, he climbs aboard the race car and slides down into the seat molded in the shape of his body. As the crew attached his safety harnesses and steering wheel, Bryce surprised himself even more. He said a prayer, asking his maker to keep him safe. *She's lost too much already.*

For the past ninety-four minutes, his sole focus had been holding off all challengers and winning the race, which he did, finishing five seconds ahead of Tony Bishop and his teammate Mateo for the second time in three races. As he drove the car to the #1 position sign in Parc fermé, he climbed up on the car, waved to the crowd, and ran to the Kazaan crewmembers assembled at the fence line. Ameer Kazaan was the first he greeted and then went from one crewmember to the next, hugging, high-fiving, and shouting all the while. As he removed his helmet and gloves, he walked to the mandatory weigh-in, handed his gear off, and surveyed the fence line again. Claudia was standing at the fence as Bishop walked to the scale. Bryce saw an opportunity and took it. He slowed momentarily, giving Bishop time, and then walked to Claudia and kissed her. Bryce turned to see Bishop approaching and said, "Looks like you take second in everything." Bishop gave Bryce a slight shove with his shoulder, but once upstairs in the driver's lounge before introductions and trophy presentations by the country's prime minister, Bishop threw a left hook at Bryce – the entire episode being broadcast live around the globe. Bryce ducked and smashed Bishop's nose with a stiff right jab that knocked the driver to the floor. Knowing the event was being broadcast, Bryce made the best of it, gesturing with his hands as he counted like a boxing referee. When he reached ten, Bryce waved both arms and then raised his in victory. The room quickly filled with security intent on breaking things up and crewmembers there to dive into the fray until everyone seemed to realize it had ended as quickly as it had begun. Then he felt something strange. His conscience suddenly bothered him as Bryce realized Mila might have been watching.

After order was established and the podium presentations concluded, Bryce sat down for the post-race press conference and opened with a statement apologizing to his fans.

"For anyone who might have been upset at the little skirmish before the podium ceremony, I," he paused and surveyed the media room. He knew they wanted something worthwhile. A sound bite. So he crushed the paper his PR team had prepared for him and adlibbed as off to the side Ameer Kazaan and his media team held their breaths.

"I just wanted to say that I have a right to defend

myself, as does everyone, and when someone throws a punch, it's only appropriate that they get one in return. I'm not big on turning the other cheek; I'm much more of an eye for an eye kind of guy. And so, I guess I can say that's a wrap, Melbourne. I'm out of here." Bryce got up slowly and smiled for the cameras, passing a frustrated PR team who had been watching from the wings.

Bryce returned to his quarters, changed into his polo and jeans, and then made the rounds of the VIP areas; surprised and disappointed, he didn't see either of the Marshalls there. He'd heard no news about a woman being found dead of an overdose, but perhaps they had. Perhaps something told them to get on their plane and return to Sydney. Hours later, as he boarded his jet for the flight out of Melbourne, Bryce wondered if he'd ever cross paths with the two again. He placed a call and grinned when Alistair answered.

"What happened to you this afternoon, Alistair? I thought for sure I'd see you after the race," Bryce said.

"I had some sad news this morning, so Andy and I opted to fly home. Didn't feel much like celebrating." Bryce buckled his seat belt as Jen delivered his coffee. He watched as she returned to her seat near the galley, ready for take-off.

"News?" Bryce asked.

"You didn't hear? Poor Penelope was found in her suite with a syringe sticking out of her arm." Bryce waited. He had nothing to say and wondered what his silence might draw from the bastard.

"Next time you're in Australia, we need to get together for sure, perhaps for a game of chess," Alistair said. "I'm beginning to think you're pretty good at it. Until next time, then."

❧

In Virginia, Kyoto heard Russo and Chadwick shout at the TV screen when they saw the fight between Bryce and Bishop unfold and end abruptly. Kyoto had been listening to the race, sitting on the floor at the door in the next room. Her former lover was in another fistfight, and she was locked in a bare room in the middle of nowhere, all because of some vendetta between the two animals on the other side of the door and this famous racer and part-time spy. Only a few books, a bathroom, and a single bed on the floor lit by a single bulb in the middle of the ceiling, controlled by a switch on the other side of the door. And there were cameras, one in the bathroom, two in the bedroom. They could watch whatever, whenever they wanted. Her food would come three times a day now, left for her when she stepped back from the door. The roadside hotel cabin had served its short-term purpose, but they had moved further into central, more rural Virginia. Roland McCarthy owned the two-hundred-acre property the cabin was set on.

❧

Roland McCarthy looked over his brunch guest's shoulder at the Intercontinental Willard Hotel in downtown Washington. He watched as the Formula One drivers accepted their trophies atop the three podium positions in Melbourne.

"For a moment, that looked more like professional wrestling than racing," McCarthy said.

His guest turned around in the booth and watched for a moment, turning back and waving to a server as he pointed to his empty coffee cup.

"There's a man with a lot on his plate, "Jason Ryan told McCarthy. "The minute you believe he has no other use to us, to you, he might just have had enough and blow his brains out. Maybe even use one of that asshole Uncle Pete's guns. It could happen."

McCarthy waited until the server filled their cups and walked away.

"No, let Russo do his thing in Miami, and then let tactical take him out."

Ryan raised his cup and nodded.

❧

At Camp David, far north of the cabin, President Zach Johnson had ordered his staff to leave two hours open so he could watch without interruption. He was so proud of what Bryce was doing representing his country, winning, until yet another fight broke out.

"He's lashing out," Johnson said to an empty living room. "Radioactive or not, he needs some help."

CHAPTER TWENTY-SIX

Bryce wanted to fly back to the States after Melbourne, but Ameer had convinced him to return to Ibiza. "Rest; let a few bikinis distract you. Work out, relax, calm," he had suggested. With two weeks before the next race, Bryce had time for anything and agreed only to appease him. Instead, he had his flight crew chart another destination, back home to his roots in the hills of Vermont. But first, there was some unfinished business to attend to in Sydney.

Susan Lee loved creatures of habit. It made her job so much easier. Away from the tight schedules of a Formula One weekend, Bryce rarely kept a routine anyone could track, but Andy Marshall, the ruggedly handsome twenty-four-year-old military sniper recently discharged honorably from the Australian Army, went about his typical day after day and that had made grabbing him easy.

Her team of three, two women and one man, simply bumped into Andy as he left the garage elevator for his car after a late-night workout at his private gym. His routine would have had him head to a local bar and depart in the early morning hours with a fresh female catch of the day, but the taser knocked him unconscious and flat on his face on the cool concrete floor. Lee leaned against a table that had been pushed back against a wall. The six meeting room chairs were neatly stacked in a corner, all but one. She watched as her captive, a black hood pulled down over his face, struggled in his chair. The restraints on his arms, waist, and ankles would hold him perfectly for what she had planned. She walked to him and punched him in the face. Andy's head snapped back as he yelled.

"What the fuck! Whoever you are, you're dead when I get free of this," he shouted. She laughed and punched him again, harder. It took longer for him to clear his head; this time, he had nothing more to say.

"Good," Lee said. "Now, we begin."

"What the fuck? Is this a kidnapping? My father won't pay you a cent, so do what you want, but you'll get nothing for this." She laughed and watched as the head in the hood turned toward her.

"Shit. You're a woman. What did I do, not call you after we shagged?" Lee shook her head and then kicked him hard in the side of the knee. Andy shouted in pain.

"God damn it!"

"So, now that we are clear on who is in charge, I have a few questions for you. Answer them correctly, and I might let you go. Lie or don't recall something, and you will never be able to fire a weapon again as I will cut off every finger, one by one, and feed them to the dogs in the street." She watched, certain the hooded man was trying to figure out how we could make it out of there alive.

"First, we are private contractors hired by the American CIA to find out why you tried to kill Bryce Winters. You were in Florida and left right after you took the shot. So remember, a lie will cost you a finger –perhaps the right thumb first, then the left."

"I didn't try to kill anyone. I'm a military sniper; I don't miss," Andy stated.

"So what was that then? Some sort of a warning shot?"

"I was sent there to get into his head, take some of his focus off his game. I did not shoot at him and was not trying to kill him."

"And who had you do this?" Lee pressed. He didn't answer. She turned, picked up a surgical instrument, a cutting one, and clamped down on his right thumb. She watched as he tried to pull it away but tightened the device, cutting slightly into his skin.

"The more you struggle, the more you will be cutting yourself," she whispered. He stopped moving. Lee paused momentarily and removed the instrument, tossing it back onto the table.

"How is your relationship with your father? After all, he sent you to boarding school when you were nine, and you've been away in schools and the army for the last fifteen years. One might think he doesn't care much about you." Lee watched as Andy's head tilted forward. She wondered if she had struck the right nerve, perhaps even brought about a tear.

"Tell me," she said softly.

"It's transactional," Andy replied. "He rewarded me

when I got good grades, gave me a car when I spied for him by dating some asshole's daughter. We aren't tight, but we are blood."

Lee walked around him and then paced the room. She looked at her watch and took a drink from a water bottle.

"Your father has a thing for Asian women, doesn't he?" The hood shook in agreement.

"Do you remember little Kantima?" The hood snapped toward her.

"Her mother cleaned your house and would bring little Kantima. You became friends."

"God, I haven't thought about her in years," Andy said.

"Well, Alistair sure did. He sent you off to boarding school so that he could have his way with her mother, and then once Kantima came of age, he had her too. He wanted you out of the picture. He doesn't like to share." Andy struggled.

"Can't believe what you are hearing, can you?" she asked. "But it's true. Ask your father the next time you see him. For now, my work here is done. I will make this as simple as possible. If anyone takes another shot at that race car driver, this will happen to you again, and your thumbs will come off before you're even awake. You cannot hide from us. Nobody can. Next, your father is involved in some shady business deals. If he were to have an unfortunate hunting accident next time he's out headhunting, that would make us forget any of this ever happened. That is unless you follow in his illegal footsteps." Lee watched. The hood didn't move.

"So we are going to cut you loose. Count to one hundred, slowly, and then you can get up and leave here. If you move one inch before you reach one hundred, you die; it's that simple." Lee leaned in close. "Do not tell anyone about this encounter. No police. Not your father. Understand?" Lee stood up and smiled as Andy shook his head in agreement. She looked at Bryce, who had sat quietly at the end of the table watching. She read his lips. *What about Kyoto?*

"One last thing," she said as she placed her hand on the top of the hood.

"Where's Kyoto? Where is your father keeping her?" Andy's head shook left and right.

"Who the hell's Kyoto?"

Lee looked at Bryce, who nodded in agreement, hopped off the table, and followed her from the room, passing the three standing guard in the hallway.

"So, how'd I do?" Lee asked.

"I guess we'll see. Now, where the hell is she?"

"No clue, but he'll be coming through that door soon. What's your move?"

Bryce extended his arm and extended his open right hand.

"Give it to me," Bryce whispered. Slowly, Lee reached inside her black jacket and withdrew her compact 9 mm pistol. She placed it in his hand. He press-checked the slide and saw the bullet resting in the chamber.

"Are you sure?" she asked. Before he could answer, Andy Marshal poked his head into the hallway. Bryce watched as Andy's eyes grew with surprise and then recognized what he was holding.

"How did you find me?" Andy asked. Without warning, Bryce raised the gun and shot the man between the eyes. He stepped over the body and stared at it.

"Warning shot my ass."

With this part of the plan accomplished, Lee's team cleaned up as she led Bryce to a black Mercedes sedan. She took his face in her hands and gazed into his eyes.

"These are dangerous, dark waters you're swimming in, and you've just entered the very deep end," she whispered. He winked and then laughed as he looked down at his hand.

"You probably want this back," he said as he untucked part of his black shirt and wiped his fingerprints from the gun. Holding it awkwardly by the barrel, he held it out for her to take. She shook her head as she laughed and took it back, her fingerprints now covering his. He climbed into the car without either of them saying another word and was driven to the airport, where his flight crew was ready to go. Sydney to New England via Los Angeles. It would be a grueling trip that included an additional flight crew who would man the cockpit as far as LA, but he wanted desperately to go home.

As Billy Reynolds brought the Bombardier in for a landing in Burlington, Vermont, Bryce's nose almost touched the window as he watched the forest beneath grow closer and closer. He loved New England and would spend the week hanging out in his late Uncle Pete's hunting cabin near Stowe. Hiking the hills, embracing the quiet, shooting the rifles he learned to hunt on, and sitting in front of a fire was just what he needed. Walking up the aisle toward the cockpit, he told the crew to get hotel rooms and then fly to Salt Lake City in the morning. Jen tried to push back, but his decision had been made.

"I pulled you away over Christmas and haven't gotten any of you back there since," he said. "Pick me up here next Monday at 6 pm, bound for Baku." Minutes later, Bryce shook hands with the charter concierge, who greeted the flight. Soon after, he was alone in a rented white SUV and driving toward Stowe.

For the next seven days, he did what he wanted; some days nothing, others filled with mountain hikes with a heavy backpack. He'd driven down to visit the Team O'Neil rally school, where he had traded work for seat time and jumped at the chance to visit with the best of the best, a group of Army Rangers and Navy SEALS who were taking the special driving courses set up in the woods for special operators. That night he posed for photos, and as the darkness came, he accepted a challenge from the cockiest of the bunch, a young SEAL from Louisiana.

"Yea, yea. Sure, you can drive F1, but think you can still go fast through the woods – at night?" the young SEAL had teased, but Bryce knew it for what it was – a challenge or most certainly a dare. Thirty minutes later, the tires and engines were steaming while the SEAL puked his lunch, and Bryce held out his hand for the five bucks they'd wagered and accepted the cheers from the warriors who had stood and watched. Before he left O'Neil, he'd ordered a dozen pizzas and six cases of beer for the group, passing the arriving delivery van as he exited the gates in his SUV.

After handing off a bag of subs and large coffees to the off-duty troopers he'd hired to watch the property while he was there, Bryce pulled up to the front of Pete's cabin and shut off the engine of the rented white SUV. He finished off half of the six-pack of the high-octane IPA he'd purchased at a C-store as he reflected on all that had happened since the first night Pete and Jack had been drawn into something deadly: that night long ago in the Middle East when Pete beat a drug dealer to death in an after-hours bar and to keep him out of jail, Bryce and Jack had helped dispose of the body. If only that damn CIA nerd Jon Watanabe hadn't been scouring CCTV feeds and had used facial recognition to identify Bryce at Langley. If only some maniac at the CIA hadn't thought it a good idea to blackmail an American hero into working for them. Once Pete got wind of what was going on, the retired career sniper took out Bryce's handlers, and after the dust settled, a lot of people were dead, and friends of those handlers had come after Bryce and anyone who had been involved.

"You just can't make this shit up," Bryce muttered as he got out of the vehicle.

Then, as he walked through the front door, feeling the quick effects the alcohol had on his empty stomach, he saw his image in a rustic mirror over the coat rack and stared. It was dark, late, and he was alone again with his thoughts. It was rare for anything to get into Bryce's head. He was a master of control and focus, but the relentless losses, not those on the track but in his personal life, were wearing on him. He'd always enjoyed coming here, except the first time, knowing Pete wouldn't be there to greet him. Now, in the near darkness, Bryce wondered if coming here had been a mistake and then asked his reflection,

"So, who else are you going to get killed?"

He shook his head and walked to the kitchen, sitting at Pete's table where he and his uncle and dad had spent so many meals talking about life, survival, and the right things to do. In the quiet, he surveyed the room, perhaps hoping, wishing one of them could somehow lend a comforting word.

"I understand why the bastards took out Jon and Jack. I get why they took Kyoto. She's probably dead now, too. If they were holding her for ransom, they'd have asked for something by now."

Bryce drank another beer and spoke to the dark, gray fireplace. Like Pete and Dad, the fire and all it symbolized were gone.

"But what about those who remain around you now? Alan's dead because of you. If you'd just gone off and hid somewhere, nobody would be dead, and nobody would be at risk except you. What about those still around you now? Those who support you, some who care about you. What about Ameer and Lilly? Claudia? Mila? The team? Danny, Bill, Lou, and Jen. And now Joan. You've put them at risk now. Is it fair? Shouldn't they have a say in the matter?"

Bryce gets up and throws the bottle hard into the hearth.

"They've opted to stand close to a moving target. They know the risks."

Bryce got up, walked to Pete's old leather chair, and dropped into it. He stared at the worn sofa, the eagle, globe, and anchor of the U.S. Marine crest sewn into an olive and tan comforter draped over its back. He thought of the night when his Kyoto had read Pete's journal, and they discovered what had really happened to Bryce's mother. Growing up, he'd been told she'd run off, but the intimate journal told them otherwise. While defending his disabled father from an angry, violent mother, Pete returned a punch that ended the woman's life.

Bryce shook his head, still in disbelief. He reached to the coffee table for his fifth beer, checked his watch, and called Ameer. Surely, the man was still up; it wasn't quite ten o'clock.

"Bryce, is everything alright?" Ameer said after answering on the first ring.

"Yes, I'm fine, Ameer. I just wanted to call you and tell you that I'm going to quit driving. Too many people have died because of me, and all of you are at risk. It's selfish of me to keep racing."

⋘

Sitting in the living room of his penthouse apartment overlooking Montreal, the lighted dome of Saint Joseph's sitting atop Mount Royal in the distance, Ameer could tell Bryce had been drinking, which is rare.

"Is this, what do Americans call it – a drunken pity party, or," he asked and waited for an answer that didn't come.

"Bryce? Are you still there? Where are you?" Finally, he heard Bryce's voice as Lilly walked into the room, seeming to have overheard the concern in her husband's voice.

"No, more of a critical analysis, Ameer. I'm not feeling sorry for myself. Just the ones that are dead and concerned for anyone who might get that way because of their proximity to me." Ameer shook his head as he gave Lilly a reassuring smile.

"Bryce, you are supported by two former fighter pilots, your bodyguard is a former Army Ranger, and the race team is made up of men and women who bravely stand on pit lane as cars fly toward them. They all know someone is after you, and not one has raised the question, shown any fear, or left us. Nobody has left you. So get some sleep and take a long walk in the morning. Clear your head, and then drive up to Montreal and have dinner. Lilly will cook." Ameer laughed as Lilly tossed a small throw pillow at him in protest and then came closer, taking a seat next to him. He watched as Lilly whispered something but he couldn't make it out. He covered the phone and waited for her to repeat it.

"He sounds vulnerable. Don't give him a hard time. Get him through tonight. You'll have time to discuss his other behavior in Baku." Ameer smiled and nodded in agreement.

"Bryce, we all care about you. Many think you should go into seclusion until they are caught, but that's not in your DNA. It's part of what makes you a champion. Now, enough of this nonsense. Get rid of the booze, drink some water, and get some rest." Ameer waited for a response and grew frustrated as he asked again.

"Bryce?"

❧

"I'm sorry to have called you this late, Ameer," Bryce finally answered. "I'll sleep on it and call you in the morning." Without saying another word, Bryce ended the call, got up, lay on the sofa, pulled the familiar comforter over him, and went into a deep sleep.

The next morning, after the best night's sleep he'd had in some time, Bryce got up and sat on the front porch of Pete's cabin, savoring the brewed coffee and bathing in the morning sun. He sent a text to Ameer that read:

Thanks for taking my call last night. I appreciate your support and needed a friendly voice to talk to. I'm fine. Not coming to Montreal. You joked too often about Lilly's cooking! I will see you in Baku, ready to race and ready for the ass chewing I'm expecting. Thank you my friend, BW

Days later, now in Azerbaijan for the next race, this would be the site of what some Americans in the southern part of the U.S. might call a "Come to Jesus Meeting." As Bryce sat across the small table from Kazaan, he knew what the team owner would say, but out of respect, he'd let the man vent. He'd heard a few versions of it before.

"Bryce, this has to stop. The sponsors are unhappy; there's nothing but negative on our social media – except in America, they still love you there. People say they want to watch a race, not a fight in the octagon." Bryce took a shot at breaking the tension. *Who knows, maybe he'll laugh.*

"That's it, Ameer. I'll kick his ass in a charity fight. We can raise millions for kids' charities on pay-per-view." Ameer wasn't having it.

"Bryce, look at this face. It is old and worn and not

accustomed to getting yelled at by anyone, especially the CEOs putting up millions to fund whatever you think you are doing. We battle it out on the track, in cars, not with our fists. This is not the wild west of America. This is the rest of the world saying calm the hell down." Bryce got up from his chair and made a coffee, offering one to his guest, his boss, who declined. "No caffeine for me, Bryce, not with my blood pressure."

Bryce retook his seat.

"How is Mrs. Kazaan?" Bryce asked.

"You are lucky she's not here. You'd be wearing that coffee," he said.

"I always admired her spunk, Ameer. Okay, now let's got get an ass chewing."

International Federation President Jacques Lafrance sat beside series president Antoine Blanc in the temporary offices set up at the circuit. Opposite them on the far end of a long, thin conference table, Bryce and Kazaan sat quietly and took it.

"Bryce, you cannot behave like this. It is unprofessional and goes against everything we stand for. This is not boxing, this is not NASCAR or the NHL; this is the pinnacle of professional auto racing," said Lafrance.

"You used to race. Are you telling me you never got into a fight?" Bryce asked.

"Never!"

"Pas de testicules!" Bryce responded with a smile.

Kazaan shot up from his chair and threw his full water bottle into a corner trash can.

"Are you trying to get a suspension?" Kazaan shouted

as he turned to face Bryce and dropped into a chair against the wall. Blanc got up, walked the table length, and sat close to Bryce.

"Bryce, we all know you've been through hell. You've lost the man who raised you, Max, and Jack in a very short period. Your home and all of its memories," Blanc said softly.

"And don't forget his girlfriend left him; I can't understand why," Lafrance shouted, his face still red from embarrassment and some temper.

"And the rogue CIA agents are still out there," Kazaan reminded the room.

"You're mistaken, Ameer; they were both captured and killed," Bryce said. Blanc placed his hand on Bryce's forearm. "No, they are still on the loose. Our security team gets updates from all intelligence services from the countries where we race. They are still out there."

Bryce's eyes scanned the length of the table and stopped at Lafrance.

"I apologize for my comment, Jacques. You raced rally cars. You have balls, and you didn't deserve that." Lafrance nodded and looked at Kazaan, Blanc, and then back to Bryce.

"Apology accepted, but your behavior is not," Lafrance said without emotion. Blanc stood up, returned to his seat, and leaned against the table to face Lafrance, his back to Bryce and Kazaan. Ameer moved back to his seat beside Bryce, still visibly shaken.

"Bryce, you should take a few weeks off and find a lovely beach or a mountain you've never climbed. Get away from all of this for a bit." Before Bryce could respond, Blanc turned to face them as Lafrance began to speak.

"Based on your recent behavior, which takes last year into account, we have decided to suspend you for one race." Bryce could feel his rage boil as Kazaan placed his hand on Bryce's forearm. "Let me speak."

"That could take us out of the championship. We can't have that, so we will appeal," Kazaan stated without emotion. Blanc walked to the window and stared down on the pit lane as race cars peeled from their garages beneath them as their first practice began.

"That is your right," Lafrance responded. "But remember to include the fifty thousand euro filing fee." Bryce got up from his chair and walked to the window, standing beside Blanc.

"So you are pulling the only American driver in F1, a world champion, out of the first race in America this season? Are you serious?" Blanc turned to Bryce.

"Yes. We are. But perhaps a penalty like this will let you, the drivers, sponsors, teams, fans, and the media, know that we do not tolerate violence."

Kazaan got up from his chair and walked to Bryce and Blanc, seeming to ignore Lafrance.

"And what about Bishop? He threw the first punch."

Lafrance joined the others at the window.

"They are waiting outside and will receive the same penalty."

Bryce opted not to shake anyone's hands. He got it but was fuming and felt deep inside he might tear an arm or two off if he did. Minutes later, Bryce was changing into his driving suit in his private quarters when a familiar knock came to the door.

"No way," Bryce said as he moved to open it. As he did, the heat of the day and the sun's glare smacked him hard, but then a friendly face stepped in to block the rays. Danny Johnson was back from burying his twin brother, unexpectedly reporting for duty.

CHAPTER TWENTY-SEVEN

Bryce had a flurry of emotions race through him. His friend, a much-needed one, had flown halfway around the world to be at his side. As he and Danny embraced, another figure came up behind him.

"Bryce, we need you in the car for the first session," the rookie team assistant called out; her Scottish accent always sounded like music to his ears. Unless, of course, she had a tone, and this message carried one. Bryce looked past Danny at Twiggy Meyers, a pert young woman from Galway with degrees in marketing and engineering.

"Ameer already told you guys the news?" Bryce asked. Tight-lipped, she shook her head yes and then pointed to her watch.

"Five minutes, mate," she said and left.

Danny stepped in and pulled the door closed behind him.

"Go ahead, get changed. What news?" he asked. Bryce changed out of his team polo and jeans to beige fire-resistant underwear and socks and then a red and white fire-resistant driving suit. He stopped and looked at Danny.

"How's your mom?" Bryce asked.

"Not good. That's one of the reasons I'm here. I could see it in her eyes. Every time she looked at me, she saw Alan, and it gutted her every time." Bryce watched as Danny choked back his feelings.

"But she's got my sister and her kids. They're her sunshine now, and they'll keep her busy until she's ready for me to come home."

Bryce stood in front of Danny and put his hands on his shoulders.

"I never expected to see you again," Bryce said. "But I'm so happy you're here. We're late, so walk with me, and I'll bring you up to speed."

⤔

Danny walked alongside Bryce, who had stepped up the pace. He looked back at the two security staffers dressed in Kazaan uniforms following from a distance. He gave them both a nod and then refocused on keeping up with Bryce.

"I wish I knew what you were planning; I could have saved your ass the 7,000-mile flight," Bryce said as they arrived at the rear of the garage and worked their way past team members moving from one task to another.

"They're suspending me for one race for the fight in Melbourne," Bryce said but stopped and leaned in.

"But I've got plans. Are you in one hundred percent?" he asked.

"Fuckin' A, Bryce, whatever you need,' Danny answered. Then, someone put their hand on Bryce's shoulder.

"In. Get in the car," Twiggy demanded. "Please." Bryce reached for his headgear and smiled at Danny.

"Let's talk over dinner. I need backup in Washington. That's where I'm headed next." Bryce leaned in and whispered into Danny's right ear. "And somebody's going to die."

CHAPTER TWENTY-EIGHT

AFTER PRACTICE AND the team's mandatory debriefing, Bryce left the room at the back of the garage and headed for the Kazaan hospitality area, with Danny and Twiggy following closely behind. His Oakley sunglasses, this pair with red lenses to match his uniform and his temperament, hid the fire that was burning behind them.

"Those motherfuckers said they'd announce the suspension before the race on Sunday, not now," he growled. Lafrance's media team has issued a press release during the first practice session, accidentally or perhaps intentionally, Bryce thought, to cause a swarm around him that could disrupt his focus and possibly cost time on the track. As he closed in on the black circular stairway leading up to the private, team-only hospitality, at least twenty reporters waving notebooks and microphones raced to intercept him. Rather than delay the inevitable, Bryce stepped onto the raised patio at the VIP area and turned to face them.

"Okay, you've all heard the news. I have one simple thing to say. Ameer has already filed an appeal with the commission and will be in Paris next week to deal with this. From where I'm standing, the car's fast, and we plan on another podium and padding our lead in the points." Bryce turned and headed up the rounding stairs. Twiggy followed, but as an overzealous reporter reached out and grabbed Bryce's arm, Danny quickly smacked it away.

"Hands off," Danny declared as he snarled at the man and smiled. "Have a nice day." Inside the second level, Bryce immediately sat at a round table overlooking the paddock with Ameer and Mateo. Twiggy and two other staffers sat at an adjacent table as Danny stood near the door.

"So, what do you think?" Ameer asked. Looking at the suite attendant who had approached, Bryce smiled and ordered lunch.

"How can you think about food?" Mateo asked. "This could cost us the title." Bryce surveyed the room and then focused his gaze on his teammate.

"If Ameer wins the appeal, no issues. If he doesn't, then you and Bishop will be one-two in points. Enjoy it while it lasts because the first race I'm back, I'm going for broke, and then I'm done." Twiggy gasped, which made Bryce smile.

"Just making sure you're back there, Twiggs," Bryce laughed as he turned and smiled at her. The worried look on her face troubled him for a second, but his wink made her breathe again. Bryce looked at Ameer, anticipating a question or suggestion that they should move into his office and discuss what he had just said privately. Ameer looked away. Perhaps Bryce's antics were wearing on the man. But at that moment, Bryce felt like fighting, and those around him smartly let him be. Servers brought lunch plates and drinks for the three sitting at the boss's table, but Ameer pushed his away, got up, and entered his office. Bryce inhaled his blackened chicken salad without saying another word and left the area, followed by his new Baku entourage, Danny and Twiggy. To their surprise, the media had taken Bryce's declaration to heart and left the area, or so he thought. But as Bryce was halfway down the stairs, he saw the commotion a few trailers over. Tony Bishop was eating it up, surrounded by a crowd of media that had grown to five deep.

Bryce watched momentarily, then returned to the garage to prepare for the second practice session. He knew the news deflated his team, and he did his best to joke around, but the enthusiasm around the car had been lost. At this point, the best Bryce could do was work hard, go the fastest, and win these lads and ladies the pole and the race. As the crowd of reporters attending Bishop's impromptu press conference disbursed and began milling about, Bryce asked Twiggy if she could play a few American tunes on the speaker system to try to revive the crew. The first song, which made many tap an appendage, was Sweet Home Alabama. Bryce smiled as he saw them move, and the smiles eventually returned. He had just delivered the first clue he had hinted at earlier. *Now, let's see if anyone can guess what I've got planned.*

After winning the pole Saturday night, Bryce insisted on taking Ameer to dinner. He felt he owed the man at least that. Over a private dinner in the dining room of his hotel suite, Bryce apologized to Kazaan for his bad behavior. As they moved from the table to opposing sofas in the living room area, Bryce moved to the edge of his seat and stared at his team owner.

"Okay, there's more going on here. What's up, Ameer?" Bryce watched as Ameer settled into the sofa, seemingly delaying a response. *Oh, shit, This can't be good,* Bryce thought.

"I know you are friendly with Claudia Werner; you, she, and Max spent much time together when you raced for him." Bryce nodded.

"Friendly, yes, but she's the enemy when it comes to racing, and now that she's fucking that Canadian dipstick, I'd say we're polite." Ameer tensed and got up abruptly.

"Polite? Do you think I'm stupid? You kissed her on the mouth in front of her boyfriend for all the world to see." Bryce sat back.

"Well, there's that."

Ameer looked at the door. It was clear to Bryce that he wanted to leave.

"Ameer, I did that to screw with Bishop, to get into his head, and it worked."

"Yes, we're not racing in Miami, so well done." Bryce got up and walked to Ameer.

"Come back into the dining room. They've laid out more food. We can talk through this, but we have to be honest with one another. What's really going on here? Tell me so I can help."

Ameer calmed and followed Bryce back into the dining room, where the staff had laid out a spread of decadent desserts. Bryce pulled a chair for Ameer to sit, and as he did, Bryce made him laugh, finally.

"That chocolate cake is mine. If you even look at it, I will stab you!"

Finally, the tension lifted, and as Bryce worked on his cake, smelling the rich chocolate before taking every bite, Ameer picked the nuts from the top of an apple caramel pie slice.

"Claudia Werner might have been an international runway model," Ameer began, "But she is also a shrewd businesswoman. Max could be an animal when it came to business negotiations, and she picked right up where he left." Bryce was intrigued and waved his fork for more information.

"Kazaan Global supplies microchips to Werner Industries," Ameer said. Bryce's jaw dropped, and so did his fork.

"The chips in question are used for weapons, guided missiles, drones, and such, but the number of chips she's been pushing us for is three times what she should need. She's up to something, and I'm not sure what, but when I pushed back, she said something that concerned me greatly." Bryce tossed his fork on an empty plate and pushed it away from him.

"What did she say?"

"She asked how Lilly was. I've known Claudia for five years, and she's never once asked about Lilly." Bryce's mind was racing. He knew what was going on but couldn't tell Ameer anything.

"Have you considered going to the authorities?" Bryce asked.

"Heavens, no," Ameer nearly shouted out.

"You did some work with your government, and look how that turned out. No, I am not sure what to do at this point." Bryce studied Ameer for a moment and then smiled.

"Sell her your company and wash your hands of this," Bryce suggested. Ameer pushed his pie plate away and stared into space.

"Maybe I should sell off everything. You hinted that this might be your last year racing, and there are well-funded parties wanting to buy an F1 team. Maybe we should sit on our boats and look at bikinis."

"Better not; Lilly will kick your ass."

CHAPTER TWENTY-NINE

THE RACE IN Baku had been a disaster, a transmission failure taking Bryce out halfway through the race. Now, back on his plane and out over the Atlantic, he was busy planning. As Jen cleared his dinner plates, Bryce looked across at Danny.

"I still can't believe you're not racing in the States," Danny said, shaking his head. "This is bullshit." Bryce smiled.

"I'm racing; it just might not be in Miami." Bryce watched as Danny tried to process what he'd just said.

"So you're racing in Baltimore?" Bryce shook his head no. His body clock might say it was around midnight, but he was already set on the Baltimore time zone, where it was just six in the evening. "Get some sleep," he told Danny as he reclined his captain's chair and shut off the overhead light. "You're gonna need it."

⤝

Hours after landing at BWI in Maryland, his flight crew headed to their rooms at the Hilton while Bryce had other plans for Danny, who followed his lead and stared in amazement as he watched his boss work.

"Dude, you know how to steal cars?" Danny asked while keeping his eyes peeled for anything or anyone. Suddenly, Bryce tossed something at him. He caught it and gave Bryce a puzzled look.

"Grab a plate; we need to switch them. Come on, act like you're on a pit crew." Danny shook his head and went to work. An hour later, Danny sat behind the wheel of the black Camaro Bryce had broken into. He slumped down and watched as a man parked his silver Jeep Wrangler and walked to the front door of #201. Danny checked his watch; it read 1:35 a.m., then placed his hand back on the gun in his lap.

Bryce heard Jason Ryan enter the security code to his Alexandria, Virginia, townhouse and sat quietly, waiting for the show to begin. From his seat in the dark living room, he sat quietly and heard keys dropping into the crystal bowl he'd noticed on the table by the door. Ryan's shadow moved across the foyer and then changed to a tall silhouette as Ryan left the light and dropped into a leather recliner near the flat screen on the wall.

"Long day?" Bryce said.

Ryan jumped up, turned on an end table lamp, and stared at the intruder, petting Ryan's cat on his lap with one hand and holding a sound-suppressed weapon with the other.

"What the -" Ryan said, his voice betraying him. He was scared. Bryce gestured toward the recliner using the pistol.

"Sit down. It's my turn to talk."

At first, he didn't move. He watched as Ryan noticed the black ball cap and something strange sticking out of it on the table beside him.

"What the hell is that – a disguise?"

Bryce raised the gun; Ryan slowly retook his seat and cocked his head, studying the weapon.

"Is that a GSH-18? Are you working for the Russians now?" Bryce didn't answer. He lowered the pistol to his right leg and continued to stroke the cat; now, its purr was the only sound in the room.

"How'd you get in here?" Ryan asked as Bryce smiled at him.

"I've learned from the best. Remember that night in Monaco when I asked how you got into my place? You said CIA. Well, you guys trained me well."

"Maybe too well," Ryan said.

"You taught me how to steal cars, evade surveillance, break into places. All sorts of things."

"We didn't teach you everything. You already knew how to kill." Bryce nodded.

"Now, you told me Russo and Chadwick were dead. I've been told otherwise. Now tell me the truth, but I'll warn you, every lie gets you a bullet, and we can start with a knee." It might have been a long day and night for them both, but the adrenaline was pumping hard in Bryce, and he wanted answers. But even more, he wanted justice or whatever this was. He wanted a head.

"So you're going to kill me," Ryan charged.

"Only if you lie a lot, in which case you'll bleed out at some point, I'd imagine. Funny, it just occurred to me that first aid was the only thing you assholes didn't teach me. Oh well, that sucks for you."

"Okay, Bryce, I told you they were dead, so you would relax and focus on racing." Suddenly, Bryce shoots Ryan in the right knee. The cat leaps from Bryce's lap as Ryan grabs his leg and falls to the floor.

"I got shot in the hand once. Hurts, doesn't it?" Bryce said. "I have seventeen to go. So the next question is, are they on the run, or are they still intent on fucking with me? They could have done it in Park City months ago if they'd wanted me dead."

"Fuck Bryce," Ryan said, grimacing. "They were intent on taking everything you gave a shit about, and yes, after that, they want to kill you on live television. Since they've taken everything, I imagine they'll be in Miami gunning for you."

Bryce shook his head no. They hadn't taken everything. They didn't know about Mila.

"You don't even watch my races?" Bryce laughed.

"What?"

"I'm suspended, so I might not be racing there."

Ryan sits up against the recliner, blood on his hands as he holds his knee.

"Do you know where they are? Are they working for you, somebody else, or are they just a couple of asshole renegades?" Bryce could see the situation taking hold of Ryan and reality setting in.

"It doesn't matter at this point. You are a dead man walking."

Bryce laughs.

"I prefer dead man driving."

Bryce studies Ryan.

"You're supposed to be smart. Take off that fucking tie and use it as a tourniquet." Ryan follows his suggestion and grimaces again as he yanks it tight around his thigh.

"What were you doing with Susan Lee in Singapore?" Ryan asked.

"Dinner date," Bryce said. "I like Chinese."

"Bullshit," Ryan shouts. Suddenly, Bryce shoots him in the left knee. Ryan grabs at the knee as he falls onto the floor.

"You dumb mother fucker," Ryan shouts.

"Me? You're the one with only one tie."

"She's playing you; that's what she does."

"That's what everyone in *your* world does, not just her."

Ryan's face touches the hardwood floor as his breathing shallows.

"Hey, dipshit, don't die on me yet. I have an offer for you. Take it, and this is over. Hand those two assholes over to me, and we're even. Anything else, and a friend of mine will release info on what the CIA has been doing to me."

Ryan laughs as he shakes his head no.

"You're not stupid. That's a doomsday move. We'd release what we have on you."

Bryce laughs.

"Oh shit, I hadn't thought of that." Suddenly, Bryce points the gun at Ryan but then shoots the flatscreen.

"What the fuck's the matter with you?" Ryan shouts. "Give me something else; I can't do shit about Russo and Chadwick. Give me someone else you want dead, and it'll be done, I promise."

"You need to answer me: Are they on their own, or are they working for someone?"

Ryan struggles as he fights the shock that's coming to stay awake and stay alive. He shakes his head, his breath visible on the floor.

"You know, the one thing you never taught me was torture. I need info, and it looks like I need to set your balls on fire or something extreme to get answers. This plan isn't getting me what I need."

Bryce got up and looked around the room. He walks to the fireplace and finds a lighter on the mantle near some candles. He flicks it to flame.

"Fuck! Stop!" Ryan pleads. Bryce takes a knee in front of Ryan.

"Listen, you have to give me something, someone. POTUS knows I killed for my country, with his signed approval. The White House is ten minutes from here; maybe I can get five minutes with him in the morning to lay the cards out. What do you think, Jason?"

"You don't get it, Bryce. Yeah, sure, POTUS might be on your side, but the Chief of Staff is the one who's really running the country. He's a puppet master on steroids."

Bryce pocketed the lighter and retook his seat.

"What's the prick's name?" he asked.

"Roland, Roland McCarthy."

"And he's running the two dipshits?"

Ryan is close to losing consciousness.

"Hey!" Bryce yells. "Tell me, or I shoot the cat!"

Bryce watches as Ryan struggles to sit up.

"Yes," Ryan whispers.

"Why?"

Perhaps gaining a second wind or realizing it might be his last one, Ryan pushed hard to sit up.

"Shoot the cat. It isn't mine. The shithead I was living with left it here."

Bryce nodded.

"I've got a better idea." Suddenly, Bryce shoots Ryan in the head and gets up as he watches the body slump to the left. He surveys the room, drops the gun on the chair behind him, checks his watch, removes the lighter from his pocket, and walks into the kitchen.

"Here, kitty, kitty," Bryce calls out.

Danny sees a person wearing a ball cap and a beard leave Ryan's house and walk quickly toward the Camaro. It's Bryce, and he's carrying something. A minute later, Danny and Bryce watch as flames appear in the front window of the townhouse.

"Let's head back to BWI," Bryce tells him.

"What's with the cat?" Danny asks.

"She needs a home, and I know just who to give her to."

"Did you get anything else, like intel or maybe some food?"

"Six cans of cat food and a name. This might get worse before it gets better. Are you sure you still want to be a part of it?" Bryce asks.

"If it means killing whoever took my brother and Kyoto, then yes, one hundred percent."

Danny turns onto Wisconsin Avenue NW, headed for Interstate 495 toward Baltimore, as Bryce strokes the cat on his lap.

"We might have to borrow a few of her lives, though. I think we're going to need them."

"So this is the fourth car we've stolen tonight," Danny said. "It's scary how good you are at all of this. This has to be a record. But the beards, mine's itchy as shit."

"Yeah, mine itches too, but they'll work. There might be cameras everywhere, but we're unrecognizable like this," Bryce said as the cat pulled at his.

"I think the best move was leaving the last one parked near the Russian Embassy. They won't find anything in what's left of any of them. They'll just find a dead CIA agent killed with a Russian pistol, and the trail of what we've left behind will take them conveniently close to where a Russian on the run might have gone for safety."

To the east, the night sky was beginning to lighten. If all went to plan, Bryce and Danny would be in their hotel rooms before the flight crew had any idea they'd left the premises, and from there, they'd head west to where Bryce had once taken another life.

CHAPTER THIRTY

"This is good," Bryce said as he surveyed the three hundred acres he'd just purchased in Utah. "We'll at least be able to see anyone coming," Bryce said as he stood with Joan Glaser and Danny Johnson.

"I like it. The builder swears he'll have it done before the first frost," Glaser said.

"So, how'd you swing this gig?" Danny asked Joan as Bryce walked toward his SUV.

"Bryce paid me to take care of a few things around town while he was gone. The more we talked, the more he realized he needed someone to look after things here, and here I am."

"He's a good guy," Danny said as Bryce arrived carrying a box. He held it out to her.

"It's not my birthday," she said, surprised.

"Girl, it's got holes in it. It's not a damn cake," Danny said. She took the box and opened it. Surprise was the first emotion Bryce read on her face, but the second looked like disappointment as she closed the lid and began to hand it back.

"I hate cats," she said. Bryce looked at Danny, who shrugged his shoulders.

"But-" Joan continued, returning the box, "My sister Dani loves them. Is it okay if I give it to her?" Bryce nodded.

"Sure, as long as she gets a good home, I'm cool."

"And you're kidding about the name, right? I'll have two people named Danny in the mix?"

"Sure sounds like it," she said.

As the three walked back to their cars, Bryce continued to take in the area that would be the site of his new home. It had everything and would have, including stables for horses, kennels for dogs, and a home for any four-legged creature that chose to wander through – as long as they didn't develop a taste for any of Bryce's collection. Then they might wind up mounted on a wall.

"You never told me you had a sister," Bryce said.

"Never came up, I guess. She trains at Olympic Park when she's not in school."

"Let me guess, another snowboarding phenom," Danny said.

"Hell no. She's a badass on skis, and there's no telling where she'll wind up."

Bryce opened the driver's door to his black Tahoe but turned and walked to Joan. He opened the box, played with the cat for a moment, and then looked at his new Park City office manager.

"So we're off to Alabama. You sure you don't want to come?" Bryce watched as she closed the box and considered his offer.

"No, I've got a lot to do here, but I'll watch it on TV.

Just be sure to watch out for - what do they call it - the Big One?"

Bryce smiled and climbed inside the SUV as Danny approached the passenger side. They waited for Joan to get behind the wheel of the new red Subaru Outback Bryce had provided as part of her employment package. It wasn't much like the race car with a license plate he kept in his garage, but it would do her just fine. She drove off, waving out the driver's window as she raced down the dirt road. Danny climbed in.

"She'll fit right in, Bryce," Danny said. "She drives a lot like you."

Bryce started the vehicle but sat quietly for a moment.

"Bryce? You good?" Danny asked. Bryce nodded, then looked at him.

"You sure you don't want to go see your mom?" Bryce asked.

Danny nodded.

"No, she needs time. But if you're cool with it, I'd like to go by Alan's grave for a bit."

Bryce nodded, put the Tahoe in gear, and drove down the dirt road toward the highway.

Late that afternoon and now back in the air, Bryce sat in the main cabin and was on the phone with NASCAR team owner Bob Jenkins.

"So you're set on your end," Bryce confirmed. "And as far as anyone knows, you've got two backup cars on board, just in case." From his phone aboard his Bombardier jet somewhere over Michigan, Jenkins assured Bryce everything was in place and ready to race.

"And there's been no leaks to the press?"

"The only other person who knows is Billy Daniels, the crew chief. We'll fly the backup pit crew in on Sunday morning, and hopefully, we'll be all smiles on Sunday night, and you'll have paid that track back."

"Nobody thought it was strange when you installed the bullet-proof panels and ballistic windshield?" Bryce joked. "That car's going to be heavy. We might have to use some cheater fuel to go fast."

"Bryce, that's not funny. Nobody's going to take a shot at you, are they? You told me all the bad guys were gone."

"Billy, I was just joking. I'll see you down there and hopefully in victory lane."

CHAPTER THIRTY-ONE

YEARS BEFORE, BRYCE had competed for the NASCAR championship driving a car prepared by a team Max Werner had put together for him. It had the best of everything. Bryce was leading the series in points when they arrived at the Talladega Superspeedway in Alabama, but by that Sunday night, Max's dreams of a championship had been shattered along with Bryce's left leg.

"The Big One," as they call it, the inevitable crash that occurs every race at this track, was notorious for demolishing cars and dreams. On that Sunday in May, twenty-one of forty stock cars that started the race were involved in the melee, and only one driver was hurt – hurt good, out of contention, and out for the rest of the season. Bryce remembered it all vividly as he told Danny and Jen the story. She'd heard it many times before but was always riveted by the tale.

"We were doing 199 down the backstretch, and somebody hit the wall, came back into the pack, and knocked the living shit out of our car. I remember flipping, spinning, flying sparks, metal screeching, and smoking tires. It was a blast."

"You're kidding?" Danny said, hanging on every word.

"Yeah, it was wild. I think we were sliding around for about ten seconds. It felt like ten minutes, but then the car stopped. I looked across at the car that came to rest beside me. He put his window safety net down just as I did to show the spotters we were okay, but suddenly, it felt like someone shoved a piece of angle iron through my thigh. Man, I was ready for a double morphine drip right there on the spot." Jen got up and walked to the galley, returning a minute later with two trays of food.

"Go on, what'd I miss?" she asked.

"I left out the part where I used every curse word I'd ever heard at least five times in rapid succession. I knew the leg was busted, but the championship was gone."

The men took a break to prep their meals as Bryce eyed Danny's burger, and Danny took in the aroma of Bryce's garlic chicken.

"Want to trade?" Bryce asked, and they did.

"Go on, finish the story; I don't have all day," Jen prodded.

"They operated on my leg that night, and I remember waking up in the recovery room. Max and Jack Madigan," Bryce stopped and collected his thoughts. He'd already said goodbye to them many times, but a story like this brought their memory and the good times they had together painfully back.

"I'm sorry. Where was I? Oh, yea, Max was pissed. I was on all sorts of painkillers, and all I could hear was Max, his German accent in full bloom, going off on how ridiculous oval track racing was. He said something like 'going around in circles is for strippers. There's no sense in it.' So Max was done. We'd won the Daytona 500 and the Indy 500; we were following Mario Andretti's path. Max didn't care about either of those series championships, but what he did care about, what he wanted the most, was to go home to Europe and buy a Formula One team. Andretti is the only American to have won both 500s and an F1 title and when Max told me he was headed overseas, with or without me, I jumped at the chance, so here we are, headed back to Talladega. She owes me one."

"I never heard that part of the story. What was it about Andretti? He stopped racing years ago," Danny asked.

"It was my dad," Bryce began. "He loved watching racing on TV, and between him and Uncle Pete, they were really into an American winning the big ones and then beating the best of the best in Formula One. I remember sitting with them, watching the races on Sundays, the smell of Budweiser and fried chicken every time, and the thought got into my head. I wanted them to be proud of me, and when I found out I could drive, I did whatever I could to win races and make the climb. Then Max Werner came along and gave me the chance."

"And then you paid him back by killing him," Jen said, or so Bryce thought. He stopped abruptly, cocked his head, and stared at her. *What did you just say?*

"You okay, Bryce?" she asked. He continued to stare at her, trying to figure out what the hell had just happened. *Now I'm imagining things. This is not the time for my conscience to start screwing with me. Get your shit together.* Suddenly, Bryce's phone began vibrating on the window sill. He looked at the caller ID; it was Ameer.

"Ameer, what's the good word?" he asked.

"They struck down the suspension," Ameer said. "Both you and Bishop are in for Miami, but they've placed you both on probation. Whoever throws the next punch gets a two-race suspension."

"Excellent. I knew you could get it done," Bryce said.

"So, where are you? That sounds more like a plane than waves crashing on a beach."

"I'm just hanging out in America this week. I bought some land I wanted to check out, and I'm visiting an old friend down south this weekend. I'll be in Miami next Wednesday."

"Bryce, SkySports wants to shoot a video with you for the pre-race broadcast. Something about taking the president for a thrill ride of some sort. We don't have much time, and if you have five minutes to spare, I can try to get them on a conference call right now." Bryce was already smiling at the news of the appeal, but if there were an opportunity to get some face time with POTUS, he'd do anything to make that happen.

"I'm all yours, Ameer. Make the call."

⁃؎

Broadcast segment producer Jackie Illings was ecstatic. Her team had files of research on all of the drivers, their backgrounds, social media posts, things they'd done for press coverage in the past, appearances at charitable events, and more.

"You must work for MI6. Hell, you probably even know my blood type," Bryce teased. A second later, Jackie responded.

"AB+," she called out. She was proud of her research

team and thrilled to work in television, especially motorsports.

"Okay, so pitch us," Bryce said.

"I know you took a tactical driving course some time ago with a bunch of security team members with your Department of State. I saw the photos they posted with the armored vehicles behind you. Did you actually get one of those up on two wheels?" Bryce smiled as he remembered that day. He'd had a blast.

"Yes, I did. The damn things weigh 11,000 pounds – 5,000 kilos, but their engines are like race engines, and their suspensions are incredible. Once you get the feel, they're pretty easy to drive, at least for me."

"That's easy for you to say, but here's what we want to do. The school has permitted us to take over the entire facility for the day there next Monday. We've booked a presidential lookalike to participate, and we can dub in a voiceover from an actor who sounds just like your president. It'll look like he's greeting you at an outdoor event, and a terrorist cell attack takes place; you jump behind the wheel and drive him to safety."

Bryce slumped in his captain's chair.

"This sounds amazing," Ameer said; Americans love this sort of thing, and it's perfect for a race in the United States. What do you think, Bryce?" Bryce didn't say a word. He had thought he would finally get to speak with the president, but now that seemed gone.

"Bryce?" Ameer asked again.

"Sounds great. I don't think anything like this has

been done before. I have a few ideas, but I'll share them when we get there. Either way, count me in."

"Brilliant," Jackie nearly shouted into the phone.

"Hey Jackie," Bryce asked.

"Yes?"

"Your group didn't have anything to do with getting the suspension revoked, now did you?"

"A girl never tells," she said. "But it would be ridiculous to have an American F1 without an American hero racing, yes? So we'll be on the scene Monday morning at nine sharp. Do you need us to set up any accommodations or security?"

Bryce looked across at Danny.

"No, I think we're good. I know the area well. But come to think of it, you might want to ask the West Virginia State Police to send a few patrol vehicles. We might be able to use them in a shot, and who knows, it never hurts to have a few guns and badges around, just in case."

"Great idea, Bryce. See you there Monday."

Ameer and Bryce ended their call as Danny stepped across the aisle and held out his phone in front of Bryce. The CNN headline read, Russian operative suspected of killing a CIA case worker in Alexandria. Bryce smiled as Danny took the seat facing him.

"So, are the shooters all set for the track?" Bryce asked. Danny nodded.

"There's a lot of firepower in Alabama already, but if some dipshit wants to take a shot at you, either the Alabama State Police sharpshooters or the rednecks partying in the infield will take care of them." Danny paused. "We're as ready as we can be."

CHAPTER THIRTY-TWO

HIGH ATOP THE main grandstands at the 2.6-mile-long, high-banked superspeedway known as Talladega, tactical units of the Alabama Highway Patrol were staged inside unique stands, one member using binoculars to scan the infield, the other, using the scope of their high-powered sniper rifle. As the designated security lead for Bryce Winters, Danny Johnson had coordinated the operation with the help of a few Army Rangers turned Troopers he had served with.

"Nobody's gonna shoot your guy, not here, not in Alabama," the lead sniper had stated through a cheek full of Copenhagen chewing tobacco during the early morning briefing. If something bad was going to happen, let it happen somewhere else; let it be some other agency's screwup that allowed it to occur. Just not here, not on our watch. Standing nearby with the race team spotters with binoculars, wearing the vibrant blue colors of Jenkins Racing, Danny's eyes were glued to Bryce. They debated whether Danny should shadow Bryce in the pits and out on pit road for driver introductions, but Bryce refused.

"These people love racing and love their drivers," Bryce had assured him. "I feel safe here. Whoever wants to blow me up will do it big, maybe just as I cross the finish line to win in about three hours. Be watching for *that*."

On pit road, Bryce had been swarmed by just about everyone looking for a photo or a fist bump. Some were thrilled to be close to the American racing hero who had made his country proud when he won the F1 world title. Others were thrill seekers, attracted like moths to a flame when danger was apparent. And today, the racing and the fact that this driver was back on home soil where someone had tried to kill him during a racing event made the atmosphere even more electric. The other drivers in the field welcomed Bryce with open arms and declared their support. One had joked, though, "Hey, if that guy does take another shot at you, be behind me when he does." Bryce thanked Jenkins and his crew as the VIPs, sponsors, and fans were cleared from pit road.

"You've given me a great car, boys. I'll do my best to bring it home in one piece."

"Just get it to victory lane, Bryce; we don't care what shape it's in," Jenkins said before shaking Bryce's hand and wishing him luck. Soon after, Bryce took the green flag at the track that owed him, and he was having the time of his life. Danny and the tactical teams on watch high above the track were on edge, peering through their optics, looking for anything unusual. With tens of thousands of fans camped out in the massive track infield, they knew that unless someone jumped out and started waving a gun and a red flag, it would be tough to stop someone determined to take a shot. If anything, they hoped they could prevent a second one.

Down on the track, Bryce had started third and taken the lead before the pack reached the line to lead the first lap. Now, with only a handful of laps to go, Bryce was in second, and then, everything seemed to be in slow motion for him as two cars ahead of him got together at over 195 mph and crashed hard into the concrete wall. He knew what would happen next; they'd bounce off and slide right in front of him. He veered slightly to the left and missed both cars by what looked to be an inch. As the yellow caution lights came to life, he watched in the mirror as the nightmare unfolded behind him. It was like he was seeing his crash again, but he'd lucked out and missed it this time. Up on the roof, Danny grew more nervous.

❧

"This might be it, boys," he said over his comms. "After they clean up this mess, Bryce will lead them down in front of us behind the pace car. At that speed, he'll be an easy target. At that speed, some asshole will have the perfect chance to deprive him of a win and maybe his life." Soon, just as Danny had described, Bryce led the field of only 14 cars still able to race off turn four and down the straightaway toward the white flag. With one lap to go, all Bryce needed to do was stay out front. All Danny and the troopers needed was a break.

"Come on, you piece of shit. I know you're out there," Danny murmured. "Show yourself. I dare you."

❧

CHAPTER THIRTY-THREE

IN A FLASH, it was over. Bryce's dream of winning at Talladega had finally come true. He'd enjoyed the sound, the heat, every minute and every lap behind the wheel, and every pass that day on the thirty-three degrees of banking. He'd shared over the radio that the G-forces he felt on the banking were thrilling compared to the grueling lefts and rights his neck and body had to endure in his F1 car. At nearly 200 mph, he passed under the flagman waving the checkered flag so fast he barely saw it, but inside the race car, he was ecstatic, pushing the comms button on the steering wheel and screaming into his helmet's microphone.

"We did it!" Bryce yelled. "I can't believe it! We finally did it!"

On the grandstand roof, Danny's heart was pounding. Looking to his right, he saw a trooper lay down his sniper rifle, and Danny yelled.

"You think this is over? If that prick's out there, he

might take the shot just as Bryce climbs out of the race car. Keep looking!"

※

Kyoto let out a silent cheer as she sat against the door, listening to the TV broadcast team shout that Bryce had won the race. Suddenly, a gunshot rang out, and then another. As she held her ears and ran from the door, she could hear shouting in the other room. It took a moment for her head to clear, but she could make it out now. It was Chadwick yelling at Russo.

"What the hell's the matter with you?" she heard. "You just killed the TV! Calm down. He's coming to Miami now, and you'll be able to shoot him for real."

Kyoto had been held captive by these thugs for four months. Their treatment of her had been very harsh at first, but over time, they had provided her with better quarters, better food, and even books to keep her busy. Russo was the bigger animal of the two, although shorter in stature. She had Chadwick to thank for the softer treatment, but regardless, she would kill them both if she got the chance.

※

At his office in the White House, Chief of Staff Roland McCarthy stared at one of the many patriotic works of art on the walls. He'd watched the race from Alabama, had seen the sea of American flags, the honor guard present the colors as a country music star had sung the national anthem, and couldn't believe what he had witnessed on the track. He wanted Bryce Winters dead, but that lucky bastard could drive, he thought. Sitting just a short walk from the most powerful office in the world, he sent an encrypted text message directing a killer to assassinate an American hero, and it was to take place in the morning. Don't wait for Miami; this was the opportunity he'd been waiting for.

FILMING A TV FEATURE. SUMMIT POINT RACEWAY. MONDAY 10 AM

᪉

Following a raucous celebration on the flight from Talladega to Winchester, Virginia, Bryce had gotten eight good hours of sleep in a roadside hotel before heading to the driving school adjacent to Summit Point Raceway in West Virginia. Danny, relieved they had gotten Bryce out of Alabama alive, was quiet but happy as Bryce drove the rental car while he slept off the cobwebs of the tequila Jen had poured him.

"Danny, you could have slept in. Nothing's going to happen here, and there's a bunch of state troopers in case anything does," Bryce insisted, but Danny had waved off the suggestion.

"By the time we get there, the Tylenol will have kicked in," Danny said. "I'll be fine."

From the back seat, Jen and co-pilot Lou Thompson were quiet, hiding behind their sunglasses and nursing the hangovers they'd engaged once they had arrived at the hotel bar. Bill Miller, who had relatives in the area, had stayed behind to meet up with them, and for Jen and Lou, the day ahead looked like an easy, fun one they wanted to witness firsthand. Everyone, including Bryce, was at ease.

Right on schedule, at the top of the hour, Bryce brought the car to a stop in front of two yellow cube vans as the production staff set up lighting and checked equipment. After catching up with the instructor he'd worked with there the year before, Bryce was behind the wheel, getting used to the armored black Cadillac limousine they'd be using for the stunt. With the presidential seal on the side rear doors and the American and presidential flags affixed to the front fenders, he put the vehicle through its paces and then, without warning, got the car up on two wheels as he ran the left side of the car up onto the concrete road barriers set up on a paved hillside made to look like an interstate on-ramp. As he drove the vehicle back toward the crew, he spun it around and stepped out of the car right in front of the project manager.

"My God, you really can put that beast on two wheels!" Illings said joyfully. "This is going to look fantastic on film." Suddenly, from behind a large RV parked near the cube vans, someone who looked like the president of the United States walked toward Bryce, his hand extended, smiling from ear to ear.

"Damn glad to be working with you, Mr. Winters," the actor said as he shook Bryce's hand.

"Call me Bryce, and I'll call you POTUS; how's that sound?" Bryce said. With the introductions behind them, Illings called everyone to the back of one of the vans and went over the script, shot by shot. Bryce and the body double-ran their lines once and then again and again until they developed a natural rhythm. Then, as they prepared for the day's first take, Bryce surveyed the area. The woods were dense and still, but something was missing.

"I thought you were going to have some state police here for this," he asked Illings. He watched as she scanned the area and then looked at her watch, shaking her head.

"That's on me, Bryce. I requested them for ten o'clock. They should be here soon."

Bryce looked at his team, Danny, Jen, and Lou, sitting on a wooden picnic table, trading barbs and drinking coffee. They looked happy, which made him smile. An hour's drive northeast of Summit Point, the real president had just ruined someone's day.

✍

"He's where?" Johnson asked over the phone from the terrace behind the Aspen Lodge at Camp David in Maryland.

"At the track at Summit Point. He's shooting a promo for the Miami race," McCarthy responded.

"Then we're going to detour there on the way back to Washington. I owe him an apology, and I will do it in person."

"But your security, Mr. President, this is too quick. There's not enough time to "

"Horseshit, Roland," Johnson said in a firm tone. "The Secret Service can send a tactical team there on one of the choppers to scope it out. It's a ten-minute flight from here. So we're going, and I don't want to hear another word about it." Johnson hung up the phone and waved for a military aide.

"Can you ask the Secret Service lead to come see me,"

he directed. Within two minutes, she was standing in front of Johnson. A twenty-year veteran of the service, Connie Termini had just assumed the role after her predecessor's retirement. She and Johnson had been getting to know each other and got along well, perhaps until now.

"We're going to stop at Summit Point Raceway on the way home. Bryce Winters is there, and I need to see him. Follow your protocols, but we're going."

"I know that look by now, Mr. President," she said. "Can you give us a fifteen-minute delay so I can get a team there first?" Johnson smiled and tapped at his watch.

"You've got ten. It's wheels up in ten," he said.

"Thank you, Mr. President," she said. He smiled and watched as she turned and walked quickly from the terrace. Johnson went inside the lodge to use the bathroom and, on schedule, stepped off a white golf cart and walked to the air steps of Marine One. Standing tall, he saluted the U.S. Marine in dress blues and went aboard. Inside, as he attached his seat belt, the shadows made by the helicopter blades began to flash at the windows, quicker and quicker.

❦

Russo's phone vibrated in his vest pocket in the woods overlooking Summit Point. He leaned the sniper rifle against the tree and read a text.

POTUS HEADED TO YOU. ABORT.
TACTICAL WILL ENCIRCLE SOON.

"Shit!" Russo almost shouted as he shoved the phone

into his jeans pocket. He surveyed the area as he placed the weapon inside the black canvas rifle bag, looked at where he had been kneeling to ensure nothing was left behind, and quickly snuck away.

෯

One hundred yards to the left of where Russo had been setting up for the shot, the cold blue eyes of a female Russian assassin inspected the weapon of choice she had brought for the mission, a suppressed Norinco Chinese sniper rifle. She worked the bolt to load a round and then lay flat on the ground, using the optic to study the dozen or so people milling around what looked to be an armored presidential limousine. Suddenly, she cocked her head. Something was coming. She could hear a helicopter coming toward them, the sound growing louder. She returned to the scope and went from one head to the next until her target lined up.

"What the," she whispered. "No way."

Was the United States president standing there, his head centered in her scope? If it was, and she took him out, leaving the untraceable weapon behind, China would be blamed for the act, and her employer's weapons manufacturing business would grow exponentially. There'd be a massive bonus for sure.

"Not enough security for it to be him," she whispered, then moved her scope to the head of the man she'd be sent there to kill, the racer – Winters. As she moved the safety with her right thumb and prepared to fire, Bryce walked from view behind one of the vans. She watched as the helicopter flew low and over them, landing in a field one hundred yards past the film crew. She scoped the chopper and counted as six men and women dressed in black tactical gear and loaded for battle fanned out, and began searching the woods. Then she saw it, what she dreaded most. A K-9 dog, a brown Belgian Malinois, jumped from the chopper. Its handler soon followed. The one headed her way, a woman, would have to pass through the film crew before entering the woods and potentially coming face to face. She thought about making a call, but there was no time. She needed to make the shot so she'd wait, determined to kill anyone in her way.

✍

Bryce stood with his team at the picnic table, watching the helicopter unload. He looked at Illings, who shrugged her shoulders and began walking toward the woman in black. Suddenly, three West Virginia State Police sedans and two SUV K-9 units stopped between them. Half stared at the presidential look-alike as the troopers exited their vehicles, while the others stared at the chopper. Bryce walked to them.

"Hi Guys, coming in a little hot, aren't ya?" he asked.

"We just got word the president is five minutes out," a trooper responded. Bryce laughed and pointed at the look-alike.

"He's already here," Bryce said as Illings and the tactical officer arrived.

"Oh my Lord, he's coming. The real president is really coming," she gushed. "Think you can get him to run the lines?"

"We're here to make sure nobody's got any weapons,

and we've got troopers walking in from the surrounding roads checking the woods," the trooper continued. "So, first things first, anyone carrying a gun or a knife?" Danny raised his hand and slowly pulled back his jacket to reveal the 9 mm semi-automatic he had holstered under his left arm.

"I'm *his* bodyguard, and I have a permit," he said. The trooper directed another to take custody of the weapon. "You'll get it back once the show's over. But we'll need to see that permit." Bryce watched as Illings and her crew huddled and then locked eyes with one of the troopers.

"Nice race yesterday," the trooper said. "Glad you still know how to drive a real race car." Bryce smiled. "Me too."

∽

The Russian assassin watched the activity from the woods and decided it was time to retreat. Slowly, she slid the Norinco into its case and began to get up.

"Freeze," a voice shouted from behind her. She turned and saw a woman in an olive green uniform standing ten feet behind her, the large black frame of a forty-five caliber handgun pointing toward her.

"Freeze means freeze," the trooper shouted. She kept the gun in her left hand and pointed at the figure on the ground as she reached for the microphone on her shoulder with her right hand. Just as she began to speak into it, the assassin rolled onto her back and drew her black gun.

∽

As the shot rang out, everyone at the film scene reacted. Danny knocked Bryce to the ground as the trooper's training kicked in, weapons drawn, hunched behind their vehicles. Illings and her bunch, including the look-alike, dropped to the ground. Bryce watched from his spot on the asphalt as the female tactical team member shouted into her comms.

"Shots fired, abort abort. I say again, shots fired. Abort!"

CHAPTER THIRTY-FOUR

RUSSO WAS SURE he wasn't being followed, at least not on the road. He'd returned to where he'd left the old white Ford pickup truck on the roadside. The trash on the dash and the fishing gear would lead most to believe some old country boy had walked into the woods and gone fishing. The last thing he wanted to do was lead law enforcement, or anyone else, to his partner and their only bargaining chip, so he drove west, away from McCarthy's cabin. He'd keep going until he could find a crowd and blend in. He remembered the truck stop near Winchester off Interstate 81. He could check the sky for drones, under the vehicle for trackers, and scan the parking lot for troopers or the FBI. He sent Chadwick a simple text, as he always did when he'd left the cabin, to restock their food and pick up necessities for their hostage.

ALL GOOD?

Ten seconds later, as had been standard for the last four months, the same response came back.

AOK

An hour after forcing down an overcooked hot dog

and Coke as he sat at the window watching the parking lot, he felt safe enough to work his way back to the cabin where everything, he'd soon find out, had changed.

◈

At the Summit Point driver training facility, the troopers stared at Bryce with disbelief.

"You want to keep shooting?" the ranking veteran Trooper with the flat top cut and the slight beer belly questioned.

"Sure, why not? Fifty troopers are still wandering around the perimeter, the shooter's dead, and that car's armored. I couldn't feel safer," Bryce said, sipping a coffee.

He turned to Illings, who was still visibly shaken.

"Come on, girl; carry on, stiff upper lip and all that, right?"

The U.S. Secret Service tactical team was already long gone. They boarded the helicopter and departed as quickly as they had arrived. Once POTUS, the real one, was waved off and flown directly back to the White House on Marine One, they had no reason to be on-site anymore.

"I've got an idea," Jen said as she stepped into the ring of troopers surrounding her boss.

"Some of these people are rattled; that's to be expected, so why not have them break for an early lunch for an hour and give them a chance to get their shit back together?" Bryce nodded in agreement and looked at the lead trooper.

"That's a great idea. Plus, that'll give me time to check out the shooter."

"What? No way, Bryce," the trooper insisted. "It's a crime scene."

Bryce shook his head, smiled, and stepped close.

"And I would have been one without one of West Virginia's finest."

Bryce nodded at the female trooper who had killed the woman she'd snuck up on in the woods.

"Look, I think you all know some renegade CIA assholes tried to kill me last year. I can't talk about it other than say that I've done work for the State Department overseas. I've come face to face with a bunch of bad actors, and so I'd like to see the body. I'd like to see if I recognize them."

Bryce focused on the trooper who may have saved his life.

"You said there was no ID on them, right?"

"Nothing. Just tactical camo, a rifle, a handgun, and a phone."

"Who has the phone?" Bryce asked.

"I laid it on her chest and left it there for forensics. They should be there any minute."

Bryce began walking toward the woods, then stopped and turned back toward the ring of troopers.

"You coming?"

Danny walked past the trooper, and within a second, six of them began to follow while the rest remained behind with their vehicles and a guy who looked a lot like the president. The female trooper caught up to Bryce and took the lead.

"What's your name, trooper?" he asked.

"Cavanaugh, Corporal Cavanaugh," she answered.

"First name, Corporal?"

"Lyndsey," she said.

"Before the day ends, I'd like your contact information to keep in touch."

"What, you want to be friends on Facebook?"

"That's funny. How far to the body?" he asked. Suddenly, Cavanaugh stopped, stepped to the left, and pointed to something in the brush twenty feet ahead.

✍

Cavanaugh watched as the world-famous race car driver walked past her and took a knee beside the body. She called out.

"Don't touch anything," but it was too late. She walked to the scene and stood over Bryce, watching his every move.

"I guess you're hard of hearing from all those noisy race cars." She grew frustrated as he didn't respond and, worse, didn't obey her order.

"Did she say anything? Anything at all? Did she have an accent?" he asked. Cavanaugh shook her head no.

"Not a word," she said. Bryce remained on one knee, the phone in his left hand. He surveyed the area and then tried to open the phone.

"The damn thing's locked. Shit," she heard him say and then watched as Bryce opened the left eyelid of the dead woman and held the phone close to it. She heard him utter something as he shook his head but couldn't make it out. He grabbed the body's right hand, pulled the glove from it, and then held the warm but lifeless index finger against the phone.

"Bingo," he called out as he stood up and began scrolling through the phone. In the distance, Cavanaugh heard someone call out. It was the state police forensics team, and someone was shouting,

"Get away from there!" Bryce didn't listen and continued working.

"Bryce, what are you doing? They're coming. You need to stop."

She watched as Bryce took screenshots of texts and sent and received calls. She looked at the forensics staff, two men and a woman dressed in dark blue bodysuits, walking toward them, faster now, still shouting.

"One more second," Bryce said as he hit the send button.

"What you do?" Cavanaugh asked.

"Just sent the screenshots to my phone. You never know. I might know some of these numbers."

Suddenly, a hand reached out and grabbed the phone from him.

"Manners," Bryce said.

"What the hell's the matter with the both of you? Trooper, you know better. You should have cuffed this guy," a male technician insisted.

"Wait, you're Bryce Winters," the second man said.

"Hey, let's take a selfie; we can use her phone," Bryce joked as he reached for it.

"Okay, Bryce, we need to head back to the cars and let these people do their work,' Cavanaugh said as she touched his arm to direct him. Bryce began walking away but stopped and stared at the body again. He stepped to it and got down on one knee as the techs shouted for him not to touch anything else. She watched as Bryce pushed the dead woman's left eyelid open and did the same to the right. Bryce didn't say a word. He stared at the dead woman's eyes for a moment, then got up and walked past the other troopers watching it all. Cavanaugh stepped closer and leaned down over the body; the life might have left the dead woman's eyes, but the color remained a vibrant ice blue.

⤜

As he reached the cabin door, Russo looked back to the dirt road he'd just driven in on. Their second car, a black Dodge Charger they rarely used and covered in fine dust kicked up from the road, was parked off to the left. Nothing seemed out of the ordinary, and he felt confident that if anyone had been on to him way back at Summit Point eight hours earlier or since then, he'd have noticed something or someone long before leading them here. As Russo turned the handle, he stopped. Most days, Chadwick would have opened the door by now, assault weapon in hand, just in case. He heard the TV blaring and shook his head.

"Fell asleep again, Chad? What the fuck." Then, as he pushed the door open and stepped into the living room, he dropped the grocery bag he'd picked up on the way. There on the floor in his underwear, his throat slit ear to ear, was his partner of twenty years. Russo drew the pistol from his hip holster and surveyed the room. He looked at his friend for a moment, shocked, and then sadness crept in for an instant and was quickly replaced by anger. He saw Chadwick's empty holster still attached to the blue jeans discarded on the sofa, and then he saw the door to Kyoto's room was wide open. He moved slowly now, entering the bedroom, and saw a white porcelain toilet tank lid lying in pieces on the floor. He checked the closet and the bathroom. She was gone. Walking back into the living room, he stared again at his dead friend on the floor and shook his head.

"Looks like somebody fucked up." He surveyed the room, studying every inch for a clue, anything, and then got moving. He ran into his bedroom and hastily threw his clothes into a duffle bag. He went down on one knee and reached under the bed to retrieve what was critical for the success of this mission: his kit of disguises. Russo then ran outside, threw the bags toward the dusty sedan, and ran to a small shed. Emerging with a five-gallon red plastic fuel jug, he ran back into the house and went from room to room, dousing them with gasoline. Then he stopped at Chadwick's body.

"You always said you wanted to be cremated," he said as he poured the remaining fuel on it and threw the empty container across the room.

"Well, I guess you got your wish." He walked to the fireplace, grabbed a log lighter, and set the cabin ablaze. He ran outside to the Dodge and opened the trunk. Their gear, body armor, rifles, flashbang, tear gas, smoke grenades, and boxes of ammunition seemed to be how they'd left it. He slammed the lid closed and then stopped. He surveyed the area again, slid into the driver's seat, and started the car. He began to drive away but suddenly slammed on the brakes, reversed toward the pickup, got out, and ran back to the shed. He returned with another jug and set the pickup's interior on fire. Quickly back in the car, he drove off, the inferno behind him set against the darkening sky and shadows of the woods. An hour later, he was near Quantico, Virginia, and driving south on Interstate 95 toward Miami.

꿍

At the Winchester Airport, Jen and Danny stood behind Bryce near the galley on his jet and listened as he asked Bill Miller how the visit with his friends had gone.

"Don't forget to ask him how *his* day went," the co-pilot said as he reviewed his pre-flight instrument checklist.

"I'll leave that for you to share, Lou," Bryce said, walking between Jen and Danny and sitting in the back of the main cabin.

"I don't know about him, but I could eat a bear right now," Danny told Jen. "Any chance you've got dinner planned?" He laughed as Jen shooed him out of the galley with her hands and a smile.

"Coffee first, and then we've got something good cooking." Danny blew her a kiss and headed back to join Bryce. As he approached him, he studied the man whose life had been at risk again today and again, not in a race car. He sat across the aisle and stared at him. He smiled as Bryce finally looked his way.

"How are you doing?" he asked. Bryce smiled.

"Looking forward to seeing how the feature we shot goes over. It was a lot of fun, all things considered." Danny returned the smile but shook his head.

"No, how are *you* doing? You've been on a non-stop thrill ride since Christmas. Are you sure you don't want just to sit on an island or climb a mountain somewhere? You've been lucky, very lucky, especially today. Even cats have only nine lives."

"That reminds me, how's Joan making out with that cat?"

"Last I heard, her sister loves it. But don't change the subject." Bryce turned and looked through the window until Jen arrived with drinks and snacks.

"I've got lasagna and garlic bread coming in ten minutes." Simultaneously, both men leaned into the aisle and smelled the air.

"Can you make it five? I'm starving," Bryce said. Danny watched the two interact. Bryce didn't have any family left on the planet, but his circle, although growing smaller as the bodies piled up, was tight, full of laughs and unspoken love. Danny had known Bryce for three years and had grown quite fond of the man. He'd had a special bond with his brothers-in-arms in the military, and that relationship was taking shape with Bryce. Danny missed his brother Alan more than he described, and while Bryce could never replace him, not that Danny wanted that, he felt a kinship with Bryce. The fact that someone was trying to kill this man infuriated him, but it also scared him. He'd already lost comrades and now a blood brother. Enough was enough.

"Dude, talk to me," Danny said as he moved across the aisle to sit facing him.

"You walked into that guy's house in DC and shot an unarmed man. Now, some sniper tried to take you out, and you're walking around like it's SOP. What the fuck? Are you blocking all of this out, or will you have a meltdown at some point? Tell me. Because I need to be prepared." Suddenly, as Jen approached with two trays of food, Bryce began to convulse in his chair. Danny jumped up as Jen screamed and dropped both trays. As suddenly as it had started, Bryce grew still and opened his eyes as he belly laughed. Danny shook his head and fell back into his seat, but Jen began shouting at them."

"You boys think this is funny? Everyone close to you is turning up dead. Nobody knows where the hell Kyoto is, and you're playing pranks. Well, I'm not cleaning up that mess, and you two can both starve for all I care. Let me off at the next stop. I'm done with this," she yelled. Danny turned and watched as Jen stepped over the spill in the aisle and stormed toward her galley. Suddenly, Bryce walked past him and followed her.

⤫

Jen stood over the galley counter, tapping her red fingernails on the stainless steel, when Bryce stepped close and put his hands on her shoulders. Her fingers stopped. Bryce whispered in her left ear.

"I'm sorry."

"How can you keep going like this? Everyone's getting killed, and you're just flying around like it happens daily."

"Well, actually-" he said, but she turned abruptly, cutting him off.

"Not in the mood for any humor right now, Bryce Winters," she said, jabbing her right index finger into his chest.

"I've been able to accept that you might get hurt in a race car, but this danger is relentless, and I'm not sure I can stand by and watch it happen again and again until someone decides to blow your brains all over the damn cabin."

"You can say you're concerned about blood on the

rug, but that lasagna seems to say otherwise." Jen turned away from him. This time, he saw her hands were now fists lying on the counter.

"I love you, Bryce, and I'm not sure how much of this I can take," she whispered. He wrapped his arms around her and held her. "I love you too, Jen," he said softly. Suddenly, Danny appeared behind them, holding two trays of food he had cleaned up.

"Should I pull the curtain, maybe hand out a few condoms?" Danny joked.

Bryce felt Jen laugh, and then he let go. He knew what was coming next. He'd seen it before. Slowly, Jen turned toward Danny, a large carving knife in her hand. Danny looked at her, smiling as he placed the trays on the counter and backed away. Jen winked at Bryce as she put the knife back.

"Listen, let's do whatever we can to get through this season, and as I've said all along, if I win my second world championship, then I'm going to retire and hang out in Park City and give young athletes and drivers a hand like Max gave me." Jen began to reset two new trays of food, removing servings of lasagna and bread from the oven.

"You have more. Sweet," Bryce said as he licked his lips.

"These were for the two up front, but I'll give them burgers instead."

Bryce took her by the hands.

"First, they get the lasagna. Danny and I are fine with burgers. Second, you know I can't quit. I just can't go hide somewhere. They always find you, Jen; they always do. I want you to stay on, and even if I retire, you and those two up front will still have jobs if you want them; you know I can't sit still for very long." Jen finished preparing the trays and looked at Bryce, standing close to him.

"I just wanted you to know how I feel about you. I know you've been through and lost a lot, but I just wanted you to know."

Bryce wrapped his arms around her and held her close. He felt her head rest against his chest as her arms tightened around him.

"You know, Danny raised a good point," he said. As he felt her grasp loosen, he stood back from her.

"Do we keep condoms on board?" He laughed as he watched Jen reach for the knife again and ran back to his seat across from Danny.

"She's fine. Just needed to vent some emotion," Bryce said as he began to scroll through his phone.

"Yeah, and that's what I've been watching for from you," Danny said. Bryce looked up and smiled as he saw Jen taking the food into the cockpit.

"I vent. Every time I pull a trigger," Bryce assured him. "I just need to vent a little more."

CHAPTER THIRTY-FIVE

BRYCE WOKE ABRUPTLY as the plane's wheels touched down in Key West. He looked further up the dark cabin and saw Danny asleep on a sofa. Jen was seated across from Danny, focused on her phone. Before taking off from the airport in Virginia, Bryce had decided on a last-minute change of plans. Rather than fly directly into Miami, where the week-long Formula One frenzy had already begun, he'd called in a favor and planned to spend Tuesday and Wednesday on a chartered motor yacht. Without telling anyone his plans, he had a van waiting to take the flight crew, Danny, and himself directly to the marina for a solid night's sleep before a day of fishing on the Gulf of Mexico. While others focused on catching the big one, he could relax and enjoy the peace before the storm. By midnight, after sharing a few beers on the back deck of the vessel, Bryce had called it a night. Once in the privacy of a spacious master cabin, he stared at himself in the mirror on the ceiling. He stared at his eyes and kept picturing the lifeless ones he had forced himself to deal with the day before, a wolf's once exquisite blue eyes. Just like the landing the night before had interrupted his sleep, the movement of the pearl-white seventy-eight-foot luxury yacht, aptly named The Pearl, caused him to sit up and get moving. Once seated at a table on the bow deck, his feet brushing the teak decking, he downed three large coffees before making a call he'd been avoiding.

"Guten tag Herr Winters," Claudia Werner said when the call answered.

"Are you in Miami?" Bryce asked.

"No, my dear, we don't arrive until Wednesday night. We have media day Thursday, as always. What about you?"

"Who's we?" he asked as he sat up in his chair. "You're not bringing Mila, are you?"

"No, no. Tony is flying in with me." Bryce sat back, happy to learn the little one would be away from the imminent danger but frustrated to hear his nemesis was still in the picture.

"I thought for sure you too were over," Bryce said.

"And what would that mean if it was? You and I and Mila, one big happy family?"

Bryce stood up and threw his coffee mug into the gulf. When he noticed a young steward standing nearby, he shrugged his shoulders and gestured for another.

"Where are you today?" Werner asked.

"Fort Lauderdale," he lied. "A friend offered me their boat, so I'm chilling for a few days before Tony and I get to have at it again."

"Bryce, please, for everyone's sake, don't antagonize him any more than you normally do. Let's race to the end of the season, and then we can sit down and discuss our future if there is to be one. But only if you and Tony race clean. Otherwise, I'll be done with both of you and will find a UFC fighter to keep me warm. At least with them, I'd know what to expect." Bryce nodded thanks to the steward as she delivered another steaming mug of coffee and a large fruit plate and croissants.

"Listen, I want to win the races and the title fair and square. But I do need to know, are you *with* him?" He heard Claudia laugh and then quiet.

"Hello?" he questioned.

"He is still kissing my ass, trying to get back in my good graces," she said. "But you've stirred something in me that I haven't felt in a long time Bryce. And with Mila, I have very mixed emotions about everything right now."

"Okay, so let's talk in Miami, and then maybe we can spend a few days together before Imola. We need to talk, one on one, away from it all.

"I would like that, Bryce. I'd like that a lot," she said.

"Good. Now last thing, any more issues in Munich? Any unwanted visitors since you upgraded your security?"

"No, everything is quiet and going as some people have demanded. I will find you in Miami, my dear. Enjoy the water."

The call ended, and Bryce attacked the food. Suddenly he was ravenous. He knew he and Bishop would put on quite a race, and although one unidentified sniper was dead, Russo and Chadwick were still on the loose and probably headed for Miami too. Bryce knew he could lose his life this Sunday but not without a fight.

Tuesday came and went in a flash. Bryce was happy he'd gone into hiding in the Keys because the news of the sniper at Summit Point had made headlines worldwide, and every media outlet was hunting for him now. As he heard the newscaster say those words on CNN, Bryce smiled and said, "Get in line."

Wednesday had been another relaxing day for Bryce, and he laughed through dinner on the bow deck as his pilots Bill and Lou told fishing stories from the day while Danny and Jen watched a rugby game on the flatscreen over the outside bar. He was happy. A thousand miles north of his location, there was a storm brewing.

⚜

"You had to torch the cabin?" Russo heard McCarthy shout into his phone as he pulled another slice of pizza from the box he'd thrown on the motel bed.

"Yes, I did. There was DNA everywhere, fingerprints on everything. You have insurance, so don't worry about it."

"You stupid son of a bitch, there's a dead body in the ruins, and any forensics team, even the local yocals down there, could show an accelerant was used to start the fire. That means murder, and my name's on the damn deed!" Russo chomped away and threw a piece of crust toward the trash can in the corner, just missing the shot.

"Listen, you have access to a clean-up team. Send them in before anyone discovers the place. I'm just north of Miami. If everything goes as planned, Bryce Winters' head will be splashed all over the papers next Monday morning, and you two can get back to business."

"Really? Are you forgetting Kyoto?"

"No, she's smart. I bet she's already used Chadwick's credit cards to get clothes and get as far away from there as possible. She knows how this works. At least she knows now. If she goes to the police, she'll be looking over her shoulder for the rest of her life. She's gone. I'm sure of it. Russo got up from the bed and took another bottle of beer from the mini-fridge. As he passed the errant crust, he kicked it under the bed.

"You've left too many loose ends, so you better do this right on Sunday, or you'll be looking over your shoulder forever, too," Russo laughed to himself as McCarthy ended the call.

"That goes both ways, you piece of shit."

CHAPTER THIRTY-SIX

THURSDAY'S MEDIA DAY at the Hard Rock Stadium, the site of the Miami F1, was a circus. Five minutes with Bryce Winters, or even one minute with him, was the hottest ticket in town, and Bryce pushed back against any media outlet or reporter that had been anything but kind in recent months. For the ones who had taken the time to offer their condolences or perhaps mentioned Jack Madigan's name with fondness and respect, he was very open to spending time with them. But first, he had a meeting to attend with the FIA and F1 again. Seated across from the two presidents once again in a temporary office designated as one of theirs for the weekend, they voiced their legitimate concerns.

"The shooter was a Russian assassin, and they haven't confirmed she was there after me or someone thought the real president was going to appear in the feature," Bryce told the men.

"And it turns out the real president was on his way there. I can't imagine what might have happened if that state trooper hadn't stumbled on the Russian and neutralized the threat," Lafrance said as he stared at a large photo taken during the 2020 Super Bowl played not far from where they were seated.

"The president has ordered a detail of U.S. Secret Service agents to protect Bryce while he is in America," Kazaan assured them. "They will be shadowing Bryce wherever he goes, some dressed as team members and others as media or race fans."

"And photos of the wanted CIA agents Russo and Chadwick are posted everywhere now including the local and national news networks, our social media, and every F1 site on the planet, it would seem," Blanc stated. Bryce got up from his seat at the table and paced the room as the men spoke.

"Bryce, please sit; you're making us all dizzy," Kazaan said as he reached out to Bryce, who moved suddenly to avoid Kazaan's grasp. He retook his seat and stared at the three men.

"And I know Miami, Dade County, the State of Florida, the FBI, and Homeland Security are swarming the place," he said. "I just can't believe it's come to this. None of these agencies have been able to find either of these two assholes in the last four months, and now my guilt meter is almost past my eyes." Bryce watched as Lafrance looked at Blanc.

"Part of me wonders if there's not something much bigger going on here," he said. "It's what keeps me up at night." Kazaan got up, walked to Bryce, and sat against the table's edge.

"Someone, a fed, told me these two bastards were killed the night before someone shot at me in Daytona, but you knew otherwise," he said. "It makes me wonder if we can trust the feds to catch them in time. Now I hear that a Russian killed that guy in D.C." Blanc shook his head in disbelief.

"So to summarize, two supposedly rogue CIA agents have been stalking you, destroying everything that matters to you, and then someone lies and says you can relax, they're dead now, only to find they are still alive, and then a Russian sniper tried to kill you, and then another Russian killed the person that lied to you. Did I leave anything out?" Blanc paused. "Bryce, what are you, some sort of James Bond? What have you gotten yourself into? This is unbelievable." Blanc walked to a server and snatched a water bottle as Lafrance cleared his throat and shouted at Bryce, "What have you gotten *us* into?"

Bryce shook his head and looked at Kazaan.

"If they don't get them here, this is going to move on to Texas and then the race in Vegas," Bryce said in a lowered tone. Kazaan shook his head in agreement and looked to the series officials.

"So, you've been briefed. Are we finished?"

Blanc's bottle left his hand and flew onto the table as he spun around quickly. It rolled to Bryce, who caught it and tossed it back.

"No," Blanc said. "There is still the issue of your driver's behavior. We all know the appeal was won only because of the pressure put on the group by our global broadcast partner, the Miami GP people, and all the sponsors. They want Bryce in the show, and so here you are."

Blanc pulled the chair across the table from Bryce and sat.

"This is not the Roman Coliseum or Madison Square Garden. We are not putting on slaves and gladiators or professional wrestling. This is the highest, most professional level of motorsport, and we cannot let it become anything less." Lafrance got up from his chair and stood next to Blanc.

"So, if you get into another fight, we can assure you that there will be an irrevocable two-race suspension imposed, and I don't care who complains about it," Lafrance said. Bryce studied the man as he spoke. He remembered his sheepish behavior in the Land Rover that night and resented the declaration he'd just made. Bryce's guilt meter had just gone flat like a tire during a race and was rapidly being replaced by anger and contempt. Bryce stood up and glared at Lafrance.

"Let's talk frankly, gentlemen, shall we?" he began. "Let's say there's some global terrorism plot going on here, and I'm an American James Bond, a friend of the president but an enemy of some of the country's top spies. Russians are trying to disrupt the show. Hell, they've been disrupting everything for the last few years. Do you think the Russians are screwing with me here because I caught their leader banging something he shouldn't have? Think about it – maybe, just maybe, they're after you, through me, for canceling the Russian GP?" He watched the two officials, who appeared stunned and speechless.

"How certain are you that *your* families are safe? That after me, perhaps they come after one of you?" Bryce turned away from them and looked at Kazaan, whose mouth was agape, and winked at him. Turning back to Lafrance and Blanc, Bryce had more.

"So, back to the threat you just made against me. Are you saying if Tony Bishop, or any other driver, wrecks me out on the track or takes a swing at me, I can't defend myself? Is that what you're telling me – the guy who has more people watching your God-damned show this weekend than ever before? Really?" Bryce walked to the door and turned to Kazaan.

"Coming?"

⋙

Only one other person on the planet could give Ameer Kazaan a tone or attitude and get away with it, his wife, Lilly. Still, he'd just gotten one from his driver, and as he followed Bryce through the door, he felt dumbfounded and exasperated. The two men pushed past some staffers and others waiting for time with Lafrance and Blanc. As Bryce slid Kazaan into an elevator, waving off two people who had tried to join them, Kazaan began to speak, but the smile Bryce presented him knocked the anger out of the man.

"You were kidding in there?" Kazaan asked as he shook his head in disbelief.

"Yes. I needed them to get their focus off of me and start watching their backs."

"But if that were me, I might have taken some of what you said as a cloaked threat, and that can't be good."

"I needed to get them to back off a bit, Ameer, and I think you'll see that it worked. But now, I need to go win this championship because the mark the CIA has on my back might be replaced by one from them." Kazaan quickly pulled the STOP button bringing the elevator to an immediate halt.

"You're not saying they'd send someone to kill you?" Bryce laughed as he released the button.

"Of course not, but they could screw with the team every race, which I won't let happen to you or the team. None of you deserve that. So let's win the title, and then you'll all be free of me." As the elevator doors opened, they were met with a throng of reporters and photographers. Luckily for them, Kazaan's media team, Danny Johnson, and four new faces dressed in team gear were there to drive the car owner and driver through the masses like a hot knife through cold butter.

Bryce waved at fans who shouted for him to stop, but he couldn't. Led by a spear of men accustomed to protecting American presidents, the group moved quickly through the sea of people until they arrived at the rear of the Kazaan garage. There, smiling at Bryce from the adjacent Werner garage, her garage, was a tanned Claudia wearing a revealing white sleeveless pantsuit. Bryce smiled as he read her lips; *We have to talk.*

CHAPTER THIRTY-SEVEN

THE RACE IN Miami had taken on a sold-out, circus-like atmosphere. Celebrities, sponsors, and the rich had flooded into the Hard Rock Stadium complex, and everyone was clamoring for that must-have selfie with Bryce Winters. As Bryce closed in on the entrance to his team's garage, he reached out at the last minute and grabbed Claudia by the hand, pulling her from Tony Bishop. Danny remained glued to Bryce as the undercover Secret Service agents spread out and kept an eye on everyone through their trademark dark sunglasses. Kazaan, who followed the two through the door, laughed as he whispered in Bryce's ear, "I get it now. You really do enjoy poking things with a stick." Bryce turned and smiled at Kazaan as he drew Claudia into a small, vacant meeting room and closed the door behind them.

"What's up beautiful? From the way you're dressed, I'd say you're here to distract me," he said as he grabbed a water and sat at the round white table. She stared at him for a moment, then helped herself to a juice and sat across from him. Crossing her long, bare legs under the table, she tapped his leg with her foot and left it there.

"Are you okay?" she asked as she struggled to unscrew the cap. He took the bottle, broke the seal, and handed it back.

"I'm fine. These past few days have recharged me completely. I can't wait to get out there. But how are you? Shaken or relieved since you saw her photo?" Claudia opened her phone, scrolled for a moment, and then turned to phone toward Bryce.

"You mean this one?" she said as Bryce stared at the photo of the dead Russian assassin, her partially open blue eyes staring back at him, which had gone viral.

"I can't believe this. The same woman who threatened me in Munich came all the way to America to kill you." Bryce sat back and thought for a moment.

"How can you be so sure it was her? All you said you remembered from that night was her Russian or Eastern European accent and her blue eyes. There's probably more than one of these running around." Claudia sat up, enlarged the photo with her fingers, and then turned it back toward him.

"Look at her right eyelid. There's a slight scar on the eyebrow. Do you see it?" Bryce sat forward and took her phone. He looked closely and then looked at her. He nodded.

"That's her, all right. I must have forgotten to mention that little detail." Suddenly a knock was heard at the door, and then Sophie, one of his team assistants, poked her head in.

"Practice starts in ten minutes, BW; time to get

dressed." Bryce smiled as the woman backed out and closed the door.

"BW? Oh, that's cute," Claudia teased. "It sounds adorable with that Aussie accent." Bryce reached across the table with both of his hands. At first, Claudia didn't move. He watched as she studied him. Unsure of what his gesture meant, but curious. She took his hands.

"Have dinner with me tonight. The FBI found some things at the crime scene up north that I want to discuss. I can have room service bring up something good. I'm in 2001 at the Four Seasons. How does eight o'clock sound?" Before she could answer, Bryce stood up and opened the door.

"So, do we have a date?" he said as he stepped into the doorway and turned, smiling at her.

"Sure, but no funny business," she said, winking as she got up. Bryce laughed as he walked from her toward the team and his race car. Danny followed without saying a word. As he joked with his crew and put on his safety equipment, he relished finally getting back into the car and turning everything off. Once seated, nearly laying down, as the crewmembers helped set up the safety harnesses, Bryce's mind wandered from the car and the hot laps to come. He thought of Claudia and how she might react tonight when he dropped a bomb on her.

After the day's second practice session, Bryce stood in the fading sunlight on pit lane talking with a journalist, or at least what most people thought was one. As the woman jotted notes on a pad, the two interacted like they did this daily. For him, that was true; for the FBI Special Agent, this was a first.

"She's a cool customer," the agent said.

"Yes, but tonight I might get to rattle her a bit. All I know is that someone told Russo and the Russian to be in those woods. Why send two professionals? I don't get it. Who knew I'd be there? Only the film crew, a few at the school, and my team, and there's no way any of my guys are dirty. No way in hell." The journalist extended her hand and shook Bryce's as she thanked him for the interview. Bryce held her hand for a moment.

"One question. I know what happens to her if we discover that Claudia had anything to do with the shooters. But what about her daughter? What about Mila?

"Not for the FBI to decide, Bryce. We're here to find out what happened and to prosecute anyone involved. Period. The CIA can't operate here on U.S. soil, but we sure as hell can."

Bryce let go of her hand and laughed.

"I wish someone would tell Russo and Chadwick that." The agent nodded.

"We'll be listening," she said.

CHAPTER THIRTY-EIGHT

The serving staff cleared dinner in his suite, and as Bryce thanked them at the door as the last one left, he threw the deadbolt and returned to the living room to find Claudia Werner walking through the sheers that were blowing in the night ocean air. He stepped to the balcony entrance and called out to her.

"You should come back in. We'll need the light." Bryce walked to the dining room table and threw a file folder on it. He sat and scrolled through his phone until Claudia finally joined him there. Taking a seat, she looked at the folder.

"Is that for me?" she asked.

"There are a few questions I can't wrap my head around, and I was hoping you could help me. Now, the FBI showed that file to me this morning. He reached across the table for it and pushed it closer to her.

"Open it." As she did, he continued.

"After the shooting-"

"Which one? You've been involved in so many, my dear," she said.

"After the shooting in West Virginia, they combed the area and found a spot where another sniper had been set up. The dumb ass left a water bottle with his prints on it."

"Who was it?"

"Russo," he said, pointing to the man's photo as she held it up. "Disgraced former CIA piece of shit John Russo." Claudia shook her head and dropped the picture on the table.

"So now, we know there were two shooters there. Were they working together? But how did they know you were going to be there? Who the hell sent them?" Bryce got up from the table and poured a coffee. He held up the pot for Claudia, but she shook her head no.

"Just another beer, the bottle this time," she said. As Bryce slid her a cold German pilsner he retook his seat and stared at his guest.

"There's more. A lot more. They found a body in a burned-out cabin in Virginia yesterday. This morning, the FBI told me they had identified it as Chadwick, the other CIA asshole that's been fucking up my world." Claudia took a long sip of beer and sat forward.

"We should order popcorn. It gets better."

"Shut up. No way," she declared.

"A woman, an Asian woman, was caught on camera at a local truck stop stealing a car. The FBI checked all the cameras in the area to see if they could find Russo, Chadwick, or your Russian on anything."

"She wasn't my Russian Bryce. She was ours."

"Anyway, the local police told the Feds about the stolen car and look at the second photo." Claudia slid Russo's photo from the top and then cringed when she saw the image of an incinerated body lying on what remained of a burned-out cabin floor. She tossed it to Bryce. He smiled.

"That's funny," she asked. Bryce shook his head no.

"They killed Jon Watanabe and destroyed my home by fire, so I think it's fitting, or do they call it poetic justice?" Claudia looked at the next photo and held it up for Bryce.

"Yep, that's Kyoto. Who knew she could steal cars."

"I thought she just stole hearts. Your heart."

"So, at this point, the FBI thinks Chadwick may have been holding Kyoto in that cabin. She killed him and got away."

"So her being in Virginia, after she was last seen in Washington, makes sense, but does anything connect the dots to Chadwick or Russo?" Bryce shook his head yes.

"Look at the fourth photo. It's her inside the C-store, using Chadwick's cards to get cash and buy food. She used his card again a few hours later to buy clothes at a mall."

Claudia took a few moments to examine each of the photos again. She chugged her beer dry and then moved to the sofa. She waved for him to join her, which he did. The two sat quietly for a few minutes, Bryce watching the sheers continue to dance softly in the night air.

"There's something I've been wondering. If something happens to you, what happens to Mila?" he asked. Claudia surveyed the room.

"Why? Do you know something I don't?" Bryce laughed and tossed a small pillow at her.

"No, but you are swimming with sharks, and there's blood in the water."

"And you aren't?" she said, settling into the cushions

but a moment later, got up abruptly and walked to the balcony. Bryce followed her and came up close behind her. She turned to face him.

"So where is the CIA in all of this?" she asked.

"Meaning?"

"They sent you to warn Max, who was dead thirty minutes after you left him. They don't want me selling arms to America's enemies either. So will something happen to me too? Perhaps I'll be found dead at some point. Is that why you are asking about Mila? Do you have plans for me too?" Bryce took a step back and shook his head.

"I loved Max and have very strong feelings for you and Mila. I don't want anything to happen to either of you. Max's death crushed me. You know that."

"So what happens to her? Isn't she what's most important? You must have made plans, just in case." Claudia shook her head no.

"Perhaps with you in the picture now, perhaps I should. She might like moving to America, growing up surrounded by the wildlife and mountains you love if you settle down. She adores animals and always enjoys our time in Zermatt. But would you take her? Do you know enough about children to raise one, especially one who would have lost the parents who were raising her?" Bryce didn't flinch.

"I'd wrap my arms around her and take care of her forever, that I can promise you." Claudia placed her hand on Bryce's chest and stared into his eyes.

"Now, enough of this sad talk. Come wrap your arms around me." She smiled and walked back through the sheers, with Bryce following close behind. They continued to the bedroom, where she began to undress as Bryce entered the bathroom and closed the door.

❦

Roland McCarthy stared at the floor-to-ceiling bookshelf that consumed the wall around the stone fireplace in his Washington mansion. He stared into the fire as he sipped at his expensive bourbon, an unreported gift from a foreigner. He was accustomed to making big decisions; he was bred for it, having come from a rich and powerful bloodline that traced back to Scottish Highlands and the mid-1500s.

He picked up the burner phone, the second he's used today and made the call.

"Yes?" the woman's voice answered.

"You're in Miami?"

"Yes, as planned."

"He's of no use to me anymore. Put him down, and don't leave a trace."

"Are you sure? He's had value in the past."

"Maybe to you, but he knows too much. It's time for him to go."

"As you wish," she said. McCarthy ended the call and dropped the phone into the fire.

❦

In the hotel room across the hall from Bryce's, Danny and Jen had been telling stories, him mostly about his time in the military and her mainly about the groping hands and other abhorrent behavior of private charter guests she'd dealt with before going to work full-time for their boss.

From his spot leaning against the headboard, he flipped open the pizza box on the bed and grabbed another slice. He gestured for Jen, but she shook her head no.

"Liquid dinner for me," she said as she raised her beer bottle. "I do this once a month, and tonight's the night."

Danny folded the pizza, inhaled half the slice, and then cocked his head as he saw a change in Jen's expression.

"What?" he growled through a mouth full of food. "It's what I do." Jen shook her head no and moved to the side of the queen bed across from Danny's.

"No," she whispered. Danny forced down the food and stared at her.

"What's with the whisper?"

"I don't want anyone to hear us," she said.

"Don't worry, I'm a quiet lover," he said with a laugh, but from the look on Jen's face, he knew they weren't headed there.

"It's okay, Jen. I swept the room when I got here. No bugs," he assured her.

"What about the phones? They say people are always listening." Danny reached his hand out, and Jen handed over her phone. He reached into the black duffle he'd thrown on the bed and withdrew a small box. Jen began to speak, but Danny gave her a look. He placed her phone in the box and closed it tight.

"Okay, my phone's secure, but just in case, your phone is now incapable of being read. So now, what's the matter? What's up?"

"Danny, that woman they found in the woods at Summit Point. How do you know she wasn't there for you?" Danny cocked his head and stared into space for a moment.

"They said it was a woman who killed your brother in Daytona, and now a woman show's up with a rifle. And there was another sniper in the woods, too – the asshole chasing Bryce. Regardless of who they were after, I want to know who the hell sent them."

Danny studied her.

"Come on, I can tell there's more," he said.

"And where's the damn Secret Service?

"That's a secret," he teased. Jen raised her empty bottle and threatened to throw it at him.

"Okay, okay. I can see you're in no mood to play. There's one in the room next to Bryce's, one watching the lobby elevators, and one at each end of the hallway standing watch inside the fire exit doors. Feel safer now?" Danny pointed to the radio resting on the top of his duffle.

"They gave me that in case we see trouble coming."

The digital clock on the dresser read 3:05 as Bryce got up from the bed and walked into the dining room. He returned a minute later and placed a glass of ice water on Claudia's nightstand before chugging an entire bottle of orange juice and sliding back under the platinum-colored silk sheets. As he pulled the covers to his shoulders, the air conditioning set at his customary chilly 65F, he felt Claudia's warmth as she snuggled in behind him.

"This would piss Tony off," she whispered. Bryce smiled. He knew it would.

Suddenly, a loud knock was heard at the front door, followed by a bang and then another.

"Speak of the devil," Bryce whispered as he sat up.

"Write a note saying I'm a better, bigger lover and slide it under the door; that will make him disappear. I'm sure of it."

"No, I can't do that. I need his head in the game. We've come all this way to win a race, remember?" Bryce watched as Claudia got up from the bed; the red lighting from the digital clock illuminated her thin, fit figure.

"This reminds me of the red light district in Amsterdam. You're all lit up like those women in the windows," he said, laughing as he sat up against the headboard and slid his night table drawer open, revealing his latest travel pistol, a black Sig compact 9mm. He watched as she dressed in the bathroom and moved the gun from the drawer to under her pillow.

"I've got it. Jump the balcony, and the Secret Service guy will hide you while I deal with the asshole causing a scene in the hallway." Claudia came out of the bathroom dressed.

"Great idea, but which balcony? To the right or the left?" Bryce shrugged his shoulders and watched as Claudia's expression showed she wasn't in the mood for jokes. As she left the bedroom, Bryce got up, slid on his black shorts, grabbed the pistol, and began to follow her, but his phone rang. It was Danny.

"You okay, boss?" Danny asked.

"Yes. Fine. How's your night going so far?"

"The Secret Service just tackled Tony Bishop outside your door. You didn't hear anything?"

"No, I'm a sound sleeper. What have they done with him?"

"They wanted to keep this quiet, so they took him into the room beside yours."

"Oh, shit!" Bryce yelled and ran after Claudia. As he reached the balcony, he looked to the left and right, where he saw his guest standing on the next balcony with two agents and an irate Tony Bishop.

"Should I order some room service? Who wants pizza?" he said as he walked to the railing, Claudia had just climbed over.

"You son of a bitch," Bishop shouted. Claudia slapped his face.

"I was talking to him," Bishop shouted. Claudia slapped him again.

"Shut your mouth. You are making a scene, and embarrassment is the worst thing you can do to me or the Werner brand. We're done. Drive the car. Don't drive the car. I don't care at this point." Claudia turned her focus to one of the agents.

"Are you arresting him?" she asked. The agent shook her head no.

"We'll escort him to the lobby or his room if he's staying here, but if he puts another foot on this floor, he's going to jail." Bryce sat and continued watching the show unfold as Claudia refocused on Tony.

"So what will it be? Leave now, right now, without another word, or your contract is canceled, and you can go back to Canada or wherever the hell you've come from." Suddenly, for some unknown reason, Bryce grew sad. He'd enjoyed his dinner, the aerobics, and a few hours of solid sleep, but sitting on a balcony watching someone cheated on get dressed down gave him a strange feeling; he felt bad for the guy.

He recalled what Kyoto had found in his late Uncle

Pete's diary, of how his disabled father must have felt when his drunken mother would bring random lovers home and have sex in his parent's bed. His father was helpless and forced to listen to it while a young Bryce slept in a crib down the hall. Bryce had experienced every emotion imaginable, or so he thought until tonight. He'd never been cheated on, at least not to his knowledge. He imagined how someone, anyone in Bishop's position, might feel. It stung. He watched as the agents escorted Bishop back into the room and noticed Claudia hadn't looked his way. He'd never seen her that angry before. Yes, he'd seen her hurt and vulnerable when she'd found Max cheated on her, but nothing like this.

In the dark under a night sky full of stars, Bryce sat and wondered how Max might have felt when he believed his friend and protege had bedded his wife. Bryce got up and walked back into the suite. He looked at the bedroom door, then at the coffee maker in the kitchen, and finally at the image staring back at him in the dining room mirror.

"You better not be regrowing a conscience because everything's been easy until now, thanks to the CIA. Everything's been like the flags you chase, black and white."

Now back in her suite and alone, Claudia Werner placed her iPhone on the nightstand, opened a flip phone, and made a call. It answered on the second ring.

"Berchtesgaden," she said and waited for the correct response.

"Revenge tour," the man answered.

"Summit Point was a complete disaster."

"It was. Nobody knew the real president was coming. It was all last minute."

"You have everything you need to finish this job once and for all? No mistakes? No fuckups," she asked.

"Yes. I have the credentials, and I've altered my appearance. The weapon, and the backup, are already inside the paddock.

"Good. Very good. Now avenge my husband and earn that million. Kill the bastard live on TV." Claudia ended the call and removed the memory card from the phone. She entered the bathroom, wrapped the card in a tissue, and flushed it away. She looked at her image in the mirror. It was late. Her makeup was gone, and her hair was barely salvaged. She could still smell the scent of the man who had killed her husband and taken a loving father from their daughter.

"And if you fail again, this time I will kill the both of you myself."

CHAPTER THIRTY-NINE

The weather for the race in Miami was perfect, low humidity, clear skies, and a thermometer reading of 73F greeted everyone as they funneled into the paddock, suites, and grandstands to witness what the promoters had guaranteed would be like nothing else anyone had seen. He was ready inside the van he had rented under an alias for this mission. He checked his watch.

"Now, just sit here for a bit, and within an hour, we'll see just how good those racing helmets are at stopping a bullet," Russo whispered.

Bryce had worked his way through the crowd and to his private quarters on the second level of the Kazaan hospitality suite. Having an entourage of professional personal security guards wedged around him had made it easy. He spent fifteen minutes mingling with VIPs and guests on the first level before excusing himself for some quiet time to get his head ready for whatever the day might bring. Sitting back in a red leather high-backed chair, Bryce relied on his usual distraction: the news. Suddenly, his phone began to dance across the round white table, bumping into an associate team sponsor's coffee mug before he checked it. A text had come in from SL: Susan Lee. It read,

SAD TO SEE THAT A FRIEND OF YOURS HAS DIED IN SYDNEY. MY CONDOLENCES.

Bryce immediately changed the channel from CNN to BBC International while scrolling to CNN Australia on his phone. There it was. Alistair and Andrew Marshall had both been found dead in the Marshall family mansion, partially burned to the ground before firefighters arrived and saved what they could of the property. Both bodies had been found burned beyond recognition, but the coroner had identified the remains using dental records and had initially ruled the deaths a murder-suicide. Bryce thought back to the moment he had taken Lee's gun and killed the sniper who had tried to kill him.

He texted Lee back simply.

THANK YOU.

She soon responded.

GOOD LUCK TODAY. WE'LL BE WATCHING.

⚜

Russo checked his watch one last time and then rechecked his disguise. The salt and pepper beard he'd grown during the previous four months was nicely trimmed and fit well with the designer glasses and freshly shaven head he'd cleaned up hours earlier in the hotel.

"Now, get through security, retrieve the gear, get up to the roof with the other photographers, and snap away," he said to his reflection in the mirror.

⤚

The morning warm-up had gone as planned; the car and Bryce were ready. After thirty minutes of greeting VIPs in the Kazaan suite overlooking the pit lane, Bryce was distracted by the look he saw on Danny's face. Bryce excused himself after taking a photo with a father and son from Taiwan with whom Kazaan did microchip business and met Danny near an exit.

"What's the matter? What's going on?" Bryce demanded. He saw heartbreak in his friends' eyes and put his arm around him.

"Danny, what is it?" Danny cleared his throat and muttered something unintelligible.

"Damn it, tell me what's wrong?" Bryce asked again. Danny took a step, so he was facing Bryce.

"Mom's had a stroke. My sister called. It doesn't look good."

Bryce surveyed the room and finally made eye contact with Sophie, who was shadowing Kazaan. She excused herself and came to them quickly.

"Danny needs to get to the airport immediately," Bryce directed. "Put him in a police car; I don't care, but get him to the airport. I'll call my crew and have them ready when he arrives." Danny put up his hands.

"No, no way I'm leaving you, Bryce, fuck that." Bryce shook his head and stepped close.

"Danny, go take care of your mother. She needs you, and so does the family. Don't worry about me; I've got the damn Secret Service looking after me here."

"But what about after? What about-" Bryce cut him off and looked at Sophie.

"Why are you two still here? Get moving. I'll hitch a ride back to Europe with Claudia. The Secret Service will get me to the plane, and then I'll have the Trudeaus meet me wherever I land. Now go!" Suddenly Danny wrapped his arms around Bryce and gave him a bear hug.

"I love you like a brother. Go win this thing, and I'll catch up to you soon."

Bryce held onto his friend until he realized people were starting to notice their emotions. He stepped back and gave Danny an understanding look.

"You're still here?" Danny laughed and followed Sophie from the gathering as Kazaan approached his driver.

"Everything okay?" he asked. Bryce focused on his phone as he watched his friend disappear through the doorway.

"Hey, boss, what do ya need?" pilot Bill Miller asked.

"Danny's mom had a stroke. He's on his way to you. Fly him home as quickly as you can. I'll call you after the race to figure out what happens next," Bryce directed.

"That sucks. We're on it, Bryce. Good luck and good-bye." Bryce slid his phone into his pocket and focused on Ameer.

"My shadow just got called away," Bryce said as he

smiled at a group of well-wishers approaching with Kazaan ball caps for his autograph.

"So I heard. We should be thankful the president sent a team to look after you then." Bryce worked the room a bit longer and then went to his personal space, his inner sanctum. While most other drivers would spend this time with their physical or psychological trainers, Bryce had his pre-race routine. Coke Zero, a few minutes on bottled oxygen, yoga postures, and a silent prayer. He always thanked God for his good fortune and the people he'd had in his life who loved him. But today, he added something. He wasn't sure why, but he did.

"Lord, please look after me today. I've got a strange feeling. I hope to meet you someday, but not quite yet, if you know what I mean."

Then, with thirty minutes to go, Sophie knocked at his door and popped her head in.

"Ready to roll BW?" she asked. Bryce smiled and got up from his high-backed chair. As he stepped to the door, he stared at the photos of him with his first love, Christy, his father, Paul, and his Uncle Pete. He paused momentarily and smiled at them fondly. Then, he moved, taking the circular steps down to the ground level, waving at the fans and media covering his every move. The undercover Secret Service agents and Sophie began to form their wedge. To his surprise, Ameer Kazaan and Claudia Werner emerged from the Werner hospitality suite next door and waved for Bryce to join them. He stared at Kazaan. *Really?* Kazaan shook his head yes and waved for Bryce. As the wedge began to move toward the garages, Bryce headed to the left toward the two. It took a second for his team to react, but they spun and took up positions near where Bryce had gone inside. The vibrant yellow and black Werner Industries trailer had been where Bryce and Max Werner had celebrated and often commiserated about the day's performance out on track. He went directly into Claudia's private office. Once inside, all three sat around a small, round black table.

"Okay, this is a little out of the ordinary. What's up?" Bryce asked.

"Claudia and I have been talking for a month or so now," Kazaan said.

"And I may be buying your contract," Claudia said, to Bryce's surprise.

He gave Ameer a questioning look.

"And you're dropping this on me just now on race day, right before we buckle up?"

Ameer shook his head yes.

"From now or the remaining two years?"

"The remaining years. I want to win the title and then sell the team. It's time. There is a lot of new money trying to get into this sport, and it is the perfect time for me to cash in and spend a little more time on Lilly."

"The wife or the boat?" Bryce teased. Kazaan looked at Claudia and laughed.

"You sure you want this guy?" Claudia smiled and shook her head yes.

"Okay, then I've got some calls to make," Kazaan said, leaving abruptly.

Bryce watched as the door closed behind his team owner.

"This is all kind of sudden," Bryce said. "How did last night go?"

Suddenly, someone knocked at the door, interrupting before Claudia could answer. An assistant stuck her head in the door and put her hands together as if begging.

"Sorry for the interruption, but one of your guests is insisting they have to speak with you straight away," the woman said in an English accent. Claudia looked at the clock on the wall.

"Don't go anywhere. I'll be right back," she said as she got up and walked toward the door, brushing Bryce's neck as she passed behind him. Bryce took it all in stride and sat quietly, surveying a space he hadn't been inside in nearly a year and a half before he had left the Werner team for Kazaan. The photos on the walls were new ones he hadn't seen. Max and Bishop, Claudia and Bishop, Claudia, Mila, and Bishop, holding race-winning trophies.

God, I wish I'd had a bug to bring. I'd love to hear what goes on in here, he thought. Suddenly, Bryce realized he'd forgotten to rinse away a hint of coffee breath before leaving his quarters. He got up and looked about the space for gum, mints, anything. Then he remembered Max always kept gum inside the center drawer for the same reasons. Bryce had reached in before and didn't think twice about doing it again. But when he did, he saw the gum and, beside it, a gun. He looked at the door and then quickly back to the drawer. "Well, that's interesting." Suddenly, the door cracked open, and he heard Claudia's German accent as she reminded someone never to interrupt her again. As Claudia walked in, he quickly closed the drawer and retook his seat. She studied him for a moment and then retook her seat.

"My apologies. Now, where were we?" Claudia asked.

"Gum, I need gum. Got any?" Bryce asked. She gave him a curious look.

"Coffee breath," he said, shrugging his shoulders. Claudia pulled the center drawer open and reached for the gum. She paused for a moment; Bryce was watching for it. A second later, the gum was tossed his way, the drawer closed tight, and Claudia was escorting Bryce from the room. Bryce touched her shoulder before she opened the door and turned her to him.

"Can I get a good luck kiss," he said as he put both hands on her arms. He watched her eyes. He saw the concern she'd shown at the drawer change to attraction. She stepped to him and kissed him passionately, then stepped back abruptly and wiped a bit of her red lipstick from the corner of his mouth.

"Use the gum, now get out of here, and enjoy finishing second today," she said as she winked at him. As Bryce emerged from the Werner transport, his team reshaped their wedge, and they hustled Bryce quickly through the crowd toward the Kazaan garage. It was now quarter to the hour, and it was time for the pre-race ceremonies to begin at the front of the grid. But as nineteen other drivers walked through the crowds to their positions in line out on the track, Bryce was hustled in another direction.

❧

Looking down now on the drivers all lined up across from Jacques Lafrance, Antoine Blanc, and other dignitaries and officials, Russo turned his brand new red F1 ball cap around and switched on the autofocus on his massive camera and lens assembly. He went from one driver to the next, naming each one, but suddenly realized someone was missing. His target, Bryce Winters, was nowhere in sight. Then, he heard the public address announcer direct the audience's attention to the screens and monitors around the facility to watch something special. *What the fuck?* Russo murmured and then joined the millions worldwide and watched the video presentation.

∽

Bryce was hurried through the garage by the four undercover team members who guided him to a black Ford window van. Moving quicker, Bryce climbed in through the side door, and the vehicle sped off. The few passersby who had remained in the area behind the garages barely had time to capture the moment with their phones. There he was, and then he was gone. Seconds later, every monitor and TV on the property came to life showing Bryce Winters dressed in a black polo, jeans, and sunglasses, standing beside the president of the United States dressed in a blue pinstriped suit, white shirt, and red tie with an American flag pin affixed to his lapel.

"We'll get you there, Mister President, no matter what," Bryce assured the man whose face showed grave concern. Suddenly, the sound and smoke from stun grenades and small arms fire caused Bryce and the president to duck alongside the driver's side of a black Cadillac presidential limousine. As suited Secret Service agents drew their sidearms and returned fire, purple smoke engulfed the limousine.

"Get in, Mister President. I'll get us out of here."
Bryce opened the thick, armored side door and shoved
the president into the vehicle. Then, as an agent waved to
Bryce to get moving, Bryce opened the driver's door. The
camera angle switched to the rider's front seat and showed
Bryce buckling his seat belt, checking the rearview mirror.
Another camera showed the president in the back seat,
connecting his seat belt and making a sign of the cross.
The front seat camera view returned to show Bryce slide
the gear selector into Drive as purple smoke outside the
vehicle got darker and darker.

"Let's go!" Bryce shouted as he punched the gas with
his foot. As the limousine took off, the outside camera
view returned to show the limousine racing toward a highway onramp. Suddenly two late model sedans, one red,
and one burgundy, pulled in front of Bryce, who threw the
transmission into Reverse, drove straight back toward the
camera, agents still firing their weapons, and spun the car
around as he slid the transmission back into Drive. Bryce
drove around the two blocking vehicles and drove the left
side of the limousine up on the ramp's concrete barrier and
around the obstructing vehicles, disappearing into more
smoke. Suddenly the sound of police sirens was heard
down on the race track. The video feed then switched to
a live feed which showed the presidential limousine, one
similar to the video car, emerge through purple smoke
and racing toward the drivers standing in a straight line
on pit lane. The limousine stopped as two black and tan
Florida Highway Patrol Dodge Chargers and three black
armored Chevrolet SUV's stopped behind the limousine.
Bryce exited the limousine, ran past his fellow drivers,

and took his spot beside a gawking Tony Bishop. Jacques Lafrance stepped to Bryce and handed him a microphone. Bryce smiled.

"Sorry, I'm a bit late, Jacques. But I had to rescue *THE* president." Bryce turned back toward the limousine and watched with the rest of the live crowd and global audience as the three Secret Service agents stood close to the rear passenger side door and opened it. Then, the president of the United States, the real one, Zachary Johnson, emerged and began waving to the crowd as he walked toward the line of drivers.

"Is that the real thing?" Bishop asked Bryce, who was smiling proudly from ear to ear. Behind Johnson, the Secret Service had taken control of the limousine and drove it slowly, remaining as close as possible to Johnson. As Johnson arrived at the line, he shook Lafrance's hand and then went down the line greeting each driver. Lafrance and Bryce followed Johnson, and Bryce laughed as Lafrance attempted to take control of the microphone once and then again.

"We're in the Wild West now, Jacques; remember that."

&

On the roof, Russo tried his best to make a discreet phone call to Roland McCarthy, who had been secretly, illegally, directing his and Chadwick's efforts since becoming the Chief of Staff.

"Speak," McCarthy shouted.

"Are you watching?" Russo whispered.

"Yes."

"Who do you want?" Russo asked.

Russo watched as Johnson took the microphone from Bryce and delivered brief remarks to the audience.

"First, Bryce, thank you for saving me back there. You're pretty good behind the wheel. Ever consider driving for the Secret Service?"

"No thanks, Mister President, this gig pays just a little bit better." Johnson laughs, shakes Bryce's hand, and then turns toward the cameras.

"The weather's incredible here in South Florida today, and I want to welcome everyone to Miami. And for those watching around the world, America is open for business, and I invite everyone to visit our country and enjoy all it has to offer. Now, I can't think of a better ending to today than having our American driver win this damn thing." Johnson looked down the line of drivers and smiled.

"Sorry, fellas," Johnson called out. Most laughed, and some waved, but Bishop turned and looked away. On the roof, Russo was waiting for instructions.

"Stick to the plan, or?" Russo asked but then realized the call had ended. He spun his hat back around, raised his camera, and took aim.

CHAPTER FORTY

JUST MINUTES AFTER President Johnson had shaken hands with the twenty drivers set to race the Miami GP, he was back inside the safety of one of the planet's most heavily fortified "passenger" vehicles. As quickly as he had arrived, his motorcade was on the move again, exiting the facility and heading to Air Force One. On the roof overlooking the starting grid, Russo was perplexed. The man holding his strings, the political puppet master Roland McCarthy had flinched. In his mind, Russo believed he could have taken out the president and maybe, just maybe, put lead in the head of the man he'd been after for months – Bryce Winters. As the cars on the grid below fired their engines and took off on their formation lap, Russo replayed what he'd learned from Johnson and Winters. For a spy, reading lips was standard, but what he had read through his camera lens intrigued him.

"Thank you for doing this, Mr. President," Bryce said as the two shook hands again.

And thank you for the detail; I can't express how much I appreciate it. I will say that it's been tough getting through to you. Your gatekeeper, what's his name – McCarthy? He's tough."

Russo maintained his focus as Johnson gestured to his lead Secret Service agent, Connie Termini, who stepped in close.

"Give Bryce your card. If he ever reaches out and says he needs to speak with me, you are to make it happen and don't let anyone get in the way, understood?" Russo watched as Termini nodded, taking a card from her pocket and handing it to Winters.

"Thank you again, Mr. President. I'll text you mine."

"You need to come visit me in the Oval, Bryce, and soon, we have a few things to talk about."

Suddenly the noise of the twenty race cars and the thousands of fans cheering from underneath him brought Russo back to the present. He quickly focused his lens, which also served as an optic for the suppressed state-of-the-art sniper rifle housed inside the eighteen-inch device. *There you are*, Russo thought. His prey was within reach, a difficult shot but a makeable one for someone with his abilities and training. But that wasn't the plan. McCarthy wanted Bryce's brain splashed against the podium's backdrop at the end of the race, no helmet, but with the world watching. Russo had agreed; in the confusion, he'd be able to exit his position and blend in with the hundred thousand screaming fans who would be running for the exits, shocked by the horror of it all.

Russo watched as the five horizontal lights stationed above the track lit red to signal the pending start, and then, as they were shut off, the drivers below raced from the grid and disappeared into Turn One. He checked his watch and smiled at the photographer set up a few feet to his left. Soon, the cars would be coming past for the first of fifty-seven laps, but the crowd gasped as the yellow flags and caution lights were displayed trackside. Bryce and two other cars had crashed hard.

Russo stared at the giant video screen across from his vantage point in disbelief as the incident was repeated. He watched his prey climb out of a badly damaged race car and knew his chance, after all these months of waiting, was gone.

"Mother fucker," he shouted as he looked back at the photographer to his left, as the man shook his head in disbelief. Russo knew McCarthy wanted Winters dead on American soil, but he wouldn't be back racing in the States until October.

"Fuck that," Russo muttered. "No way I'm waiting until then for my money. I'll get this prick in Montreal next month, and if the asshole doesn't pay up, I'll take his picture too." Russo began to pack up his gear. The photographer came closer.

"What are you doing?" he asked. "You're not leaving?" Russo smiled as he shook his head no.

"My boss wanted some shots of Bryce on track, so since he's out, I'll lose the big stuff and work pit lane instead." The photographer seemed puzzled but shrugged and focused on the race. Russo studied the man briefly but then finished packing and headed for the stairs.

∽

Bryce and two other drivers rode in the back of a white and red ambulance to the medical center for a mandatory post-crash examination. On the way, Bryce couldn't believe his chances had been extinguished so quickly while he half-listened to the Italian and the German drivers curse at each other in their native languages, blaming the other for the crash. Once the vehicle came to a stop and they climbed out, fans and reporters shouted requests for autographs and questions about who was to blame.

"Who caused the crash Bryce," a Brit called out.

"This could hand Bishop the points lead Bryce, any comment," came from another.

Bryce ignored the questions and went inside to have his vitals checked. Upon leaving, Sophie and the four agents were there and again formed the wedge that would guide him back to his quarters where he could change, regroup, and prepare to face the media. Once inside, he took a few minutes and watched a replay of the crash from many angles.

"Nobody's fault," he muttered. "Just another racing accident." As he changed into his red Kazaan polo and blue jeans, he phoned Bill Miller.

"Hope you're out over the Gulf of Mexico by now," Bryce said. Inside, he wished the plane was still at the Miami airport, delayed somehow just long enough for Bryce to get to it and fly away from this place. In three days, he was supposed to be in Italy for the next race, but the unexpected detour to Park City would allow him to check on the new property and the builder's progress. He'd been moving about the world without a proper home for four months and felt unsettled. But he was still alive; the crash hadn't killed him, and neither had Russo if he was here. At least, not yet.

"Hey Bryce," Miller came back. "We just got in the air. Air Force One had us all on a ground stop, but we watched her take off and then got moving too. Jen told us what happened on the first lap. That sucks."

"How's Danny?" Bryce asked as he drank an orange Powerade without flinching.

"Quiet, as expected. He's in the back drinking coffee and counting clouds. We'll take good care of him, but what's your plan? Want us to turn right around and come back for you?"

Bryce thought for a moment as he put on his Tag watch and checked his face and hair in a wall mirror.

"No, you'll be out of hours if you come back to get me. I'll hitch a ride overseas with Claudia Werner, and if that doesn't work, I'll shoot up to Montreal with Ameer. You could grab me there tomorrow afternoon, couldn't you?"

"You're the boss," Miller said.

"Okay, I've got to go do press. I'll call you in a few hours. Have a safe flight, and tell Danny I was asking for him. Safe travels."

As Bryce approached the door, he thought about thanking his maker for keeping him alive but knew better; the day was still young. Then a strong feeling of emotions swept over him.

❧

Russo had made it. He had managed to hand the black gear bag to his inside man in the paddock, Max Werner's nephew Felix, the logistics crewman dressed in black and yellow Werner apparel. Young Werner had seen to it that the special gear was there when Russo came to retrieve it and would stow it away, hidden within the maze of parts and pieces that traveled the world by cargo aircraft, until he was told to make it available again, or if needed, make it disappear forever. Inside a stall in one of the Hard Rock Stadium's restrooms, he altered his appearance once again and kept moving. A new yellow Pirelli ball cap replaced the F1 cap he'd shoved into a trash bin. The salt and pepper beard is now more of a black goatee. His sunglasses are also different now, with Oakley gold lenses replacing the green ones and the Tommy Bahama floral blue shirt also gone, a basic black tee shirt now on display. Once he cleared the pedestrian exits and headed for his rented van in the parking lot, Russo was all smiles. His friend was dead, but the man screwed up, so he got what he deserved, and his vendetta was delayed yet again. But he was a free man and could now disappear for thirty days until it was time to cross the border sixteen hundred miles north of his present location in sunny Florida. McCarthy would have to wire more operating money. The sun was baking the asphalt, and all Russo could think of was the bucket of ice-cold Budweiser's that would be his dinner date somewhere north of Lauderdale. As he approached the van, he smiled at people who were tailgating, listening to loud music, tossing footballs, cornhole bags, or cold ones to their friends. Then, as he opened the driver's door, a blinding reflection of light flashed through his windshield, and everything went black.

⋰

Bryce felt like a caged animal, and even worse, he felt alone. His race had ended prematurely, and other than talking with the press and still feeling that today could be his day to die, he felt lost. His plane and his crew were gone, and his security was set to end the minute they dropped him off at Miami's charter terminal. Where the hell was Russo, and although he shouldn't care, where was Kyoyo?

He took a few more minutes to gather his thoughts, did some deep breathing exercises, and then left the safety of his private quarters, following Sophie and the security wedge toward the press line. Soon after, as the race was nearing its finish, Bryce entered Claudia Werner's VIP suite and stood slightly behind her, quietly releasing a sigh of relief as Tony Bishop crossed the line in fifth. He watched as she shook her head in apparent frustration and turned, her expression first a look of surprise which changed quickly to a curious one.

"What are you doing here?" she asked as her guests all streamed out of the suite to head for the exits or down to the track to watch the champagne showers soon to come.

"What? You didn't see the first lap?" he asked, "I crashed my car, and I need a lift back to Europe. Any chance you're heading over tonight and without Tony?" He watched as she appeared to consider her options.

"I do owe you a ride, so sure. We're scheduled to take off at seven sharp and straight to Munich. It'll be just us. Tony is returning to Canada to visit his family. Do you want to rendezvous at my plane or?" she asked.

Bryce stepped away momentarily to pose for photos with a dozen or so Werner guests who had spotted him arrive and remained behind. After that, he caught up to Claudia as she thanked the suite staff and prepared to leave.

"I'll meet you there. This Secret Service detail can get through traffic like a hot knife through butter." He kissed Claudia's cheek, held the door for her, and watched as she and her two assistants headed for the elevators. Bryce paused for a moment and then went back inside. He walked to the suite's balcony and went outside, taking a seat and watching the podium celebration as thousands of people crowded the track and pit lane. He surveyed the rooftop across from him and wondered if a shooter had been on site or was perhaps still there.

Suddenly, fireworks exploded high over the facility catching him off guard. To his surprise, two members of his protection detail, now dressed in lightweight tan jackets, polos, and khakis, were beside him instantly.

"Where the hell did you two come from?" he asked with a laugh.

"We need to get you out of here, Bryce," the female agent said, her Maine accent catching him for a moment and making him think of New England and home. "A body's been found in the parking lot, and they think it's Russo."

CHAPTER FORTY-ONE

THEY WERE IN the air, headed northeast off the coast of Georgia, when Claudia finished her call list and walked to the main cabin to sit with her guest. Bryce watched as she approached his seat and dropped into the black leather chair facing him.

"You look tired," Bryce said as a young attendant delivered their drinks. As he smelled the freshly brewed coffee, savoring the hazelnut aroma, he kept his eyes on her. Despite being exhausted, the natural German beauty still looked like a cover girl and downed her whiskey in one fast draw. She shook the ice cubes in the crystal tumbler and then raised the glass in the air, signaling she wanted more.

"Yes, I might not be much company tonight," she said as she yawned. "An account in Seoul is causing some problems, and they demanded I be on the call, or they were switching suppliers." Bryce laughed and raised his black and yellow Werner mug.

"That's why you get the big bucks." She forced a smile.

"So what will you do once we land in Munich? Mila is

away in Norway with my best friend and her family on a cruise, and I've got a full schedule until the flight to Italy." Bryce felt the disappointment wash over him and knew she saw it as well.

He shook his head, and then his mood changed again.

"I was surprised your team wanded me and went through my bags," he told her. "We didn't do that from Daytona." Claudia shrugged her shoulders as she accepted her drink from the attendant.

"It's a protocol, so shoot me," she said. He laughed.

"Well, I would have, but they took my gun." She laughed.

"Oh, and the inflatable doll they found wasn't mine. I was just holding it for a friend," she laughed again, nearly snorting, and then hid her face with embarrassment. She collected herself and explained.

"We've had so many people on board since we got this one. Some of our more interesting customers aren't worried about guns; they worry more about bugs. Max always said it's better to be safe than dead," Bryce watched as Claudia squeezed her glass.

"Ease up, Claudia; you don't want to get cut." She threw the drink back and placed the tumbler hard on the cabin ledge.

"So what will you do in Munich? You're not the type to drown yourself at the Hofbräuhaus."

"If I can borrow a car, I'd like to drive to Salzburg and get into the mountains. I only have a few days." He watched as Claudia processed his request.

"You know, we haven't touched the estate where Max

died, where you saw him last. You could stay there if you wished," she said. Bryce shook his head and stared at her.

"And things were going along so nicely. What a buzzkill." Claudia shrugged her shoulders and got up from her seat. She stood beside him for a moment, patted him on the shoulder, and then walked toward the galley. Bryce sat quietly as he watched her speak with the attendants. As she walked back toward him, she looked sad. He stood up to embrace her, but she took his hands and held them instead.

"Believe it or not, I have one more call to make. They will serve dinner soon. I'll take mine in the rear cabin, and then I need to sleep." She placed her hands on his face and gazed into his eyes.

"One of my drivers will take you to my place so you can shower and change clothes. You'll have the choice of any car in the garage, but if you break it, you bought it."

"You're not going home after we land?" he asked.

"No, I'll change here and head straight to the office. Have to keep production going if you know what I mean." Bryce took her right hand and kissed it. As he focused back on her stunning but tired brown eyes, she reached up and kissed him softly. Then, as Bryce heard the attendant clear his throat behind them, he turned to see that his food had arrived. As Bryce turned back toward Claudia, he saw her disappear into the rear cabin and close the door behind her.

Hours later, Bryce woke and slid the window shade open to reveal the first signs of light glowing from the horizon. He rubbed the sleep from his face as he stared at the door to the rear cabin, still closed. He looked to the front of the cabin and saw an attendant, their face illuminated by a Kindle. He yawned, got up quietly, and walked to the spacious bathroom at the front of the cabin. He smiled at the attendant and then went inside. There, he began opening cabinets in search of eye drops, but as he opened and closed one small door, he stopped and reopened it.

"This is kid's stuff. This must be Mila's," he said as he stared at what he'd found. It was a mix of pink Barbie and white unicorn toiletries, including toothbrushes and paste, hair brushes, play makeup, sunblock, and hair tyes in a dozen colors. He smiled and closed the cabinet. After continuing his search, he found what he needed, took care of business, and reached for the door handle. Suddenly he stopped and turned.

"DNA, that would have her DNA," he said as he shook his head. *Why didn't you think of that before*, he thought as he looked at his image in the mirror. *Oh yea, been a bit distracted.*

He picked up one of the brushes and pulled a few strands of hair from it, beautiful blonde hair from the head of an angel he'd been told was his. He wrapped the hair in tissue and shoved it into his pants pocket. As he went for the door again, he smiled. *Now I'll know for sure.*

On the tarmac, Bryce hugged Claudia and thanked her for the ride. He sensed something was different, and he asked her about it.

"What's up? Did I do something wrong?"

Claudia laughed and surveyed the area before answering.

"Here, I am all business, and I don't want photographs of us splashed all over the internet. We haven't decided how we should approach Mila with what we know, but the last thing I want to do is confuse or upset her in any way until we have. You understand, I am sure," she asked.

Bryce smiled, stepped back, and extended his hand in jest. She smiled and shook it.

"Madam, thank you for everything. Guten tag," he said and followed the driver she had pointed to as they exited the plane. As he rode off in a black Mercedes sedan, he watched as Claudia was escorted to another Mercedes, this one a limousine. As the side door opened, he saw someone inside, but the view was lost as his driver sped away.

Hours later, Bryce listened to the gravel as he brought the black Mercedes sedan to a halt near the front door of the home where he had killed Max Werner. At first, as he drove east on the A8 from Munich toward Salzburg, he'd ignored the envelope left on the passenger seat by someone on Claudia's staff. After he stopped at a roadside coffee shop and obliged requests for photos or autographs from a few truck drivers and a young couple who had recognized him, he tore the envelope open and found a key. A single key and a card with what he assumed was an alarm code, and he knew immediately what it opened. He sat quietly behind the wheel and surveyed the area, with the Königssee Lake bookending his view of the one-level mansion. He'd spent the last four hours driving there through Salzburg and taking as many mountain roads as possible. There was no hurry, and he wanted and needed to savor the ride and the spectacular views. But then a text hit his phone: ANY CHANCE YOU'LL BE IN LONDON SOON?

Bryce didn't recognize the sender but responded. WHO'S THIS?

The answer came quickly. RED-HEADED ROOM SERVICE.

Bryce laughed until he remembered the last time he'd seen Jonathan Sproul; the man had just shot Penelope Clark in the throat in Australia. Now in Austria, until then, his day had been going great, despite where he had just parked. As Bryce continued to text, he saw an older man walking toward the car, carrying a double-barrel shotgun. He lowered the driver's window and smiled. The man, perhaps in his seventies, wore a faded Werner Industries ball cap over sharp gray eyes that looked more like lenses and a white beard that would have made Santa proud. As he grew closer, he placed the butt of the gun in the gravel and held the weapon by the barrel.

"Mrs. Werner said I should be expecting you." Bryce exited the car and slid his phone into a pocket before extending his hand.

"Bryce Winters," he said, but the man didn't accept it or answer. He simply made a sound, perhaps a growl that would have been fiercer in his younger days, but Bryce got the message.

"I shouldn't be here long. I just want to pay my respects and look at the photos in the office if that's okay," he told the man.

"Not my decision," the man said, his tone softer now. "Please tap the horn when you leave so I can chain the gates behind you." Bryce nodded and watched as the man took up his shotgun and sauntered off. Bryce looked at the trunk of the car, pleased he hadn't needed any of the weapons he'd brought along for the ride. He felt his phone vibrate and remembered he'd left the MI6 case worker hanging. Rather than continue the texting, he called the number.

"Not back in England until Silverstone; I'm headed for Imola and then Monaco the week after," he told whoever answered.

"Glad to hear from you too," the Brit said sarcastically. "Imola's going to be a rain-out. Flooding's expected." Bryce shook his head no.

"No way," he said, "How the hell would you know?"

"You know where I work. We know everything, including there was something suspicious about what happened to the Marshalls down under." Bryce lowered the phone to his side and shook his head in disbelief.

"Sad thing that was, a father and son gone in a flash, but that's all I have to say. Come find me if you need anything else but wait, I need something from you." The men spoke for another minute, and then Bryce ended the call. He retrieved the key and alarm code from the front seat and let himself in. Max had loved this property, Bryce recalled, and now that he was there again, he remembered why. The location was special as it overlooked a long, thin lake, but the house had been designed and built from scratch and maintained a warm, Bavarian style. It reminded Bryce of some of the homes he'd known in Vermont, particularly the von Trapp property near Stowe. The air conditioning was running, and if the place had been unused since Max's sudden death, that wasn't evident. It was as if it was waiting for his return, which would never come. Bryce didn't bother to tour the space; he was there for one reason: to walk back into Max's office and say goodbye once again.

Bryce stood quietly in the doorway and stared across the room at the dead man's desk. Past Max's brown leather upholstered chair, the view of the lake, the sun now casting shadows as it continued its journey west, was beautiful. Bryce walked to the chair and stood beside it. Claudia was right; nothing, absolutely nothing, had changed. The crystal tumbler Bryce had poisoned Max with was there, the slight stain of dried scotch its only color. He wondered if the room was bugged; it probably had been at some point, but for whatever reason, he didn't care if anyone was listening.

"Surprised they didn't check that," he said softly. "It shouldn't matter, but then again, they could have been trying to frame me." Bryce picked up the glass and saw a mosaic of fingerprints mixed together, Max's and Bryce's. He picked up the glass and turned to the sliding door behind the chair that led to the lake. Bryce threw the bolts and walked outside. He surveyed the property and wondered if the old man with the shotgun was watching from the woods. Without another word, Bryce threw the glass as far as he could and watched it reflect a ray of sun before it splashed into the water. He checked his watch. It was nearing six in the evening, and his phone vibrated again; this time, he recognized the caller immediately and answered.

"What's up, Sheriff?" he asked.

"Well, nice to hear from you too, Bryce. I have some news for you."

"Let me guess, there's an issue with my building permits," Bryce joked.

"No, you wanted me to call you if she ever showed up, and she has."

"Who? Who are you talking about?' Bryce felt his heart rate increase. He was usually a cool customer, especially in a race car or under fire, but the last few days, and this one in particular, had been emotional. Then the sheriff answered.

"Kyoto. She showed up this morning."

CHAPTER FORTY-TWO

Sitting across from Max Werner's desk, in the chair he'd occupied after handing his friend, the illegal weapons international trader, the drink that killed him. He stared at the darkening sky over the lake and checked his watch. He'd been sitting there, his phone turned off, for two hours.

"She's there in Park City?" he remembered asking the sheriff.

"No, she showed up at the coroner's office in Salt Lake, and they called me. I did what you asked and headed on down there, but by the time I arrived, she'd already gone."

"You didn't tell them to hold her?"

"On what grounds, Bryce?"

"Fuck, you could have made up something."

"Remind me to write you a ticket for that mouth of yours," the sheriff had said sternly.

Bryce shook his head and continued to replay the conversation.

"I apologize, Sheriff, I am sorry, but she was kidnapped by the bastards who killed her brother and my friend Jack."

"I understand that. The Feds have kept me in the loop just in case, but the coroner told me she said she'd told the FBI everything. Said she'd come to claim her brother's body, have it shipped back to Tokyo where she was going to have it buried with their parents, I think."

"Wait, they're shipping the body to Japan?"

"No, she claimed it but was having it cremated and then shipped to Tokyo, where they're from originally. That made better sense to me. Hell, he was already cooked, so they're just finishing the job."

"Do you know where she's staying?" Bryce remembered asking.

"Nope. The coroner said she took an Uber to the airport right after she signed the papers."

Bryce got up from the chair and flipped a wall switch to brighten the room. He thought of the last thing he'd asked the sheriff before ending the call.

"How was she? Did the coroner tell you how she looked? Was she okay?"

"You know, come to think of it, he did. Said she was the most attractive Asian woman he'd ever seen, even on television, but she had some bruising. It was fading, but it was there."

Then, Bryce looked across Max's office at the wall of mounted photos the two men had reminisced over during that last visit. He walked to them and took time with each one, them standing together after winning Daytona, Indy, Silverstone, Austin, Sochi, Brazil, and so many more. The centerpiece, the largest, photo was of him and Max standing beside the Formula One World Championship driver's trophy. There was another photo there that, at the time, hadn't meant much to Bryce until now; Max and Claudia standing proudly outside the church in Crailsheim, Germany, holding their infant Mila following her christening.

"Their baby?" Bryce asked. Bryce remembered the hair he'd found on the little brush on the flight over. *We'll know soon enough.*

With that, he was done. He walked to the doorway and surveyed the office one last time. He flipped the switch and headed for the front door. After reactivating the alarm, he stepped outside and walked to the borrowed Mercedes. He found himself wondering if he'd ever see Kyoto again and what Sproul had said of the flooding now forecast by the race series for the next venue. Then, without warning, a shot rang out, and Bryce collapsed to the ground.

CHAPTER FORTY-THREE

STUNNED, BRYCE LAY on the ground and watched someone approaching the car from the opposite side. As they
came closer, he could only see their hiking shoes; it wasn't
the old man. He knew he needed to move, get to the bag
in the trunk, and get a gun, or he'd be dead. He felt the
warmth of his blood running across his neck. There wasn't
any pain, at least not yet. *Am I dying?* He wondered as he
fought to control his breathing and stared at the darkening
sky. *Is this the way you go? Damn it, Bryce, Move!*

Suddenly, a shotgun blast rang out, and Bryce saw
whoever was approaching drop to the ground. In an
instant, the old man with the Santa beard was standing
over Bryce, staring down at him. Bryce could see a hint of
smoke still coming from one of two barrels that had been
fired, and he tensed when he realized the other barrel was
pointed at him.

"I have to apologize, but I didn't get your name,"
Bryce said, hoping this man was there to help and not
leave two bodies lying on the ground.

"Americans," the old man said as he shook his head in anger, his German accent very clear.

"My name is Hans. Every time an American has come here, someone has died. But the most interesting part, at least for me, is that you were the American both times there was a death." Bryce stared at the unused barrel.

"So, is that for me?" he asked. Hans shook his head no.

"Now, you must excuse me. I need to finish this, and then we will get you fixed up." As Hans walked away, Bryce realized he could feel everything now, the good and the bad. He could feel his hands and feet, but the pain in his neck and shoulder had come and was becoming more and more excruciating. He struggled initially but got up in time to see Hans standing over the person who had shot Bryce. The man on the ground was on his back, both hands raised, begging in German for his life as Hans braced the shotgun against his shoulder.

"Wer hat dich geschickt?" Bryce called out. "Who sent you?"

The man on the ground turned his head and stared at Bryce. He recognized him but didn't know from where. Without flinching, Hans emptied the second barrel, erasing the front of the man's head. Hans turned to Bryce, who was moving toward his gear in the trunk, and slowly shook his head no. Hans looked past Bryce and gestured with his chin to look behind him. As Bryce turned, he saw another shotgun, this one in the hands of a woman, an older woman, perhaps Hans' wife, he thought. Bryce froze.

"Come with me, and we'll see about that wound," the woman called out as she waved her free hand. Bryce looked back at Hans, who was going through the dead man's pockets.

"Are you going to call the authorities," Bryce called out. Hans looked at him with surprise.

"Why? Did you want me to?" Bryce shook his head no and followed the woman.

The woman pulled a dish towel from her apron, pressed it hard on the wound, and told him to apply pressure. He struggled initially but followed her inside the guest house to the right of the main building, where he collapsed onto a chair at the kitchen table and let her work. He was lucky. After she removed his shirt, she saw the damage. The bullet had struck above the right collarbone close to the neck. It had torn through muscle and exited; it had been the shockwave so near his spinal cord that put him on the ground. Soon, Hans joined them there.

"Are you okay," Hans asked as he looked at the woman. She shrugged.

"I feel like I got punched in the head, but not near as bad as the other guy," Bryce said. Hans nodded and then went to a cabinet and pulled out a brown bottle. He poured himself a drink and offered one to Bryce, who politely declined.

"What did you find on him?" Bryce asked. Hans shook his head no.

"Nothing; there was nothing on him besides a second pistol magazine. You are lucky. I am surprised he didn't take a second shot. If that were the case, you'd have been done."

Bryce watched as the woman gave Hans a questioning look.

"I would prefer it if you didn't call the police," Bryce said and then cringed as the woman began suturing the entry and exit wounds closed. Hans laughed and stepped close.

"You've done this before?" he asked as she continued to work.

"Yes, I worked for years as a nurse at the hospital in Crailsheim before we moved here."

"No need to call anyone. The body is gone, and so is the gun." Bryce shook his head, cringing as he did.

"You've done this sort of thing before?" Hans nodded. As the woman applied bandages over her stitches, Bryce apologized.

"I don't know your name. I'm Bryce." Hans laughed.

"She is my wife of fifty-seven years. She is Greta. Greta Werner."

Bryce stood up in shock but immediately dropped back into the chair.

"Take it easy, Bryce Winters," Greta said as she resumed her work with the bandage.

"Max was my son," she said. Hans took a seat across from Bryce and stared at him.

"My wife and I moved here after Max died. He left it to us in his will. We left everything the way it was when he left us."

Bryce watched as the man's expression showed pride, perhaps disappointment, and then sadness.

"He was a good boy but at times a bad man," Hans continued, but Greta interrupted, pressing on Bryce's shoulder as she took exception with her husband. He cringed.

"Do not speak of that dead that way. Not of our son, not here!" she shouted.

Bryce took a few deep breaths, hoping to calm his nerves and enable him to think more clearly. The parents of the man who had once been a great friend, the man he killed for the CIA, had just saved his life.

"God," Bryce uttered as he looked at Hans.

"What did you do with the body?" he asked. Hans reached across the table and picked up a pipe, flicked a matchstick to life, and began puffing away.

"A neighbor heard the gunfire and came running as Greta took you inside. I told him this man had tried to rob us, so he and his sons are disposing of the body. You have nothing to worry about; either way, you haven't killed anyone." Bryce and the old man locked eyes, and Greta put her medicine kit away. When she returned to the kitchen, she sat at the head of the table.

"You should see a doctor," she suggested. "You will need antibiotics and perhaps more. I think much more."

"You can stay here tonight if you wish," Hans said, "but all things considered, with who you are, it might be best to get as far away from here as possible and soon. No need to go to Italy; the race will be flooded." Bryce shook his head in agreement.

"Can I ask one favor before I go? I could really use some coffee." He watched as she prepared his drink and surveyed the room as Hans continued to smoke and study their guest.

"Do you get to see Mila very often?" Bryce asked. He watched as Hans's expression grew sad, and for that, Bryce wished he could have taken the question back.

It was dark now, the property lit by a full moon in a beautiful clear sky as Hans walked with Bryce back to his Mercedes. Bryce stopped and took a moment to take it all in. He looked to the now empty spot where the shooter had met his demise, then to the doorway where he had said goodbye to Max, and finally, he turned to see Greta standing at the door of their little Bavarian cottage.

He smiled at her and then heard his car door being opened. He turned and looked at Hans, who motioned with his head for Bryce to get in. As he did, Hans shut the door abruptly and leaned down to speak.

"Don't ever come back here, Bryce Winters. You were lucky today, but someday, like all of us, your luck will run out." Bryce stared into the man's eyes. In the moonlit darkness, they were more piercing than ever.

"Sounds like good advice. I'll take it." Bryce told him as he started the car and slowly drove off. As Bryce switched on the headlights, he saw three men standing near the open gates, two held shotguns, while the oldest of the three kept his hands in his pockets. They were dressed like caretakers, farmers, and as Bryce drove through the gate past the men, he nodded at them; their stone faces didn't budge. It was clear to Bryce that they had all done this before.

Back on the road, Bryce quickly realized he was hurt worse than he thought. Raising his right arm to the steering wheel of the Mercedes didn't just bring pain; it was a struggle to grasp it and hold it there.

"Shit," he shouted as he realized another bullet may have just cost him another championship. It was now just past ten at night as he drove past the Salzburg airport, and he had a decision to make; try his best to make it back to Munich and seek Claudia's help or head south for his home in Monaco. He needed additional medical treatment that was clear, but what he wanted most was something to kill the worsening pain. He pulled into a roadside petrol station and made a call.

"We were hoping to hear from you, Bryce. Where are you?" Elaine Trudeau said happily.

"Parked on the side of the road near Salzburg. I got shot a few hours ago and was wondering if you had any ideas on how I can get to Monaco tonight without being seen."

The call went silent momentarily as Bryce squinted from the glare of a trucker's passing headlights.

"Hello?" he asked.

"Bryce, it's Toby. You're on speakerphone. Are you joking, or is this real?"

Bryce relayed what had happened and the shape he was in and, despite the coffee, found himself tiring very quickly. He checked the bandage and was relieved when he found he wasn't bleeding.

"Now," Toby asked. "Are you in danger sitting where you are?"

"Only if I eat the truck stop food."

"Where's the shooter?"

"Wood chipper's my bet."

"Good. Send me a pin, and give me ten minutes. We know people there. Stay put."

Bryce ended the call and then texted the pin. Within seconds the phone vibrated again. He read the caller ID and dropped the phone. It was Frank Dini, probably calling, Bryce imagined, about the upcoming twenty-four-hour race at LeMans they had entered. He stared at himself in the mirror and realized that unless he woke up to find this had all been a nightmare, he would probably miss that race as well. He closed his eyes and passed out.

Three hours had passed since Bryce spoke with the Trudeaus, and suddenly, he heard Elaine calling out his name as someone was banging on the car door.

"Bryce, wake up! It's Elaine and Toby. We're here."

Soon after and still under darkness, Bryce woke up lying on an examination table in an outpatient surgical suite. Groggy, he raised his left hand to shield his eyes from the overhead lamps.

"Where am I?" he asked. He felt someone place their hand on his left shoulder. He turned to see Elaine smiling at him and then heard Toby's voice.

"Hey, you two, knock it off. I'm standing right here."

The three of them laughed until a doctor, Sebastian Haas, a former corpsman with the Austrian Army, moved the overhead light away and slowly sat Bryce up.

"So what's the prognosis Doc? Will he ever play the piano again?" Toby asked

Bryce wasn't in a joking mood and made it clear immediately.

"Screw the piano, Doc. Can I drive?" Haas stared at Bryce and then let him have it.

"No."

CHAPTER FORTY-FOUR

Luckily for Bryce, the Italian Gran Prix had been canceled due to intense flooding in the region, so as he sat on his balcony overlooking the Monaco Marina in the warmth of the mid-day sun, he had every intention of proving the Austrian doctor wrong. It was now Thursday, and he had a week to do it. Bryce had been visited by two medical experts found by Ameer Kazaan, one flown in from Paris and the other from Zurich, and all had said the same thing: You need time to heal. Electrical stimulation and therapy would help, but they weren't optimistic. "You could spend much of your days in a cryogenic chamber and the nights in a hyperbaric one," they told him. "But time is the answer. That torn muscle and severed nerves need to heal. Ready for the next GP? Impossible." To Ameer, the man paying their fees, their prognosis was much worse. "He's done. At least for this year."

His friends, the Trudeaus, had gone above and beyond getting Bryce emergency care and back home, and based on what had happened at the Werner Estate, had surrounded their client with a dozen former special operators who knew how to blend in but, more importantly, keep their charge safe. Hoping to draw from the sun's healing powers might have been what Bryce intended, but an hour later, a photo of him sitting there with his right arm in a sling made headlines on every racing and celebrity site on the planet. Frustrated, he threw things as best he could with his left arm inside his high-rise condo and had his phone ready for launch until he felt it vibrate and read the caller ID. It was Ameer. After asking about his rehab, Ameer said what Bryce expected to hear.

"Bryce, I hate to say this, but I know you will understand. We are also chasing the car constructor's championship, so we need to field your car and remain in the lead, whether you can drive it or not. I know you understand. We're talking nearly $150,000,000." Bryce leaned against the counter in his rarely used stainless steel kitchen and shook his head slowly. He got it.

"Ameer, I'd do the same thing. But don't give up hope on me. I hope you'll let me get back in the car if I can drive." He listened and tensed as Ameer's response took longer than Bryce expected.

"Of course, my friend, but we will need another driver there starting on media day, just in case." Later that night, the Trudeaus were able to stage a move that led fans and pesky photojournalists to believe Bryce had escaped to his motor yacht and sailed off for Capri.

Remaining in his high-rise condo, Bryce spent the next few days inside and away from any prying eyes, moving back and forth between physical therapists and the healing chambers in his private gym. He kept in touch with the people he wanted to, his flight crew, his new assistant and project manager Joan Glaser, and was happy to hear from Danny Johnson that his sick mother was on the mend. He spoke with Claudia Werner daily, usually late at night, and was anxious to see her. After nearly being killed, he wanted to look into her eyes when he demanded answers.

A week had passed since Berchtesgaden, and as the partygoers below celebrated the return of Formula One to Monte Carlo, Bryce got up from the white sofa in his living room and checked the spy hole in the door. It was Claudia, and it was late. After an embrace and her gentle inspection of his injured shoulder, Bryce led his guest into the living room, poured her a drink, and sat at one end of the sofa. She sat at the opposite end, three feet away, and studied him.

"You're lucky the shooter wasn't that good. An inch or more toward your center, you'd be dead," she paused. "Or paralyzed," he added.

"So, how do I explain this?" Bryce asked as he moved his arm slightly.

"What Ameer's team said was perfect. You had a freak accident on the mountain roads on a bicycle." Claudia reached into her large bag and removed a card, handed it to him as she said,

"This is from Mila."

"I told her about your accident, and she thought that might make you feel better." Bryce opened the card and stared at the beautiful drawing the little girl had made for him, perhaps his little girl. He fought back the emotion trying to take him and looked at his guest.

"Let me ask you something. If anything happens to you, what happens to Mila?"

He'd caught her off-guard with the question; she looked stunned but recovered quickly.

"Why? Do you know something I don't?" she asked as she surveyed the living room.

"If you need a good housekeeper, I can recommend a few. This place looks like a bomb went off."

"Well, the way things have been going, that might be next. Look, you know, with me out of the game, your chances of winning the driver's championship just improved exponentially," he said as he got up and walked to the balcony window. Claudia reacted immediately.

"Wait a minute. I'm here to see how you are, not talk about points." Bryce turned and stared at her. He was done playing games and let her have it.

"You were the only person who knew I was headed to Berchtesgaden," he charged. She pushed back.

"Not true. One of my staff, the one who put the key and the alarm code in the car, knew where you were going, and of course, Hans and Greta had to be informed. Bryce and Claudia stared at each other; their glares slowly eased.

"And by the way, where's that car?" Bryce had to slow down and process what she was saying. He had a hard time with it and figured it must be the painkillers he was on. With that in mind, he knew how to play it better, or so he thought. He took a few deep breaths and softened his tone.

"I'm sorry, Claudia, they've got me on some powerful meds, and they mess with my head. Like now." He walked to her and sat down close.

"I'm sorry," he said as placed his left hand on hers.

"And I'm sorry to say, I'm ravenous." She gave him a curious glance.

"I need to order some food. What are you in the mood for? My security team can grab whatever we want." She shook her head and smiled.

"Okay, pizza. Lots of pizza and some wine. I'm starving too."

"Should I get anything for your guys?" he asked.

"Not necessary. I snuck away. I knew you had a team here, and with any luck, you'll let me spend the night."

Seated in a dark blue Mercedes sedan, Elaine Trudeau wrote down what Bryce wanted and reminded him he was due for another pill. He resisted, but she kept at it.

"Yes, I know you don't want to get addicted, so let's start to wean you off of them. Just take one tonight, not two. Perhaps tomorrow you can man up and be done with them for good," she teased and ended the call. As she entered his food order on the restaurant's app, she shook her head as she thought of Bryce's injury and the conflict it was bringing him.

"Numbness and sharp pain, numbness, and pain. His nerve endings are trying to heal. This is crazy," she whispered. Ten minutes later, as the streets around his building grew quieter, she left the car and headed for the restaurant, texting Toby as she walked. Knowing Monaco like the back of her hand, she took a shortcut through an alley that ran behind a row of high-end stores and suddenly came face to face with the barrel of a gun.

⁓

Bryce removed the sling, showed Claudia the arm's limited range of motion, and then tried to pick up a book from his coffee table. He couldn't.

"You're in a weird spot, aren't you," he suggested.

"How so?"

"You care about me, but my bad break is good for you. I know you had nothing to do with the shooter, and you'll probably win at least the driver's title, but the question for both of us then is, who sent the prick? Was it someone tied to Russo back in the States, and this CIA bullshit isn't over, or was it someone else? I knew the guy's face. I just wish I knew from where. Something tells me he's on one of the teams, but I can't remember which. Your father-in-law didn't help when he blew his head off. But that wasn't enough; he had the body taken away. Hans is a little too good at his job. I just can't figure out why." Claudia got up from the sofa and went into the kitchen. Bryce called out to her.

"It makes me wonder what would have happened if I'd been killed. What would Hans have done then?"

Claudia didn't answer but returned with a beer.

"Where's mine?" he asked.

"Not when you're on those meds, my dear. We don't need you falling from your balcony." Bryce laughed but wondered if that was a hint of what might be in store. *She didn't answer my question. What does it all mean? How do I play this? God, I can't think straight. I can't accuse her, not here, not with this damn arm. Keep your cool, Bryce. Make it through tonight.*

"I want to leave an impression on Monte Carlo, but not that way." Bryce walked to the kitchen and returned with a sealed white envelope. He handed it to Claudia as someone knocked at the door. He checked his watch and smiled.

"Pizza's here!"

Claudia studied the envelope.

"What is this?" she asked as he walked down the hallway toward the door.

"Open it," he called out, throwing the deadbolt and turning the knob.

As he opened the door wide, he was stunned. His eyes moved from the woman's exquisite face to the gun in her hand. He began to speak, but she placed an index finger to her lips and motioned for him to return to the living room. As Bryce did, he heard the door close behind him and the bolt thrown. Walking back into the living room, he stared at Claudia, still seated on the sofa, the white envelope and its contents now resting on the coffee table.

Claudia had read the test results, and now there was little doubt about who Mila's father was. She heard Bryce return and began to get up, anticipating the pizza party she was starving for. But she saw a confused look on his face. Suddenly, a figure holding a gun stepped out from behind him. It was Kyoto.

It had been a long time since Kyoto had first walked into Bryce's condo, alone, past the stunning nature and motorsport prints that Bryce loved by the American lensmen Mangelsen and Rebilas and took in the vibrant blue and white décor that reminded everyone, as intended, of Mykonos. She was standing there tonight; her world had been turned upside down and nearly destroyed since then. As she stepped clear of the man she had loved, Kyoto quickly raised her gun and shot Claudia in the neck.

CHAPTER FORTY-FIVE

BRYCE WAS STUNNED, but not as much as his German guest. He stood over Claudia Werner's body and stared at it. Whether still a bit off from the pain meds, the shock of being shot and the ramifications on his career, or seeing the woman he loved suddenly appear out of nowhere, it had been a night, and it was just getting started. Bryce stared at Kyoto, looking past the fading bruises on her face and remembering how stunning this woman was.

"What the hell Kyoto? Did you have to kill her?" he said in a low tone.

"Happy to see you too, lover boy," she joked as she went to the body and checked Claudia's pulse.

"She's not dead. Just knocked out. It's a dart gun," she said as she tossed it to him, "Check it out." Bryce reached for it with his left hand but suddenly relented and let it fall to the floor.

"I'm not putting my prints on that thing, no way," he said. Kyoto got up and stood right in front of him. "You couldn't have caught it anyway." She bumped him as she walked past, down the hallway to the door. Seconds later, she led Jonathan Sproul and four men and women dressed in black from head to toe into the room. Bryce studied each one of them. He nodded at Sproul, sat on the sofa, and stared at Claudia.

"Okay, clearly I'm not in the driver's seat anymore, at least not tonight, so what happens next," he asked. Sproul checked his watch, and a slight grin cracked the corner of his mouth as he began to explain the plan.

"Right about now, the four factories Werner Industries was building weapons in, all of their weapons, from knives and semi-auto pistols to guided missile systems and jet fighters, are being blown up. Claudia there, who had led you to believe she didn't want any part of it, kept it going and even ramped up production in the last six months, will be distraught when she learns the news and will, or at least it will appear, that she snacked on an entire bottle of sleeping pills, some of which might have a good bit of Fentanyl in them, and die of suicide in her hotel bed."

"You're kidding? You'll move her from here to her suite at a five-star hotel two nights before the GP, and don't think you'll be seen?" Sproul laughed as he went into the kitchen and surveyed the room.

"She snuck out of her hotel without her team and got in here without being seen. We simply plan on reversing the trip. Unlike the screwups at CIA who made a mess of all this, at MI6, we are very good at what we do." Bryce turned to speak to Kyoto but saw her facing a corner bookshelf, running her fingers across the titles. He got up and joined her there.

"Aren't you forgetting something, actually someone," Bryce said.

"Who?" Sproul asked.

"A little girl named Mila, damn it," Bryce shouted, "And don't tell me she's collateral damage." Kyoto turned to face Bryce. She took his hand and guided him to the back of the sofa, and had him lean against it.

"Bryce, did Claudia ever tell you who she left Mila with when she traveled?" Bryce shook his head no.

"She had a girlfriend, someone she went to college with. They became like sisters and also lived in Munich. They both had children around the same time, and that's who looks after Mila and where she's been since Claudia left Munich. Her Will names the woman as Mila's legal guardian if anything happens to her, and she designated a lot of money and properties Mila is familiar with to be left to them. She's very used to being with that family, and she'll stay with them now unless someone else challenges the Will." Bryce dropped his head. At first, Kyoto began to move closer but waited. Sproul and Kyoto exchanged glances and waited. Suddenly, Bryce cleared his throat and stood up, wiping his eyes with his left sleeve.

"I am so sorry about what happened to your brother," he said softly. "I feel it's my fault." Kyoto turned quickly, her eyes full of fury, and spoke her piece.

"You weren't responsible; the American government is. They had every available asset and could not track down, capture, or eliminate those two animals. Bullshit. Jon and Jack got killed, and I got the shit kicked out of me repeatedly for a few months until they finally got tired of it and left me alone. That's when I could regroup, begin to heal, and let what my father taught me come back to life. Those bastards had no idea what they had woken up in me, but they do now, or at least that piece of shit Chadwick does, dead in his tidy whities.

"You forgot about Alan," Bryce said as he turned to face Sproul.

"Who the hell's Alan?" she asked.

"You remember the identical twins you met in Park City? Danny and Alan Johnson. They were my security in Daytona, and someone killed Alan in his hotel room." Bryce continued to eyeball Sproul.

"Nobody ever discovered who killed him or who sent them," Bryce said directly to Sproul.

"CIA or one of the assholes tied to her company," he said as he looked again at Claudia on the floor. Sproul walked to Bryce and stopped close.

"Put it together, mate," Sproul began. "Claudia told you that a Russian woman with cool blue eyes snuck into her house and threatened her life if the weapons flow was interrupted. Then, a woman with cool blue eyes gets taken out in West Virginia while pointing a sniper rifle at you. You don't see a connection? The call and text records you sent to me from her phone were very informative, and I can tell you that Claudia Werner was the one who sent old blue eyes after you. Without a doubt." Bryce was stunned.

Sproul suggested they move into the kitchen so his team could finish up. As Bryce turned, he saw an olive green housekeeping cart parked in his living room, with Claudia's left arm hanging from the side of it. He took a beer from the refrigerator, popped the top, and drank it down.

"Are you sure you should be drinking on those meds?"

Kyoto asked. Bryce raised the empty bottle and went for a second.

"With the week I'm having, I sure as hell do. You should join me. The both of you, come on." He fell silent for a time but sat up and held his fresh bottle.

"A toast the fallen. To Jon, Jack, and Alan. May they be having in heaven what they didn't have here on earth." Bryce watched as one of the men in black entered the kitchen.

"We're all done here. I'll text you when we're finished in her suite." Sproul patted the man on the shoulder. "Well done."

The room grew quiet as Kyoto picked at a bowl of red seedless grapes on the white island and Sproul made coffee.

"You two moving in or?" Bryce asked, the mixture of painkiller and alcohol now slurring his speech. Sproul laughed.

"No, we'll be out of here shortly once we get word that she's been tucked in and the fireworks all took place. You do understand that everything you've seen and heard here and up until tonight is still covered by your relevant clearances and confidentiality and non-disclosure agreements." Bryce nodded and walked from the barstool in the kitchen to where he'd been seated in the living room before Kyoto had interrupted the party.

"So, how did you two connect? A U.S. State Department lawyer based at the Embassy in Tokyo and an MI6 case worker. That doesn't happen every day." Kyoto followed Bryce into the living room and sat a few feet from him on the other end of the sofa.

"Jonathan and I were classmates at Oxford," Kyoto said, smiling fondly at her college chum. "We kept in touch, and we've helped one another a time or two. Once I got free, knowing there was nobody in the States I felt safe calling, I called Jonathan."

Sproul walked to the bookshelf and began studying it.

"Kyoto, what did your father teach you? What were you talking about," Bryce asked. Kyoto began to answer but was interrupted.

"A lover of thrillers, I see," Sproul remarked. "All the good ones, including Ian Fleming. Makes sense, I guess, considering you've become the James Bond of F1." Bryce turned in his seat and grimaced as he did.

"I spend a lot of time in the air, so between books and movies, they keep me busy. But you're not here to play librarian. What's the plan? Claudia's taken care of, or she will be, but for one thing, what about her daughter? We also need to talk about two or three other people." Kyoto went into the kitchen and returned with a hot mug of coffee, with hazelnut just as Bryce liked it, sat down, and began to drink.

"Where's mine?" he asked with surprise.

"No caffeine, mister. You need to get some sleep. We can have you on a plane and out of here before midnight." Bryce struggled for a moment but was finally able to stand.

"I can't leave. Not yet. I have press commitments down there through to the pre-race show on Sunday." Sproul pulled a book from the shelf and began paging through it.

"What time can you leave with us on Sunday," Sproul asked. "I want to get you on a plane and away from here as soon as possible. If you insist on staying here, we can come back tomorrow night and talk more or wait until we're away from here."

"What? Why? I have the Trudeaus to look after me, but you think I'm still in danger? Russo's gone, and Claudia's about to be. Who else could be after me?" Kyoto moved to the sofa and sat closer to Bryce.

"Someone was pulling strings. Someone other than just Claudia. We need to address that, and there are also the countries whose weapons flows are being cut off tonight. With all this happening, they might be curious about your proximity to Max when he died or how much you've been seen with Claudia and want to discuss that with you in person. And then there's what happened to Penelope and the Marshalls."

Bryce dropped his head back on the sofa and sighed his exhaustion.

"Kyoto, you said 'we' – are you working for the CIA now?"

"God, no. I've made a deal to work with MI6, with Jonathan as my handler. I'm done working with the USA; finding someone to trust with your life is nearly impossible."

౨

Kyoto made a *psst* sound, which caused Sproul to turn. Bryce was out cold, and she motioned for the door. Sproul slid the book back into its place and followed Kyoto down the hallway, where she opened the door and gestured for him to keep moving.

"You're staying here?" he asked with surprise. She nodded.

"Yes. I want to keep an eye on him, and we need to talk through a few things."

Sproul began to protest her decision, but she put up her hand to stop him.

"I know where all the guns are, and between the Trudeaus, their people, and yours, I feel pretty safe here." Sproul nodded in agreement.

"Do you think he understands he might have to give up racing and go hide on an island for the rest of his life," Sproul asked in a hushed tone.

"No, I don't think that's registered yet. Now, get out of here and text me when it's done," Kyoto whispered as she smiled at her friend and slowly closed the door. She threw the latch but froze when she heard someone sneaking up behind her." It was Bryce.

"We need to talk," he told her but she shook her head no.

"Not in the shape you're in. You need to get some sleep. We can talk tomorrow."

The next morning, Bryce was showered, dressed, and standing at the coffee maker in his kitchen. He'd already downed three cups, poured a fourth, and savored the aroma as if it were his first. He checked his watch as he walked past the living room sofa and slowly drew back the vibrant blue curtains that turned the room from the dark night to a sun-drenched Mykonos morning. But it was Monaco, and he needed to get down to the circuit for interviews, and his guest needed to get up.

"Hey," he called out. "Are you going to sleep all day?" Suddenly he saw Kyoto's face appear as she pulled the blanket down she'd been hiding from the sun under.

"Jesus," she declared. "I hate morning people." Bryce laughed as he walked back into the kitchen and returned with a mug of steaming hot coffee. Setting it down on the coffee table, he sat on the sofa's edge and tapped Kyoto on the forehead.

"Go back to sleep," he said. "I'll be back at noon, and we can have lunch if you want."

Staring at the woman he once wanted to marry and still did, he was thrilled to see her there, with him, once again. With her eyes still closed, she asked Bryce about his shoulder.

"I called out a few times from the shower that I needed help, but you mustn't have heard me." Bryce looked down at his arm, formed a fist with his right hand, and then released it.

"It's okay. But I still need your help." He smiled as Kyoto opened her eyes and sat up against the end of the sofa.

"With?" she asked. He smiled and stood up, displaying a red, fully unbuttoned, button-down shirt and watched as she remembered the six-pack abs he knew she admired.

"Buttons. If you can help me with these," he asked. He got up, and soon Kyoto stood face to face with him, slowly fastening one button after another.

"We have a lot to talk about. About being held prisoner, about Jon, and." Kyoto placed one hand on his mouth to quiet him and the other gently against his chest.

"Not yet. I've been through hell and back. I spent four months mourning my brother, mourning losing you, and wondering if I'd ever make it out of there alive but I'm not ready to talk about it, not yet, not with you. The shrinks who checked me out said I'd be fine but it would take time. So if you can be patient, that day will come, I promise."

Bryce placed his left hand over hers, kissed it, and then gently pulled it away.

"Okay, whatever you need."

Kyoto finished the buttons and ran her hands over his chest, chasing a few wrinkles.

"So, does the fact that I have samurai blood coursing through me scare you at all?"

"No, not at all. I think it's sexy. It's incredible that you repressed everything your father taught you until you'd had enough, and their violence brought it all back." Kyoto nodded.

"Yeah, and neither could Chadwick. I could tell the one liked me, so I used that weakness against him. He's the one that grabbed me in the Watergate garage. He was almost the opposite of that asshole Russo. After being together for four months, he lowered his guard just once. I made a move, he went for his gun, and I killed him. Now get going.

"Yeah, and neither could Chadwick. Now, get going. I need some more sleep." Bryce leaned forward, wrapped his arms around her tight for a moment, kissed her forehead, and then walked to the front door. As he opened it, he was greeted by Toby Trudeau standing guard.

"You ready?" Trudeau asked. Bryce shook his head yes and then turned back toward Kyoto.

"That whole samurai thing. It doesn't bother me at all. Puts me in the mood for sushi."

Kyoto laughed and quickly threw an end pillow toward Bryce, hitting the door as he yanked it closed.

CHAPTER FORTY-SIX

LIKE BLOOD TO a vampire, Roland McCarthy wasn't just drawn to power and pageantry; he had to have it, and on this June moonlit evening during a brief holiday in Northern Scotland, he had much to consider. Sure, he'd become the Chief of Staff, the gatekeeper and policymaker to the most powerful man on the planet. Still, they'd been at odds in recent months, and McCarthy was taking the time away to plot and plan how he could repair the rift or, perhaps even better, replace the man. Returning to the stone structure, a more miniature castle of sorts, in his family dating back to one hundred years before the United States had been assembled, his frustration continued. A neighbor to the west of there, the Queen of England, had died at the Balmoral Estate in the past year, and with her, at least he felt, much of the prestige of boasting about the place and inviting people there he wanted to impress and often sway. Tonight, as he sat in his black Jaguar SUV, he watched as his guest, a tourist he had met that evening in a nearby hotel bar, gushed with excitement about the estate he had just taken her to. He reached inside the center console, withdrew a Faraday bag, and directed her to place her cell phone inside it. He watched as she thought for a moment and then looked at him.

"Really?" she asked. He nodded.

"You're not going to lock me in a dungeon in there, are you," she asked and then laughed as she slid her phone from her bag and dropped it inside. McCarthy grinned as he sealed the Faraday and placed it back in the console. He was glad she hadn't noticed the black handgun inside the compartment. That might have caused a much longer conversation and derailed his plans.

As he left the vehicle and walked around to open the woman's door, he felt a chill in the air and was pleased. His guest would also feel the cold, perhaps 55° Fahrenheit at this hour, and be drawn closer to him for heat. Once inside, he hung his tweed sports coat on a wrought iron hook in the foyer and did the same for his guest's black designer leather jacket.

"Would you like a scotch?" he asked his guest. She smiled.

"No reason to stop now," she laughed and paused momentarily to survey her surroundings.

McCarthy walked into the main room and was immediately off balance; something was wrong. He knew he'd left a light on and that the flames in the massive stone fireplace should have died long ago. The room was dark, except for the glow from the small inferno. Perhaps it was the scotch at dinner. He'd had more than his share. But he wasn't sure. She took a step past him and turned. She studied him.

"What's the matter, Roland?" she asked. Suddenly, another voice called out.

"Yea, Roland. What's the matter," a voice called from somewhere in the darkness. McCarthy struggled to adjust his eyes from the fire's glow to the movement in the flickering shadows. Then he saw it, the barrel of a gun.

"Tell your guest she needs to go. We have a few things to discuss," the voice said, the tone benign, not threatening. Suddenly, the lights in the room clicked on.

✥

Sproul had agreed to let Kyoto back up Bryce, but as she sat quietly in the dark kitchen, her blood had begun to boil. The man ultimately responsible for her brother's death and her brutal encounter with the "CIA twins," her nickname for Russo and Chadwick, was in the next room, and she needed to change the script. "Enough already," she whispered and stormed into the main room. Her gun may have risen as she did, but her jaw dropped with shock.

"Susan Lee? Is that you?" Kyoto asked in disbelief. "What's a Chinese spy doing out on a date with the president's Chief of Staff?"

✥

Bryce walked to one of two opposing brown leather wingback chairs and took a seat. The gun in his left hand remained pointed at McCarthy, but his attention was laser-focused on the date the bastard had brought home. Known for quick thinking and reactions in the race car, it took little time to make an assessment.

"Yeah, what she said," Bryce said jokingly. "What are you doing with this piece of shit?" Bryce glared at McCarthy.

"And you, while she's making something up, take a seat," Bryce commanded as he gestured toward the other wingback using the suppressed gun barrel, but McCarthy didn't move.

From the tip of his suppressed pistol, a flash appeared as a bullet from Bryce's gun smashed into the doorframe behind the couple.

"I meant now," Bryce shouted. McCarthy began to move toward the fireplace, but Lee didn't move. She hadn't flinched. They'd talked about it before, over their dinner in Singapore recently. She'd been shot at too many times for it to bother her. Bryce kept the gun trained on McCarthy but focused on Kyoto. She'd gone off script and was walking slowly, gun in hand, toward Lee.

"Why would anyone live here? It's cold, and it's the middle of summer," she complained.

§

"You're making small talk?" Kyoto shouted at her. Lee smiled.

"That's what old acquaintances do," Lee responded as she stared at Kyoto's gun.

"And that's not necessary. I'm a friend, remember? I saved your life."

§

From his chair by the fire, Bryce had a ringside seat and, for once, was happy to sit back and watch whatever was playing out. He looked at McCarthy.

"What's your bet? She'll put the gun down, and they'll hug it out or a big-time catfight?"

"How'd you get in here?" McCarthy demanded. Lee laughed as she looked at him.

"He's a spy, you idiot."

"And you," McCarthy glared. "You're not a tourist from Taiwan here to see Balmoral and St. Andrews; that's clear now, but what's your game? What's all of this?" McCarthy said with contempt.

"She's from China all right, but the big one," Bryce stated and then cocked his head toward Lee.

"So what *are* you doing here? You may have stumbled onto something you shouldn't have," Kyoto asked. Her demeanor appeared to settle, at least for now, Bryce thought.

Lee smiled at Kyoto and then focused on Bryce and his gun.

"Your hand, you're shooting with your left hand," she observed. Bryce looked down at his right hand, sticking out of the end of a black sling. He struggled but formed a shaky fist, if just for a moment, and then watched it crumble.

"The CIA taught me a lot, but my Uncle Pete taught me long before they ever did. He always told me to use both hands. If your best hand is compromised, you might still need to fight. So I learned to shoot a gun and handle a knife with either hand before I hit sixteen." Bryce turned his attention back to McCarthy.

"I'm not sure what this is or what you want, but you do know who I am. My security checks in every half hour. This will end badly for you if you don't get up and walk out of here right now," McCarthy said after finding some courage. Bryce laughed.

"I doubt that. I made one call to your boss, and he pulled them just as we arrived at the gate. He told me he'd done that to you once before. They'll be back once this is over. So stop with the lies; they will determine how you die."

"Getting right to it then, I prefer it. Now, how much do you want? I have millions, " McCarthy asked. Bryce smiled. He recognized the charisma powerful men like this had in their toolbox, but nothing could fix this tonight.

"And so do I," Bryce laughed, "But I earned mine. You've been taking money from the Werner's for a long time. First, with Max and then with Claudia, you kept the illegal trading going and got your cut. I'll bet you were double dipping with all the bad guys paying you. Bastards like you are already sucking money out of America's war machine. That wasn't enough. What else did you deal with our enemies?"

Lee cleared her throat, drawing Bryce's attention.

"He's been a very busy boy," she said. Bryce studied her for a moment.

"So where does China fit into all of this?" he asked. Lee shook her head.

"It's complicated."

"Really? So tell me why you lied about Russo." Bryce's comment seemed to catch Lee off-guard, which surprised him. He'd never seen that before.

"You told me you killed him the day you saved Kyoto in Singapore. But the truth is you nursed him back to health and traded him for some shithead spy of yours that Washington was holding."

"Yeah, tell us about that, Susan!" Kyoto demanded.

"Bryce, I never said I killed him. I said I shot him."

"And then you sent a sadistic killer back to America, and you know what he did," Kyoto shouted as she stepped closer to Lee, who looked to Bryce, perhaps for help.

"Bryce, you owe me," Lee said.

"Don't look at him. I'm talking to you," Kyoto shouted. "Do you know the first thing Russo did when he got back home? He killed my brother, and then he kicked the shit out of me over and over again!" Without flinching, Kyoto raised her gun, pointed it at Lee's face for an instant, clenched her jaw with rage, and then lowered it slowly.

"God damn you for doing that," Kyoto screamed and then broke into tears. Bryce watched as Lee stepped closer to Kyoto and embraced her.

"Well, so much for the catfight." Bryce focused on McCarthy again.

"What kind of a name is Roland anyway?" Bryce asked as he tapped the gun barrel on his knee. "I looked it up. Some idiot named you after Charlemagne's' eight-foot-tall nephew? Really? Guess they couldn't have known you'd grow up to be a five-six piece of shit who betrayed his country and had innocent people killed. People like her brother, Jack Madigan, Alan Johnson, and who knows how many more." McCarthy began to protest, and without warning, Bryce fired two bullets into the floor at his feet. McCarthy yanked his legs up and wrapped his arms around them.

"Fetal position," Bryce chuckled. "It suits you."

"You'll never get away with this; the people Werner was supplying, they'll all figure out it was you, and then you're a dead man. There will be no place on earth where you can hide and they'll keep Kyoto around just like Russo and Chadwick did for fun and games, only worse, until she's no fun anymore." Bryce aimed the gun at McCarthy's face.

"Actually, the NSA has been able to hack your phones and email accounts, even what you thought were the highly sophisticated encrypted ones, and they've shared a lot of what they've found with MI6, Mossad, and even a few of America's enemies who have in turn, as of tonight, initiated some interesting countermeasures. Nobody will be coming after us; they'll be coming after you for killing Claudia and blowing up her factories. My bet is that after learning this, you set this fine Scottish castle on fire and killed yourself." Bryce watched McCarthy squirm. There was no getting out of this one, and he knew it.

"Now, you could screw up our plans and make a run for it. I'd have to shoot you, and then we'd have to figure out a Plan B. But it's late. We're all tired, and I'm hungry, so be a good little traitor and play along." Suddenly, McCarthy made a run for it, and halfway to the door, Kyoto stood in his way and shot the bastard in the neck with the same tranquilizer gun she had used to take down Claudia Werner. As McCarthy hit the beautifully maintained wood floor, Bryce looked at Lee.

"So what *were* you doing here tonight?" he asked as he got up from his chair and approached her, his gun now tucked into his belt.

"Bugs," she said. "I was in London, and when we heard he was coming, my boss sent me here. He was so dirty with all of his electronic contacts that he never let the Secret Service scan any of his homes. So we planned to take advantage of that until you two showed up."

Lee, Kyoto, and Bryce stepped close and stared down at the unconscious bastard.

"So what's the plan?" Lee asked.

"I'm an eye for an eye kind of guy," Bryce confessed. "Kind of puts me in the mood for a good, old-fashioned Scottish barbeque. I say let's stick to Plan A."

"I could use a drink," Lee said and walked to the shelves that housed a dozen or so bottles of liquor and wine, flutes, wine glasses, and crystal tumblers. She grabbed a bottle and three glasses and walked back to the pair, laughing as she read the label.

"Macallan James Bond Series 60th Anniversary Decade II Highland Single Malt Scotch Whisky. The guy thinks he's a spy," she said.

"No scotch for me," Bryce said as he shook his head, feigning disgust. "I'll wait for the beer." Lee placed the glasses down on a table and poured one for herself. She looked at Kyoto, who nodded. Feeling left out, Bryce went looking and returned with a beer bottle.

"I had no idea you knew your way around any of this," Lee said as she raised her glass and clinked theirs. Kyoto took a sip of the expensive liquor and then explained.

"My father came from an interesting bloodline. One hundred years before, some of the men of the family were samurai. He was with the PSIA in Japan; I am sure you know of it." Lee nodded.

"He wanted his children to join and help protect our country. He tried to teach us everything he knew, but Jon pushed back and focused on computers while I studied international law. Jon refused to learn anything that involved violence, but I embraced it. I learned everything my father knew. But then, my mother was killed in our home by someone my father had been investigating. It sent him into a deep depression. The only thing he showed interest in after that was baseball games and Formula One races until he died of a broken heart. For me, I internalized everything and didn't want to have anything to do with violence ever again. But after a few months in the care of those two bastards, it all came back, everything I learned. I used it to take out Chadwick, and now here we are, standing over this pile of sheep shit." Bryce finished his beer and suggested it was time to get moving. Footfalls were heard coming toward them from the kitchen, and soon, three men dressed in black entered the main room and began staging the scene. Lee smiled.

"Well, that's my cue." She walked to the doorway, grabbed her jacket, took McCarthy's keys from a crystal bowl, and pushed the button to unlock the SUV. Once there, she reached inside and took back her phone. She waved to Kyoto and Bryce and began walking toward the team's vehicles, now idling near the gate.

As the fire inside engulfed the majestic stone castle, Bryce and Kyoto exited the front door and began walking down the gravel driveway. As they came close to McCarthy's SUV, Bryce stopped and, with his left hand, removed a folded white envelope from his jeans' back pocket. Kyoto turned and walked back to him.

"What's that?" she asked. At first, Bryce struggled, but he managed to unfold the envelope and began to remove the contents, a white piece of paper, using his right hand.

"It's the DNA report comparing mine to Mila's," he

said as he looked back at the growing inferno, the sound of wood beams crashing to the floor inside.

"So what's it say? Open it?" Kyoto encouraged. Bryce looked at her. He thought of the love and joy Kyoto had brought him, but then the heartache he had felt when Kyoto had left for what she said was the last time. He forced a somber smile and then walked back to the house, crumbling the unread report as he grew closer and tossed it into the fire. Returning to Kyoto, he saw Jonathan Sproul walking toward them and members of the MI6 team and McCarthy's U.S. Secret Service protective detail waiting alongside their idling vehicles further down the way. Both organizations had been forced to terminate the employment of some troublesome government employees in recent years, and once his detail learned what McCarthy had done, they switched from protecting the traitor to opening the door to let a doctor in to kill this cancer. And it had come with the president's sanction.

"Did you read it?" Kyoto asked. Bryce shook his head, cleared his throat, and wrapped his arms around her.

"No. She's better off," he whispered. "She's safer and happier being where she is with the woman and family Claudia's will dictated, whether I am her father or not."

Bryce tightened his grasp around her, felt the familiar warmth he had longed for, and then released. He began walking toward the vehicles, passing Sproul without saying a word. Bryce was focused on heading home, unsure of what his injured hand had in store for him or what the future would hold, but it was time to move on. Without looking back, Bryce stepped into the back seat of a dark green Land Rover for the drive back to the Aberdeen airport, where the jet that had brought him there was now at his disposal. Suddenly, the door opened, and Kyoto got in.

"What's this?" Bryce asked, feeling surprised, cautious, and hopeful all at once.

"I heard you were headed to the airport," she said. "Me too."

The ride took longer than expected; the rain and traffic had slowed the driver's efforts just enough to turn the sixty-minute trip into a ninety-minute one. The entire time, Bryce and Kyoto didn't speak and instead took turns scrolling their phones, resting their eyes, and scrolling some more. Navigating his way to a remote area of the airport, the driver brought the Land Rover to a stop near the government jet; Bryce smiled as he saw another plane, his Bombardier, parked nearby. The driver opened the door for Kyoto as the bodyguard riding shotgun did the same for Bryce. As Kyoto and Bryce met in front of the vehicle, he watched as she recognized the second plane. She'd spent countless hours on the white Global 6500 and smiled fondly, looking at the familiar red stripe and tail markings, N500BW. Bryce stood beside her as a light but cold drizzle began to sweep the area.

"So there's two planes. I had my team fly to Nice after I got shot and had them on standby. They followed Sproul's plane here, and if anyone asks, we were here for an after-hours private tour of Balmoral. And now we're on the move again," Bryce began. "The coffee and the food's better on my bird. Jen's seen to that, and we can fly farther than theirs. So now we'll take you wherever you want to go—Tokyo, Park City, or somewhere else, anywhere else. You can get on that one or come with me. You decide."

"Not Munich," she suggested. He clenched his jaw as he shook his head no.

Bryce leaned in, kissed Kyoto on the cheek, and then began walking toward his plane. He didn't look back, he just kept walking, but just as he got close to the jet stairs Kyoto barged in front of him and walked up the steps, struggling a few times, and entered the plane. Bryce just stood there in the rain, at the base of the stairs, and watched as Kyoto and Jen shared a tearful embrace inside the cabin entry. He watched as his pilot and co-pilot Bill and Lou abandoned the cockpit, hugging Kyoto, laughing and crying. Bryce felt those same emotions inside and was glad the rain was hiding his tears. Then, as quickly as the reunion had started it ended as the crew retook their seats in the cockpit. Bryce watched as Kyoto walked through the main cabin and dropped into a window seat. After a few moments settling in, he saw her spot him standing in the rain on the tarmac and shook her head, waving for him to come in. Suddenly, a familiar voice called his name.

"Hey, Bryce. I know you've been shot and are probably all doped up, but how about getting your butt on board so we can get the hell out of here," Jen shouted from the doorway.

He looked up at her, cleared his throat, and took the stairs. Once inside, he stepped into the cockpit and thanked the two men for standing by him through it all.

"You two are the best," he began. "I'll never be able to thank you enough for putting up with everything I put you two through." Suddenly he felt someone knocking on the back of his head. He spun around and stared at Jen; she'd done that a dozen times before to get his attention.

"And what about me? You do remember I prepare your food," Jen said as she broke into laughter. Bryce turned and wrapped his arm around her. After a time, she stepped back and stared at the arm she hadn't felt. His right arm strapped into a black sling. He watched as her expression slid from joy to sorrow.

"It'll be fine. You just might have to cut my food for me," he joked as he watched Jen step back into the galley and smiled.

"No, that's what *he's* here for," she said, turning to watch Danny Johnson walking quickly up the aisle toward them. Bryce dropped his head and shook it left to right until Danny got to him and wrapped his arms around him.

"I leave you alone for one minute and you get shot," Danny whispered.

"How's your mom?" Bryce asked. Danny stepped back and frowned.

"Sad to say she's back in the kitchen burning everything, which is why I'm here if you still need me." Bryce placed his left hand on Danny's right shoulder and smiled.

"I sure as hell do." Bryce looked past Danny and saw Kyoto, still seated, peering out the window as the rain beat harder on the plane.

"Did you meet her?" Bryce asked. Danny nodded. "Yes, I introduced myself and offered my condolences. She's a class act, Bryce; she offered the same for Alan and asked how my mother was."

"She sure is." Bryce turned to the pilot.

"Hey, fire this baby up. I'll have a destination for you in a minute."

Bryce tapped Jen on the shoulder, and as she turned, he began to ask for coffee but smiled when he saw the steaming mug in her hand. He took it from her and took a sip, savoring the hazelnut flavor, and then watched as Jen delivered a mug to Kyoto, half coffee, half Bailey's, remembering the way she liked it.

"Give us some time after wheel's up, okay," he said to Danny, who nodded and then pushed the button to retract the jet stairs. As Bryce approached Kyoto, Jen slid past him in the aisle and closed the door between the galley and the main cabin. Bryce took a seat facing Kyoto but didn't say a word. He looked down at his right arm and flexed his fist once and then again. It was a struggle, but the grip was stronger, giving him hope. They sipped at their drinks a few times, and then he told her she had a decision to make.

"So we're all fueled up and ready to go," he said. "Where to?"

Kyoto placed her drink on the window sill, removed a compact pistol from a black shoulder holster, and placed it in her bag. She looked at Bryce, studied him for a moment, and then picked up the cabin phone.

"Captain, how quickly can you get us to Park City? Our guy needs a lot of rehab, and I hear he's having a new home built there, and I'd love to see it."

Bryce settled back into his seat and stared at her.

"What?" she asked as she hung up the phone.

"You know I'm not done racing or done helping

MI6." She grinned, kicked off her shoes, and engaged the footrest.

"Neither am I."

⁓

The White House, Washington D.C.

Nearing midnight, President Johnson sat back into his favorite recliner, a brown leather where he'd found solace since his earliest days in politics as a U.S. Representative from Austin, Texas. He'd just arrived in the residence after making a brief statement to the press in the White House Briefing Room regarding the tragic loss of his dear friend and Chief of Staff, Roland McCarthy. It was time for an escape, perhaps a few hours on Prime Video and his favorite series, Jack Ryan. But as the steward delivered his glass of milk and a warm slice of pecan pie, Johnson reached for the remote, then stood up suddenly, knocking the tray to the floor, and stared at the CNN Breaking News headline:

BRYCE WINTERS PLANE MISSING
OVER THE ATLANTIC

THE END

EPILOGUE

Bryce stood calmly on the cold, wet grass and stared at the plane he loved; flames and heavy smoke now enveloping her. He'd escaped injury and death in race cars over the years, but tonight, he and the rest had survived a harrowing crash landing after their rapid descent to the small Váger Airport near Sørvágur in the Faroe Islands, east of Iceland. He shook his head as he studied those closest to him and replayed what had happened in the air. After an explosion had taken place below the rear cabin at 40,000 feet over the dark Atlantic Ocean, Bryce had run to the cockpit to find Bill and Lou wearing their oxygen masks, struggling to gain control of the plane and trying to find somewhere to land. The aircraft hadn't lost cabin pressure - yet, but communications were gone, much of the hydraulics were unresponsive, and the smell of smoke permeated the cabin.

"We can't dump the fuel," Lou had called out after removing his oxygen mask. Bryce stood in the cockpit doorway to ask what he could do. "Hardly anything's working. Go strap in and get everyone to put on their oxygen masks. We could lose pressure at any time." With enough fuel on board to make it from Northern Scotland to America's Mountain West, everyone knew they were essentially strapped inside nothing more than a big fuel tank with two jet engines roaring on either side. Bryce sat across from Kyoto and watched as she worked her satellite phone.

"Who are you calling?" he asked. At first, she didn't respond, but as she tapped in another number, she looked at Bryce.

"Sproul. I'm trying to get Jonathan to tell him what's happening, but he's not picking up!" Bryce sat back in his captain's chair and stared out the window into the darkness until he heard Lou shout from the cockpit.

"We've got lights in the distance. Jen, get everyone ready. If we make it to land, we'll need to get the hell off this thing fast!"

Jen had already given everyone their life vests and prepped the rafts for deployment if they went down in the water, and after that, all they could do was wait - and pray. With their landing gear crippled, once they touched down, they skidded through a shower of sparks and finally stopped after sliding off the runway into a dark field. Bryce, Kyoto, Jen, Danny, Bill, and Lou jumped to the ground from the pilot-side forward cabin door and ran as fast and as far as they could. After taking a minute to process what had just happened, Bryce shook his head as he walked to the flight crew and wrapped his arms around them.

"Any idea where we are," Bryce said to the pilot, who had just ended a call to his wife, assuring her they were safe.

"Somewhere between Inverness and Reykjavik is my best

guess. Lou spotted the lights, and we just aimed for them. As we got close, we picked up the runway's signal on our IFR. If this had been a stormy night, we'd never have seen the lights and gone down in the water for sure." Kyoto leaned in close to Bryce for warmth and stared at the two. Despite being mid-summer, the night air was just shy of fifty degrees. As the breeze changed direction, for a moment, they felt the warmth of the distant inferno, the smell of smoke, and the kerosene-like aroma of jet fuel. Lou and Danny began walking toward the runway as they pointed to the blue flashing lights of the small airport's emergency equipment that were now racing toward the flames.

"You do know that was a bomb," Bill said as he stared at Bryce.

"So, who did this," Jen asked. As the fire reflected in his eyes, he stared at her.

"Only the fuel tanker driver and the food concession truck put a hand on us back there. Nobody else got close, and nobody got inside," Lou said, "And." Danny interrupted him.

"It would have been easy for the fuel guy to step to the landing gear and attach something, right?" Bryce looked down at his right hand and flexed his grip.

"Well, it sounds like we know how, but she asked who." Bryce looked at Kyoto.

"Would Sproul have done this?" Kyoto broke away and shook her head at the suggestion.

"No way, no f-ing way," she shouted. Bryce turned to Danny.

"Secret Service?" he asked. Danny shook his head no. "Doubt it."

"So who then?"

As two red and neon yellow fire trucks arrived, pumping foam onto the plane before their rigs stopped, two POLITI cars and an ambulance caught the survivors in their headlights and sped toward them. Bill and Lou began waving at the police cars while Danny wrapped his arms around Jen to help keep her warm. With only one working arm, Bryce did the same for Kyoto and whispered in her ear.

"So who then?"